# THE LIFT

R J Hilton

# ACKNOWLEDGMENTS

I would like to express my thanks to my family, especially my wife Mary, for putting up with me while I put this book together.

# CHAPTER ONE

The phone rang in Fred's office. "Hello, this is Fred Bates."

"Fred, this is Linda. Your daughter is on the phone." Linda Taylor is the receptionist at Insurance Innovation Incorporated or I3 as it is called by most everyone.

"Thank you, Linda. Please put her through."

"Hello Dad?" Kristine Bates is Fred's only child.

"Hey Kris. What's up?"

"All my activities this afternoon have been cancelled and all my homework is caught up. How about we walk down to the river? We haven't walked in that park in a while."

The park borders the property next to the building where Fred works. The river is about a mile away.

Fred thought for a moment and said, "Sure. I have a pair of sneakers here at the office and a polo shirt. Do you need me to drive home to get you?"

"No, I will meet you at work. I will ride my bike down. We can toss it on the back of your car for the ride home. Okay?"

"Sounds like a plan. See you in a bit."

A couple hours later Kristine knocked on Fred's office door. Fred looked up. "Oh, hi. I got into something and lost track of the clock. Give me a couple minutes."

Kristine smiled and said, "No problem. I will meet you in the lobby." She turned and headed toward the elevators.

Fred saved the work he was doing and signed off his computer. He changed his shirt and his shoes. As he walked by the reception area, he told Linda he was going for a walk with his daughter. He walked to the elevators and pressed the down button. A bell sounded and he looked to see which of the four elevators had arrived. He noticed it was the number four elevator.

After the elevator car doors opened, he entered. The number four elevator had padding on the walls. The owner preferred the tenants use this one for moving large objects such furniture and office equipment. Fred noticed the floor near the doors was wet. Someone must have spilled something.

When the doors opened in the lobby Kristine was at the door with her mom. As Fred stepped out Kristine shouted "Surprise! I asked Mom if she could come too."

Fred gave them both a hug and said, "This is great. My two-favorite people. Let's stop in at Clara's and get a water bottle."

Kristine held up two water bottles. "I brought some from home. Besides, the shoppette is closed."

Fred looked at his watch. Clara's, the shoppette on the first floor of the building, closes at 2 PM and it was now nearly 3. "Well let's go."

Kristine took off toward the building entrance. Fred hung back with Jill, his wife. They had met in college. She is about 5 feet 7 with a runner's build. She was a runner in high school and college. She still runs the odd 5K or 10K when she has time. She has dark blond hair which she wears about shoulder length. Her eyes are a bright emerald green. Jill is a veterinarian. Fred took her hand as they walked out of the building.

The grounds around the building are well maintained and landscaped. There is about twenty or thirty feet between the parking lot and the property boundary. This is all grass and trees. The building owner hires a landscaping company to make sure the grounds are well maintained. It is one of the reasons businesses lease space in the building. Even though the building is older it has been well maintained.

One side of the building has a small picnic area with a barbeque grill, so people working in the building or visiting can sit outside during their breaks when the weather permits, which is often during the spring, summer, and autumn. A sidewalk encircles the entire building. A pathway from the sidewalk leads to the city park adjacent to the building property. Kristine was already heading toward the park.

Jill was the first to speak. "So, what is the occasion for this outing?"

"No idea. Kris called me at work around noon and asked to walk down to the river. She didn't tell me she called you."

Jill feigned being hurt, "I know when I am not welcome, I should leave."

Fred started to apologize when Jill squeezed his hand and said with a big grin, "Gotcha!"

They both laughed and caught up with their daughter. They walked the half to three quarters of a mile of open space to the edge of the woods talking about those things families talk about. The river was another half mile or so through the woods.

After about 30 minutes, they reached the edge of the river. Walking along the river downstream they reached a bridge that crossed the water. The path split here, one across the bridge and another that continued along the river's edge.

Kristine said, "Let's go to the waterfall" and took off across the bridge. Kristine was going to be the spitting image of her mom. She had the same blond hair and green eyes. She also loved sports of all kinds, and even though she was still young she was becoming quite athletic. Jill and Fred followed her across the bridge.

Across the bridge, the path followed the river both up and downstream. Kristine had turned right to head downstream toward the waterfall. A few minutes later, they arrived there. As waterfalls go, it was not Niagara Falls, but it was about 30 or 40 feet high. Just above the falls there was a historical marker. Kristine was at the marker when Fred and Jill caught up to her.

"Dad, look at this." The marker was describing a rock formation that was nearby surrounded by a low fence. The

4

marker read, "The rock formation is believed to be a pre-Columbian Native American monument documenting the death of one of the natives. No date has been determined for the creation of the monument."

An enhanced photo of the rock formation was below the words. In the photo, there were many flat rocks piled on top of one another. Etched into the rocks were weather-worn stick figure diagrams of what appeared to be someone going over the waterfall and landing splayed out at the bottom. Next to the stick figures was what is believed to be a symbol. No one had ever been able to understand what the symbol was or what it could mean.

Kristine asked, "Dad what do you think the symbol is?"

Fred looked at the symbol. "I have no idea. There have been many historians and symbologists that have studied this, and all have come up empty. The only thing they say is it looks like a bunch of letters combined. The problem with that is this was created before the alphabet was invented." He took a long sip from his water bottle. They walked over to the monument and looked at the scratching on the rocks. The weather over the centuries had nearly obliterated the figures and the symbol. Fred wondered what it must have been like back then.

Jill said, "We should probably head back. I have some things I need to get done this afternoon."

Fred added, "I need to pop in the office for a few minutes. Can you take Kris with you?"

"No problem, I can do what I need to do from home." With that, they headed back.

Halfway across the open space, Jill was looking at the building. "Why in the world did they build an 8-story building way out here?"

Fred explained. "It was built in an area the original owner had thought would soon become part of the growth of the city. Unfortunately for the original owner, the town grew in the other direction. The big city was closer to that side of town. The owner's dreams of multiple buildings all full of tenants and him becoming a millionaire land mogul were not realized. He ended up only having the one building. The building provided good income but not the great income he hoped for. He ended up selling it to the current owner."

As they entered the parking lot Fred noticed a new model BMW convertible in one of the visitor spaces. "That's odd."

Jill had started to walk toward her SUV but stopped and said, "What is odd?"

"That BMW over there. It was there when we left. It is most likely a sales rep.'s car. Whoever it is has been here a lot longer than the normal sales call."

Kristine joined in, "Nice car, he must make a lot of money."

"A good sales rep can make a nice living. Part of my job is to sell our training classes and software."

"So why don't you drive a BMW convertible?

"Because we need more room for our stuff than will fit in one of those cars."

Jill decided to end the discussion. "We will see you at home in an hour or so."

Fred answered, "Yeah, I won't be too long." He turned and headed for the building entrance.

# CHAPTER TWO

Fred turned and watched Jill and Kristine get into the SUV and pull out of the parking lot. He waved as they went by. He turned back toward the entrance to the building.

The entrance is a set of two glass doors that open from the center. The glass on the right-hand side is imprinted with the address of the building at the top of the door. 1680 Hilltop Rd. The entrance opens on the main foyer of the building. To the left is the entrance to Clara's shoppette/deli. On the right is the security desk. Just beyond the shoppette is the West End Orthopedics office. Opposite is found the West End Medical Group. On the left just before the elevators is the directory of the building. The directory is of an older generation. Individual white letters are placed in evenly spaced slots on a black background.

There are four elevators in the center of the building situated a little closer to the rear of the building. One of the elevators has light brown padding attached to three of the walls to indicate it is the one to be used for deliveries of larger merchandize and equipment.

At the rear of the building just past the elevators are two utility closets, one on each side of the lobby. To the left of the hallway behind the utility closet is the building manager's office. Beyond the utility room on the right-hand side is the building maintenance office. At the rear of the building in each corner is a restroom. The far-left corner has the men's room, and the far-right corner has the lady's room. Next to the entrance to the restrooms is a door to the emergency stairway. The stairways on the first floor also have an emergency exit out of the building. These doors do not have knobs or levers of any kind on the outside as they are for emergency use only. The stairways themselves are available for use from the first floor all the way to the eighth floor.

Fred got off the elevator on the seventh floor and headed through the I3 lobby toward his office. Linda welcomed him back as he passed her desk. She is an older woman with slightly graying hair cut in a bob. She has a pleasant face with gentle brown eyes. She was wearing a casual skirt with a white blouse covered by a blue blazer. "Did you have a nice time?"

"Very nice, thanks. We should do that more often. Sometimes a nice leisurely walk, especially with those two, is just what the doctor ordered." Fred replied with a pleasant smile, and then headed to his office.

Fred's office was the largest outside of the executive suite. There was a bookcase with one shelf dedicated to scouting artifacts. Off to one side of the shelf was a framed certificate signed by the president. It was a scanned signature, but he was still proud to have it because it was given to him at his Eagle Scout ceremony. There was one curious "award" in the middle of the shelf. It was a square knot on a green colored board with routed edges. Above the knot were the words "Troop 74 Knot Tying Champions." The knot was painted black, however. Fred always needed to explain his patrol won the knot tying championship by finishing all the Tenderfoot required knots faster than all the other patrols. The square knot was painted black because his patrol actually accomplished the feat blind folded! They also came in second for the lashing championship.

Fred's desk was a medium size wooden desk. On the desk was a phone, two computer monitors, and two coffee mugs. One mug was full of pens and pencils and the other was used for coffee. He liked to keep his desk clear unless he was working on something. He signed on to his computer and opened his class schedule.

Fred was the training coordinator for 13. He also developed much of the training material for the classes. After he checked the schedule he got up and walked over to the wall opposite his bookshelf. He opened the credenza and pulled out the hard copies of the materials the instructors would need for the next day. He placed the materials on the small table in the corner of the office. The credenza was completely covered with framed pictures he took of Jill and Kristine on various adventures. There was also a photograph with Jill and Fred from their wedding.

With that finished, he got up and walked to the stairs at the rear of the building and headed to the eighth floor. The classrooms were all located on the eighth floor. He took a quick look in all the rooms. All had been in use and were now empty. He checked to make sure no materials were left out or computers left on. All was in order, and he reminded himself he has a great training staff making his job that much easier. He then walked back downstairs and closed his office.

When he left the building, he noticed the BMW still parked in the visitor spot. "That is very odd." He said out loud as he continued the short walk to his SUV. He unlocked the door, climbed in, and headed out of the parking lot toward home.

# CHAPTER THREE

Fred got up early the next day. He made his normal power breakfast of Rice Krispies and a sliced banana. He finished it off with a tall glass of orange juice. After breakfast he brushed his teeth and got dressed for work. He wore straight leg trousers, a white oxford shirt, and a sport jacket. He was once asked why he wore white shirts most of the time. He replied, "A friend once told me white goes with everything, so you don't have to worry about matching anything."

Fred has a computer science degree from the state college a few hours drive from his hometown. He started out as a computer programmer directly out of college. He has worked for I3 the last fourteen years. His current job is the head of the training department. They have a small number of employees that hold training classes in their training classrooms on the eighth floor. Sometimes they travel around the country to larger insurance company offices to train the insurance company employees in the I3 products. He enjoys his job. He has always liked teaching, and this allows him to teach and make use of his technical skills at the same time.

He is not a big man. He is about 5' 8". He is stocky but not heavy. He is currently 40 years old. His hair has not started to turn or recede although all of the males in his line have turned grey as they approached 50. Most kept their hair, however. He has mostly European ancestry. His hair is a deep brown, and his eyes are a deep blue which is quite a contrast.

He is one of three boys. He has an older brother (Francis but he goes by Frank), his younger brother (James) lives a couple towns over. His mom, Norma, lives around the corner from James. Frank lives in the next state. All three were at one time in the scouts but Fred is the only one to achieve the highest rank.

When Fred was 16 his father, Will, died which necessitated his getting a job at the local hardware store. There was life insurance which paid for the house and gave his mom a little money to live on and provided the essentials for the boys. However, Fred had to work to save money for college and to buy the little things boys his age needed.

He flirted with smoking for a bit but decided spending his meager earnings from the hardware store on smokes was a bad use of the money. He never got back into the habit. Of that he was glad because he does not want Kristine to be influenced at home into that habit. There is enough pressure to smoke from some of the kids at school. Fortunately, so far there has been enough pressure in the opposite direction from the peers she cares about.

As Fred pulled into the parking lot, he saw four police cars. Police tape was draped around the BMW. Two officers were taking photographs of the car from different angles. A short distance away a tow truck was idling. Fred suspected the driver was waiting to take the car somewhere.

Fred parked his SUV and headed toward the building. He needed to pass near the BMW to get to the front entrance. As he approached the door a police officer called to him. "Excuse me sir but do you work here?"

Fred looked at the officer, noticed his name tag and said, "Officer Taylor is it? Yes, I do work here. What can I do for you?"

Officer Taylor took out his note pad and asked, "Could you give me your name and where you work?"

Fred told him his name and where he worked.

Officer Taylor continued, "Did you notice anything strange yesterday? We suspect it would have been in the mid to late afternoon."

Fred paused and then said, "What do you mean by strange? It was just a normal day here."

"Anything that may have seemed out of place. Anything resembling a struggle, strange unusual noises. Anything you can think of."

"Well, all I can say is that car you have surrounded was here a lot longer than usual."

Officer Taylor asked, "What do you mean longer than usual?"

Fred continued, "I went for a walk with my family about three and noticed the car when we headed out. Nothing strange about that because cars are using the visitor spaces all the time. Most of the time they are sales reps. Cars rarely park there for hours at a time. For example, when we have people in for our training classes, we specifically request they not use the visitor parking spots."

Officer Taylor interrupted, "You said you and your family took a walk?"

"Yes sorry, we left about three. We headed over to the park and walked to the waterfall and back. We were gone, oh, let me think, about 90 minutes. When we got back my daughter saw the car and asked who drove such a nice car. It struck me as strange it was still in the lot. I went back to my office for about a half hour. It was still here when I came out. Has something happened?"

"Thanks for everything." Officer Taylor closed his notepad and put it in one of his pockets. He grabbed a business card from another pocket and handed it to Fred. "Give me call if you think of anything else."

Fred looked at the card and put it in his jacket pocket. "Sure thing." Fred headed back toward the building.

The police with all their gear and the police tape around the BMW were in stark contrast to the building grounds. The area around the building was well maintained. In the spring there are two flower beds, one on each side of the entryway, with seasonal flowers. For a few days, the grounds have the musky smell of fresh landscaping mulch.

During the winter, the lots and sidewalks are cleared by the same landscaping company. This company has been a contractor for the building for a couple of generations much like the building shoppette. The current owner of the landscaping business is the son of the original owner. He worked for his dad for years. Now his dad works for him on a part time basis.

Fred walked into the building, past the shoppette, and to the elevators. He rode to the seventh floor.

Linda looked up from her desk as he walked into the lobby. "Did you see the police downstairs?"

"Yes, what is going on? They asked me if I had seen anything strange. When I asked them about it, they were pretty                    tight                    lipped."

Linda with a bit of a conspiratorial look on her face said in something close to a whisper, "One of the salesmen visiting the building yesterday has gone missing. That BMW is his car. He was supposed to be calling on the dentist upstairs. He never made his scheduled appointment. There is no sign of him?"

Fred looked at Linda in mock amazement. "How do you find out these things?"

"Hey, we ladies of the reception desk need to stick together!"

They both laughed.

Pulling out the officer's business card and reading the name Fred said, "Hey, the officer asking all the questions is named Pete Taylor. Any relation?"

"Not that I know of. All three of my children live out of state. Two in California and the other in New York."

Putting the card back in his pocket Fred headed toward his office.

When Fred got to his office Bob French, one of his instructors, was waiting patiently nearby. "Hey Fred, I thought I would get an early start today."

Bob was of Ethiopian decent. He had jet black hair, brown eyes, deep brown skin, and was a very handsome 6 foot 2. He was originally from Detroit but had gone to school in Baltimore.

Fred smiled and said, "Hang on a second while I get the office opened up. I have a stack for you to pass to the rest of the team."

Bob said, "No problem. Did you see the cops in the parking lot?"

"Yes, I did. We talked for a couple minutes. Did they ask you anything?"

"I couldn't help them. I didn't even notice the car was there when I left yesterday. I musta been blind. I walked right past it."

Fred handed Bob the stack of papers he had retrieved from his credenza the previous evening. "I noticed the car and thought it strange to be in the visitor space for so long. Kris was asking questions about who drives that nice a car. We walked down to the waterfall yesterday afternoon. Let me know if you need anything today. I should be here all day."

Bob took the stack of printout and as he headed toward the stairs said, "I wondered where you had gotten yourself to yesterday. Someday, I will have kids and take off early."
Fred smiled and with a wave turned, sat down at his desk, and turned on his monitors.

Lunch time came and went. By the time Fred realized he had not eaten lunch it was nearly 1:30. He locked his computer screen, grabbed the book he was reading, and headed down to Clara's.

The shoppette was empty when he walked in. Lara was in the process of closing. She looked up and saw Fred. "Hey Fred. In a bit late today."

"Yeah, I was in the middle of something and I lost track of the clock."

"Most everything is already put away. The usual?"

Fred looked up from the book, "Yes if isn't too much trouble."

"Not at all. The sandwich makings are the last to be put away. What is that you are reading? Another thriller from that guy whose last name you can never pronounce?"

Fred looked at the cover of the book and held it up for Lara to see. "Yep, one of those Italian sounding names."

Fred went back to reading as Lara prepared his sandwich. Lara owns and runs the shoppette. She took over for her mother, Clara, about 14 years ago. The shoppette is just inside the entrance to left as one enters. It is open Monday through Friday from 7 in the morning until about 2 in the afternoon. Lara has one person that helps out during the busy morning hours and when she takes her one or two short holidays each year. The shop stocks a small selection of business supplies just in case someone needs to get something.

Lara does a very good breakfast business with a small selection of bagels and egg-based sandwiches. She usually has three or four different flavors of coffee brewing each day. Lunch time has a variety of deli sandwiches, salads, and soups. There is a standard set of special sandwiches every day. Tuesday is always Italian sub day.

Most of the people taking the classes at I3 get breakfast, lunch, or both at Clara's almost every day. Lara is grateful to Fred and his team for keeping her in business.

Lara finished the sandwich. "Anything else Fred?"

"Just an iced tea if you have one."

"Just the one in bottles in the fridge." Lara pointed to the refrigerator with the glass door containing a variety of sodas, teas, and energy drinks.

"Right." Fred took out a cold bottle of tea. "What's the damage?"

Lara said, "On me today."

"Are you sure?"

Lara smiled and said, "You must have all your classrooms full this week. I have been slammed. You have more than paid for that sandwich. Have a great afternoon!"

Fred thanked her and headed back upstairs.

Fred was at his desk eating the sandwich when his phone rang. "Yes Linda."

"Fred, Jill is on the phone."

"Thanks. I will get it." He waited for Linda to put Jill's call through.

"Hi Babe, what's up? Oh, you do know you can use my cell."

"Hi, yes but I like saying hello to Linda. She is such a sweet lady."

"That she is." Fred agreed.

Jill said, "Don't forget Kris has a game tonight. I thought we would all go to the game and catch dinner at Jessie's afterward. I tossed a couple chairs in the car this morning."

Jessie's was the Bates family's favorite restaurant. The staff there is friendly, and the food is good. Fred usually orders the fish and chips, Jill the Cobb Salad, and Kristine one of the various pasta dishes.

Fred said, "Sounds like a plan. I will meet you at the field. Remind me what time."

"You are hopeless. The game is at 5:30 at the elementary school. See you in a bit. Love you."

"Love you too. Bye." Fred hung up.

The rest of the afternoon was uneventful. The classes wrapped at 4:00. The rooms were all made ready for the next day by 4:30. Fred met with the training staff for 20 minutes before he left for Kristine's soccer game.

Kristine had been playing soccer since she was 5. While not the best player on the team she held her own and was beginning to have a real sense for how all the positions on the team should be played. Fred thought she would probably follow in her mom's footsteps with a scholarship for college. Of course, that may have just been Fred being a proud dad. Kristine also liked running like her mom.

Fred arrived at the field just before Jill and Kris. He waited in the car so he could help carry the chairs. Jill pulled up on the street and parked behind Fred's SUV. Fred got out and walked to the back of Jill's car to grab the chairs. They were folding captains chairs with the logo from one of the local hardware stores. He set them up on the sideline next to all the other parents of kids on Kristine's team.

The game lasted about 40 minutes. Kristine's team won by a goal. Fred never played the game, so he had to learn the rules over the years since Kris had been playing. She played defense in this game and from what he had learned, she played well.

Walking back to the cars Kristine's coach was talking with Jill. Fred and Kristine were a little ahead so they could not hear the conversation. Once at the cars, Fred put the chairs in the back of his SUV. He turned to see Jill and the coach still talking. He interrupted them, "Jill, I will take Kris and meet you at Jessie's. Okay?"

"Go ahead. I will only be a few minutes behind."

Kris ran around to the passenger side and hopped into the car. Fred got in and started the engine. "Kris, seat belt!"

"Dad! I was getting to it."

"Okay. You played well today."

"Thanks. It was fun. The team we played has some of the best players on it. I can't believe we beat them." Kristine said with no little excitement.

"Well, I am not an expert, but I think you and the players on your team are pretty good too."

"I heard some of the girls talking they were being asked to play in the travel league. That is where they play better teams from other parts of the county and state."

"I do know what the travel team means. Good for them. I think some of the girls on your team would be good for that team as well. I think you are good enough to play on that team." Fred said.

"Come on Dad. You are just saying that because you are my dad."

"No, I am not. You are a good player, and you can run forever. Thank your mom for that by the way. She is a great runner."

"I know she is. When I run with her, she doesn't get much of a workout because I am so slow compared to her."

"Don't worry Kris. When you are older you will be able to keep up. There will come a time when she will have a hard time keeping up with you. Fortunately, that is a long way off. The two of you will have a long time to run together before that. Oh look, we are here."

Jessie's restaurant was in a little strip mall just down the street about halfway between the school and their townhouse. Fred parked the car and they walked to the front door. He held the door open for Kris. The hostess greeted them both by name.

"Hello Mr. Bates. Hello Kris. Where's Mrs. Bates?"

Kris spoke first, "Mom is on her way. She will be here in a few minutes."

The hostess said, "Booth or table?"

Kris looked at Fred. She said, "Booth."

Jill arrived a few minutes later and sat next to Kris. "Well that was an interesting conversation. They are making kind of an all-star team to travel to other parts of the county and state to play the all-star teams there."

Fred said, "Kris and I were talking about that on the way here. She said some of the players on the other team were talking about moving to that team."

Jill said, "Yes they are asking the best players from all of the teams. They selected three girls from our team. They want to know if it is okay with us for Kris to be one of those three."

Kris nearly jumped out of the booth. "What?"

Fred smiled, "I told you." Looking at Jill he said, "Well, what do you think?"

Jill thought for a moment. "I don't mind, but it will be a time and financial commitment. If we say yes it won't be fair to back out later." This last bit was said to both Fred and Kristine.

Fred looked at Kristine. She sat back down on the bench. "Kris, do you want to play? Like your mom said, if you say yes, you are committed. No slouching on schoolwork either. School comes first."

Kristine looked at Jill. "Mom, what do you think?"

Jill said, "I am all for it as long as nothing else suffers. I agree with your dad about school coming first. Also, chores still have to get done."

Kristine made a fist on her outstretched arm and pulled it back to her waist as she said a little too loud, "Yes."

Fred laughed and said, "Well I take that to mean you want to play."

They finished their "usual" meals and left Jessie's. Kristine road home with her mom. Fred thought she needed a few minutes with her mom because he really could not relate to the sports thing. He rode a bike but never played sports. He followed them out of the parking lot and the rest of the way home.

While he was following them, he said, "I am truly the luckiest guy in the world. What a great kid Kristine is and Jill …"

# CHAPTER FOUR

Jill Sandstrom, an only child, grew up in one of the more affluent families in her hometown. It was a small town in central Ohio. Her father Martin, a son of Swedish immigrants, commuted to work in Columbus. Her mother, Elena, was also of Scandinavian descent. She was a stay at home mom. Martin and Elena were both in their early thirties when Jill was born. Elena suffered complications at childbirth and could not have more children.

They lived in a comfortable three-bedroom house in the nice part of town. Mr. Sandstrom bought a new car every three years. They had enough money to allow Elena to have her own car. Not many families in their town could afford a nice home and two cars.

Jill was different from most of her classmates. Most families in the community were blue collar families. She did have a growth spurt when she was about fourteen but until then she was a bit on the small side.

The kids in her class never ceased to let her know she was an outcast. She did not get invited to play with most other kids.

To give Jill a chance to play with children her age, her mom and dad took her on frequent visits to family at the other end of the state. Jill always looked forward to those trips so she could play with her cousins.

Her parents realized she needed a companion and allowed her to have a dog. When Jill was 8 years old, they drove to an animal shelter so she could pick out a dog. She walked up and down the aisles looking for the perfect pet. She was on her third trip through the maze of cages when a fluffy golden cocker spaniel caught her eye. Jill knelt next to the cage and the dog stuck a paw up to the fencing while vigorously wagging its tail. Jill stood and looked from her mother to her father and said, "Can I have this one?"

Martin and Elena both nodded. Martin left the room returning soon with one of the shelter volunteers. Elena asked, "What is the dog's name?"

Looking down a chart held in his hand the volunteer said, "Let me see. Ah yes, the cocker. Her name is Lily."

Jill said, "That is a pretty name. Can we keep that name, or do we have to change it?"

"Of course, you can keep the name. Some people do change the names, but it is not required. She already answers to Lily so it will be an easier transition for her if you keep the name."

Soon, the Sandstroms were in the car heading toward home with a new fourth member of the family. Lily was the start of a lifelong love of animals for Jill.

# CHAPTER FIVE

Jill started running when she was eleven or twelve. She does not remember the first time it happened, but she knows she was in the sixth grade. A bunch of kids were picking on her at the playground and she had to run home. This would happen every few days. She finally decided to stop going to the playground. She did not stop running.

High School arrived and Jill tried out for cross country. At the tryout no one would talk to her. She even got strange vibes from the coaches. The tryout was held over two days. The first day started with a 100-yard dash. Jill wondered why they did this for cross country. The coaches grouped the students by grade.

When it was time for the freshmen she stepped up to the starting line. There was a lot of pushing and shoving at the line. Mostly kids pushing their friends into Jill. The assistant coach walked over to the line and separated the kids doing all the pushing. Then the whistle blew. Jill was not a sprinter. She came in third of the ten freshmen. She was always amazed, although not really surprised, no matter what she did the kids would taunt her. She was jeered because she

26

came in third. She was also jeered because she beat seven others.

The students were put into two groups for the five-mile run. Seniors and Juniors in the first group to be followed 5 minutes later by the Sophomores and Freshmen. The first group left. A couple minutes later the assistant coach reminded the second group of the route. At four minutes they were told to line up. The assistant coach stood at the line so there was no pushing this time. At five minutes they started their run. Some of the freshmen took off very fast. Jill started in the middle of the pack.

After the first mile every one of the kids that had started out fast had fallen back, and Jill was now running second. Once past the second mile she began to increase her pace. Soon she was in the lead of the second group. By the time she had a mile left she was about to pass runners in the first group. As she crossed the finish line the coach was calling out times. One of the volunteer parents was recording the times. Jill went over to see her time and was extremely disappointed. She thought her pace would have given her a much faster time.

Once all the first group finished the times being called for the second group were adjusted by the five-minute difference in the start time. Jill went to the coach and asked why her time was worse than those now finishing in the second group. The parent that recorded the time said, "What grade are you?" Jill replied, "Ninth." The coaches standing around the finish line looked at each other. The head coach walked over to the parent recording the times.

"Let me see that." He looked at the time recorded for Jill's run and mentally subtracted five minutes. "Oh my God." Was all he could get out.

Jill made the team. Since there were only a set number of slots they could fill at any event, Jill was continuously reminded she had someone else's spot on the team. Even when she scored points for the team there was no relief. She became very closed off from her teammates and basically ran for herself.

During high school Jill blossomed into a beautiful young woman. Her grades were excellent. Cross country and distance running on the spring track team provided her with a partial scholarship to college.

# CHAPTER SIX

One evening in the fall semester of her freshman year at college Jill bumped into Fred, literally. She had just finished practice and was in line at the cafeteria for dinner. She dropped her gym bag and as she bent over to pick it up, she banged her head against Fred's. He was also bending over to pick up her bag. They both grabbed their heads and stood up. They looked at each other and started to laugh. "Hi, my name is Jill."

"Mine is Fred, you have a hard head!"

A few days after the encounter in the dining hall, Jill was having trouble getting comfortable with the notion she was not the best runner on the team. She was having a particularly bad day. Fred noticed her from across the quad and jogged over. "How are you doing?"

She replied with a subdued "Okay."

Fred said, "Right, convince me! Shoulders slumped. Grumpy expression. Where is that normal bouncy stride you have? If this is your version of okay, then I will need to get a new dictionary. Although, I don't think the bookstore has one with that definition it."

Jill relented with a weak smile. "You're such an asshole!"

"Finally, a true statement" he said. "Want to talk about it?" After a nod from Jill, he led her to the library. They found an empty seminar room. He opened the door, let her in, flipped the sign next to the door to occupied, then closed the door after following her in. The room was just big enough for the table and chairs. There were twelve chairs surrounding the table all in various stages of being pushed under the table. There was a white board on the wall opposite the door. It had been erased but it looked as if the eraser had been damp, because it looked more smudged than erased. They walked to the far end of the room to hide from view as much as possible.

Jill set her bag down on the table and plopped onto the floor. Fred set his bag next to hers on the table and sat next to her on the floor, back against the wall.

"Would you turn off the lights?"

"Sure, be right back. Don't go anywhere."

"You are such a jerk!"

Fred stood up. "Just trying to keep it light." He walked back to the door and flipped off the lights. A window made up the top half of the door, so it was still light in the room. It appeared the library staff wanted to know what was going on in their rooms. Fred walked back to the far corner and sat on the floor next to Jill. "What's going on?" Jill leaned over and laid her head on his shoulder and started to cry. "We have plenty of time. No rush."

They sat there for about thirty minutes. Jill cried off and on for much of it. Fred spent the time stroking her blond hair. Neither spoke a word and none were needed. A bond between them had begun to grow much as a flower seed germinates.

Jill dried her eyes and straightened. She then told Fred about her hometown and high school and running. "I used to be the best at school and that was the only way I got anything resembling acceptance. Now I am not the best. I don't know what to do. Running defined me!"

"So, what are you studying here?"

"General Studies because I don't know what I want to do. All I thought about was running and they asked me to come here and run for them. They even gave me a partial scholarship."

"Okay, are your times, or whatever you measure improving?"

"Of course, I'm still young and the coaches here are the best."

"So, you love running and you are getting better. Do your teammates think you're dragging the team down or that you are not pulling your share?"

"That's just it. They like me, I think. They encourage me, and when I turn in a personal best they cheer and hug me. In high school all I ever got was scorn from the teammates and false praise from the coaches because they knew they were winning because of me."

"What do you want out of running? I understand it probably saved you in high school, sort of. I don't think you need that kind of safety net here. Now that you are not in that toxic high school environment, you have a chance to really think about what you want. From running, from a career, and from all other aspects of your life. I am here any time you want to talk about it." Fred gave her shoulder a squeeze.

Jill leaned over and kissed Fred on the mouth. She stopped as Fred pulled back. She said, "Did I do that wrong? I never kissed a boy before."

"No, I just wasn't expecting it. Let's try it again." After the kiss Jill put her head back on his shoulder. About an hour later the door opened. One of the library staff was checking all the rooms before closing. Seeing them in the corner, she told them the library was closing. Fred and Jill stood up, grabbed their bags from the table, and walked sheepishly out of the room.

Fred walked Jill to her dorm. "We missed dinner. Do you want to get a bite somewhere?"

"Rain check? I have a lot of homework."

"No problem. I have something in my room."

"Fred, thank you for your shoulder." She kissed him on the cheek. "Tomorrow? Dinner?"

# CHAPTER SEVEN

The next evening Fred met Jill back at her dorm. "So where to?"

Jill said, "I have a favorite place just a little off campus. I can drive."

Fred said, "I didn't know you have a car? I don't have one. My mom told me I didn't need one since my classes, my room, and the cafeteria are all on campus."

"Since I got most of my tuition as a scholarship, my parents bought me a car. It's a little Honda so it was not too expensive, and it gets great gas mileage. Since I am on the cross country and track teams, I get to park it over at the field house. I drove it here after practice today. It is just across                          the                          street."

Jill was right. The car was little. It was maroon on the outside and beige on the inside. Jill unlocked the doors and Fred got in on the passenger side while Jill got in behind the wheel. She started the car and put the radio on low.

Fred started the discussion, "I know it has been only one day, but have you thought about our talk yesterday?"

"Yes, I did. I am not all the way through it yet. Like you said it has only been one day after all. But I think I can accept the fact I won't be able to make running a career. So, I need to give what I want to be when I grow up some serious thought." She turned left. "I have been so focused on running for so long. I never thought about what life would be like after running. I never had Olympic aspirations or anything like that. I just like to run!" She turned left again.

"Yesterday, I think you woke me up from what was years of me being withdrawn from anything other than schoolwork and running. I know it will take a long time to really come to grips with it. I may even need to do some therapy. I thought about all of this today as I was running. The run seemed to be over as soon as it started. I wasn't even tired after the run! I was exhilarated. It was like there was a trip I was looking forward to with great anticipation and it was finally here. I thought about repeating the run because I was on one of those runner's highs."

Fred did not want to break the spell she was in, but he asked, "All this from yesterday?"

Jill was excited now, "Yes, it was like a baby getting slapped on her behind on her birthday. All of a sudden, I was awake and crying! Literally! I have a new energy because I know I will have a future other than running. I will still run but it won't be the sole reason I exist. I don't know what it will be, but I know it is out there somewhere. I just have to find the path. And, I have you to thank for that!"

Fred had not realized it, but the end of the conversation took place in the parking lot of the restaurant. He was watching her in amazement and had not even noticed they were no longer moving. Jill had been looking straight into his eyes with all the new found passion for her future.

Jill opened the door, "I hope you like Italian!"

"Sure do."

# CHAPTER EIGHT

After dinner, Jill and Fred got back into the maroon Honda and headed back to campus. This time the conversation was more casual and centered on class and campus activities. They were both exploring the likes and dislikes of each other.

Nearing campus Jill said, "I have to take my car to the field house. I can't park it next to the dorm overnight. I will drop you at your dorm."

"No, I would like to go with you and walk with you back to your dorm."

"Are you sure? I would love the company."

"Most definitely!"

Jill drove to the field house. They both got out and she locked the car. They had just under a mile to walk to Jill's dorm. The streets were well lit and busy. A hundred yards or so down the sidewalk Fred reached down and took Jill's hand in his. Jill did not flinch at the touch but accepted his hand in hers. They walked hand in hand the rest of the way to Jill's dorm. They did not seem to be in any hurry, and the walk took about twenty minutes. Neither one said much during the walk. They were pretty much talked out.

When they reached the front door of the building Fred gave her a kiss. He then leaned over and whispered in her ear, "I am so glad I bumped heads with you!"

Jill said, "Me too." Then added nervously, "Do you want to come in?"

"This is going to sound corny, but I really like you and I really do want to follow you to your room. I am worried we might do something I really want to do but I am not sure either of us is ready. I for one do not want rushing into this to spoil what we have started. I am looking at the long game. I want what we have to grow and last. I want to make sure we both are one hundred percent certain and ready. Know what I mean?"

Jill engulfed Fred in a hug and said with tears welling up in her eyes, "Thank you for not rushing. I don't know where my head is just now. I will tell you though, I am one hundred percent certain. I will let you know when I am ready." With that she squeezed a bit harder, gave him another kiss, and winked as she ran giggling into the dorm.

Fred walked across campus to his dorm. He took the elevator up to his floor. He got out of the elevator, turned right, and walked to his room. The door was unlocked. He opened the door and announced to his roommate he had found his soulmate and that Jill would marry him someday. Looking up from his studies his roommate said with a touch of sarcasm, "Right." He then returned to his books.

Fred flopped onto his bed. He could not study. He could not sleep. All thoughts were of Jill and the last two days.

# CHAPTER NINE

This morning Fred was reading the novel by the mystery writer on his way into the building from the parking lot. He walked onto the elevator without noticing Harry, his boss, following him. Harry accidentally pressed the button for the sixth floor instead of seven. He looked at Fred, deep into his book, and said "Sorry about that!" But Fred had not noticed. The doors closed and they began the ride up.

Just after the light for floor three lit up, the elevator had a slight bump. Harry said "I hate it when it does that. I know these elevators are getting old, but they do get regular maintenance. They get a checkup about every six months and a complete overhaul about once a year."

Then the doors opened to the sixth floor. Harry said "Sounds like a storm is raging in there. Sounds like wind and rain. Weird music track. Could it be the Doors song 'Riders on the Storm?'"

Fred looked up at this and said, "It even smells like a spring rainstorm. Funny, because the sun is out this morning."

The doors began to close, and the sounds and smells vanished as they came together and the climb to the seventh floor began. When the doors opened Fred followed Harry out of the elevator. Neither one noticed fresh water at the edge of the floor just inside the elevator.

# CHAPTER TEN

Fred looked up from his monitors and reached for his briefcase. It was not behind his desk. He stood up and walked to his table. It was not there either. After a quick examination of his office Fred decided he must have left it in the car. He looked at his watch, it was just after 9:30. A bit too early to grab lunch.

Fred locked his computer screens and headed out of his office. As he walked through the reception area on his way to the elevators, he told Linda he was heading to his car and would be right back. He pressed the down button and waited a minute for an elevator to arrive.

Once in the lobby, he headed into Clara's. He walked to the refrigerator with the glass door and grabbed a bottle of iced tea. After paying for the tea he walked out of the building and headed for his car.

When Fred reached his SUV, he took out his keys and unlocked the doors. He looked in the passenger seat and he did not see his briefcase. He then remembered he put it in the back before leaving home. He closed the passenger door and walked around to the back of the car. As he was opening the hatch, he noticed a man wandering the parking lot. The man appeared to be mumbling to himself. Fred was too far away to make out any of the words.

The man looked completely disheveled. His clothes were tattered, and his hair was completely unkempt. He had what appeared to be a beard. It was thin and as untidy as the rest of his hair. He was looking around as if he was searching for something he lost.

Fred turned to his car and reached for his briefcase and closed the hatch lid. When he turned to start for the building the man had begun to walk toward Fred. Fred called out, "Hey, are you okay?"

The man said, "Where's my car?"

"Your what?"

"My car."

Fred then asked, "Can I call someone for you?"

Then man started to walk away. As he did he said and then repeated over and over until Fred could no longer hear, "Sixth floor. Use the stairs."

Fred watched the man as he walked out of the parking lot and headed toward the center of town. Not knowing what to do Fred shook his head and headed back to his office.

When Fred got home that evening, he mentioned the parking lot encounter to Jill. "He reminded me of Michael Palin at the beginning of the Monty Python TV program. I half expected the guy to say 'Its' when he walked over to me."

Jill said, "Do you know who that was? I heard on the news on the way home. It was the guy who went missing at your building that day we went for a walk to the waterfall. That was, what, a month or so ago. Where do you think he was?"

Fred said, "And why did he get dropped off back at the building. He said a few things to me. I didn't think much of them at the time. He said he was looking for his car. He also said something like sixth floor and use the stairs. This last part he kept repeating over and over as he walked away. I just thought he was some poor guy that was lost. He headed out of the lot and walked toward downtown."

Jill said, "Well at least he is back and hopefully well." Changing the subject, she said, "Shall we go out for dinner tonight or get carry-out? I don't feel like cooking."

Fred said, "Let's order Chinese. I don't feel like going out."

# CHAPTER ELEVEN

A week after his encounter in the parking lot, Fred arrived at the office about 7:30 in the morning. The first thing he did was make sure all was ready for the classes. Since it was Wednesday, the classes had been going for a couple days. The instructors had everything organized. Back at his desk the phone rang.

"Hello Fred? This is Linda. Bill Hansson from TPR is on the phone. Remind me what TPR means again?"

Fred said, "Great, I was hoping he would call back. Put him through. TPR stands for Technology Personnel Recruiters. Bill Hansson is one of their Software Engineer recruitment representatives. You know, a headhunter!"

Fred pressed the outside line button and said, "Hello Bill. I am glad you called back. I was hoping to get together to discuss a couple holes I have in my staff."

Bill added, "I think I have the perfect people for you. Would you like to get together and talk about them? I am free all morning if you can get away today. Tomorrow morning works as well."

Fred looked quickly at his calendar. "I can get away this morning. I can get there about 8:30 unless that is too early."

"That works perfectly for me. I will see you then. Bye."

"Bye." Fred pressed the button on the phone to hang up. He then let go and dialed Linda on the intercom.

"Yes Fred."

"I have a meeting with Bill Hansson at 8:30 to discuss a couple of developer needs. I should be gone no more than a couple hours."

Linda said, "I will add it to the office calendar. Good hunting!" She rang off.

Fred hung up the phone and gathered his notes he would need for his meeting with Bill Hansson. He opened his briefcase and tossed the notes in. He picked up the book he was reading and headed for the door.

The meeting lasted about an hour. Fred was heading back into the building just before ten. He was nearly finished with the book and was reading it every chance he got to get to the end.

Fred reached the lobby and pressed the up button to get an elevator. The second one on the left arrived first.

As Fred was getting onto the elevator several guys from the insurance company on the fifth and sixth floors joined him. They were in the middle of a heated discussion about something. Fred was really more interested in his book than eavesdropping on their conversation. He pressed 7, they pressed 5 and 6. The guys from the fifth floor convinced the guys from the sixth floor to join them in the conference room to finish the discussion. The doors opened on 5 and they all got off.

The doors closed. There was that bump between floors again. The doors soon opened again. Fred stepped out. He looked up from his book. The lobby looked different. He heard the doors closing. He turned to get back on to see them close, and then disappear.

Fred was standing in the middle of a meadow.

"What the hell!" Fred looked in all directions. He appeared to be in a meadow. He could see trees in every direction. There was a small rise nearby. No sign of the building. No sign of the elevator lobby. Just a grassy meadow and then trees. Lots of trees. He dropped the book and the brief case and started to call out.

"Hello! Is anyone there?" Fred walked around in a small circle calling out again. "Hello!" After a few minutes he gathered himself. He looked for his briefcase and the book. He found them lying in the grass. He sat next to them.

"What has happened? Am I dreaming?" He pinched his arm. "Well I felt that. Does that mean I am awake, or can I just feel the pinch in my dream? If this is a dream the detail is much clearer than usual."

Fred sat there for what seemed like hours. He was hoping to either wake up or for whatever dropped him in the middle of the meadow to reappear and take him back. He did not wake up because he was not asleep. Whatever dropped him there did not come back to get him. So, he waited. And then, he waited some more.

# CHAPTER TWELVE

Fred noticed the sun was getting low in the sky. He wondered if it would be dark long. He knew he needed to find shelter. The closest wooded area was just over the hill. It looked to be a half mile or so away. He headed that way. Fred hoped he could find some dense trees like pines to provide some cover. It was slow going since the grass in the meadow was very thick and his feet kept getting tangled.

By the time he made it to the tree line, some stars were beginning to show. Fred said out loud, "I wish I was better at recognizing constellations." He was hoping for something familiar. There was no moon, and the sky was getting dark quickly. He had never experienced this type of darkness. The was no light pollution here. He had not walked very far when he looked back at the sky and saw more stars than he had ever seen before.

Fred reminded himself he needed to find shelter. He could look at the sky later. Every couple of minutes he caught himself looking back up at the stars. He was walking along the tree line. He wished he had spent some time exploring earlier, while the sun was still out. Was it the "Sun"? A few more minutes and he was looking at the sky again.

Something looked familiar. Were those stars forming a giant "W"? Could that be Cassiopeia? "Am I still on Earth? Stupid question. Where else would I be?"

Suddenly, his foot got snagged on something and he realized he was falling. He tried to put his hands out to brace his fall but one of them was still holding his briefcase. He hit something hard. Then it went dark.

# CHAPTER THIRTEEN

"Jill, close the blinds!" Fred said as the sun hit his eyes. He rolled over to close them himself. "Ow!" He reached for his head. He felt a small lump on his forehead. Opening his eyes, he saw he was outdoors.

Looking around Fred saw he was at the edge of a meadow where it meets a forest. "What the hell!" He went to stand and noticed his feet were tangled in what looked like a pole with vines wrapped around it. He freed his feet from the tangle and stood up. "God, I thought this was a dream."

He looked back down at the pole he had apparently tripped over. His gaze followed the pole toward the forest. It looked like the pole was connected to something resembling a lean-to. It was in bad shape if that was indeed a lean-to. Taking a closer look, it looked man made for sure. Even if was not in bad shape the construction was not done well. Taking another look around he exclaimed "Where the hell am I?"

He began to remember the day before. The elevator, the grassy field, and then the stars. He remembered walking while looking at the sky and then falling. As he remembered falling, his hand reached to his forehead seeking out the newly created lump.

He reached down and picked up the pole. It looked to be from a hardwood tree of some sort. The bark that was left on it looked rough and Fred thought it was probably oak of some kind.

He remembered he had his brief case with him. He looked around and saw it lying in the grass about five feet from where his head hit the ground. The book he was reading lay next to it. He walked over to it, bent down, and picked up both. He opened the briefcase, put the book inside, and made a quick search. He found what he needed, his pocketknife.

"I need to get back." He looked near the edge of the forest and noticed the grass looked slightly trampled. He retraced his steps along the edge of the meadow. After a few minutes, the path in the trampled grass turned left toward the middle of the clearing. He continued to follow his track from the previous day until he reached a small hill. He walked up the hill and noticed the path ended a short distance from the other side of the hill.

Fred surmised this must be the place he arrived. He walked around an area about twenty feet by twenty feet trampling the grass. He wanted to be able to easily find this place again. When he was satisfied the grass was sufficiently flattened, he plopped down on the ground and waited.

He sat there, and he sat there. After what seemed like hours, he looked at his watch. It read 8:15 AM. Was he on the same time schedule here? Where is here? This got him thinking.

"Did that elevator send me here? Where is here?" He felt an odd familiarity as he looked around. "That is the dumbest thing in the world!" He stood up and looked around. He looked along the path he made toward the forest. He could see the tops of the trees showing above the crest of the hill. They must be at least a half mile away.

He looked up at the sky. There were small puffy clouds moving slowly across the sky. The sun, "Is it the Sun?", was low in the sky. Again, he had the feeling of something familiar. Why did this feel familiar? He continued to look around. There was forest in the distance in every direction. Strange there is a meadow here. How did that happen? The closest trees were where he went yesterday. He thought out loud, "That would be why I went that way!" There was that feeling again.

He looked at the clouds again. What are they called? As he watched them float across the sky, he noticed there was a slight breeze blowing toward the closest part of the forest. There is that feeling.

Fred sat back down and opened his briefcase. There was not much in there. He had already taken out his knife. He found a couple sets of class notes he had been editing, his notes from the meeting with Bill Hansson, a box of CDs with his backup copies of the class presentations, the book, and finally there was a small pack of matches he brought from home to light the grill at the last lunchtime company barbeque. Turns out he did not need them. Harry already had the grill lit before Fred left his office to head downstairs for the picnic area. He took the box of matches out and opened the box. The matches were an inch and a half long and made of wood. He counted seventeen matches.

He thought of the initiation he had for one of his scouting organizations. Breakfast was an egg and a paper cup of water. He was given 2 matches, strike anywhere, and was told to boil the egg in the paper cup. He gathered a bunch of kindling and other sticks from the nearby woods. He then set about clearing a place to build a fire. Soon he had a small fire burning. He let it burn down until he had a good set of coals. He placed the egg in the cup and let the excess water spill on the ground.

He watched as the water in the cup began to boil. As the water level dropped, the exposed part of the cup would dry and then burn away. After ten minutes or so Fred decided the egg must be done. He toppled the cup over so the water left in the cup would start the process of dousing the fire. Using a couple of sticks he retrieved the egg and set it aside to cool. While the egg was cooling, he stirred the damp coals to get the fire as close to being out as he could. Finally, he took handfuls of dirt from around the fire to finish the job. The fire out, Fred sat down and enjoyed a perfectly hardboiled egg cooked in a paper cup!

Snapping back from his thoughts Fred realized he had not eaten anything since lunch the day before. More importantly he had not had anything to drink either.

Fred though out loud, "Where would I find water around here?"

There was that feeling again.

"I wonder if that shelter is near a water source."

Looking at his watch it was getting close to noon. He looked up toward the sun. It was high in the sky. Not exactly overhead, however. That feeling again. Fred is sensing something he just cannot put his finger on it.

"How did we use the sun to find directions?" At noon, back home, the sun was always a bit to the south. At noon, shadows ran south to north. He looked at his shadow. It was not very long, but it was enough to give him an approximate bearing toward the North. All the rest of the compass points would follow per usual. There goes that feeling again. Something is familiar. What is it? He looked toward the forest. "Could it be?"

With a sudden burst of energy, he got up, grabbed his briefcase, dropped the pole on the ground, and took off in the direction of the lean-to. Running through the grass proved to be difficult. His feet kept getting snagged. He reached the tree line in about ten minutes. He turned right to head toward the shelter. He had taken a different angle than the night before and was closer to the shelter. Soon he was there and stopped to catch his breath. He took a long look at the forest.

The forest looked like the hardwood forest he was used to seeing at home. Mostly oak, with beech, maple, and ash thrown in. It was a mature forest with a thick canopy and therefore a minimum of undergrowth. He could not remember the differences between red and white oak or red and sugar maple, but it really did not matter.

After a few minutes, his breath caught, he put his briefcase in the lean-to and headed into the forest. "How far is it? Will it be there?" The farther he went into the forest the faster he walked. He found himself running.

Dodging the trees and the few brambles able to grow under the dense canopy of the trees. He only stumbled once. That made him realize he was at a dead run, so he slowed. Soon he could hear running water. Suddenly, there it was. The river. Right where he thought it should be.

Fred now understood what the feeling was. Everything around him appears to be where his office building was and the park next door with the river. He wondered if there would be a waterfall just down river. May as well confirm it. He looked around and gathered a few sticks to make a sort of marker so he would remember where to turn back into the forest to get back to the shelter. He turned right to head downriver.

A hundred yards, or so he thought, downriver the bank was low enough for him to get to the water. He was quite thirsty. He took off his coat and laid down so he could get some water. As he drank from the river, he thought to himself, "this is the best water I have ever tasted!" After he satisfied his thirst he stood back up and continued down river.

There was the faint sound of the waterfall. Fred began to get excited. The closer he got to the precipice, the louder the sound. The water was beginning to move faster. Then, there it was! The waterfall. It did not look exactly like he remembered, but there it was right where he expected it to be.

Fred sat on the forest floor overlooking the waterfall. "What the hell has happened? Why am I here?"

Fred sat staring at the waterfall and listening to the crashing water. He was trying to sort out what to do. Was this really where he thought it was? If so, what brought him here? Is it a different time? A different, what do they call it, dimension? Was he selected to be here or was it random? How long would he be here? How will he survive? Most importantly how would he get back?

All these questions ran through his head over and over. It was as if he was in some sort of a trance. After what seemed like hours, he shook his head and stood up. He looked at his watch. He had been sitting there less than an hour. He was still hungry. First thing was to get something to eat. But what?

He had seen a lot of fish in some of the pools in the river. He had some matches in his briefcase. He would catch a fish and then cook it near the lean-to.

Fred headed back upriver to look for a fish to catch.

He did not have to go far before he saw what he thought was the best place to catch a fish. Near the bank of the river was a shallow pool bathed in sunlight. There, fish appeared to be sunning themselves. Their tails moving only to match the current to stay in the sunlight.

Fred stripped to his underwear and stepped into the river. Unfortunately for him, he immediately stepped on a rock covered with a slimy something and slipped and fell into the water. This startled the fish and they all disappeared. He climbed out of the river soaking wet. He sat next to the pool in the sun to stay warm and dry off. Soon the fish began to return to the pool.

He decided to give it one more try. More carefully this time. He slowly entered the water. Sidestepping the offending rock from his first attempt, he approached the pool. He picked out a fish nearby and put his hands into the water to grab the fish. He crept closer to the fish with his hands out in front of him. The fish apparently had not noticed him yet. Fred lunged, clasping his hands around the fish. Problem was the fish was not in his hands when he took them out of the river. Fred chased after the fish as they scurried away from the pool.

Now the fish were gone and the water in the pool was completely clouded with bottom sediment Fred had stirred while chasing after the fish. He climbed out of the water and sat back down in the area illuminated by the sun. Once again soaked he said out loud to no one in particular, "Well that was stupid. I need to think this through better." He sat there until he was dry enough to put his clothes back on.

He needed a plan. Once dressed he headed back toward the lean-to.

Once back at the lean-to, Fred entered the shelter for the first time. The support poles and walls we completely tangled up with weeds and undergrowth. He began to pull the plants to clear the inside. The shelter was about twelve feet by eight feet. It took twenty minutes to clear the plants from the inside. The ground now nearly bare revealed the walls and support.

Fred examined each of the poles that were left. One was still in the middle of the meadow. He pushed against each one to test how sturdy they were. They all had varying degrees of wobble to them. He would have to put them farther into the ground and maybe put support on the outside. Weeds and vines had been used to attach everything together. They would all need to be replaced with fresh since they were coming undone.

Next, he looked at the walls. He could see through all three of them. More repair was needed on the roof as well. He wondered how long it would take to make the shelter viable for protection from the weather. He also wondered if he would be here long. He needed to figure out how to get everything done and still spend most of each day at the spot in the middle of the meadow.

The afternoon was waning, and he knew it would be dark in a few hours. Fred was still hungry, but he decided he did not want to go chasing after fish again today so, he would wait until the morning. This made him think about where he was going to sleep. He was not sure he wanted to sleep directly on the now mostly dirt floor of the shelter.

He looked around at the forest. What could he put together quickly to get him somewhat off the ground? He also looked at the meadow. An idea came to him. He headed into the woods. He found a couple branches from the trees six feet long and two inches in diameter. He also picked up two half as long.

Back at the shelter, Fred laid them on the ground to form a frame six feet by three feet. He would need to lash them together but he did not have anything handy to do that, so it would wait. He then headed for the meadow. He started pulling up grass. It was hard work. Most of the grass would come up with the roots. He had to pound the root balls against the ground to knock the dirt off.

He filled the frame with the grasses. It was not much, but it was not dirt. Fred thought it would be enough for one day. He was tired. The sun, if it was the sun, was getting low in the sky. If this was a dream, he sure was working hard. He lay on the grass bed and fell asleep.

# CHAPTER FOURTEEN

Fred woke on the third day inside the shelter. It took a few minutes for him to realize he was still in the foreign place, or more likely, foreign time. He did not understand why he was here, or for that matter, how he was here.

The sun was streaming into the lean-to through gaps in the foliage. Fred decided, if he was going to be here, he would need to shore up the structure. First, he needed to get something to eat. As for catching fish, yesterday was a lost day. All he did was get wet when he slipped into the river. He needed to think. He needed to remember. He had training when he was younger.

Did he see signs of wildlife yesterday? "Concentrate" he told himself out loud. The problem was he still was not sure he really and truly believed this was not a bad dream. Even if it was a dream, he needed to be smart and calm. He needed to remember. He needed protection from the elements and potential wildlife. If his hunch was correct, somehow, he was transported to the same place but a different time. There may be wildlife the area had not seen in centuries, or maybe even millennia. Who knows when this was?

He looked around inside the shelter. He had cleared most of the undergrowth out of it yesterday. He began a mental list of what needed to be done. Yesterday, he inspected each of the shelter support poles. Every one of them wobbled a bit. He would have to put them further in the ground and replace the one he left in the meadow. The roof and sides would need to be rethatched. He needed to go back to the spot in case whatever brought him here returned. That meant less time during the day to work on the structure.

He stepped out of the shelter and looked around. He would need to clear some of the area around here as well. He needed a fire pit, unless he was content to eat raw fish. He also hoped to be able to catch some small animals. Are there any? He was not really paying attention too much yesterday. It was a bit disorienting to think he was just in a different time at the same place. But the distances to the river and the waterfall were about what they should be. He had just walked to the waterfall with Jill and Kristine a couple weeks, no it was a couple months ago. "What the hell is going on?" he said out loud.

He looked at his watch. It was early, 6:30. He headed toward the river. He needed to drink something. He needed to eat something. He did see plenty of fish in the river. Catching them could be a problem. He had no line, no rod, and no hooks.

Think!

Fred started looking around as he was walking. He was not even sure what he was looking to see but he thought he might know when he saw it. Then he saw it. He did indeed know what he needed. Lying on the ground about two feet to his right was a branch that had fallen from a tree. The branch was about eight feet long with a diameter of about an inch and a half. It must have broken off the tree because it had a jagged point on one end. That is what clicked in Fred's head. A stick with a pointed end.

He bent over and picked up the stick. He put one end on the ground and pressed down hard. The stick snapped in two. "Well, that one won't work." He thought. But now he knew how he was going to catch the fish. He set out looking for a stick that would not snap in two when he pressed it on the ground. It took a few minutes to find a suitable replacement. It did not have a sharp end, but he would make quick work of that with his knife.

Fred made his way to the river. He found a fallen tree trunk nearby and sat down. He took out his knife and began to sharpen one end of the stick. It had not been on the ground long making it easier to whittle the end down to a point. He got up and began walking upstream. He might as well get to know both directions.

He was beginning to remember some of the survival training he received when he was in scouts. Fish were easier to catch early in the day and later in the day. Was that right? Well it did not matter, he needed to eat and other than going back to the spot in the field, he had all day.

There were many pools along the banks of the river. Most were shallow enough to see the bottom. So far, all he saw, were small minnow sized fish. The day before he went downstream. He saw larger fish that way, so he turned around and headed downstream.

Shortly after he passed the path toward the shelter, he began to see larger fish. They were a little too far from the riverbank for him to reach with his rudimentary spear. He kept walking. There were many places he had to walk around fallen trees. One tree had fallen with branches in the river. When he looked closer, he noticed there were fish swimming around the branches.

Fred leaned against the tree trunk and watched. Soon there was a fish close enough for him to reach with his spear. He waited, steadied himself, raised his arm and then plunged the spear into the river. Missed! The fish scattered.

"Damn", Fred said out loud. "This is harder than it looks on TV." He rested on the tree trunk and watched. After a short time, the fish started to return to the area around the branches in the water. All he had to do was be patient. Another fish came within range of his spear. He repeated the process with a splash. Another miss.

He thought maybe the fish were too deep and there was distortion by the depth of the water. He decided to wait until one was closer to the surface of the river. It took a few more tries, but he finally caught his first fish. He looked at his watch. It was now 8:30. It had taken him nearly an hour and a half since he got to the river and started on the spear. He cleaned the fish, putting all the scraps in the water. No sense attracting any unwanted wildlife. He then headed back toward the shelter.

Fred needed to get back to the spot in the field. However, he was not too keen on eating raw fish. He decided to clear a place for a small fire. He pulled up the undergrowth clearing an area of the ground six feet in diameter. He searched the forest for a half dozen logs to use as a temporary barrier. He would make a barrier with rocks later.

He gathered some kindling and small sticks and set to building a small fire. He broke a branch off a nearby tree and stripped off part of the bark. He slid this branch through the fish and held it over the fire. In five or ten minutes he had freshly cooked fish for breakfast. Once finished eating he stirred the fire to allow it to go out faster. Once it was out, he headed for the spot in the middle of the field.

The path to the spot in the meadow was easier to follow today than it had been yesterday. It also took less time since the grass was becoming trampled enough for easier walking. He looked at his watch. It was after eleven. When he reached the spot, he picked up the pole he left there yesterday. He sat down and began to wait.

As Fred waited, he took out his knife and sharpened one end of the pole. Once it had a pointed end, he stood up and drove it into the ground. The ground was hard and it did not go in very far. He let go and the pole immediately fell over. He tried it again with the same result.

He knelt and using the awl on his knife began to dig a hole. It was slow going, but he did not have anything else to do. It took him 20 minutes to get a hole he thought was deep enough to hold up the pole. He put the pole in the freshly dug hole and filled in the space around it with the dirt from the hole. Holding the pole, he stood up and packed the dirt down with his foot. This time when he let go of the pole it did not fall. Now he would be able to find the spot from any direction.

After a few hours he was getting thirsty. He realized he was going to need something to hold water. He was also getting warm. He took off his jacket. Fred wondered if he should build a small shelter here to block the sun. How long would he be here?

Fred stood up to stretch his legs. He started to walk around the clearing swinging his arms. He immediately caught his feet on some of the grass and stumbled. This gave him an idea. He ripped up a handful of the grass. He took two of the stalks and placing one halfway down the other began to twist them. He added a third and then a fourth. Soon he had a strand of woven grass ten feet long. It was a bit stiff, but it appeared to be quite strong. He spent the rest of the afternoon weaving grass to make pieces of rope. He would need a lot of this to strengthen the structure of the lean-to.

He looked at his watch and it was getting on toward three. His hands were tired, but he had quite a bit of his rope. As he gathered it up and headed toward the forest, he thought to himself, "survival is hard work!"

When he reached the shelter, he dropped the rope and picked up the spear he made earlier in the day. Time to go fishing again. This time it only took a couple tries. He had a fish and his fill of water and was back at the shelter in just under an hour. This is when he realized lighting two fires a day would use up all his matches in a week. With any luck he would not be here that long. But what if he was not that lucky. Fred needed to keep a fire going to save his matches.

Fred knew this would be dangerous and could lead to a forest or brush fire. He decided as long as the weather cooperated, he would keep a fire going all the time. To do this he needed to make a better fire pit. So, before he cooked the freshly caught fish, he set to making a fire pit he was comfortable using for a perpetual fire. Once done, he gathered kindling and other dry wood for the fire. He started the fire using another of his matches and as it burned down, he cleared a wider area around the pit.

After he ate his fish, Fred headed to the river to look for some rocks he could use for a barrier around the fire. By the time he made a few trips to the river and back with rocks, the sun was getting lower in the sky. He arranged the rocks around the fire. He added a couple larger pieces to the fire.

By now, he was quite tired. He went into the shelter and straightened up the grass bed and before he knew it, he was asleep.

It was still quite dark when Fred was startled awake. "What the hell was that?" he asked the night. He crawled over to the edge of the lean-to. There was still a faint glow near the bottom of the fire pit. He got up and put a couple more pieces of wood into the fire. Soon they were aflame, and he went back to the shelter and listened.

He was amazed at how quiet it was here. At home in the evening there always traffic noises or air conditioners or airplanes or any number of other noises from the number of people around. Here there was nothing but the faint sounds of the river. Other than that, all he could hear was the crackle of the fire.

Then he heard the sound that made his skin crawl. There was the sound of what he thought was a growl of a large cat. He had never heard that sound before, other than in a movie or TV show. It did not sound very close, but it could not be that far away if he could hear it. Fred wondered what the cat was growling at. He began to have second thoughts about the fire. Was he making it easier for the cat to notice him now that the fire was going again? What did he do with the left-over fish parts from dinner? Could the cat smell them, and would it be drawn to the smell? He needed to either toss them in the river or bury them from now on.

He searched in the darkness for the spear he used to catch the fish. When he found it, it seemed to be quite lacking in what he thought it would need for protection against predators. He wondered how Native Americans protected themselves against these animals.

Fred did not hear the sound again the rest of the night. He did not get any more sleep either. He tended to the fire. When the sun finally came up, Fred knew what he had to do that day.

# CHAPTER FIFTEEN

The sun had not been up very long when Fred headed straight for the river. If the timeline was tracking, it would be Saturday, and he didn't think the elevator would show up, since nobody would be in the building to push the buttons.

When Fred got to the river, he wondered why the shelter was not closer to the water. Should he build a new one here? He spent a lot of time down here getting water and food. Maybe if he ended up here for a long time, he might think of moving closer. "What is a long time? A week? A month? Longer?"

At this moment, he was worried about the cat he heard last night. Fred was wondering if he was at the top of the food chain or just somewhere near the top. He was not hungry yet, but he needed to drink. After drinking, he set out looking for something he could use for weapons.

The sticks he had sharpened for fishing did not look as if they would hold up against a determined predator. He searched the woods for some poles he could use to attach some pointed rocks. How would he attach them? What else could he use? He looked for a branch about three feet long and three to four inches in diameter.

After an hour of searching he was back at the riverbank with a few 7-feet long sticks he planned to use for spears, a three-foot log, and a few flat rocks with pointed ends. He took out his knife and started on the 3-foot log. He planned to use it like a club or a baseball bat. On one end, he started to carve away some of wood to make the diameter a bit smaller. This way he could get a better grip while still having the large size at the opposite end. He was not far along when he noticed the sky getting darker. He quickly gathered everything and headed for the shelter.

Reaching the shelter, Fred was able to get a better view of the sky. The clouds were getting darker and it smelled like rain. He dragged the log he used for a chair into the shelter. He also grabbed most of the firewood he had gathered and stacked it in the shelter. Some of the rest he added to the fire in an attempt to keep it burning even in the rain.

He was just finishing moving all the firewood when a slight breeze picked up from the direction of the far side of the meadow. To the right, the upriver direction Fred suspected was north, the clouds were much darker. The shelter did not seem to be bothered by the little breeze. Fred walked around the perimeter pulling on the vines and grass rope he made to make sure all was as secure as he could make it.

The rain started as a sprinkle but soon was a steady rain. The fire outside of the shelter stayed lit until the steady rain had fallen for about ten minutes. Fred suspected it would be a cold night. The inside of the shelter, closest to the meadow, had less cover from the forest and began to leak from the rain. Fred used what little cover there was from the forest to gather additional branches full of leaves to shore up the portions of the shelter leaking the most.

After an hour, the leaking was mostly stopped, but Fred was soaking wet. He stripped to his underwear and put on his jacket. He had the good sense to leave it in the shelter. Now that the shelter was mostly dry, Fred sat down on the log and went to work on the club and spears.

Fred wondered where he would be without his knife. How did people manage before there was tempered steel for knife blades? His knife was making short work of the handle he was carving in the club. With the club finished, Fred started on the spears.

First, he cut the two sticks down to a manageable length. Next, he notched one end where he would put the sharpened rock. The hard part was going to be securing the rock in place. He first tried the rope he made out of the grass. Fred was not convinced this was going to hold. He thought he needed something more pliable, closer to to the size of thread.

Late in the afternoon, the rain eased somewhat allowing Fred to venture out. He took off his jacket and put his shirt back on. Near the river, now a little swollen with runoff from the rain, Fred found some vines he thought might work. He cut a few strands and headed back to the shelter.

Fred stripped individual fibers from the vines. He wrapped the fibers around the rocks on the end of the sticks and secured them in a little grove he had carved in the handle. He grabbed the rock on the tip of the spear in one hand and began to try to wiggle it from side to side. He felt there was too much play in the rock, so he undid the fibers and tried it again. After a few tries he thought it was a good as he was going to be able to make it. He repeated the process with the second spear.

When finished Fred said out loud, "I hope this works. I really hope I don't have to find out!"

The rain stopped just before dark. Fred went to the fire pit and put his hand near the logs in the center. He could not feel any heat at all. He went back into the shelter for a handful of dry wood. He placed the wood on top of the logs and using one of his matches got a fire started. Soon it was hot enough for him to try and dry out his clothes.

# CHAPTER SIXTEEN

Fred decided to spend much of Sunday working on the shelter. The rain the previous afternoon made it clear more work was needed. While he did make it a bit sturdier, the roof definitely needed more work. His priority the day before had been creating a couple weapons. He had been able to fashion something resembling a baseball bat. He also made two new spears. He felt confident he could defend himself about as well as could be expected given the materials he could find.

He examined the roof a bit more critically than he had up to now. The entire roof had a layer of green leaves. He had patched the holes yesterday. However, one layer did not appear to be enough. He reached up and wrapped his hand around one of the cross members and pulled down. Because the weight of the branches and the rain already made it sag in the middle, the first task was to brace the middle of the roof. It was not nearly as sturdy as it needed to be for the additional weight he thought would be needed.

He went about the shoring up the roof and adding additional layers of foliage to block the rain. The sun was high in the sky by the time he was satisfied the inside would remain dry during the next rain. While admiring his handiwork, he wondered how he would have done this if the trees were bare of leaves.

This thought made him think of home and Jill and Kris. How were they doing? He was here trying to survive. How were they surviving now that he was gone? If he is truly in a different time, is time tracking at the same rate for them? If he ever gets back, will he have been gone the same length of time he experiences here, or will he get back the same time. The guy he saw in the parking lot, he was gone for a while. Was he the one that was here before? If so, was he here the same length of time he was gone?

Finally, Fred shook his head to clear these thoughts away. "I need to concentrate on surviving until I can get back." He heard himself saying. He then thought, "If I ever get back. But I must hope for that. The other guy got back." This last thought gave him hope. He looked around and took stock of his resources.

Inside the shelter he had his briefcase with the matches, some papers, and a box of CDs. He had four spears. Two he made for fishing. The other two he had made for protection. He also had the bat he made. The firepit was about as big as he dared make it. There was a big log he rolled out next to the fire. The pocketknife was in his pocket.

Looking at the firepit, a thought came to him. What would happen if the fire got a bit out of hand? He needed to keep some water nearby. What could he use to store water? He headed off into the woods. Not quite sure what he was looking to find, he looked left and right as he walked toward the river. Fred decided to walk a bit off his usual path. He thought about what he would use to carry water if he was home. "I need to make a bucket. How the heck to I do that?"

All he had was his pocketknife. Maybe he could make something to carve wood out of a rock or stone. He had found some yesterday. He fashioned them for the tips of his new spears. Once at the river, he headed downstream looking for something he could use.

Fred reached the place where he had found the sharp stones the day before. He found three rocks he thought may work as tools. He took them over to a large boulder at the edge of the water and began to scrape them back and forth. It was the same process he used to sharpen his pocketknife. After an hour, he had two of the three as sharp as he could get them. He had to stop because his hands were getting beat up. He was not used to this type of labor.

Heading back toward the shelter, he was searching for pieces of wood he could use for the buckets. With any luck, he would find some already partially hollow. Finding two possible logs, he struggled to carry them, the rocks, and the bat to the shelter. He left one of the logs behind and made the round trip to the shelter and back to retrieve the second log.

Fred was about to pick up the second log when he noticed some vines hanging from a nearby tree. He went over to the tree to get a closer look. As he did, he said, "These would make great handles." He took out his knife to cut a strand of the vine. Just as he was about to cut the vine, movement off to his left caught his eye.

Suddenly, there was a rush of movement. Fred bent over to pick up the bat he dropped beside the tree. By the time he had the bat in his hand, the cat was on him.

Fred swung the bat but missed. He ducked, but one of the cat's paws raked his back. Fred let out a scream. The cat's momentum, coupled with Fred's sideways movement, caused the cat to overshoot. Fred had another chance to swing his homemade bat. This time he connected with the cat. The cat seemed momentarily dazed, giving Fred time to look at it.

The look was brief as the cat rebounded quickly. A little more wary of his opponent, the cat began circling Fred. Fred wished he had brought the spear as well. He had the bat in his right hand and his knife in the left. "So, are we going to fight or are we going to be neighbors?" Fred heard himself say.

The cat looked to be about the size of a female German Shephard. Nearly four feet from head to hind quarters. Fred was not able to tell if it was a male or female. The cat continued to circle. Fred thought the cat was trying to decide if this fight was worth the effort. The cat stopped circling and looked to be getting ready for another lunge. Fred dropped the knife, grabbed the bat with both hands, and turned as if he were standing at home plate waiting for a 3-2 pitch. "Come on! Let's get this over with!" he yelled at the cat.

As if on cue, the cat lunged, and Fred took a swing with everything he had. He heard a big crack, and his left arm went numb. He looked to his left and saw the cat lying on the forest floor. There was blood behind the cat's left ear. Fred regripped the bat and noticed it was cracked. He bent over and picked up his knife, never taking his eyes off the cat. He slowly backed away. He could see the cat's chest moving, so he knew it was still alive.

Fred was mesmerized by the animal lying just a few yards away. He stopped backing away and took a long look at it.

The cat was a deep tan color with a tail at least three feet long. The cat seemed to be flexing its paws as it lay on the ground as if checking to make sure he could still control them. Suddenly, the cat stood up and looked Fred square in the eyes. Fred spread out his arms and as loud as he could he yelled, "Ahh! Get out of here and don't come back!"

The cat seemed startled by Fred's outburst because it recoiled away from Fred. Then as fast as it appeared it took off heading toward the downstream direction of the river. Fred hoped it would keep going until it was miles away.

The whole event had taken less than three minutes. As Fred put down his arms, he realized his left arm felt like it had taken the hit from the bat instead of delivering it. He tried to touch the sore spot. As he reached a searing pain in his back told him something else was wrong.

Fred took off his shirt. The pain in his left arm and back made this quite difficult. Once the shirt was off, he examined it. There was a bloody gash about 3 inches long in the middle. He folded his knife and put it in his pocket. He put his shirt back on and then bent over to pick up the log. Lastly, he took the now broken bat in his left hand and headed slowly toward the shelter. He thought he was now a prime target for the cat and hoped it would stay away. At least it left in the other direction.

Once at the shelter, he dropped the log and the bat. He grabbed one of the new spears and headed for the river. He wanted to clean off the wound on his back the best he could. The first thing he did was to lie down at his drinking spot and drink his fill. When finished, he took off his clothes. He dropped everything but his shirt on the ground and headed into the river.

Fred scrubbed his back using his shirt to reach the middle. When he was satisfied, he dunked his shirt in the river. He went over to a rock and scrubbed it like he had seen women do in those documentaries on TV. He rinsed it thoroughly and wrung out as much of the water as he was able. He opened it up to see a stain still there. At least the matted blood was washed away.

Fred climbed out of the water and sat down on a patch of moss to dry off before putting his clothes back on. The walk back to the shelter took a little longer this time. Fred was beginning to feel tired. When back at the shelter, he sat down on the log next to the firepit. He tossed a couple logs on to get the fire going a little better. After about five minutes, he nearly fell off the log. Even though it was early, Fred got up and headed into the shelter and lay down on his makeshift bed.

All in all, Fred felt quite lucky. He survived an attack from what appeared to be a mountain lion, or at least a distant relative. He still feared infection, but there was nothing he could do about that. He closed his eyes and fell into a fitful sleep.

# CHAPTER SEVENTEEN

The next day was Monday, if the days were tracking correctly. Fred woke up in pain. His left arm was quite stiff and when he raised it up it took effort. His back was quite sore. He hoped it was not getting infected. He struggled to get up.

Looking out of the shelter he noticed the fire was all but out. He tossed a few small branches on top of the coals. He bent down and blew on the coals to reignite the branches. Soon the fire was going strong. Again, he struggled to stand up.

"I know I may regret this, but sitting down in the field all day is probably a bad idea. I need to move and loosen up this tightness in my arm and back." He was not really sure that was a good idea either, but he did feel better when he was moving. Fred decided a little exploration was in order.

Walking around the meadow seemed a bit silly, so Fred picked up one of the spears and headed toward the river. He was also wondering about how far things were apart. He was not quite sure why he cared about that all of a sudden.

How could he measure distance? He knew his normal stride was a little over three feet. Starting upriver, he looked at his watch and started timing himself. Counting his steps for three minutes gave him a very inexact estimate for how far he walked per minute. All he had to do now was keep track of how long he walked from one place to another and he had some sense of the distance.

It was slow going along the riverbank. He could only take about 30 steps a minute. That meant 30 yards, 90 feet per minute, tops. It would take at least 15 minutes to go a quarter mile. An hour to go a mile. He normally could walk a mile in 15 to 20 minutes.

Fred decided to walk an hour upstream and back and the same downstream. It would take 4 hours and cover a mile or so in each direction, assuming he did not stop to rest along the way.

The river was about how Fred remembered it. The banks were not as steep, except downstream of the waterfall. He assumed if he had traveled back in time, less erosion had taken place. The river was between 30 feet wide in the narrow sections and over 50 feet in the widest sections.

Upstream, the river meandered in gentle curves with long straight stretches. Most of the time, you could barely tell there was a current. The water was smooth and the flow gentle. The water made very little noise, just the faint gurgling of water rushing around a fallen tree branch or a rock protruding through the surface. Thirty minutes into his walk, Fred became mesmerized by the quiet flow, so he sat down to enjoy it.

Fifteen minutes later, he stood up. Now he remembered why he was moving. His back had tightened up again while he was sitting down. His left arm seemed to be getting better. The soreness had already diminished.

Another five minutes walking, he noticed the noise from the river ahead becoming a little louder. Rounding a bend, he saw why. There the water was flowing down a little incline. The water was crashing over the exposed rocks. There was a small pool where the incline ended. There the water swirled around before settling down and joining the march downstream.

Twenty minutes later, he reached a point where two streams combined to make the much larger flow. He guessed he was almost a mile upriver. Back home, he never really went upriver. He and Kris normally ventured downstream, toward the waterfall and the glen beyond. That was up next. He turned downstream and headed back to where he started.

Fred did not stop on the way back downstream. He reached the place he started an hour later. The way to the waterfall was already familiar and he made better time during that stretch.

When Fred reached the waterfall, he started looking for the paths he and Kris had used to explore the glen. Finding none, he assumed they must have been man made over the years. He would have to stay on the rim of the glen. Most of the walls of the glen were much too steep to climb down. The base of the waterfall looked to be reachable.

He walked for about 15 minutes downstream of the waterfall, when he noticed a small area of runoff from the rainstorm. There was a muddy patch about four feet wide that appeared to have been a stream when there was rain. The stream appeared to come from somewhere in the forests and flowed over the side into the glen. Fred crossed the wet area and continued downstream a little farther.

Every few minutes, Fred studied the river at the bottom of the glen. Very few places between the wall of the glen and the edge of the river had any dry rocks or soil. Travelling up stream or downstream through the glen on foot would not be possible. To make matters worse, the grade inside the glen caused several small rapids, removing any thoughts Fred might have had to walk up through the water.

Fred was about to cross over another small stream, when he noticed some animal tracks in the mud near the edge of the glen rim. He walked over to the rim to take a closer look. When he got a good look at the tracks, Fred decided he had gone far enough downstream. The tracks looked to be from a large cat. They appeared to be headed downstream, but Fred had enough of cats.

As he headed back toward the waterfall, Fred came to the realization this trek downstream past the waterfall had been a bad idea. The last time he had seen that cat, it was headed this way. He hoped it had kept going and was only looking for a place to get a drink where he had seen the tracks in the mud.

When Fred got back to the waterfall, he had been exploring for just under four hours. He had not eaten anything yet. He continued up to the place where he normally drank from the river and lay down on the bank and drank. He then back tracked downstream just a bit, to the place he caught fish. Thirty minutes later, he was heading back toward the shelter with two freshly cleaned fish.

# CHAPTER EIGHTEEN

Fred was adjusting the supports to the shelter. He had been here about two weeks and he was settling into a routine. He would spend most of his days sitting at the spot. He could not stay there all the time, as he needed to get food and water. There was also firewood to collect. As he was working on the lashing for the support, he thought he heard a voice. He said, "Now I know I have been here too long. I am hearing voices. Is this what it means to go crazy? Am I beginning to lose touch with reality?"

A little bit later, he thought he heard a voice again. This time it was a bit clearer. "Hello, Hello, does anyone hear me?" Clearly, if the voice was real, the person behind it sounded scared. It also sounded a bit like him when he realized he was no longer in the building.

"Oh hell, I should get back to the spot for another hour or two anyway. I will just head that way and prove the voice is just my imagination playing tricks on me." With that, he gave up the work he was doing on the shelter support and headed toward the voice.

The voice was actually getting louder as he approached the spot. He started thinking. "Okay, how do I do this. The person sounds scared. It sounds like a woman. Do I just burst over the hill, or do I take it slow and find out who it is? She sounds like she is alone. That can be good or that can be bad. Does she have a weapon? If so, what kind of weapon? Does she have a knife, mace, a gun? If so, how will she react when I make myself known?"

Real close now. "Hello, anyone there?"

Cannot quite see her yet. Again, "Hello, anyone there?"

Well Fred thought, "Just go for it." He said, "Hello back at you. I am stranded here please do not be afraid. My name is Fred."

"Stay away." Came the response.

"Wait," Fred said. "You have been shouting to see if anyone is here. I am here. I thought you wanted help."

"Show yourself slowly."

Fred thought, "How does one do this without getting shot these days." He then said to her, "I will walk slowly over the hill so you will have time to make a fight or flight decision. Although, I must tell you, as best as I can determine, there really is no place to run. Here I come." He proceeded to ease himself over the last remaining hill. She saw him first.

"Stop! I need to look at you."

Fred stopped.

"I know you. You are the guy that went missing."

"And I recognize you. You are a sales rep. You sell stuff to our company."

"You work at 13 don't you?"

"Yes." Fred has never talked with her, other than to say hello as they passed one another in the office or the lobby of the building.

"I was heading to your office. How did I get here?"

Fred tried to ease the tension of the meeting. "First, my name is Fred. Fred Bates. I am not a threat. I have been here a couple weeks as far as I can tell."

"Where is here?"

"Well, this may be hard to believe, but I think it is more a question of when is here. I think this is the very spot where the building will be some time in the future."

"What?" Gail was dumfounded by Fred's theory. "Are you fucking crazy? I just got on an elevator in a huge building. When I got off, I was no longer in the building. I must have bumped my head and passed out. This can't be real." She started walking around the meadow. "Wake up! Gail, wake up!" She began slapping her face.

All Fred could do was stand there and watch and wait. He remembered his first day. He felt much the same way. It was midafternoon, so he could wait for her to calm down for a while.

She continued to walk in circles around the spot shouting for herself to wake up. Interspersed among her wake-up calls were various expletives. "Wake up! Wake up! Where the fuck am I? Who did this to me? Wake up. Who the fuck did this to me? Why am I here?"

Fred thought, "Wow, does she have a dirty mouth or what." But then he remembered the anger he felt when he arrived here. He said a few choice words as well. At least she appeared to be reacting how a normal person would react.

The grasses in the meadow were two feet high in places. She was stomping around leaving paths through the grass much as kids do when they play tag in the grass. Eventually, she wore herself out walking around shouting. Some of the grass wrapped around her feet and she stumbled to the ground.

Cautiously, Fred walked over to her. "Are you hurt?"

She looked up at Fred and said, "Is this a dream?"

Fred said in his calmest most reassuring voice, "As far as I know it is real. If it is a dream, I have been in it for quite a while. My name is Fred. What is yours?"

"Gail. Gail Miller."

"Okay Gail, nice to meet you. I wish the circumstances were different. I know leaving this spot is not what you want to do, but it is late afternoon and soon it will be getting dark." He pointed toward the wooded area and the river. "About half a mile that way there is a shelter. We should be there before it gets dark. I am not sure spending a night out here is a good idea." Fred was reaching down to help Gail stand.

Gail reached for Fred's hand, but she abruptly pulled her hand back. She stood without help, moved away from Fred and asked, "Why is a shelter so important. I don't know you. How do I know I can trust you? I think I should stay here in case whatever dropped me off here comes back!"

Fred thought to himself. "How do I get her to trust me and understand I am not a threat?" He said to Gail, "What day is it?"

"What?"

"What day is it, or was it when you were heading to 13?"

Gail, confused, fought competing thoughts and finally said, "Tuesday."

Fred smiled, "Wonderful, that is consistent with the days I have been tracking since I got here. Were you visiting 13 in the mid-afternoon?"

"Yes, I had, no, have a 2:30 appointment with Harry."

"Okay, do you wear a watch? I do let's compare."

Gail looked at her watch as Fred approached her with the dial of his watch facing her. As he got closer, he said, "Mine is an analog watch. Fortunately, I just had the battery replaced a few weeks before I ended up here. What time is it by your watch?"

Gail took her eyes off the approaching stranger and looked at her watch. She had a small digital display. As she looked at the watch, she heard herself saying, "3:14."

"Mine says just after 3:15. Either I am fast, or you are slow." Fred was showing her the time on his watch. He was now standing next to Gail. She was about to move away when Fred continued. "Look, I know you don't know me from anybody. I will not harm you in any way. However, the days here appear to be tracking with the days we left behind. It will begin to get dark in a few hours. Between now and then we need to get to the shelter, and you will need to eat something. Come on, follow me." Fred was now walking toward the trees in the distance and beckoning Gail to follow.

Gail stood still for a few moments, thinking. Finally, she decided to trust this guy to a point. She was a bit hungry, and the mention of something to eat made her stomach rumble a bit. She began walking behind Fred.

As they were walking toward the shelter, Fred studied Gail. She had light brown hair, cut just below her shoulders. He guessed she was about 5'6". She had dark brown eyes that look as though they could cut you in half when she was angry. Gail was wearing a green blouse and tight-fitting blue jeans. On her feet, she was wearing what looked to be a pair of designer sandals.

She also had the lean look of a runner. Not a jogger but a runner. There is a difference in look and in attitude.

Fred broke the silence. "You look like a runner."

Gail was a bit suspicious of this question. "What makes you say that?"

"My wife is a runner. Long distance, college scholarship. Runners walk in a certain way. A lot of runners also fit into a particular body type. From what I can see in your arms and legs, you have runners' muscles."

Gail was indeed a runner. She had run in a number of charity 5Ks in the area and was currently training to run in a half marathon in the state capital later in the year. Her goal was to work up to a full marathon and, then, one day finish the Boston Marathon. "I run. I don't have as much time now with work and all, but I do want to run the marathon in Boston someday."

"That's great. I hope you get there. Boston is a great city. My wife ran the marathon there. I waited at the finish line. I am a geek, not a runner. Although, I do ride a bike. Geeks are allowed to do that."

Gail changed the subject, "You said staying out here wasn't a good idea. Why? Are there dangerous animals here?"

Fred looked her in the eyes and said, "I have not seen any, but I have heard some. But, if this is truly the area where the building is or was or will be, I know at some point in time there were black bear and large cats. I have only seen small animals like rabbits, so far. The river also has a lot of fish." Fred regretted saying this as soon as he said it. He knew it was a lie. He would have to fess up sooner or later.

"I am a vegetarian." Gail announced. "What else is there around?"

"Wow, that may be a problem. I don't know much about edible plants. About the only wild plants I remember eating as a kid were wild raspberries. I also had to eat dandelion leaves once when I was in scouts. They were bitter. Think arugula and multiply the tartness tenfold or more. You may have to wave the vegetarian regimen while here."

Gail looked crushed. "I don't know if I can do that. I haven't eaten animal flesh of any kind for decades. I was a kid when our whole family went meatless. My mom is an animal rights activist. I don't even own leather shoes. Do you know how hard it is to be fashionable and be totally leather free?"

Fred, not knowing how this was going to come out, answered, "Actually, I don't have any idea. I do know however, that here we don't have the industrial animal farming. We only have survival. I do not kill anything unless

I need to for my own survival. Most of my meals have been fish from the river. The river is about a half mile into the woods."

They were quiet for the rest of the walk to the shelter. When they arrived there Gail stopped and looked at it. "That is safer than sleeping in the open field back there? Really?"

Fred, knowing exactly how she felt tried to reassure her. "Most of the protection the shelter actually provides is from the weather. The inside stays surprisingly dry. Believe it or not, it was here before I got here. A month or so before I ended up here, I saw a guy come out of the building looking very haggard. He was looking for his car and mumbled something to me that sounded like sixth floor and take the stairs. I don't remember the rest. What floor did you get off?"

Gail said, "I was heading to 7 to meet Harry at 13. I got a call from Linda that Harry was available. Even though I had taken the day off and was out and about, I agreed to meet him. While on the way up to 13 I was on the phone and not really paying attention. Why?"

Fred continued the thought, "Do you remember which elevator you were on? Was it the one with the wall padding?"

"Yeah, I think so. I think it was the second one on the left as you walk in from the front door."

"Me too."

It was Gail's turn to change the subject. "Where do you sleep?"

Fred said, "Let me give you the tour. The shelter is made of all-natural materials."

At this Gail rolled her eyes and said, "Really, I am surprised you didn't just go down to the Home Depot and pick up something. Or maybe Dick's for a tent. You said this was here when you got here?"

"Oh yeah, that's what I was talking about. The guy I saw. I think he was here before us. I think he built the shelter. It wasn't built very well, but it was essentially a lean-to with a roof made of leaves. The lashing sucked and it was a bit unsteady. I have modified it a lot. I re-lashed everything, made it a little bigger, and enclosed all four sides. I also anchored it better. It is quite sturdy. There have been a couple storms since I arrived, and the shelter has stood strong. "

Gail was amazed, "How do you know how to do all this? I can barely tie my running shoes."

Fred stood up a bit straighter as he told her, "Well, I was a boy scout for a long time. I spent a lot of time camping with my troop. We had to build shelters out of what we could find in the woods. We were not allowed to cut down any trees if there were items already on the ground we could use instead. Our scoutmaster was all about only using what was absolutely necessary and killing anything unnecessarily was forbidden. That included trees. My patrol also won a number of awards and contests. One of them was a knot tying contest. I have a plaque in my office for that one. The knot on the plaque is painted black because we tied all the knots blind folded. Have to be able to tie knots in the dark."

"So, were you an Eagle Scout or whatever you call it?"

"Yes, I am an Eagle Scout. Once an Eagle, always an Eagle. It was close, because my dad died, so I had to spend more time working. So, the final few merit badges I needed to qualify were a struggle. Then there was the time needed for the Eagle project."

Fred continued the tour, "So, I sleep on that raised pad over there. Not the most comfortable thing in the world, but I am off the floor. I also have smoothed out a couple of logs to use as a chair. I don't have tools other than a pocketknife and rocks to carve wood. It is hard work but the one log over there was shaped like a chair with a back, so I scarfed that one for a chair with back support. That is really all that is inside. Most of my time I am outside. Surviving takes work."

He led Gail back outside. "I have cleared a place for the fire. Don't want to start a forest or brush fire. But, a fire will keep animals away or at least that is what we were all told when we were younger. I try to keep a fire going all the time. Lighting fires without a lighter or matches takes a lot of effort. I have a few matches left from a box I had in my briefcase. I want to keep those for emergencies as long as possible."

Gail noticed a couple hollow logs about eight inches in diameter near the fire. "What are those hollow logs for?"

"They are not hollow all the way through." Fred picked one up and handed it to Gail. "Those are two of my water buckets. I found logs the right size and using my knife and a sharpened rock, I hollowed these out. I keep them near the fire just in case a spark settles somewhere it can start a bigger fire. I refill these almost every day from the river."

Fred noticed Gail was beginning to waiver a bit. He walked over to her and helped her sit down on one of the chairs, logs, near the fire. "I need to go to the river to catch something to eat. You are welcome to join me or you can crash inside. Your choice. I know you have had quite a shock. It will take more than an hour or two to come to grips with it."

"I think I will stay here. Suddenly, I am very tired."

"Okay, I shouldn't be too long. I am getting good at catching the fish."

Fred returned from the river with a couple fish. He had cleaned them at the river to give Gail a little extra time alone. He also thought she would not want to witness the cleaning, since she was a vegetarian. He was gone about an hour. Gail was no longer sitting near the fire.

Fred looked in the shelter and saw Gail curled up on the sleeping pad in the corner. Fred put two additional logs on the fire, so they could add to the coals to cook the fish. While the logs burned, down Fred went about getting the fish on two fresh sticks being used for skewers. He tried to be as quiet as he could to let Gail sleep undisturbed.

Fred was cooking the fish over the fresh bed of coals when Gail came out of the shelter. "I smelled the fish. I realized I was hungry. Is that all there is?"

"Yes sorry, like I said earlier I don't know much about edible plants. I haven't seen any berries since I have been here. Full disclosure though, I haven't really been looking for them."

Gail looked at the fish over the fire and asked, "How long does it take for them to cook?"

Fred said, "With the fire this hot, 5 to 10 minutes. They aren't very big. It is up to you how much you want or don't want. Unless we do find some edible plants, you will need sustenance of some kind. Since it has been a long time since you have eaten something other than plants, I suggest you take it slow."

Fred took the fish out of the fire. He held one of the skewers out for Gail. She looked at the fish and then at Fred. He shrugged his shoulders. "Sorry, I understand if you don't want it."

Gail contemplated the fish. She took the stick from Fred. "Well, you don't need to hold it for me."

"Careful, it will be hot."

Gail sat there in front of the fire, looking at the fish. Fred slowly took a bite out of the fish. He smiled as he slowly chewed it. When he finished chewing the bite and swallowed it, he said, "It isn't too bad considering that is all there is. No fries, no lemon, no malt vinegar."

"Are you trying to get me to eat it or throw it away?"

"Sorry, I am just trying to lighten the mood. It really isn't bad, for fish."

Eventually Gail took a small bite.

Fred suddenly remembered something he meant to say earlier. "Be careful of the bones. I haven't learned how to do a proper fillet. I don't think the knife I have would be sharp and thin enough anyway. Either toss them into the fire or put them in a pile on the ground. I have to make sure we don't leave anything that could attract animals lying around."

Gail looked at him, a bit surprised. "I thought you said there aren't any big animals around."

"Actually, that isn't precisely what I said. I will explain better after we are finished." Fred wanted Gail to finish eating before he told her the truth about the cat. He knew she would probably be upset and not finish eating, and she needed to eat.

While they were eating and cleaning up, Fred was hoping Gail would forget the subject. Fred gathered the fish bones. He asked Gail if she wanted to walk to the river with him. To his surprise, she said yes. Fred grabbed one of the spears and they set off for the river. Neither said much on the way. Fred described the path he took and pointed out some of the trees he recognized along the way. Once at the river, he tossed the bones downstream from where he went fishing. More importantly, far from where he filled the water buckets.

Fred showed all the locations to Gail and explained why he picked each one. This one for water, that one for fishing, that one for bathing.

Gail did not have any questions until he mentioned bathing. "What do you use for soap?"

"Ah, soap. I don't have anything. I know there are natural things to make soaps, but I don't know what they are. I do know that you can use dirt, kind of like a scrubbing pad. If you use the silt in the bottom of the river, it isn't too bad. I don't recommend it for the hair. That is going to be a problem. At least mine is short so it is less of a problem than for you. Unfortunately, there is nothing to heat water with either. We should probably head back before dusk. The woods seem to quicken how fast it gets dark."

The two headed back upstream to the path back to the shelter.

They were about halfway to the shelter when Gail asked the question Fred was not looking forward to hearing. "So, big animals? What did you say, precisely?"

"What I said was something like I have not seen any. Yet, if this is truly the area where the building is, at some point in time there were big cats and black bear in the area. I also said I had not seen any and that, unfortunately was not exactly truthful."

Gail grabbed Fred's arm and turned to face him. "Excuse me? You lied to me?"

"Well, at the time it seemed like a good idea. You had just experienced something quite traumatic. I didn't want to add that on top of everything. I am sorry"

"Sorry! I just met you and decided to trust you. Now, I don't know what to believe. How can I believe anything you tell me?" Gail backed away from Fred. "How do I know this is real and not some bigger lie? Maybe you drugged me and drove me way out in the country somewhere."

Fred was stunned at this accusation. "Wait a minute. I have not drugged anybody! Here, look at this." Fred pulled his shirt up to expose the gash in his back from his encounter with the cat. "I got this from a big cat. This happened about a week ago. I think the cat really got the worst of it. I have not heard it since that day. If I remember correctly, their territories can be up to 600 miles. I think it is long gone."

Gail gasped at the mark on Fred's back. "How did that happen, and you are still alive?"

Fred straightened his shirt and said, "It is a bit of long story. Let's get back to the shelter and I will tell you."

Gail looked Fred in the eyes and said, "Don't ever lie to me again. I am counting on you. I have to be able to trust you. Now I know why you took that spear as we left for the river."

"Again, I am sorry. I really thought it best to wait to tell you. I won't let it happen again."

They walked the rest of the way to the shelter in silence.

# CHAPTER NINETEEN

Fred added wood to the fire. Gail was sitting on the log next to the fire pit. Fred went into the shelter and rolled out the log he used for a chair next to the fire. He was not expecting company, so he only had one log next to the fire to sit on. He sat down across the fire from Gail.

Gail was studying Fred. She watched as he rolled the log next to the fire across from her and sat down. She spoke first, "I have some questions."

"Ask me anything." Fred replied.

"You said survival takes work. If you are so busy surviving, how will you get back?"

"Well, remember when we compared our watches? I said the days appear to be tracking here. Days when I think people would be in the building, workdays, I spend most of the day in the meadow waiting. I take projects there, so I am not being idle. I carved those two water buckets out while waiting there. I have a lot of rope made of grass and some from vine strands. I made them there as well. I do need to eat and do other things, so I am not there 8 hours straight, even though that is the best option. If I always stayed there 8 hours straight, I would have been there when you arrived. Shows a flaw in my plan, or at least the execution. I was working on the shelter when you got here earlier."

"Okay, that all sounds reasonable. What happened with the cat?"

Fred let out a sigh. He was not sure he was ready to relive this experience yet. "I believe it was a Friday night. I heard what sounded like a mountain lion growl. I had never heard one in person. But I had heard them on TV and in movies. It sounded just like that. The next day, I spent making weapons. The spear you mentioned was one of them. I also made something like a baseball bat. I actually broke that hitting the cat."

Fred spent the next thirty minutes explaining what he did to prepare for an encounter and then the actual attack and the aftermath.

When he finished Gail said, "You really yelled at the cat and it ran away?"

"Yes, but it was sore and bleeding. I don't think it expected to get much resistance. I suspect the animals it goes after don't resist the same way I did. They also don't make much noise or at least noise that loud. I think I scared it. It did not just slink away. It was running with its tail literally between its legs." At this Fred let out a nervous laugh.

"What is funny about that?"

"Nothing actually. I hadn't thought about it running away with its tail between its legs until just now. I guess some clichés are based on truth. I am not sure who was more scared, me or that damn cat. I just hope the wound on my back doesn't get infected."

Gail stood up. "Let me take a look at it."

Fred stood up and pulled up his shirt. Gail studied his back. She ran her fingers across the wound several times. "Did that hurt?"

"You mean now or when the cat scratched me?"

"Just now."

"Not really."

"Good. It is not red like I would expect if it was infected. Washing it off in the river as soon as you did probably made the difference." Gail went back to her log and sat down.

Fred sat down as well. "One more question before we have to get some sleep. You can use the makeshift bed."

Gail wondered what to ask. "Will you teach me how to do this survival stuff? I don't want you to have to do all the work. I need to contribute."

Fred said, "I think the best way to do that is for you to go with me and watch everything I do. Maybe even try some for yourself, when you are ready. Most of what I do is common sense. Like I said earlier, I don't kill or destroy anything, unless I need it to survive. That makes things simpler at least on some level."

Gail nodded. She seemed to understand even though she still was not sure she really believed what was happening and where, or when she was. She waited for a couple minutes before standing and heading into the shelter.

Fred stood and followed her inside. He grabbed his coat and handed it to Gail. "Here, you can use this as a blanket. I will sit outside for a while. I like to keep the fire going as long as possible. If there is a bed of warm coals in the morning it is easier to restart."

Gail took the coat and watched Fred head back out to the fire pit. She covered herself with the coat the best she could. In spite of all the thoughts swirling around in her head, she fell asleep after only a few minutes.

When Gail awoke in the morning, she reacted just as Fred had on his first morning. She was quite disoriented. She started yelling again. "What the fuck is going on? Where am I?" Over and over.

Fred had anticipated this would happen and made sure he was out of the shelter while she was still asleep. Last thing he needed was for her to wake up with a strange person in the shelter with her.

It did not take long for Gail to storm out of the shelter. She saw Fred sitting on the same log he was on the night before, stoking the fire. She said, "I was hoping this was all a bad dream. Now I see you sitting there. So, this is really real?"

"Afraid so. I know exactly how you feel. I had almost the same exact reaction as you the first morning I was here. Except I didn't swear quite as much." He spent a couple minutes recounting the afternoon and evening he arrived and how he got his feet tangled in the grass and fell.

Gail looked at him. "You have been beaten up a bit by this place. I hope I have better luck than you."

Fred smiled. "I guess I have a little. The bump on the head wasn't as bad as the encounter with the cat. So, I need to head down to the river to get something for us to eat. Sorry, it looks like it will be fish again. And I promise to not say that very often. Anyway, feel free to come with me. No time like the present to start learning how to survive here."

Gail nodded and handed Fred his jacket. Fred stood up and walked to the shelter to hang his coat and grab his fishing spear.

He looked at Gail and said, "Well, then, on we go."

The path to the river was being used enough for it to be recognizable. At the river's edge he reminded Gail where to get water, bathe, and the best fishing spot. There he demonstrated how to catch fish by spearing one on the first try.

Gail said, "That doesn't look too difficult. Let me try."

Fred took the fish from the spear and handing the spear to Gail, he said, "Give it a try. Wait until they are close to the surface. Less distortion from the water that way."

Gail mimicked the way Fred stood near the water's edge. Soon, there was a fish within her reach. Splash went the spear. No fish. "Damn, I missed. I almost lost my balance and fell in."

"When I first tried to catch fish, I was using my hands. I was splashing all over. I got soaked. Take your time. You will get the hang of it."

Gail stood at the river's edge again, waiting for a fish to come within reach. Again, splash. Only this splash was much larger. Not only did the spear enter the water, but Gail slipped and fell in.

Fred walked over to the water and stretched out one hand to help her out of the river. When she was safely out of the water he said, "Are you okay?"

Gail was more than a little flustered. She was embarrassed and soaking wet. She said a bit more harshly than she intended, "I am fine. I am soaking wet and pissed off. But I am fine."

Gail noticed Fred was smiling at her.

She said, "What is so funny?"

"Nothing, but I guess you have been officially baptized."

"Not at all funny." Gail said. A couple of minutes later as she sat on the ground trying to dry, she started to laugh. "Baptized? Really? I think I will try again later. I have had enough for this morning."

"Yeah, this spot won't be good to catch anything for a while. The fish were all scared away, and the water will be murky for a bit."

Gail stood up and took off her blouse. And peeled off her jeans.

Fred said, "Gail, what are you doing?"

"I needed to get out of these wet clothes. They will dry faster with me out of them. I will dry faster as well. Don't worry I am wearing a sports bra. As for the panties. Sorry that is all I have." She wrung as much of the water out of her blouse and slacks as she could.

Averting his eyes, Fred picked up the spear, the one fish, and started walking. "Just make sure you keep your sandals on. Stepping on something would be bad. What are they made out of anyway? They look like leather. You said you don't wear leather."

Gail said, "I don't know exactly, but I got them in a shop that only sells leather-free apparel. They are quite comfortable."

Fred shrugged his shoulders and said, "I need to clean this fish."

Fred headed a short distance downstream where, using his knife, he opened the fish and took the guts out and tossed them into the river. He cut off the head and did the same. When that was finished, he headed back upstream toward the path to the shelter.

Gail was never more than a few feet behind. She decided to stay behind Fred to lessen his embarrassment at her state of undress.

When they reached the shelter, Fred grabbed his coat and handed it to Gail. He went about preparing the one fish for the fire. She sat on the log closest to the shelter and laid the coat across her lap.

Fred propped the fish over the fire. He went over to Gail and said, "Let me have your things."

Gail looked a bit surprised at this request. "Why?"

"I am going to hang them up. They will dry faster. I fashioned something like a clothesline between these trees. I wash out my clothes from time to time. They smell better and I am hoping they will not wear out as quickly." He said pointing to two trees on the opposite side of the fire from the shelter.

Gail handed him her blouse and jeans and watched as he arranged them on the line.

He said, "There. They should be wearable in no time. I don't think it would be a good idea for you to be waiting for the elevator to return to the meadow in your underwear."

Gail blushed at this. "How do we do that? Will we take turns, or should we stay together?"

"Let's stay together, at least today. We can see how you feel tomorrow. Once your clothes are dry enough to put on, we can head over to the spot in the meadow. That is what I call the place. It is the spot I, now we, got dumped here. I have some vines to tear apart and make a rope. Let me get them and I will show you how I do that. It is kind of like spinning wool, only the fibers are stiffer."

Fred started to walk over to the place he left the vines, when he realized the fish was finished cooking. He took it out of the fire and handed it to Gail. "Eat as much of this as you can. I can wait until later."

While Gail nibbled at the fish, Fred walked over and selected a vine that was a few feet long.

Fred sat on the log next to Gail. When she was finished eating, he said, "See, I pull these strands off the larger one. And when I have a few I can weave them together. I stagger the starting points so I can make it longer than the original vine."

Gail said, "That doesn't seem too difficult."

"It isn't. It just takes a long time to get something with a useful length."

The two of them sat there in an uncomfortable silence. Fred finally broke the tension, "So, we have a few minutes. Tell me about Gail."

"Are you sure you want to know about me? I really am not that interesting."

Fred said, "Everyone is interesting in their own way. I teach people how to use the software our company develops. I also write some of the code. There are plenty of people that say that is not very exciting. I enjoy it, and I make a decent living for me and my family. I think that is all that matters. Are you happy? Well, except for being stuck here."

Gail started, "Okay, remember you asked. Starting at the very beginning. I was born on the other side of town. Went through school locally. I went to college first at the community college where I got an AA in Business Administration. I did the last two years at State. I got my BA in Business as well. I had worked for the company where my dad works since high school. When I graduated a couple years ago, they kept me on. I decided to try my hand as a company representative. That is how I ended up with I3 as a client."

Fred asked, "How did you get started running? Did you run in school?"

"No, I didn't start running until toward the end of college. I didn't run on any team or anything like that. My boyfriend at the time, ran for exercise, and he asked me to join him. I found it to be a great way to blow off steam and get my head straight at the end of the day."

"I take it you guys broke up since you said "at the time"?"

"Yes, we didn't last. As it turns out someone dared him to take me out and get in my pants."

Fred glanced briefly at Gail's chest, barely covered by her sports bra and her lap covered by his jacket. He looked away before Gail noticed. He immediately became angry with himself for the reaction to her admission.

She continued, "We had dated for a few weeks. I always had an excuse for not getting into a situation where he could press an advantage."

Fred interrupted. "Gail, this is a bit TMI. You don't need to talk about this."

Gail looked at Fred and smiled. "Actually, I haven't really talked about this to anyone before. I hope you don't mind, but it feels like I am freeing myself from something by talking about it."

Fred smiled back. "Well then go ahead. I promise it will go no further."

"Thanks for that Fred. Where was I? Oh yes, then one night after our run he got a bit too familiar. It sounds a bit cliché but he said the 'if you really care about me' line. I couldn't believe he actually said it like that. Well, I pushed my way out of his grasp and said, 'well I don't really care about you that much' and walked away. I was about twenty feet away from him when he started yelling shit at me. The last thing I heard him say was that it was all a bet anyway and he thought I was boring."

Fred said, "He really said that crap. What a loser. I know there are people like that out there. I am so sorry you had to experience one of them."

"I was glad to be rid of him, but it really messed me up. I stopped seeing guys and wondered if I should try women, thinking they would be more understanding. I tried to make some friends, but I couldn't find anyone I thought I wanted to be intimate with."

Fred said again, "Are you sure this isn't getting a bit too personal? Afterall, we only met yesterday."

"No, this is like I said, liberating."

Fred asked, "But you still run."

"Yeah, sounds a bit strange because of how I got started, but I really do enjoy it. I guess part of it is spiteful as well. By the time we broke up I could run farther than he could. I don't want to give up that lead."

"No one in your life just now?" Fred asked.

"Nope, I am happily single. I have my work and training keeping me quite busy. Not that I am against having someone in my life. I just am not actively seeking anyone. So, that about sums up my life. Tell me about you and your family."

Fred said, "Okay fair is fair. I am married to the best woman in the world, sorry."

Gail laughed, "Don't worry about that. She better be the best in your eyes!"

Fred continued, "Her name is Jill. She is a veterinarian. We have a daughter named Kristine. I have two brothers. My mom is still alive and lives on the other side of the state near one of my brothers. I have been at 13 for nearly 15 years.

Like I said earlier I oversee the training software development and our training staff. I get to travel to some of our clients when they prefer a class to be taught in their facilities. My life revolves around my family and I3. I do ride my bike, sometimes even to work."

Gail looked at Fred, "You know you light up when you talk about your family. How did you meet your wife?"

Now it was Fred's turn to laugh, "Well, I literally bumped into her at school."

Gail said, "What does that mean?"

"Jill was in front of me in line at the dining hall and she dropped her bag. We both bent over to pick it up and we banged heads."

"Really?"

"Yep, it took some time, but I helped her through some tough times she was going through with the track team. We have been together ever since."

Gail said, "That sounds wonderful. I am happy you two found each other. Maybe I can use that approach."

"I don't recommend it. She has a very hard head. I had a lump for a few days. Let me check to see if your clothes are dry." Fred stood and walked over to the makeshift clothesline and checked Gail's clothes. They were a bit stiff but dry enough. He took them off the line and carried them to Gail.

Gail took her blouse and jeans. She stood up handing Fred his jacket. Fred walked to the shelter while Gail got dressed. After he hung up his jacket he waited.

A few minutes later Gail said, "It is okay, you can come back out. I am dressed."

When Fred returned to the fire pit, he tossed a couple logs onto the fire. He looked at his watch. It was already mid-morning. He picked up a few of the vines and one of the spears and said to Gail, "We should spend some time at the spot."

Gail said, "Right, lead on."

With that they headed to the spot in the middle of the meadow.

The two settled into a routine over the course of the next few days. Gail was able to catch fish, so not only could they split the time at the spot in the middle of the meadow, they could also share getting food.

Fred was working on the shelter and gathering wood when Gail was at the spot in the meadow. Once he had plenty of wood, he decided to go to the river to fill water buckets. Once the buckets were full, Fred stripped off his clothes, and waded into the river. He scooped up a handful of the silt from the bottom of the river and scrubbed his legs, chest, and arms. He dove under the water to rinse off. When finished, he climbed out of the water to retrieve his clothes.

He went over to the opposite side of the river where there was a large rock exposed to the sun. He scrubbed his clothes the best he could hoping this really would make them last a bit longer. He stretched the now soaking wet clothes out on the rock to dry. He climbed out on the rock and sat to wait for his clothes to dry.

Fred must have fallen asleep because he was startled awake by a large splashing sound. He sat up and saw Gail swimming across the river toward him. She appeared to be as naked as he was. He grabbed for his clothes and quickly put on his underwear. Before he could get his pants on Gail was standing next to the rock.

Fred said, "I thought you were at the spot in the meadow."

"I was, but I got bored. I walked back to the shelter and noticed a couple of the water buckets were missing, so, I thought you were probably here filling the buckets. I didn't think you would be lying here getting a suntan. Mind if I join you?" Gail started climbing out of the water.

"Nothing personal, but I wish you had some clothes on."

"Why? You don't."

"I didn't know you were going to be stopping by and I needed to wash the clothes."

Fred could not help but look at Gail as she climbed up next to him. Before he knew it, he said, "Damn, you are gorgeous."

"Why thank you Fred. You aren't so bad yourself."

Regaining his composure Fred said, "I gotta get the water buckets back." He gathered his clothes and slid down the rock into the water and began to cross back over the river.

"Fred, did I do something wrong? Why are you leaving?"

Fred turned and looked at Gail. "I am leaving because you are gorgeous, and, like I said earlier, I am married to the best woman in the world."

Gail said, "What if we never get back? What if it is just the two of us for the rest of our lives?"

Fred was taken aback by what Gail said. "Gail, I have to believe we will get back. I have to believe I will see my wife and daughter again. I cannot live believing otherwise. I would not be true to myself if I lived any differently. I hope you understand. It is not about you! It is all about me! Jill is the love of my life. I can't ..."

Fred could not finish the thought. He turned away from Gail and climbed out of the water. He wiped himself as dry as he could, got dressed, and headed back to the shelter water buckets in hand.

An hour later, Fred was sitting by the fire having added a few logs when Gail arrived with two freshly caught fish. She set them next to Fred. "Peace offering. I meant no harm. I hope you can forgive me."

Fred looked up at Gail now dressed and said, "Nothing to forgive. Please, don't worry about it. I know it seems like we should get together. All the story books, movies, and TV shows with two people stranded on an island, or in a spaceship, or wherever always seem to get together. We are all led to believe it has to happen. Maybe it does, but I just can't."

Gail said, "Okay Fred. It will be difficult for me with us essentially living together."

"Think of me as an older brother. I am older than you. Maybe that will help."

"Yeah, an older brother. I don't have one of those. I will try. Thanks for being understanding."

Fred smiled, "Let me get those fish ready for the fire."

# CHAPTER TWENTY

Gail and Fred had assumed a more brother – sister relationship. All seemed to be going better since the episode at the river. Gail was taking on about half of the time at the spot in the meadow and some of the food and water duties. Today, Gail was in the meadow and Fred was gathering wood for the fire and checking out the shelter.

Fred heard Gail calling his name. Why was she calling? Fred dropped what he was doing and started running toward the spot. Maybe there was an elevator car waiting for them, and she was holding the door. Would it stay open long enough for him to get there?

"Fred, hurry!" She was calling again.

A few minutes after he first heard Gail calling, Fred crested the small rise before the spot where the elevator left them. What he saw stopped him in his tracks. Standing a few feet from Gail, was another person.

Gail saw Fred and called out. "Fred, this is Jason. He just got here."

Fred was confused. Gail was supposed to be here to catch the elevator. How did someone end up in the meadow with her waiting nearby?

Before Fred could ask Gail what happened, Jason spoke, "Who are you? Where am I?"

Fred said, "My name is Fred, and you are?"

Gail interrupted, "I tried to explain but he doesn't believe me or understand."

Fred looked at Gail, "Well it has been what, 5 minutes. It took both of us much longer than that to come to grips with our situation."

Now looking at the new person, Fred said, "So your name is Jason, correct?"

Jason just nodded.

Fred continued, "Okay, this will sound a bit crazy, but you are exactly where you were when you got on the elevator, just earlier in time as far as we can tell. I don't expect you will believe it, but it is true. I didn't believe it at first, but I think I met someone who was here before."

Jason looked around and said, "Someone is playing a joke on me. Who is paying you two?"

"Fred and I are telling you the truth. That elevator has somehow transported us here. The river that is near the building is just over there." Gail said pointing in the direction of the shelter. "A little farther is the waterfall from the park."

Jason looked at Gail and then at Fred. He looked back at Gail, and with sudden recognition he looked back at Fred. "I know who you are. You are the guy from the software company upstairs that went missing a few weeks ago." Then looking at Gail again, "You must be the sales rep that went missing a week or so ago."

He paused for a few seconds. "Did you two run off together or something?"

Fred and Gail looked at each other. Fortunately, they both laughed at the same time.

Fred spoke first, "No, we did not run off together. As you said, I went missing before Gail did. I did not know her until she arrived here early last week. It took me a while to get her to believe what happened. Hell, it took me a couple days to really believe it myself."

Jason reached into his jacket and pulled out a pack of cigarettes. He said almost as an apology, "Sorry I am a bit stressed." He used a lighter and inhaled a long drag.

As Jason puffed on his cigarette, Fred took a long look at him. He had a slender build and was about 5 foot five inches tall. He looked to be in his early to middle thirties. His hair was cut short and appeared to be graying already. He was wearing a nice suit and tie.

Again, Fred broke the silence. "Well we should head for the shelter. We can explain everything in more detail and get to know one another better."

With that Fred tapped Gail on the shoulder and motioned using a slight head nod that she should follow. Like Gail when she arrived, Jason did not immediately follow them. They were twenty or thirty feet away when he decided to follow.

Fred slowed and Gail did likewise. Jason caught up to them. Fred began a conversation, in part to take his mind of the situation, but also to introduce themselves to each other. After Fred told him about his work and homelife, Gail did the same.

Jason waited a few minutes but then told them he works on the sixth floor. That made Fred think it strange more folks on the sixth floor have not gone missing. Jason continued that he works for the insurance company as a claims administrator. He is 33 years old. Pointing to his suit he feels he must dress nice, meaning he wears a suit or a sport jacket with khakis every day. Sometimes, but rarely, he will wear casual clothes on Friday. That usually only happens when his boss reminds him the company allows casual Friday. Jason will usually wear casual clothes on Friday for a week or two but then it will be back to shirt and tie every day until the next time his boss corners him and says employees are encouraged to "dress down" on Fridays. He was born and raised in New York City but ended up in this area after college.

When he was finished Fred asked, "So, if you feel up to it, tell me what happened today."

Jason gathered his thoughts, then said, "What the heck, I got on the elevator after grabbing something quick at Clara's. There were a bunch of people going to the eighth floor. You guys have a bunch of classrooms up there, right?" He said looking at Fred.

Fred said, "Yes we have classes every week. Usually at least thirty people, sometimes as many as sixty."

Jason went on, "Well they were all having a good time laughing about something. There was one other person going to I think the third floor. In any case I forgot to push the button to the sixth floor. When the person got off on three, I noticed the light for six was not lit and pushed the button. The doors closed, and the elevator did that little lurch thing it does sometimes. All the people going to your classrooms laughed and joked the elevator must be broken. I was getting tired of the noise they were making and when the door opened on six, I practically ran off the elevator. When the doors closed, the field appeared, and I stumbled over Gail, and fell down."

Gail picked up the story from there, "I had fallen asleep waiting for the elevator to return. It was warm and I was bored. Sorry. When he fell over me, obviously, I woke up. He helped me get up. He looked around and realized something was wrong. Then I tried to calm him down the way you did with me. I introduced myself, and got him to say his name. Then I called for you and well, you know the rest."

Just as Gail was finishing her part they arrived at the edge of the woods. Fred, trying not to get too animated at Gail admitting she had fallen asleep at the time when the elevator had actually arrived, pointed at the shelter. "Well Jason, humble as it is, here is home. I found this here when I arrived. It was in pretty bad shape and I have made some improvements. It keeps us dry when it rains."

Seeing Jason was fading a bit, Fred walked over to him and helped him to one of the logs they used for seats. "Jason you should sit. You look a bit wobbly."

Gail came over and helped Jason sit. Looking at Fred she said, "I will try and calm him down. You did your bit with me."

Jason was looking around with the finished cigarette in his hand. Fred looked at the two of them and took the cigarette from Jason's hand, walked to the fire pit, and tossed the cigarette butt among ashes. "I will see about getting something to eat and topping up the water buckets."

Fred walked over to each of the water buckets. Two were next to the fire pit. They were both full. The other two were just inside the shelter. One of those buckets was nearly empty. Fred reached down grabbed the handle he had fashioned from some vines and picked it up. He felt his pocket to make sure he had his pocketknife, grabbed a spear, and headed into the forest.

Fred had two reasons for heading off alone. The first was he really did need to fill the water buckets and get something for them to eat. But he needed to be away from Gail. He was a bit angry and he knew saying something just now would not be at all productive.

He looked back at Jason sitting on the log with Gail softly talking to him. Jason looked dazed. Gail had looked like that just a hand full of days ago. Fred thought he probably did the first day he was here as well.

# CHAPTER TWENTY-ONE

Fred did not want to show his anger toward Gail. He remembered the time he got angry at Jill and raised his voice during the ensuing argument. He had no recollection of what started the argument. Jill told him he was acting like a prehistoric cave man the way he was trying to loudly control the argument. That had stopped him mid argument and he had to think about what she had said.

Fred immediately stopped and apologized for his behavior toward Jill. The point of the discussion suddenly became secondary to the way he was acting. He never had treated his life, his soul mate. He told her he needed a few minutes.

Fred walked out of the house and sat on the porch. He wondered how he could ever behave the way he did toward Jill. He took a deep breath and said out loud, "I am married to the best woman in the world. What the hell am I doing."

He did not notice Jill standing behind him on the other side of the door. She heard what he said and turned away, tears welling up in her eyes. She did not want Fred to see her crying because he might misunderstand why. She was crying because of what he said, not the argument that already seemed to be ages in the past.

After five minutes or so, Fred returned inside and again apologized to Jill. She also apologized for not understanding he would be upset over the situation. He still could not remember what the argument was about. That was the last time he raised his voice to Jill.

Fred realized he had walked all the way to the river. How was he going to explain to Gail he was upset they had missed their chance to get back to their own time. He was upset that he, Fred, had missed his chance to get back to Jill and Kris. They must be going crazy with him being gone. He was keeping himself distracted from thinking about being away by working on the shelter, and providing for the now two people sharing his situation. Gail was helping some, but now he had to see how Jason would handle survival.

Fred walked along the bank of the river until he found the pool he used to fill the buckets. He dipped the bucket into the river and the swirled the water around. He then poured it out behind him on the bank. He refilled it with fresh water, and then headed back upstream to his favorite fishing place. That time of day there were plenty of fish around, and before long, he had enough for everyone. He did not think Jason would be ready to eat much.

Heading back toward the shelter, he began to wonder why the elevator had brought them all together. Was there some reason these two people had been paired up with him? He had to teach Gail almost everything she needed to survive. Fortunately, she was a quick study. Would Jason learn as quickly?

Why was he the one having to teach these two how to live off the land? Was that the reason he was here? To teach these two? Was there even a reason, or was it just coincidence that the three of them happened to be in that elevator at three different times when it decided to travel to a separate time?

His ire was now directed toward the elevator instead of Gail. That was probably a good thing because he was nearing the shelter. He could hear Gail's voice gently reassuring Jason all would be well. Fred thought he could see some renewed confidence in Gail. Maybe she was feeling she could now help someone else the way Fred had been helping her.

Fred interrupted her when he entered the space outside the shelter. He set down the water bucket and went about getting the fire ready. Soon the fish was roasting over the coals and Fred sat on one of the other logs. He took a long look at Jason and Gail. Jason had only been here for an hour or two, and it looked like Gail was already forming some type of a bond with him. Fred was not sure if it was a motherly type of a bond or something else. In any case it may prove to make Fred's job a bit easier. He suspected Gail would be spending a lot of time with Jason.

Fred did not say anything until the fish was ready. "Jason, are you hungry?"

Jason looked at Fred. He seemed to focus on Fred for the first time since Fred had returned from the river. "What?"

"I asked if you were hungry. There isn't much to eat around here except fish and some small game. The fish are much easier to catch. All there is to drink is water. There is fresh water in the bucket I set near the two of you"

Gail chimed in eagerly, "You won't believe how clean this water tastes. There is no pollution, and no fluoridation, just clean water. It is amazing. The fish isn't so bad either. It is about as fresh as you can get. You will get used to it. I did, and I am a vegetarian."

With that Gail got up, took one of the skewers they had fashioned out of tree branches from the fire, and blew gently on the fish attached. A moment later, she broke off a piece of the fish and in an exaggerated motion, placed it in her mouth and ate it.

Fred smiled as he watched her. It reminded him of times when he and Jill were trying to get Kris to eat. They would put food on the spoon and hold it in front of Kris' mouth. Then they would open their own mouths to try and get Kris to open hers. Every parent he had ever seen trying to get their young children to eat, did the same thing. Now he was seeing Gail doing the adult equivalent to show Jason it was okay to eat the fish. Not bad for a vegetarian!

Gail saw Fred smiling and said, "What?"

"I was just remembering trying to get my daughter Kris to eat. Then I was remembering you are a vegetarian, and I had to smile."

Gail displayed a sheepish smile and said, "Hey we all have to survive."

Gail took a second piece of the fish and held it out to Jason. Jason looked at it for a long time. He then looked at Fred and then at Gail. When he caught Gail's eyes, she nodded and moved the piece of fish a little closer to him. After what seemed an eternity, he took the piece of fish from Gail's hand. He studied it for a minute, rolling it around gently in his fingers. Finally, he put it in his mouth and ate it.

Gail let out a sigh and said, "See that wasn't so bad was it?"

This comment made Fred roll his eyes. Gail noticed this and waved him off. She then turned her attention back to Jason.

Jason did not eat very much that first meal. It was probably best since he was quite a bit out of sorts from the realization he was not dreaming. Fred gave him his sleeping pad to use when it was clear Jason was going to crash. Reluctantly, Jason took off his jacket and laid down. He was not sure he wanted to go to sleep. But if this was really a dream, maybe, if he went to sleep, he would wake up in his own bed.

# CHAPTER TWENTY-TWO

Jason fell asleep quickly. Fred wondered if he was truly that tired physically, or if it was emotional. Gail made herself busy but did not stray too far from the shelter. Fred went about is normal evening chores of gathering wood for the fire, checking the water buckets, and disposing of the dinner trash.

Fred was finally settling down near the fire relaxing and staring into the fire. Suddenly there was a huge commotion in the shelter. Jason was awake and was not reacting very well to where he was. He was shouting again and becoming increasingly demonstrative.

Gail rushed into the shelter before Fred could stop her. It was dark in the shelter. As she entered the shelter, the fire cast her shadow against the inside of the shelter, adding to Jason's disorientation.

"Jason, it's me Gail. We met earlier this afternoon in the meadow."

Jason, his heart racing from startling awake, not recognizing where he was, reached out for Gail. "Who the hell is Gail? I don't know anyone by that name. Where am I? Why is it so dark? I don't remember going camping! Ever!" As he said this his leg bumped the makeshift bed and he started to fall.

Gail reached out to try and catch Jason as he fell. All she succeeded doing was getting her head in the way of one of Jason's arms as he was flailing toward the floor of the shelter. Gail was momentarily stunned and fell on top of Jason. Jason reacted angrily and pushed Gail off roughly.

Fred entered the shelter just as Jason pushed Gail away. He said, in a voice a little more forcefully than he had planned, "Stop! You are going to hurt yourself or someone else!" Fred was surprised at the force in his voice. He did not remember ever having to do that, even with Kristine.

Jason immediately stopped and looked at Fred. "What the hell! Who are you?"

Fred a bit softer now, "Jason, I am Fred. Remember we met earlier in the meadow. You are not dreaming. The woman trying to help you is Gail." With that Fred went over to Gail and helped her to her feet. "Gail, are you okay?"

"Yes, I think I caught an elbow or something when he fell. I will be alright." She turned to Jason. "Jason are you okay? You need to remember!"

Jason looked at Gail. Then he looked at Fred. He peered out at the fire. He listened. It was deathly quiet, except for the crackling of the burning logs in the fire pit. He was trying to make sense of where he was. Gail and Fred just stood there not moving or talking. They both had been in the same position as Jason. He was going to have to come to grips with the situation in his own time.

After a few minutes Jason said, "I came out of the elevator in the middle of a meadow."

Gail started to answer what she thought was a question, but Fred shook his head stopping her.

Jason looked back and forth at Gail and Fred again. Pointing at Gail, "I fell over you there. So, this is real?" He stopped and looked at the two of them for some type of confirmation.

Gail looked at Fred. This time he nodded, and she said, "Yes, it is real. You fell asleep a couple hours ago and you just woke up. I know how disorienting this is. I had the same experience a week or so ago."

Now mostly calmed down Jason said, "I hope I didn't hurt you. I am truly sorry. I don't know what came over me. I am not a physical person."

Gail walked over to Jason, put her arm around his shoulder, and said, "Don't worry about it. No harm done. Come sit next to the fire. Tomorrow I will show you around."

As Gail and Jason headed toward the fire, Fred wondered if Jason was going to be a problem. He seemed a bit lost even when considering the situation. One thing he did know, his workload was now a lot bigger.

# CHAPTER TWENTY-THREE

Fred was sitting by the fire when Jason came out of the shelter the next morning. Seeing Fred already at the fire Jason said, "I was hoping when I went to sleep last night, I would wake up today and find out this was all a dream. If it is a dream, it's a doozy. What do you do here all day?"

Fred looked up at Jason as he talked. "Well, we survive. We catch food, keep a fire going to cook the food, and maintain the shelter. We also sit in the meadow, or sometimes fall asleep there, in hopes of catching the elevator so we can get back to our own place or time."

Jason thought about this. "I don't know how to do any of those things, except sitting in the meadow. I have never gone hunting or fishing. I haven't been camping either. I was raised in the city. We never went out of the city. If the train didn't go there, we didn't go there. Hell, I never left the city until I went to school. Even then, it wasn't that far away. I got my driver's license when I was in school. Do you know how many places won't accept a college ID as proof of age?"

Fred let out a sigh. "Don't worry about it. I can teach you everything you need to know. Gail has picked up everything pretty quick."

Gail came out of the shelter. "What did I do?"

Fred turned to Gail. "I was telling Jason not to worry about learning how to survive. I said you picked up everything fast."

She said, "Right, Jason I like I said last night, I will show you the ropes."

Fred said, "The best place to start is getting familiar with the area. You know the meadow. Through the woods there is the river. That is where we catch the fish we eat. We will need some for breakfast."

Gail said, "I will take you down to the river and show you how to catch the fish. Do you mind Fred?"

"No not at all. I have a few things I need to tidy up on the roof anyway."

Gail tapped Jason on the shoulder and said, "Let's go. It isn't that hard."

Fred watched as Jason tentatively followed Gail down the path toward the river. Maybe, this would not be a lot of additional work for him. Maybe, Gail would take a lot of that burden. Afterall, catching fish is not that hard, it just takes patience. Fetching water is not hard. The hard part was making all the spears and buckets and the shelter. That was all done by Fred. Gail has made some additional lengths of the rope. They have plenty of that now.

Fred went about shoring up the roof of the shelter. An hour or so later he heard Gail talking and looked to see them walking back up the path. Jason looked to be wet.

When they reached the clearing next to the shelter Gail saw Fred and said, "Just like me, he fell in the first time he tried to catch a fish. Fortunately, I caught some first."

Jason sat down next to the fire and took off his shirt to let it dry. Gail saw this and took the shirt and hung it on the line Fred had used earlier to dry her clothes.

Jason looked at Fred working on the shelter. "You mentioned yesterday you found this shelter here. How is that possible?"

Fred stopped what he was doing and walked over to the fire and sat on one of the logs. He picked up one of this fish and began to prepare it for the fire. As he cleaned the fish, he told Jason about the guy he saw in the parking lot, how before that there was a car left in the parking lot, and the police were there.

When Fred finished Jason said, "So you think that guy was here before us and built this shelter. That sounds like too much of a coincidence."

Fred looked puzzled, "Really? More of a coincidence than the three of us being brought here at the same time. I think it is entirely plausible. But it really doesn't much matter. It was here regardless of who made it. It saved me some work. The only thing wrong with it is maybe the location. There are times I wish it was closer to the river. But then, there are other times, I wish it was in the middle of the meadow. I suspect it was built here for the added protection, little as it may be, from the surrounding trees. We may never know why."

After they ate Fred said, "I need to dispose of the scraps from the fish. Jason why don't you come with me. I will explain a little of the geography, and some of the little things we do to survive and pass the time.

Jason went over to the line and grabbed his shirt and followed Fred down the path. A moment later Gail jumped up and shouted, "Wait for me." She ran after both.

The three of them spent the day going through all the things they had to do just to stay alive. By the end of the day Jason was visibly tired. Jason went in the shelter and was soon asleep.

Gail followed soon after saying, "I think he will eventually get it. Remember, it is only his first day?"

Fred said, "That's okay. No need to apologize for him. He will get it, or he won't. At least he has the two of us to help him. Not everyone is cut out for this. I will be along after I take care of the fire."

Gail said, "Thanks for everything Fred. Sometimes I forget how hard you work here."

Fred just waved her off, and she headed into the shelter.

# CHAPTER TWENTY-FOUR

The next morning after they ate, Fred said he would take the first shift in the meadow. Gail and Jason were going to fill the water buckets and gather some wood for the fire. Gail also said she would show Jason how to weave the grass together to make the rope.

Gail and Jason headed off down the path toward the river, buckets in hand. Gail was talking about all the things they would be doing during the day. The two of them were becoming quite chummy. They had only known each other for a day and a half. Fred remembered how Gail reacted toward him, culminating in the incident in the river. He was sure she was latching onto Jason in the same way. This time, there would not be another family getting in the way of her desire to not be alone if she never gets back.

Fred looked at his watch. It was still a little early to head to the meadow, so he spent the time gathering some materials to make another spear or two. Since there was another person now, he thought it we be better to have enough so everyone had protection should they be separated. He thought about carving a club like the one he broke, but he decided that could wait for another day. Afterall, he would need something to do tomorrow!

The path toward the center of the meadow was much easier to follow. The grass had been trampled nearly every day for over three weeks. Usually, Fred would think about Jill and Kris as he was walking through the grass. Every now and then he would also wonder about I3 and how the people at work were getting on without him. There was plenty of work on the schedule before he left. That should last a couple months anyway.

Today he was thinking about Jill and Kris. He was feeling a little selfish for thinking about them all the time. Here, he had two people that were relying on him just to stay alive. Shouldn't he spend most of his time trying to make sure those two were safe? Gail was doing okay but he was not sure Jason would make it on his own.

He was just over halfway to the spot when he thought he heard voices. Why were Gail and Jason following him. He thought they were headed for the river. He turned around and saw no one behind him. He then heard the voices again. This time they sounded behind him. He turned back toward the center of the meadow. The realization struck him. There were people up ahead.

Fred shouted at the top of his lungs, "Hold the elevator!"

He took off running. He shouted again. He was almost to the small hill just before the spot, when he heard a sound. It was the sound you hear when an elevator door has been open too long and is now trying to force itself closed.

Fred crested the small hill just in time to see what looked to be a building hallway begin to fade away. He could just barely make out an elevator door close as the image changed completely to the meadow.

128

Fred dropped everything and sank to the ground. There had been an elevator right there! He missed it by twenty steps. People heard him calling and tried to hold the doors, but the elevator had forced them to close. As he sat there staring at the place the elevator had been just moments ago, he wondered if the people had seen the meadow or if all they could see was the hallway. He then remembered the day he and Harry were in the elevator and heard what sounded like a rainstorm. He saw the hallway.

Fred wondered if the elevator knew he was coming and decided to tease him? He said out loud, "Man you have been here too long. Thinking the elevator has a mind of its own."

Fred gathered the things he brought with him and moved to the place he usually sat when waiting for the elevator to arrive. He set to work making another spear. As he worked, he wondered if he should mention anything to Gail and Jason about his near miss. After much debate with himself, he decided telling them would not be a good idea.

He sat in the meadow for a little over five hours. He had finished two new spears. They were getting better each time he made one. Deciding he had been there long enough, he grabbed the new spears and headed back to the shelter. He wondered how Gail and Jason were doing.

# CHAPTER TWENTY-FIVE

"Fred!"

"Fred! Come quick!" startled Fred awake.

He had taken a short nap after examining the exterior of the shelter. Fortunately, only minor repairs needed to be made to the roof.

It was Gail's voice that brought him out of his daytime slumber. "What is it?"

Gail replied quickly, "There has been an accident. Jason fell down a waterfall. He is in a lot of pain."

"Where is he?" Fred asked as he grabbed his homemade rope and his knife. He also grabbed one of the weapons he made.

"Down at the river, about a quarter mile downstream."

Following the path, they headed toward the river. Once there they turned right and headed downstream along the bank. There was surprisingly little underbrush to navigate and they reached the top of the water fall in a little over fifteen minutes.

Jason was at the bottom of the waterfall thirty or forty feet below. Fred called to Jason and was rewarded with a tremulous wave.

Jason was on a flat rock next to the pool created by the falling water. The rock appeared to be a type of slate and was worn smooth by the stream. There had not been a lot of rain in the recent weeks, so the water level was lower. Otherwise, Jason may not have found a dry place.

The side of the river here had formed a small glen. The glen was made by erosion of the waterfall and had receded similar to the Niagara River Gorge downstream from Niagara Falls. The banks down to Jason were quite steep. Fred had scouted this part of the river before and knew the easiest way to get to Jason was to climb down. The walls of the glen went all the way to the river for some distance before opening on a flat space. It would be too hard and dangerous to try to reach Jason from downstream. The river was too deep in places to wade through. Getting Jason out that way would be harder still.

Fred called to Jason "Jason can you walk at all?"

Jason's voice was obviously strained as he replied, "I don't think so. My leg may be broken. I landed awkwardly on the left side."

Fred could barely hear Jason over the sound of the waterfall. "Okay we will be down there real soon. Are there any critters like snakes down there?"

"No."

Gail said, "Why did you ask that?"

Fred told her "If he was in that kind of danger, we would have to address that first. Now we can concentrate on getting the things we need to get him up and back to the shelter."

Fred looked around and said to Gail, "We need to find two branches about 6-8 feet long and 2-3 inches in diameter. Did you see any vines on the trees we passed?"

"I was concentrating on getting back here and didn't pay any attention."

Fred said, "That's okay. I didn't notice either. Go look for the branches. I am going to make a quick trip down to Jason, and then I will look for some vines."

Fred made his way down the steep slope to Jason. "How are you doing? I am going to try and get you out of here. I need to make sure you are breathing okay and are not in immediate danger. I will be back in a few minutes to get you out of here. I don't see any blood. Were you bleeding?"

Jason said, "I don't think I am bleeding. My leg hurts."

"Okay, I am heading back to the top to get some things. I will be back in a couple minutes. Okay."

"Okay."

Fred climbed back out of the glen. After a few minutes Fred returned with a large bundle of vines. Gail was waiting for him with a small pile of branches. Fred picked the two he thought would work the best and set to assembling a makeshift litter.

Using small pieces of his rope he attached the vines to the two branches. He wound the vines around the branches forming a "bed" about six feet long. He then started looking for the best place to get Jason back up. He found a place where he could use trees as leverage.

"Gail grab a couple of the smaller branches. They need to be a couple feet long and about an inch in diameter. We may need a couple splints."

Gail selected two small branches and held them up for Fred to look at.

"They will do. Are you up for the climb down and then back up?"

Gail looked down the slope of the glen and said "It's kinda steep?"

"Yes, it is, but there is no choice. We can use the trees like steps only we will step down with our hands. I used to do this at the gully just outside my hometown when I was a kid." Turning to look at Jason he called out "Jason you still with us?"

"Yes" came the faint reply.

Fred turned back to Gail and said, "Follow me! No need to rush. All that will do is raise the probability you or I will join Jason on the DL."

Fred made his way down the slope with the litter in tow. He managed to find a path among the trees keeping the distance Gail had to travel between the trees to a minimum.

Once he reached the floor of the glen Fred rushed over to Jason. He needed to make a more thorough evaluation. He felt his forehead and it was cold and clammy. He hoped Jason had not gone into shock.

Bending over close to his face, Fred said in as calm a voice as he could muster, "Jason, are you still with me?"

Jason looked at Fred and gave a slight nod.

Fred continued looking over Jason. "I am going to examine your leg. Left one correct?"

Another nod.

"It may hurt a bit okay?"

Still another nod. Jason added, "Go ahead. The pain is just below the knee."

Fred gingerly slid Jason's pant leg up. Jason gave a muffled cry as it passed the painful spot. There was a large bruise visible. Fred set his hands on either side of Jason's leg just above the knee and began to feel gently. He worked his way down the leg toward the foot. As he passed the bruise, Jason let out a faint cry. "Sorry Jason." Fred did not feel anything leading him to think there was a clean break. Also, there was no bone broken through the skin so it would not be a compound fracture. That would have been much harder to deal with.

Fred returned to the bruised spot and squeezed a little bit harder trying to feel the bone. Jason cried out again. Fred said, "Sorry, I am not a doctor, but I need to know as best I can what we are dealing with. Can you raise your leg?"

Jason tried to raise his leg, but the pain was too much, and he gave up.

Fred then said, "Okay, when my next-door neighbor broke his leg, his grandmother asked if he could wiggle his toes. She said if he could wiggle his toes the leg wasn't broken. Jason, can you wiggle you toes?"

Fred saw a slight wiggle. "Great, that is a good sign?"

Gail looked puzzled. "Is that really true?"

Fred just looked at her and shrugged his shoulders.

Fred turned back to Jason. "We have two options to get you to the top of the glen. We can put you on the litter and pull and push you up. The other option will be faster and probably a bit easier. I can tie a bowline around your shoulders and pull you up with you helping as best you can with your good leg. At the top we will load you onto the litter for the journey the rest of the way to the shelters. Think you can do the second option?

Jason thought for a minute and using his right leg pushed himself a bit farther from the water.

Fred said, "Perfect! I will still do most of the work. Gail, you follow us up in case he starts to slip."

Gail replied, "Okay, I will try."

Fred said, "You will do fine.' He then took the two sticks Gail selected and fashioned a splint. He tied it onto Jason's left leg with a small piece of rope from below the bruised area to just above the knee.

"Okay, let's get started. I am going to tie the rope under your shoulders. I will then use the trees for leverage to help me pull you up. Gail will follow in case you slip a bit. After we get to the top, I will let you rest a little while I climb back down and retrieve the litter. Ready?"

Jason nodded and Fred wrapped the rope around his chest under his shoulders. He secured the rope with a bowline. Jason said, "Are you sure this will hold me?"

"I have been tying this knot since I was about 10 years old. I even had to tie it blindfolded. In fact, my scout patrol won a knot tying contest. I have a plaque in my office to prove it. Don't worry Jason, it will hold. I am also tying it around my waist. So, if you fall, I will too." He said this last bit with a big grin.

Gail said, "Fred be serious, Jason's hurt."

"Sorry, I was just trying to lighten the mood. Really though, the knot will hold."

They then started up the hill. Fred went up to the first tree on the path they came down. Bracing his feet against the tree, he pulled and told Jason to push with his good leg. It took a few minutes, but Jason was up far enough for Fred to move to the second tree. They then repeated the process, tree after tree.

They were about two thirds of the way up when Gail noticed Jason was no longer pushing with his leg. "Fred, stop! Jason passed out!"

"We need to hurry" was all Fred could immediately get out. He scrambled to the top and gestured for Gail to join him. He braced hid feet against a big tree. They both pulled dragging Jason the rest of the way to the top.

When Jason was finally at the top, Fred moved him a little way from the edge of the incline. He made a quick examination. Jason was still breathing but he was no longer cold. He was warm and no longer clammy. "We need to get him back quickly. I will get the litter because I don't think I can carry him on my back all the way to the shelters. I don't think that would be good for him anyway. Rest while you can, Jason is going to need us both to get him back.

Fred removed the rope from around his waist and Jason's chest. He slid back down to the river to retrieve the litter. He went down a little faster since he did not have to worry about Gail following. He took off his shirt and soaked it in the river. He tossed it on the litter. He then tied the rope to the litter and repeated the climb up the slope pulling the litter this time, instead of Jason.

When he reached the top, he gave Gail his shirt. "Here, use this to try and cool him down a bit. I am afraid he may have overexerted himself on the climb out. I need to rest a minute."

After a few minutes rest, Fred got up and spread out the litter. Using the rope, he made a harness, of sorts, he could wrap around his chest to pull Jason. He and Gail maneuvered Jason into the litter. He secured Jason using some of the left-over vines, donned the harness, and set off retracing there steps back to the shelters. The going was slow but without the paths worn by their frequent trips to the river, it would have been much harder.

# CHAPTER TWENTY-SIX

Once back at the shelters, Gail took over. She told Fred to put Jason onto his cot in the shelter. She tossed Fred his shirt and asked him to dip it in one of the water buckets. Instead of dipping it, Fred poured water from a bucket onto the shirt to rinse it and cool it down again. After he gave it back to Gail, she suggested he get cleaned up. While he was away doing that, she turned her attention to Jason.

Jason woke up and asked, "Where am I and why is it so cold?"

Gail explained where he was and filled in the gaps of the rescue. As she did this, she noticed his clothes were still wet from the fall in the river. She decided she needed to get him out of the wet clothes. She carefully removed the splint from his leg and slowly took off his pants, underwear, and shirt. She then took Fred's damp shirt and wiped him down as best she could. During this Jason had passed back out. She was nearly finished when Fred walked in.

She turned to him and commanded, "Out."

Fred turned around and walked out. He sat down on one of the chairs he built out of fallen logs. A few minutes later Gail came out and sat next to him.

"He woke up for a few minutes and was complaining about being cold. So, I took off his wet clothes and tried to put on something drier. Unfortunately, there isn't anything else. All I could find was your jacket. I just covered him up using it like a blanket. I laid out his clothes to dry. What are we going to do if this place has a fall or winter season?"

Fred looked at Gail and asked, "So, are you going to tell me what happened?"

# CHAPTER TWENTY-SEVEN

Gail began, "While you were working on the shelters, Jason and I decided to go to the river and fill the water buckets. We got to the river and Jason asked me if I had seen the waterfall. Apparently, you had mentioned it to him when you first took him to the river. I told him I had seen it and offered to show him."

"We walked along the river as best we could since the path is not as good as the one between the shelter and the river. It took us about 20 minutes. We weren't in much of a hurry and as you know there are a lot of trees even though the underbrush isn't too thick. We got to where we could see the top of the waterfall. We heard it before we saw it."

"Jason led the way to the bank. It isn't very steep a little upstream from the waterfall and Jason decided he wanted to see it from the river. I told him not to get in the river, but he was playing the macho guy. As he was stepping down the bank he slipped and dropped one of the buckets."

"The bucket started bouncing and rolling down toward the water as if in slow motion. Before Jason could grab it, the bucket tumbled into the river. Jason tried to grab it, but the river had it in its clutches as it raced toward the waterfall. I yelled to him to leave the bucket."

"He didn't listen. The water wasn't very deep, so he started after the bucket. He was trying to stay in shallow water. He nearly reached the bucket about 20 or 30 yards from the waterfall. He sped up a bit and reached down. As he did, it looked like he stepped on a rock that was a bit slippery, because he lost his footing and fell into the water."

"Before he could get his bearings, the current was pushing him toward the edge. He went over awkwardly. I was running along the bank the whole time. I saw him slide down the first part to the place where it has a small landing before the final fall. That is where he hit his leg. He was flailing around, and his leg slammed into the rock. He went still as he plunged over the final ledge."

"He landed in the pool and struggled to the nearby rocks. I called down. He answered he may have broken his leg. I told him I would get help. He said hurry. I ran back here. You know the rest."

Gail finished and Fred sat silently for a few minutes. She was about to get up when he said, "If the days here are sync'd up with those we left, I make tomorrow to be Monday. You and I will have to sit longer shifts. That will last until Jason is able to walk again."

Fred started to stand. "I need to find another log I can turn into at least one more water bucket. I also need to check the snares to see if we will be eating tonight."

With that Gail, feeling dismissed, went to check on Jason. Her attention to Jason made Fred feel how much he was missing Jill and Kris. What must they be thinking? He had

never been away for more than a couple hours without Jill
knowing his whereabouts, and when he was expected to
return.

# CHAPTER TWENTY-EIGHT

Fred was trying to be strong, in part for Gail and Jason, but his thoughts now, after the events of the day, put him in a state of depression. He was glad he had things to do away from Gail and Jason. He was afraid his current mood would lead him to snap at the two of them for being foolish. He also had to spend time replacing the lost water bucket. It would take a long time to replace the bucket using his pocketknife and the stone age tools he created. How did the folks back then survive? The fact of the matter was, not all of them did.

He also was experiencing some resentment that he now had to sit at the spot longer periods each day. When he was done there, he had to find food for all three of them. Granted, Jason was not much help even before he did his trip over the waterfall. Gail helped, but he still did most of the work as he was much better at the minimal survival skills.

While each of these thoughts was racing through his head, he systematically checked the snares he had laid out. He was about halfway through, when one had a rabbit. No fish tonight! He quickly killed the rabbit. He then checked the rest of the snares to make sure they were empty. No reason to make an animal suffer any longer than necessary stuck in a snare. The rest were empty.

He decided the extra bucket could wait. They still had a couple. He wanted to get the rabbit cleaned and dressed. As he cleaned the rabbit, he began thinking about what Gail had said about the seasons and potential for changes in the temperature. She had a good point. They had nothing to keep them warm other than the clothes they wore when they arrived here. How long had he been here? He had never considered this. He was so busy trying to survive, and now helping two others survive, he had not thought about what they might need if they were stranded here for a long time.

The shelters were fine for fair weather and rain. What would happen should this place have winter? If this was truly the same place just a different time, winter's storms would wreak havoc with them. He would have to think about something sturdier. Hopefully, Jason would recover quickly because all three of them would be needed.

His thoughts changed to clothing. He had only caught a few rabbits. They ate mostly fish from the river. Could he catch enough rabbits to make warm coats? How did the Native Americans and early settlers prepare the pelts to be worn so they did not decompose? Could he figure that out? Were there larger animals? Deer? Bear? He knew there were cats. He wondered if the weapons he made would be sufficient to kill a larger animal.

By the time he was finished dressing the rabbit, he was feeling a bit hungry. He also told himself he was beyond the resentment. It was not their fault they ended up here, any more than it was his fault he was here. He went into the shelter to see Gail and Jason. He immediately wished he had waited a little bit longer.

Apparently, Jason was feeling better. Fred found Gail straddling his mid-section and slowly rocking back and forth. Quiet moans were escaping her lips. Jason was rocking in rhythm. Gail noticed Fred as he was walking back out. She turned away from the opening and continued her rocking. A short time later when they were both finished, Gail straightened her clothing and walked outside to talk with Fred. He was nowhere in sight. All she could see was a rabbit on a makeshift spit atop the fire.

# CHAPTER TWENTY-NINE

The resentment came flooding back in a flash. Fred was angry. The problem was, he did not understand why. Jason and Gail were both unattached adults. They clearly had an affinity for each other. They would always go the river to fetch water together. The episode with the waterfall was the latest example of that. Before Jason arrived, she always went with Fred.

Before!

Was that why he was angry! Really! Was he jealous of Jason and the time he spent with Gail? And now they are screwing!

"I am married to the best woman in the world", he heard himself saying out loud. A bit louder than he would have liked. He was almost shouting. Is he angry they have each other and he is alone? He started thinking about Jill, his soulmate. Where is she? When is she? He kept asking these questions.

Fred was wandering the woods, stewing, thinking, reflecting. He realized it was getting dark and he was not near the shelters and the relative safety of the fire. He looked around to get his bearings. He listened for the river. The river is the best landmark if he needs to figure out where he is. He knows the path of the river at least a mile both upstream and downstream of the shelters.

The river was close. He made his way to the river. He was surprised to see he was about a mile upstream just below where the two streams join to form the river. He turned to follow the river and started walking back.

# CHAPTER THIRTY

Fred got back just as Gail was helping Jason out of the shelter. She had his arm slung over her shoulder, so she could take his weight off the left leg. He would sort of hop on his right leg. She positioned him next to one of the logs and helped him sit down. He was back in his clothes. Gail sat down and they both looked at Fred as he came into view next to the fire. When he looked at them, they dropped their eyes and looked at the ground.

Gail got up walked and walked over the Fred. She whispered in his ear, "I am so sorry. It was our first time. I went in and he was awake. I gave him a hug and one thing led to another. Sorry you had to see that!"

With more edge that he meant or wanted Fred said, "Hey you are both single. Just go easy until we know how the leg is really recovering. We can't afford a more serious medical condition just now." With that said he cut up the rabbit and passed it around. The events of the day made them all hungry. Some more than others. The rabbit did not last long at all.

After they ate Fred had to bury the remains of the rabbit. Even though he had not seen the cat since his encounter, he knew in his heart it was still out there somewhere. It was a long day. They turned in. Tomorrow was Monday and they had to monitor the spot.

# CHAPTER THIRTY-ONE

A couple days later Gail approached after her shift at the spot. "Fred, come and see what Jason and I did this morning."

"What is it? I do need to get the fire going for the fish. I take it Jason can walk better."

"It won't take long. And yes, Jason's leg is almost back to normal."

"I am glad it wasn't more serious than a bruised leg and a bruised ego. I do want to take one last look to make sure the bruise isn't spreading. I seem to remember that may be bad for some reason."

Gail was leading him down the path toward the river. Once they reached the river, she turned right to head downstream. About halfway to the waterfall she walked down to the river. "It is shallow here and the current isn't strong, so we can cross."

Fred was astonished. "Seriously, you two didn't have enough adventures with the river, you had to go back in."

"We are going straight across. Don't worry, we did it earlier today without any trouble. Just follow me."

Fred did not bother to remind her he had done an extensive reconnaissance of the area the first few days he was here. Finding a safe river crossing was something he felt was necessary. He had crossed here before. He was still surprised Gail and Jason thought going into the river after the events of a few days ago was even remotely a good idea. They crossed without incident. They managed the short climb up the opposite bank. Gail continued farther downstream.

As they reached the waterfall, Gail said, "Jason and I thought the little adventure we all had here deserved some sort of marker. Look over here. It took us a couple of hours to gather everything. We wanted to write something but weren't sure of what to write so we just..."

Fred took one look at the marker they had built and said before Gail could finish, "There is a stick diagram of someone on this pile of rocks. The top diagram shows the person standing. The figure is shown falling until lying flat on the lowest rock. On the top rock is a symbol with what appears to be a G, J, and F all written over each other. It is hard to tell that is what it is. Looking at it now with the scratching on the rocks fresh, it is easy to make out."

"How the hell do you know that!"

"I have seen this before. My daughter and I hike the trails along this river now and then. There is a historical marker next to these rocks indicating they thought it is, was, the earliest found example of Native American art. They couldn't determine a good date of the structure. They also could not figure out the symbol on the top. The assumption was that someone fell over the waterfall and died, because the last figure showed the person lying down. I guess that analysis was flawed. I can't believe I am actually seeing this, now. I do think the lines need to be deeper or the weather will wear them away."

Fred turned away and started walking back. He was fighting back tears. Would he ever get to walk the trail with Kris again? If he got back, would he even want to?

Gail chased after him. "Wait, you mean to tell me this pile of rocks survives? It is famous? I wasn't sure I believed this was actually the same place, just an earlier time. How the hell did we get here? That elevator car is really some type of portal between different times? The only reason I believe it is possible is I am living it. It all seems so fantastic. Do you think we will ever get back?"

Fred had been trying to hide his face so Gail would not see the evidence of the emotions he was struggling with since seeing the rock marker. "I don't know, but I plan to continue to sit where the elevator car opens just in case it comes back. I have to believe it will happen. I have to believe I will see Jill and Kris again."

He continued, "I told you about the person I saw before, and the shelter was already here. I just made it stronger and added on to it. So yeah, I think we will get back. All the more reason for us to stay within shouting distance of the spot during what we think are workdays back in our own time." This last comment was said with a little bit of parental scolding that went unnoticed.

Gail was excited, almost giddy, thinking the pile of rocks she and Jason had created was identified as a historical site. "I can't wait to tell Jason. This is so cool. What else can we build to make last?"

Fred looked at her still reeling from learning the marker survives, "I think that is plenty. You have all the archeologists wondering how that marker was made earlier than any other known record of humans in the area. That symbol you created out of our initials has them completely baffled. I have half a mind to send them an anonymous note when         I         get         back."

Gail continued to bounce along the riverbank. They waded across at the same place they crossed before. Soon they were back at the shelter. Gail immediately sought out Jason.

"Jason, Jason, you won't believe it but ... ", that is all Fred heard because he was headed back into the woods to gather firewood. He found an assortment of different sized branches. He was having to walk farther and farther from the shelter to gather the wood. He was not inclined to cut down any trees. He was not sure if he would be able to cut one down with the tools he fashioned anyway.

As Fred was walking back to the shelter, he wondered why the rock marker was the only historical site found. Did they not find the site where the shelter is? Did none of that get buried well enough for some to be preserved? What about all the coals from the fire? Surely some of that must have been buried by time. Maybe when he got back, he would suggest they look for it. He also thought about all the animal and fish bones he buried so they would not attract other animals. Some of those must have avoided becoming completely decomposed. Would he be able to find them also?

When back at the shelter he was preparing the fish for everyone when Jason and Gail came out to help. They had ear to ear grins on their faces. Their excitement at the prospect of creating the historical marker only made Fred think more and more about his family, how they were surviving in his absence, and if he really would see them again.

# CHAPTER THIRTY-TWO

It was early on what Fred thought to be a Wednesday. He was sitting in the middle of the clearing working on a new water bucket to replace the one Jason dropped in the river. Thoughts of Jill and Kris were into and out of his head.

All of a sudden, he realized he heard a bell. He looked up in time to see the car of an elevator appear in front of him. Dropping the bucket, he jumped up and ran to the car. It was empty. He put his hands against the crash bar to keep the door from closing.

He started to yell, "Gail" "Jason." He yelled three times. No response. "I hope they aren't fooling around down at the river again!" he thought. He tried yet again. Still silence. Then a buzzer began to sound followed by the doors forcing themselves to close. Fred pushed back but his strength was lessened by the time he had spent here eating less regularly than usual. The motors on the doors were too strong for him. As the doors closed, the meadow and the water bucket were replaced by the hallway between the elevators on the sixth floor. Fred felt a little lightheaded. He was afraid he might pass out.

Before Fred knew it, the elevator door was opening again. He looked out the door of the car to see the building lobby. He looked around the lobby. It was empty. Tentatively, Fred stepped out of the elevator. Was he really back? He slowly walked toward the door. He decided he should call Jill. Would she be at work?

He was passing the door to Clara's Shoppette. He turned and walked in. Fortunately, Lara was the only one there. She looked up and saw him.

"Get out of here", Lara said pointing toward the exit.

"Lara, can I borrow your phone?"

She grabbed her phone and said, "Get out of here before I call the Police!"

"Lara it is me, Fred Bates! I just got back, and I need to call my wife to come and get me."

"Fred? You look like hell. Where have you been?"

"You wouldn't believe me if I told you. Can I borrow your phone?"

Ten minutes later he was standing outside in the parking lot when Jill arrived, driving a little faster than she should. She pulled up next to Fred, got out of her car, and ran over and gave him a huge hug. She let go and said "Where have you been? You look like hell, and you need a bath!"

"Can we get out of here? I don't really want to see anyone else just now."

"Sure, let's get you home." With that they got in the car and drove away from the building. Jill pulled out of the parking lot and turned toward home. After a few minutes, Jill broke the silence. "What happened to you? Where have you been?"

"Do you promise to hear me out and not make any judgements until I am finished? The problem is, I don't know if I really believe what has happened to me, and I was there."

Jill thought for a minute, eyes focused on the road. She said, "I will listen, and I promise not to interrupt."

Fred was not sure where he should start. Finally, he said, "Do you remember the day Kris called us to go for a walk to the waterfall? We saw that car in the parking lot and Kris asked about it? It belonged to that guy who went missing. Remember?"

Jill said, "Yes. I remember. Why?"

"I am getting there. Remember I saw him the day he came back. He was looking for his car in the parking lot. He said something to me. Something like 'Take the stairs' and 'Sixth floor'. Remember?"

Jill, eyes still focused on the road said, "Yes, vaguely. I still don't get the connection."

"Remember how I described his appearance? I likened it to how Michael Palin looked at the start of the Monty Python TV show. His beard was a bit shorter though."

"Okay, but I am still not getting it."

"Jill, look at me. What do you see?"

Jill took her eyes off the road and looked at Fred. "What? I'm driving."

Fred was getting a little impatient. "Pull into the parking lot of that convenience store."

Jill put on the turn signal and drove into the lot and parked away from the other cars. "Okay, we are stopped. It has been a hard few weeks with you gone, and I am just not understanding you."

"Sorry but look at me. My clothes are all tattered. My hair is a mess. I haven't shaved since the morning I went missing. Look at the back of my shirt." He took off his jacket and turned so Jill could see his back.

Jill cried out, "What the hell did that?"

"It was a large cat, but we are getting a little ahead of the story. Back to the other guy. I think I was at the same place he was. Here comes the unbelievable part. I think it was near the waterfall and where the office building is. Just a long time ago."

Jill, stunned, looked at Fred. After a minute, she said, "Excuse me? Are you saying you went back in time? I am supposed to believe that? Fred, what really happened?"

"I said I find it hard to believe, and you promised to hear me out. Let me start at the beginning."

Jill seemed to calm down a bit. "Alright, you have never lied to me and I owe you the opportunity to tell the story. I promise to listen, regardless of how fantastic or improbable it sounds."

"Thanks, I swear to you, this is the truth."

Fred stopped to realign his thoughts. "Okay, from the beginning. I forget what day of the week it was, but I went to work normally. I got a call from a company I use to get technical folks. I went over to their office and reviewed the resumes of some candidates. When I got back to the office I got on the elevator. A few others got on with me. As usual, I was reading something and not really paying attention to the other people. For some reason I must have gotten off on the wrong floor. The hallway looked different. Before I realized it, the doors were closing. I watched the doors close, and once closed, the building dissolved into a meadow."

Over the next hour and a half Fred told Jill the whole story. "I know it sounds crazy, but it really happened."

Jill looked at her watch and turned to look out of the car windshield. She stared out of the window for a few minutes. She turned back toward Fred. "I can't believe I am saying this. But I have no reason to not believe you. Those other two people really made that monument at the waterfall?"

"Yes, Gail and Jason. I even know what that symbol means. It is our initials. A G, a J, and an F. But Gail and Jason are still there!"

"But if they were left behind, they would be long dead by now wouldn't they? I mean it was hundreds maybe thousands of years ago. Did you see any signs of Native Americans?"

Fred said, "No, I saw no sign of anyone else. Well, other than the shelter I found. As I said, I think the other guy built that. The entire area I explored couldn't have been more than two miles up and down the river by two miles, if that.

I guess for such a short period of time, it is possible we would have not bumped into one another. I don't remember hearing of any major Native American settlements in this exact area. I think the closest one was twenty or thirty miles from here. So, it is possible we could have been there at the same time."

Jill looked back out the front of the car. "We should get home. Kris will be home from camp soon. She will want to see her dad. I suggest you bathe and put on some clean clothes." She started the car and pulled back onto the street.

After a few minutes she asked, "You really fought a mountain lion or whatever it was?"

"Yes, more scared than I have ever been in my life. Well, maybe not as scared as I was when I was walking across campus to your dorm the night we went out for Italian food. Remember?"

Jill gave Fred a little punch in the arm and said, "And you are still an ass!"

"Yep, that's me!"

"I need to take a look at the wound on your back when we get in the house." Jill said as they pulled into the parking spot beside their townhouse. They got out of the car and went inside.

Checking the clock, Jill said, "Kris will be home in an hour. Take off your shirt and turn around." She went to the cupboard and took out the first-aid kit.

Jill examined the mostly healed gash in the middle of his back. "This doesn't look too bad. No signs of infection. How did you manage to clean it?"

"Well I immediately went to the river and washed as best I could."

Jill took a closer look. "You are lucky on many levels. I can't get over this cat encounter. Not many have a story like that to tell."

She turned Fred around and looked him in the eyes. She kissed him hard. "I have missed you. Come on, let's get you cleaned up." Grabbing Fred's arm, she led him up to the master bedroom. Walking past the bed she took him into the bathroom.

"Get undressed. I will start the water." She commanded.

Fred did as he was told. By the time he had all his tattered clothes off, the shower was hot. Fred got into the shower and sighed. "I haven't had a hot anything in a long time."

Fred noticed Jill getting in the shower with him. She said in a whisper in one of his ears, "We need to make sure you are good and clean before I dress that wound on your back. No fooling around. Save that for later."

Fred responded by expanding on his previous thought, "This is the first hot water I have touched since I left. All the bathing I did was in the cold river."

Jill said a little playfully, "So, did you and Gail bathe together?"

Fred turned to look at Jill. I told you Gail and Jason have a thing for each other. No, Gail and I did not bathe at the same time. She did catch me in the river once. When I saw her naked and all of her clothes on the ground, I got out of the river and headed to the shelter. When she saw I was leaving, she said I should join her, but I just kept walking. All I could think of was why was she stuck with me when the only person I wanted to be with was you. Every time I saw the two of them together, I was jealous because they had each other, and I was away from you."

Jill got out of the shower abruptly. She took a towel out of the linen closet and began to dry off. Soon Fred was taking her towel and gently drying her. When he looked into her eyes, he noticed they were moist with tears.

"What's wrong? Are you crying?"

"Yes, I am. You get stranded with a gorgeous woman who asks you to join her in a swim in the river and you walk away thinking of me. Of course, I am crying."

"All I could do was think about surviving so I could get back to my two favorite people."

Suddenly Jill said, "Oh God, what time is it? Kris will be here soon. Let's get that scratch fixed up and we need to get dressed."

While they were getting dressed Fred had a thought. "What are we going to tell Kris? I am not sure the whole time portal thing is a good idea just now. What do you think?"

"Let me think about that for a bit. For starters let's just play it by ear. We will say you aren't ready to talk about the experience just yet. I think she will be glad her daddy is home."

Fifteen minutes later the back door opened. Kristine saw Jill's car in front of the house and as soon as the door closed called out, "Mom? Mom? Are you home?"

"Yes honey. I am in the living room. Come on in I have a surprise for you."

"Well, camp sucked today so it better be good." Kris said as she was heading toward the living room. She turned the corner and saw Fred. She rushed at him and leaped into his arms. Fred nearly fell backward onto the sofa.

"Dad, when did you get back? You have a beard. Where have you been? Why didn't you call us?" Were all said in in one quick breath, like kids do when they are excited.

Jill interrupted, "Dad has had quite a time the last few weeks. He will tell you all about it, just not now. Let's let him adjust to being home. Maybe we should take him out to dinner."

Fred turned to Jill and said, "How about we get takeout. I am not sure I want to go anywhere tonight. I have been hoping for the time when I could be back with you two, and I don't want to share that with anyone else tonight."

Fred regretted saying that almost as soon as it came out of his mouth. Now he had two people tearing up in front of him. Jill walked over to the two of them and made it a true family hug. She whispered to them, "Not a problem. What should we get?"

"Anything you want, except no fish!"

Jill burst out with a laugh. Kris said, "What, why is that so funny?"

"Most of what I had to eat while I was away was fish. I am kind of tired of it. I will explain, but like your mom said a bit later. You know what sounds really good right now is a pizza. What do you guys think? I know Saturdays are typically pizza nights, but let's make an exception today."

Jill broke away from the family hug. "Sounds good to me, Kris?"

"Me too!"

Jill headed toward the kitchen. "I will call and have it delivered. I also should call the sergeant."

Fred said, "Who?"

"The detective that led the missing person case. I should let him know you are no longer missing."

"Can it wait a day. I don't feel like dealing with that today."

"Don't worry about it. I will just make an appointment for us to meet sometime tomorrow or the day after. No way I am letting you out of the house tonight."

While Jill was on the phone, Kris filled Fred in on everything that was going on at camp.

Jill was only gone a couple minutes. When she returned, she said, "The pizza will be here in half an hour. No cops tonight. We will meet with them tomorrow afternoon."

True to the pizza restaurant promise, dinner arrived in exactly 30 minutes.

# CHAPTER THIRTY-THREE

Jill paid the delivery guy and carried the pizza boxes to the kitchen counter. "I got one veggie and one with pepperoni and mushrooms. You didn't have any mushrooms while you were away, I hope."

Kris looked at her mom and then her dad. "Why would Dad have been eating mushrooms?"

Fred said, "No, I wasn't eating any mushrooms. I don't remember seeing any I thought eating would be worth the risk of getting sick. Let's eat. I haven't had a true meal in a long time. What do we have to drink that isn't water?"

Kris said, "What's wrong with water? Dad why are you acting so weird? No fish, no water, but mushrooms are okay because you don't remember seeing any? Where were you, on some sort of survival thing? I thought you were kidnapped. Were you taken somewhere and escaped and had to live off the land? What?"

Fred had picked up a slice of pizza and was about to bite into it when this barrage of questions came from Kris. They were a little too close to the mark for comfort. Putting down the pizza slice, Fred said, "Slow down Kris. You are sort of correct. I did end up at a place where I had to fend for myself until I made my way back here. Let's just say, I spent most of the time I was away fishing for food."

Kris was not done with her questions. "Did you know two other people went missing, and were last seen in your building?"

"Your father is aware of the two others." Jill interrupted. "Let your dad have something to eat."

Fred, knowing the best way to get Kristine to stop asking questions was to get her taking about other topics. "So, what happened to you while I was away? Besides your summer homework. Did the police talk to you? How did your friends react?"

Jill gave Fred a glance with a wink and a smile only he could see.

"Well, the night you left, Mom called your office when you were not home at the usual time and had not called. You always call when you will be late."

Jill added, "Linda answered the phone. Does she live there? Does she have a life outside the office?"

"Yes, she does have a life outside the office. Harry pays her very well to manage the front desk. She loves the people in the office and believes they are her second family. You know her kids are all grown and have scattered across the country. She does take time off to visit them. Back to you Kris!"

"Anyway, Mom talked to Miss Linda. She said you were not in the office. In fact, you had left early in the morning and didn't return."

Trying to keep her talking, Fred asked, "Then what did you guys do?"

"Well, Mom tried your cell, but it went directly to voice mail. It was like you had turned it off. Do you ever turn it off?"

"No, I don't. I need to be available should someone from the office call."

"So that was weird." Kris replied.

Fred interrupted thinking out loud, "Although I seemed to have lost my phone. What did you do after that?"

"If you lost your phone how did you call Mom?"

"There are other phones in the world you know." Fred said with a big smile.

"Dad!" Kris said exasperated.

"Sorry, go on."

"Mom said we should head down to the office to see if your car was there."

Now Jill interrupted Kris, "Right, and if I remember you thought it was silly because Linda said Dad was not there. So why should his car be there." Turning to Fred. "We jumped in the car and headed to your office. And ..."

Kris picked up from there, "We pulled into the parking lot, and sure enough your SUV was parked right where you always park it. Mom drove over to it."

Jill's turn again, "I got out of the car and looked inside yours. Obviously, you weren't inside. It looked quite normal, nothing looked disturbed. I put my hand on the hood, and it felt cool like it had been there all day."

Kris said, "After Mom checked out your car, we went inside to see if you were there. When we got to your office it was locked up. We even tried the top floor to see if you were in one of the classrooms. They were all locked up as well."

Jill said, "Now I was getting worried. This was not at all like you. I remembered the guy you mentioned before."

Now Kris interrupted, "What other guy? You didn't say anything about another person."

Jill regretted saying that now. "I didn't mention it because I didn't want to get you upset. I forgot about it until just now. Well, that got me to thinking. So, that is when I called the police."

Fred asked, "What did they say?"

Jill continued, "They said an officer would come over and get a statement. We waited, how long Kris?"

"It was 15 minutes. I can ride my bike there in less than 10. What takes them so long?"

Fred said, "Well if it didn't sound too urgent, they probably just took their time to make sure they could send someone that wasn't doing anything."

Jill said, "When the officer arrived, we described what had happened. He had a notebook and wrote everything down. When we were finished, he said he had to make a call. He went over to his police car and was talking on his radio. He came back over to us and said a detective wanted to come out and talk to us. So, we waited for the detective to show up."

Fred asked, "How did that go?"

Kris said, "It was so dumb. The detective asked all the same questions the first officer did. He wrote everything down in his notebook."

Jill said, "Well he did do a few things differently. He asked if we had a key to your car and if we had opened it. I said yes to having a key, but I didn't open the car. He said it was good I hadn't opened the car. I did tell him I looked in the windows and felt the hood."

Kris jumped in, "Wait a minute. He asked if we knew somebody. I think he said Bruce or something. Is that the other guy you were talking about Mom?"

Fred said, "I don't know anyone named Bruce. Do you Jill?"

"No, I don't, and I told the detective that as well."

"Was that it?"

Kris said, "They wouldn't let us take your car. They said they had to take it to the station to have the experts look it over. A tow truck showed up and they took it."

"That's right. They called us a week or so later to have us come and get it. They could not find anything that gave them any clues to what happened."

Jill realized Fred had not taken a bite of his pizza. "Fred, you aren't eating. Let's eat and finish after we are done."

Fred started eating his pizza. Between mouthfuls he continued, ignoring Jill's request to wait. "What did you do after the police left the office?"

Jill said, "I thought we were going to wait. Well, we left before the police were finished. The detective said there wasn't anything else they needed. He gave me a card and asked me to call if I thought of anything. The two of us climbed back in the car and left the parking lot."

Kristine said, "We just drove around for about an hour. Mom was really quiet."

"I didn't know what to do. Finally, I called your brothers and your mother. They all wanted to rush over, but I told them not to come. Francis would have to fly, and it was getting late. By the time Jack and your mom would have arrived, it would have been nearly midnight. We all agreed to meet later the next day."

"Mom also called Gramma and Grampa." These were the names Kristine used for Jill's mom and dad. "They came to town for the weekend."

"Everyone was really fantastic. Family, friends, and everyone at 13, especially Harry and Gretta. People brought us meals and called every few days to make sure we were okay. I don't know how to thank everyone properly."

Fred shook his head. "I am so sorry you had to go through this. Yes, Harry and Gretta are the greatest. I only hope Harry will take me back on somehow, doing something. I really like 13. What a great place to go to work."

Jill sat the slice of pizza she was eating down suddenly. "Have you called your mom and brothers?"

"No, I haven't."

"You better do that right now."

"I need your phone. Mine is missing."

Jill got up from the table and went to the counter where she left her bag. She took the phone out of the bag and handed it to Fred. "Why don't you go to the living room. Kris and I will get the kitchen cleaned up while you talk to your family."

Fred got up and went into the living room. Jill and Kris heard him talking to his mother and then each of his two brothers in turn. He assured each of them he was okay. After 30 minutes he came back into the kitchen and gave Jill her phone. "The battery is getting a little low. Mom was a mess. I can only imagine how it must have been when you called her to tell her I was missing."

Jill said, "She pretty much had a major melt down. She adores all her boys. Thinking she could have lost one, well, as a mom, I know I would fall apart completely."

Jill's eyes became a bit moist at this admission. Fred looked at her and smiled a sad but reassuring smile. He glanced at Kris and noticed the same moist eyes. "The two of you are quite a pair. I missed you both more than you will ever know."

They had a second family hug. Once done they spent what was left of the evening talking about friends and other goings on while Fred was away. Finally, with both Kris and Jill getting sleepy they all decided it was bedtime. Kris headed upstairs to her room first. Jill and Fred waited a few minutes before heading to their room.

Fred's exhaustion was beginning to show. He sat down on the bed and started to get undressed. Jill sat next to him and helped him with his shirt. He looked her in the eyes and the emotions finally caught up to him and tears ran down his cheeks. Jill used his shirt to dab his face dry. She kissed him.

"I am so glad you are home. You need to get some sleep." She gently pushed him onto his pillow and without getting undressed snuggled in behind him. Fred was asleep in less than a minute. Jill smiled and pressed herself to him. She soon followed him asleep.

# CHAPTER THIRTY-FOUR

Fred had been back for almost an entire day. He called Harry first thing in the morning. He told Jill he did not have a good feeling about the tenor of the call. Harry seemed a bit distant to him.

"Get some rest and eat something. I'll be back in an hour or so. I have some errands to run. We will need to talk to Sgt. MacDuff later this afternoon. He wants us to meet him at the station." Jill said as she was grabbing her car keys.

"Did you say Sergeant MacDuff? Really?"

"Yes. He is a bit sensitive about it, so I recommend you don't mention it. You should probably shave before we go to the station." With that, she headed out the door. She was glad Kristine was at camp. Kristine wanted to stay home to hang with mom and dad, but Jill knew Fred needed some time to decompress. Jill was going to be away for part of the day, and then there is the trip to the police station. Also, Fred was not the only one to call Harry this morning.

Jill pulled into the parking lot at 1680 Hilltop Road and parked in one of the visitor spots. She wondered if it was the same parking spot the other guy had used the day he went missing. As she walked into the lobby she wondered when the last time she was here. She walked past the shoppette and the security office. The shoppette was just beginning the lunch service and the few people in line did not seem to notice her.

She continued to the elevators and pressed the "up" button. The first car to arrive was car number four. She saw the padding against the walls and let those in the car exit. They were all talking about where they were going to have lunch. Jill started to get in the car but stopped suddenly and backed away. "This is the one!"

Once the elevator doors closed and it headed off to a higher floor, she pressed the "up" button again. The doors next to the first opened and she entered the empty car. She pressed seven. The doors closed and the ride to 13 began. The bell in the car rang and she started out of the car. Just before crossing the threshold she looked up at the lighted floor designator above the door opening. 7 was illuminated. She took a deep breath and stepped out of the car.

She walked into the 13 lobby and up to Linda Taylor and said hello.

"Jill it is so nice to see you. I hear Fred is back. News travels quickly, especially in the office. You tell him to get his self in here as fast as he can", was the rapid-fire response from Linda.

"Thank you, Linda. I will be sure to tell him when I get back home. I believe Harry is expecting me."

"He is. Let me go in and tell him you are here. There is coffee, water, and soda in the break room if you would like something." She then disappeared through the door to the executive suite.

Linda was not gone more than a minute when she appeared in the doorway and beckoned Jill to follow her. Jill was beginning to feel nervous. "Why am I shaking?" she thought. "I know Harry. Fred and I have dinner with Harry and Gretta two or three times a year." They also see each other at the company picnics in the summer and the holiday party in December.

Suddenly, Jill realized she was in Harry's office sitting on the sofa. Harry was getting up telling Linda they were not to be disturbed and mums the word on Jill's visit. He closed the door and sat at the other end of the sofa. "I was very glad to hear from you this morning. Gretta and I have been very worried. How is he, truly? He sounded a bit out of sorts on the phone."

"He is doing better today than last night. Before I forget, thank you for the calls, help, and support you, Gretta, and the other I3 family members gave us while Fred was away."

"You and Fred, and Kristine of course, are I3 family as you put it. My only concern is for his and your wellbeing. When will he be able to come in and see me?"

"He wasn't sure after your conversation earlier this morning. He said he got a strange feeling during the call."

"Well, I was quite surprised by the call. I guess it took me a while for the realization he had returned to set in. The call was short so maybe I hadn't fully recovered from the shock, albeit a good one, during the call. So, what did you want to talk about?"

"I was hoping you would consider giving him a job. Anything, he is going to need to get back into some sort of normal routine to help him back into life here. He has had a very interesting experience that even I find hard to believe."

Harry held up his hand, "No details now. Do you believe his story or not?"

"The story sounds fantastic."

"Don't tell me. Let Fred in his own good time. Do you believe him?"

"Sorry, yes I do believe his story. He has never lied to me. We are soul mates. I know that sounds corny, but it is true."

Harry patted Jill's hand. Standing he said, "I will have Linda call later to set up a time for him to come in and talk. I will also tell her that you were not here today. Thanks for the talk."

Jill stood up and gave Harry a big hug. Harry led her to the door and said, "Remember you were not here today!" He winked and walked to his desk.

Jill walked back to the 13 lobby. She waved goodbye to Linda as she went by. Linda was on the phone but put her finger up to her lips as if to say, "Mums the word."

Jill pressed the elevator button. A minute later the bell rang and one of the elevator doors opened. She entered and pressed the button for the lobby. The elevator stopped on the 6th floor. As the door opened Jill tensed up. She relaxed as two people rushed into the elevator car. They all said polite hellos. The doors closed and soon Jill was walking out of the building toward her car. "That happened very fast."

# THE LIFT

Jill thought about Harry and Gretta as she drove to the store and how they had come into her and Fred's life.

# CHAPTER THIRTY-FIVE

Harry Esposito, Fred's boss, was a third generation of Italian ancestry. His father, called Joe by everyone, was named Giuseppe. His mother, also of Italian descent, was named Anna. Most of her friends called her Ann. Harry was an only child and was born and raised in a suburb of Cincinnati in southwest Ohio. Harry was born toward the end of the baby boom after World War II. Like most boys his age he played sandlot baseball and football. He was good enough to play both in high school earning varsity letters in both sports each of the last two years.

When Harry graduated High School, he was not sure what he wanted to do with his life. He was not sure he wanted to go to college. Joe suggested he join the military. The Vietnam War had been over a few years so there was little danger of Harry actually serving in a hostile area.

Harry thought about it, and with the blessing of both Joe and Ann, decided to join the Army. He went to a recruitment center in Cincinnati. There, the sergeant asked him what he wanted to do in the army. With the draw down after the Vietnam War, coupled with the attitude much of the country held toward the military because of the war, most of the MOSs, Military Occupational Specialties, were available.

Harry explained one of the reasons he was joining the service was because he did not know what he wanted to do with his life just yet. The recruiter said he understood. "A lot of the people coming through this center are in the same situation. You can decide after boot camp. You may discover something you like while in basic training."

Harry was to report in 30 days to start basic training. He spent this time saying goodbye to friends, teachers, coaches, and most importantly Ann and Joe. He arrived for basic training and was assigned to a barracks with the group of young men with whom he would share the next eight weeks.

Basic training taught him all the things a soldier in the army would need to do. He learned to shoot a rifle and the proper way to throw a hand grenade. They spent a lot of time marching and on physical conditioning. Harry was glad he had played football and baseball in school. He was in much better shape than many of the men in his barracks. Two of the men were mustered out of the Army for medical reasons, discovered because of the conditioning.

Harry began to show an aptitude for organization and leadership and was soon named a squad leader. By the time basic was finished his drill sergeant recommended him for additional leadership training.

Harry was asked if would like a domestic or overseas assignment. Having never been out of the country, he requested an overseas assignment. He received two weeks leave before he needed to report for his first tour in Germany.

Harry spent the two weeks back home with his parents. He thanked his dad for recommending the service. He felt like he now had some direction in his life, and fully expected his calling was waiting for him in Germany, or wherever the Army sent him after that.

Harry had to make his way to Fort Dix, New Jersey to catch his transportation to Germany. Joe and Ann decided they would like to visit New York City for a couple days before Harry had to leave. The three of them drove to New York and spent three days visiting all the sites. They saw the Empire State Building, the Statue of Liberty, wandered through China Town, and rode a Hansom cab through Central Park. They even visited the FAO Schwartz toy store.

Three days flew by and it was time for Harry to go to Fort Dix. After checking out of the hotel, they again climbed into the car, and drove to Fort Dix. Harry got out of the car followed by Ann and Joe. Joe shook Harry's hand. Harry shrugged that off and gave his dad a huge hug. "Dad, thanks for everything. I wouldn't be here without the support from you and Mom."

Joe, never really very emotional, was not able to say anything. Damp eyed Joe broke from the hug and stepping away pointed to Ann.

Ann sensing what Joe was going through took over the hugging with a big squeeze for her son. She gave Harry a big kiss on the cheek. "You be careful over there! You hear me?"

"Yes Mom. I love you guys."

Both Ann and Joe were now tearing up. They both waved as Harry picked up his bags and headed into the building lobby. The two got in the car and drove off. Harry turned and watched them go. He had a very strange feeling like he would never see them again.

Harry landed in Germany and was detailed to the Landstuhl Army Regional Medical Center. Now it is called the Landstuhl Regional Medical Center (LRMC). It is an overseas military hospital operated by the United States Army. LRMC is the largest US military hospital outside the continental United States. Near Landstuhl, Germany, LRMC serves military and dependents stationed throughout Europe and Africa. Currently the medical center treats service members from the entire region, some being flown into nearby Ramstein Air Base before being transferred to the United States.

Harry was detailed to the medical records department. He started out doing rather menial clerical work. He rapidly gained responsibility until he oversaw an entire section of soldiers and civilians maintaining medical records.

Harry noticed many inefficient processes used by the hospital. He was able to change some, but by the time he moved on to other duties there was still a lot of work to do.

While stationed at Landstuhl, Harry took full advantage of the opportunities to travel and explore the local area. One evening Harry was enjoying dinner and a beer at a local restaurant. He noticed one of the German women from the hospital staff having dinner with some of her friends. He had seen her around the hospital and town but never had a chance to say hello. Their eyes met and Harry sensed interest on her part. He smiled at her and the smile was returned.

When Harry finished his dinner, he got up and walked to her table as he was leaving. "Hello, my name is Harry. I work at Landstuhl. I have seen you there. Do you work there?"

The woman looked up a bit embarrassed by the attention, "Yes I do. I have seen you there. You work in the medical records department. I have to pick up records from time to time. I work in the admissions office. My name is Gretta."

"Well, Gretta, nice to finally meet you. Auf wiedersehen!" Fred used the German term usually used for goodbye. He really meant it a way it is often translated into English, "until we see each other again." Because he really hoped he would see Gretta again. As he walked away, he could hear Gretta and her friends speaking excitedly in German. He could not make out what they were saying because his German was spotty, and the ladies were talking very fast.

The next time Gretta had to go to the medical records office was a few days later. At the desk she asked if Harry was in. The soldier at the desk said, "Harry? Do you mean Corporal Esposito?"

Gretta was taken back by this question. Again, she was a little embarrassed because she did not know Harry's last name, or even his rank. She did know he was military because she had seen him in the records department. She said, hoping there were not two people named Harry in the medical records department, "Yes, I believe that is correct."

The soldier picked up the phone, "I will see if he is in." A few rings later he said into the phone, "Corporal Esposito, there is a German national at the desk asking to see you."

After a minute of listening to the person on the phone he said to Gretta, "Who shall I say wants to see him?"

"Gretta, Gretta Hollberg." She answered.

"She says her name is Gretta Hollberg. Yes Corporal, I will tell her." Hanging up the phone he continued speaking now to Gretta. "Corporal Esposito has time to see you. I will take you to his office." The soldier stood up and led Gretta through the maze of offices until they reached Harry's.

Harry was standing outside his office waiting. "Thank you Private. I will take her from here. I will also see to it she is escorted out of the area when we are finished. You may return to the desk."

The private now gone, Harry waved Gretta into his office and closed the door after he followed her inside. "Well this is a wonderful surprise. Please have a seat." Harry was pointing to a chair on the opposite side of the desk from his chair. After she sat down, he sat as well.

Gretta said, "I hope you are not going to get into any trouble letting me in your office."

Harry was a bit surprised by this comment. "Not a problem. As long as you are escorted it will be okay. So, let's complete the introductions. I am Harry Esposito. My full name is Harold Giuseppe Esposito. My father's first name is Giuseppe. I am a Corporal in the US Army. I go by Harry. And …" Harry made a gesture toward Gretta.

"Oh, I am Gretta, Gretta Hollberg."

"Nice to finally meet you Gretta. I apologize for the restaurant. I saw you there and I felt I needed to say hello. But you were with your friends, and that must have been a bit uncomfortable. I am sorry."

Gretta smiled and said, "That is okay. When I saw you at the restaurant, I was glad you stopped by. I have been trying to figure out a way to get your attention, but it is hard here. I didn't want to seem too forward."

Harry smiled back, "Well it seems we have both been admiring each other from afar. By the way, you speak English like a native speaker, there is almost no accent."

Gretta did in fact speak particularly good English. She grew up in a home where English was a second language. Both her mother, Margot, and her father, Wolfgang, made sure she spoke English well.

Gretta's father grew up in a small town in south western Germany called Kaiserslautern. He was conscripted into the German army at the age of sixteen during the summer of 1944. The war was not going well for Germany. The Allies had landed in France in early June and were making steady progress toward the German borders.

After a short training period, Wolfgang was assigned to the 5th Panzer Army. In December of that year the German forces broke through the Allied lines in what they called Unternehmen Wacht am Rhein or in English "Operation Watch on the Rhine". The Allies called it the Ardennes Counteroffensive. Most people today know it by the named coined by the press at the time, "the Battle of the Bulge".

Wolfgang was captured by the American army when they relieved those besieged at Bastogne. He was taken to America and placed in a POW camp inside an Army base. While in America he worked as labor at farms near the base. He learned English and made friends with some of the local people. On occasion, he was allowed to spend some of his earnings at local stores. POWs were paid for their labor per provisions in the Geneva Convention.

Wolfgang spent the rest of the war as a POW. He was not repatriated to Germany until 1948. He left America in early

1946 only to be placed in a work camp in France for two years. He returned to Kaiserslautern to begin his post war life. He soon met and married Margot. Soon after, Gretta was born. Gretta was named after Margot's great Aunt. Her Aunt Gretta died as a result of the fire bombing of Dresden.

Wolfgang saw American bases sprout up all over West Germany. The east was occupied by the Soviets and the west was occupied by the Allies, mostly America. Realizing how important America was going to be for the future of Germany, he insisted his house understand and speak English.

Gretta was enrolled in English classes from an early age. By the time she finished her Gymnasium at age 19 she spoke English like an American, and as Harry had noticed with very little German accent.

Gretta was taught everything about America. Her father told her stories of his time as a POW, and how his life as a prisoner was far different from those in Japanese POW camps and many of the camps in Germany and Poland. Her parents bought picture books about the US, including some about the National Parks. They even subscribed to some English language versions of magazines like National Geographic and Life.

After Gymnasium, Gretta was looking for a job. Her father suggested she look at one of the American facilities in the area. Her mastery of English would be an advantage for her. She applied to several of the bases and accepted a job at Landstuhl. She rented an apartment near the hospital so she would not need a car. Most days she rode her bicycle to work. She enjoyed her job and all the people she met. She found most of the Americans to be quite nice, in spite of the fact that a couple decades previously they were enemies.

She had seen Harry a few times when she was in the medical records office. She also noticed him about town from time to time. She never had the nerve to cross the street or go to his table at a restaurant to introduce herself. She was not even sure he had ever noticed her. As it turns out he had noticed her. She was glad he finally stopped to say hello.

Harry and Gretta began to see each other a little more often. They both had a good feeling about the relationship. Wolfgang and Margot both liked Harry and were very accepting of him. He spent hours talking about America whenever he and Gretta would visit them.

They were visiting Gretta's parents, a few months after the encounter at the restaurant, when the phone rang in the house. Margot answered the phone and questioningly looked at Harry. "Harry the phone is for you."

"I am sorry, I am on call this weekend. I needed to leave your number so they could reach me if I need to go into work. I hope you don't mind."

Margot handed the phone to Harry, "Of course not. I understand."

Harry took the phone and said, "This is Harry, er, Corporal Esposito." After listening Harry said, "Thank you I will." He hung up the phone.

Harry turned to Gretta and her parents and said, "There has been an accident. I need to get home."

Gretta said, "Home, do you mean America home?"

"Yes, I need to get to the office to make arrangements. I am sorry to cut our visit short. My mom and dad have been in an accident."

Gretta jumped up and took his arm led him toward the door. Looking at her mom and dad said, "I will call you later."

The drive to the hospital took 30 minutes. Harry went to his office and made some calls. Gretta waited in the lobby. When Harry got back to the lobby he was visibly upset.

Gretta walked over hugged him and whispered in his ear, "Are you okay?"

"They're gone. I can't believe it." Was all he could say before collapsing into one of the chairs sobbing.

Gretta put her arm around his shoulder and said, "Let's get out of here." She helped him up and led him back to the car. She was glad the lobby was empty, so no one saw him like this.

Harry calmed down an hour later. He explained to Gretta his parents were in a car accident. They were driving through an intersection and a delivery truck from a large trucking company ran a red light and hit their car. They were both killed instantly. The driver of the truck had been drinking and was legally drunk.

Harry was given funeral leave by the Army and headed home to take care of all the arrangements. Gretta asked for time off so she could join him in America. She did not have a passport. She would not be able to join him for a couple days while her travel documents were completed.

Harry's father made a decent living. The house was paid off and there were some savings. There was also a decent life insurance policy and Harry was the sole beneficiary. Harry was also besieged by lawyers all wanting to represent him in his case of wrongful death against the truck driver and the trucking company.

After a lengthy legal battle Harry was awarded a generous settlement in the case. Adding that to the worth of the house and the savings, Harry eventually had a small fortune. He talked to Gretta about what to do with it. The first thing Harry decided was he and Gretta should get married. She accepted his proposal and they got married shortly after returning to Germany.

# CHAPTER THIRTY-SIX

Harry left the Army when his current enlistment was up. He and Gretta moved to Ohio. They lived in his old house while they decided what to do. They both got jobs in the medical field. Harry went to work for an insurance company, processing medical insurance claims. Gretta got a job at a hospital working in admissions, just as she had in Landstuhl.

Harry was having a hard time with the processes and forms used by the insurance company. There had to be a better way to do things. He talked about the problems with Gretta. They discussed different ways to do things better. They decided to use Harry's money to start a company to make record keeping and claims filing better and easier for insurance companies and patients.

It was about this time he decided he could no longer live in his parents' house. They started looking for a place to build their company and their future.

The search for a place to start their company led them to a small community outside of Ohio. There, most of two floors of an eight-story building were available for lease. Harry and Gretta went to look at the property and fell in love with the area. The building was older, but, had a bit of old charm about it.

The owner was very flexible in how they used the space. He would build it out to suit their needs. They started out with just one floor, with an option to use the unused portion of the floor above if they needed to expand. The address was 1680 Hilltop Road. They leased the seventh floor with hopes for the unused part of the eighth floor in the future.

Harry and Gretta had ideas of how to automate the forms and processes. They got a business loan from one of the local banks based on their business model and set to hiring the staff needed to develop the technology. Insurance Innovation Incorporated or I3 as it was mostly known was off and running.

Harry set about working with the staff to develop the requirements and the software needed while Gretta set to all of the administrative details.

The tools and technology developed were well received by the industry. Patent applications were filed, and patents awarded. As the years passed and the company grew in reputation, more business came their way. Eventually it was clear Harry could no longer work with all the customers himself. He also needed to change his staff from a development staff to a maintenance and training staff.

He advertised for someone to lead and grow his training staff. He came across a young engineer with experience working with people. Harry thought this young engineer may just be the person to do it. He was smart and had experience writing software with human interfaces. He also was newly married and therefore should be stable and not looking to jump from company to company.

Harry made some subtle checks of the young man's references. They were all very positive. Even inquiries to those for whom he worked were positive. Harry talked with his current manager. The manager said he knew the young man in question would not be staying at his company for ever. He was too good to just sit at a desk and write code all day without prospects for something better.

Harry had heard enough and called the young man in for an interview. Fred arrived on the seventh floor of 1680 Hilltop Road to be greeted by Gretta Esposito. She smiled and led him to Harry's office.

Harry winked at Gretta and shook Fred's hand. "Mr. Bates, I am very glad to meet you. My name is Harry Esposito. This beautiful woman with you is my wife Gretta. Please, let's sit down." The three of them sat in the chairs around Harry's desk.

Harry started the interview, "So Mr. Bates, tell me about yourself."

Fred began listing all the projects he had worked over the few years since he graduated college, and the programming languages and operating systems used for those projects.

Harry interrupted Fred before he had gone very far through his resume. "Mr. Bates, may I call you Fred? I have read your resume. I have also contacted all your references. And if you will forgive me, I talked with a few people you did not list as references. One of those people is your current manager. I know I may have outted you as looking for a job, but your manager said he knew you were either looking or would be soon. I know your technical skills. I want you to tell me about you."

Fred was caught completely off guard by Harry. "Sure, Fred is fine." Stumbled out of his mouth. He looked at Harry and then Gretta and then back at Harry.

Gretta laughed, "Well Harry, I think Mr. Bates, sorry Fred, does not understand how we conduct interviews. Let me try to explain. Fred, we understand most people tell the truth on their resumes. We also know people usually only write the good stuff there. That is why we ask for references and follow up with each one."

"If we find someone we want to interview, we then do a little more digging, as Harry mentioned. So, by the time we ask someone in for an interview we know they are able to do the job. What we want to find out is, are they a good fit for our company. That is why we want to know who Fred Bates is. What are his aspirations? What is he looking for in a position? What does he want out of his life? So, let's back up a little. Tell us why you sent us your resume."

"I sent my resume because you are looking for someone and I think I would be a good fit for the job."

Harry's turn to smile, "We know that part Fred. What is it about this job that makes it more, oh what is the word I am looking for?" He looked at Gretta.

She said, "I think Harry is looking for desirous."

"Yes, that is perfect. Thanks Gretta. So, Fred, why do you think this position is more desirous than the one you currently have? So much so, you have taken the leap of applying, which taken to a logical conclusion, means you are content with the prospect of leaving said current position?"

Fred was not sure what was happening. This was surely one of the strangest job interviews ever. "Well, my current position doesn't require much thought. I get handed a set of requirements that are quite detailed. All the real thought has already been done. All that is left is basically punching in statements. All the art in coding is removed. I sit with a pool of coders. We all just sit there and write code with little imagination involved. I am hoping to be able to make decisions and make a difference by doing something and not just acting like a dog that had been taught to catch the same stick over and over."

Harry said, "Well that does sound a bit boring. Are you saying you don't enjoy writing software any longer?"

"No, I am not saying that. I would like to have some input into what gets written, why it gets written, and how it gets written. Not just here write this this way. I also think there is more than just writing software. I want to understand how it fits into the business it is written for. I am not sure I am expressing it properly."

Gretta said, "Fred, we do understand what you are saying. Many of the reasons you expressed are the same as those Harry and I had when we started this company. Go on Harry explain."

Harry took over the discussion by giving a brief background on the company founding and added in some of the details of his and Gretta's background that led up forming the company. When he was finished, he looked at Gretta and then refocused his attention on Fred. "So, Fred, Mr. Bates. Do you think this is a company where you could be happy? We want to grow our staff more into a sustainment and maintenance direction. Focusing more on training our growing customer base on how to use our tools more effectively. We are looking for someone we can groom into one day leading that part of our business. Are you still interested?"

"Mr. and Mrs. Esposito." Fred began.

Harry immediately interrupted. "Stop right there Fred. I am Harry."

Gretta added, "And you must call me Gretta."

Fred now a little nervous started over, "Harry and Gretta. I think this would be a perfect place for me to work."

Harry clapped his hands, "Fantastic, let the two of us talk for a bit and we will put a formal offer together. Can you wait a few minutes?"

Fred said, "No problem, I took the afternoon off, so I don't have to rush. I would like to talk to my wife though."

Gretta said, "Follow me, I will take you to a place where you can call your wife with some privacy. In fact, if she can stop over why don't you ask her to come by. We would love to meet her." This last thought she said while looking at Harry. He nodded in agreement.

Gretta led Fred to an empty office. She left and closed the door behind her. Fred called Jill at her office. He told her about the strange interview, and that the Esposito's would like her to stop by so they could meet her.

Jill said, "What, right now? You really like these folks? It seems a bit strange they would want to meet me before they even give you their job offer. What if the terms are not satisfactory? What if they really aren't how they seem?"

Fred said into the phone, "You know babe, I really like these two. They are so into each other and this company. I don't think their behavior was a show at all. I think that is the way they are. What a great pair of people to spend time with every day."

Jill looked at her schedule. "It is nearly 3:00, I have a 3:15 appointment that should take 15 or twenty minutes. I can be there by 4. Let me know if that works."

Fred said, "I tell you what. Plan to come by at 4 unless I call you back to say otherwise. I have to go. Someone is at the door. Love you."

Jill said, "Love you too. See you in an hour!"

After he hung up the phone, Fred opened the door to see Harry Esposito waiting just outside.

"Did you get through to your wife okay?"

"Yes, I did. Thank you. She is a veterinarian and has one last appointment this afternoon. She can get here by 4 if that is okay."

Harry made a bit of a show of thinking for a minute before he said, "No problem, I think I can find something for you to do until then. By the way what is your wife's name?"

Fred said, "Jill."

Harry asked, "Is that short for Jillian?"

"No, it is just Jill."

Harry led Fred through the reception area to a small conference room on the other side of the building. Laid out on the table was a 4-inch binder full of PowerPoint slides.

"Okay Fred, I know you do not work for me. I haven't even given you a job offer. Gretta and I decided to wait for when your wife, sorry, Jill gets here to give it to you. What is in this binder is the current state of the training we give to our customers for our tool suite. I would like you to take a look through it while we wait for Jill to arrive. I will not ask you for any opinions unless you accept our offer. Even then, I will not listen to anything until you are on the payroll. I am not expecting anything for free. Agreed?"

"I guess." Was all Fred could say.

Harry gently slapped Fred on the back and said as he walked out of the room, "I am so glad you sent us your resume and came to talk with us. I will come back in an hour. Gretta and I have a few things to do."

The hour passed quickly while Fred was reviewing the training material in the binder. He noticed a note pad and a pen conveniently placed on the center of the conference table. Using both, he began taking notes on the material and how he would change them.

A knock on the door made Fred look up at the wall clock. It was 3:50. The door opened and someone he had not met came in. "Hi, Mr. Bates, I am John. Mr. Esposito asked me to come by and get you. He and Mrs. Esposito are in his office with your wife."

John led Fred to Harry's office. Fred entered to find the three in a pleasant conversation.

Harry stood up and walked to the door. "Fred, come on in. Jill just arrived. Please, let's all sit and talk."

Fred looked around for an empty seat. All he could find was one on the sofa. Sitting on the coffee table in front of the sofa was an envelope with his name on it. The whole meeting appeared to be a bit choreographed. Fred sat on the sofa.

Gretta said to Jill, "Jill, why don't you sit next to Fred and look over the package we prepared."

Jill got out of the chair and joined Fred on the sofa. Fred opened the envelope and took out the typed page that was inside. The page contained the offer of employment at I3. The salary listed on the page was a 30% increase over what he was currently making. That alone would have been a deal maker in Fred's mind, but that was not all. There was also a generous amount of vacation and personal time included. There was also life and health insurance that was at least as good as his current position. The last item on the page listed an option for part ownership in the company should he stay with the company at least 10 years. The total share of the company would come out to about 5%.

Fred looked at Jill and saw tears in her eyes. He looked at Harry and Gretta. They both had big smiles as they watched Fred and Jill. Fred wondered why these two people were offering him this much. He said, "This is a great offer. Can I ask you a question?"

Harry said, "Absolutely. I would hope there would be some questions."

Fred pondered how to ask the question. "This is going to sound very strange. Why do I feel like my mom and dad just handed me the keys to a new car?"

Harry and Gretta burst out laughing startling both Jill and Fred. Harry, still laughing a bit said, "Fred, when we got your resume and started finding out about you, we decided you are exactly the person we would like to have here. That piece of paper reflects that sentiment. Now that we have met Jill, we are double sure. Take some time to think about it and get back to us."

Fred looked at Jill. He had not realized she had taken his hand. She squeezed it gently and gave him a slight nod.

"Well Harry and Gretta, I think Jill and I have already decided. When would you like me to start?"

"Hot damn!" Harry exclaimed.

"Harry! Language!"

"Sorry Gretta. Fred, tell me when any obligations you have at your current company will be satisfied. We would like you the very next day. Let's go to dinner and celebrate."

That was the first of many evenings Jill and Fred spent with Gretta and Harry. Now nearly 15 years ago.

# CHAPTER THIRTY-SEVEN

Fred had indeed shaved by the time Jill returned. He helped her bring the grocery bags in from the car. When they were done, he gave Jill a huge bear hug. "I hope I never get tired of these chores. Believe it or not, I missed these little things we do together."

Jill laughed and teased, "Who are you? Did you take my husband's place?"

Fred started to object but Jill planted a big kiss on his lips. When she pulled away after the kiss she said, "Nope, it's you! We have to get going."

The drive to the police station took about fifteen minutes. It was getting close to rush hour so there was some traffic. They found a parking spot around the corner from the front door.

The police station was a new building. There was a fire in the old building. Even though the fire only damaged the kitchen area there was enough smoke and water damage the building was deemed unsafe to use.

The holding cells in the basement had the most water damage. Those in the cells at the time of the fire were evacuated to the county jail across town without incident. The biggest worry was the records office. Most of the records were digital but, the evidence area was kept near the records department. The desk sergeant, once he knew the fire was localized to the kitchen area, had one of the officers guard the records and evidence areas. The officer happened to be a volunteer firefighter. He borrowed an extra suit from the fire company.

The new building is a two-story building. The second floor has the department offices. The first floor has all the facilities those not in the department would use. Just inside the door was the reception desk. It was not raised on a platform like you see in the movies or on TV. It was like a little room to itself because it was surrounded with bullet proof glass.

Two doors led out of the reception area. One to the left and one to the right. The door to the left of the desk led to the interrogation rooms, conference rooms, and the fingerprint area. The other door, the one to the right of the desk, led to the suspect processing area and the holding cells. There were six holding cells. Four were usually reserved for male prisoners and the other two for females. Most of the time they were empty. Once arraignments were finished, those being held were transferred to the county jail.

Jill and Fred walked into the station. Sitting at the desk was a stern looking police sergeant with Bland stitched over his right shirt pocket. Over his left pocket was a badge showing the number 433. His hair was cut short as if he were in the Marines. He looked like he could have been a body builder. As they walked up to the desk, he gazed at them with two dark brown eyes.

"May I help you?" His voice boomed out in that serious police tone, making sure Jill and Fred knew he was the one in charge.

Jill spoke before Fred had a chance. "Yes, we have an appointment with Sergeant MacDuff."

A small smile escaped from Sgt. Bland's face. He caught himself and looked around to make sure no one saw his reaction. "May I tell him who is here to see him?"

"Yes, I am Jill Bates, and this is my husband Fred."

Sgt. Bland picked up the phone and tapped a few buttons. A moment later, he said, "Mr. and Mrs. Bates are here to see you." A short pause then, "No problem, I will buzz them through."

He placed the phone in its cradle and said, "He will meet you in the conference room just inside. First door on the right after you leave the lobby." He was pointing to their right.

Jill and Fred started toward the door and they heard a click. The door opened toward them. They waited as the door opened and walked through the opening. The first door on the right was about ten feet down a hallway with doors on both sides. The door was open. They entered the room. It was about 12 feet by 10 feet. Just large enough for a table and four chairs. There were no windows.

To Fred's surprise there was no mirror on the wall. The walls were decorated with photos of local landmarks and buildings. Fred let out a quiet laugh.

Jill looked at him and said, "What is funny?"

Pointing to a picture on the wall opposite the door Fred said, "See the picture of the waterfall? That is the one Jason fell over."

Jill looked at the picture with a sad smile but was startled when a voice behind her said, "Please have a seat."

Jill and Fred turned to see a man about 45 years old about 5 feet 7 inches tall standing in the doorway. He had dark brown hair that was trimmed and neatly combed. He was wearing a grey suit with a blue striped tie. His badge was hanging from the left breast packet of his jacket. Half of the wallet containing it inside the pocket. His badge number was 254.

Jill said, "Sergeant MacDuff, it is nice to see you again. This is my husband Fred."

Fred walked over and shook his hand. "Good afternoon Sergeant."

Sgt. MacDuff repeated, "Please, let's sit."

They all took seats. Jill and Fred on one side of the table and the sergeant on the other.

Sgt. MacDuff started the discussion. "You were talking about a waterfall when I came in."

Fred replied leaning his head toward the wall behind them, "Yes, the picture on the wall is of the waterfall at the park near my office. Kristine and I hike there often."

"Kristine?"

Fred said, "Yes, she is our daughter."

"Right, I bet she is happy to see her dad again!"

Jill said, "She wanted to come with us today, but I made her go to camp. She can spend time with Fred once we get home."

Sgt. MacDuff again looking at Fred, "So, when did you get back?"

"Yesterday afternoon. Jill called you once she recovered from the shock of my return."

"That was at 5:45. How long before that did you return?"

"I don't know exactly. I remember the shoppette was empty so it must have been after the lunch time rush. I would guess 1:30 or 2. I borrowed Lara's phone to call Jill."

"And Lara would be the owner of the shoppette? I thought it was called Clara's." Sgt. MacDuff was writing everything down.

"Clara was Lara's mother. Lara took over for her mother some time ago. Clara passed about two years ago."

"I will talk with Lara to get the time stamp from her phone."

Fred was puzzled by this. "Is that really necessary?"

Sgt. MacDuff said, "We opened a missing person investigation when Mrs. Bates reported you missing. We have to document all relevant facts related to the case until it is closed."

"But I am back now. I am no longer missing, so you can close the case."

"I'm afraid it isn't that simple. We have not determined if anything criminal transpired with your disappearance. That is part of what I want to talk about today, or at least get it started. The sooner we get the details of your disappearance and return, the sooner the department can make a decision to continue the investigation or close the case."

"What do you need to know?" Fred and Jill had decided as unbelievable as his story sounds, the truth is always better.

"Before we get started, I want to inform you we will be recording the conversation. This is for your protection as well."

Fred said, "I was wondering why there were no mirrors. You have microphones and/or cameras."

Sgt. MacDuff showed a hint of a smile. "We installed the electronics when this building was built." A short pause, then, "Shall we start at the beginning or work backwards from the day you returned?"

Fred looked at Jill, let out a sigh, and looked square at Sgt. MacDuff. "I went to work that day like any other day. I had to run out for a meeting with a vendor in the morning. It was a Wednesday."

"Who did you visit that day?"

"Let me think. If my memory serves me correctly, I was looking to get some help for my software team. It would have been Technology Personnel Recruiters (TPR). I met with Bill Hansson. He has helped me find good folks in the past."

Sgt. MacDuff jotted down TPR and Bill Hansson in his notebook. "I will give Mr. Hansson a call to verify your appointment."

Fred wasn't sure he appreciated the appearance of mistrust.

When Fred hesitated to continue Sgt. MacDuff said, "Mr. Bates, I can tell you don't understand this process fully. I have an obligation to check out everything you tell me. The more information I get from you, the easier and faster the process will work. It isn't that I don't believe you. Please continue."

Fred thought about what the sergeant said and realized he was being too suspicious of his motives. "Sorry, I got back to the office about 10. I walked into the building with a bunch of the guys from the insurance company on the two floors below us. We all piled into the elevator. I wasn't paying any attention to those guys because they are usually kind of loud and obnoxious. Besides, I was reading a book."

Sgt. MacDuff asked, "You were reading a book?"

"Yes, I always read when heading places. Sometimes I read books, sometimes technical journals, and sometimes the newspaper. I was reading a book that day. The only reason I remember is because I was nearly finished. Oh shoot, I left it behind. Now I have to buy the library a new copy!"

"So, you were in the elevator with the guys from the insurance company."

"Yes, a lot of time guys from the sixth floor will get into a conversation with guys from the fifth floor and will get out on five to finish the conversation. Many times I have almost gotten off on six instead of seven. Well on that particular day I got off on six."

Fred stopped for a second and looked at Jill. She smiled and nodded ever so slightly giving Fred the encouragement he needed to continue.

"The instant the doors closed behind me I was no longer standing in the building, but in the middle of a meadow."

Sgt. MacDuff's head sagged imperceptively and he said, "A meadow? But you got off on six!"

"I know it sounds fantastic, but there I was in the middle of a meadow."

For the next two hours Fred told Sgt. MacDuff the highlights of his ordeal. The only two times he was interrupted were when Sgt. MacDuff wanted to make sure he had the names of Gail and Jason correct.

Fred concluded with, "Jill picked me up and shortly after called you."

Sgt. MacDuff sat at the table and flipped through the notes he had taken over the last two hours. The first thing he asked was, "Do you know Brad Myerson?"

Fred looked a bit puzzled. "Who? The name doesn't ring a bell."

Now reading from his notes Sgt. MacDuff said, "No matter. So, you say this Gail Miller and Jason Lake were with you. You realize both have been reported as missing, and you have now admitted to being with them after their respective disappearances. And neither of them is known to have returned."

"That is all correct."

Sgt. MacDuff continued, "If this were an ordinary case, I would be recommending you be held on suspicion of kidnapping. However, since you came here willingly, I am going to recommend to the District Attorney that you not be held but, you should have a psychiatric evaluation. I am sure she will agree. I will also recommend you stay local."

Fred was a bit taken aback by this. "Do you think I am crazy or something?"

Jill reached for Fred's hand and gave it a slight squeeze. He looked at her and immediately took a deep breath.

Fred spoke again, "Well I guess the story does sound a bit out there, and I can understand why you wouldn't believe me. I am going back to I3 tomorrow to see if I can get a job, so I will not be going anywhere. I will agree to submit to a psychiatric examination if requested."

Jill added, "Sergeant MacDuff, for what it is worth, Fred has never lied to me and while I agree the story sounds fantastic, I believe him."

This comment took Sgt. MacDuff by surprise, and for a brief moment he lost his professional bearing and said, "Maybe you need that exam as well!"

He immediately knew he should not have said it, and attempted to recover. "I am sorry Mrs. Bates. I did not mean that. The story is indeed fantastic and as Mr. Bates told it, very compelling. There are extenuating circumstances I am not currently at liberty to discuss. Please forgive me."

"That's quite alright Sergeant. Fred and I will cooperate with you as much as we can."

Fred nodded his head in agreement.

Sgt. MacDuff rose and said, "Well, thank you both for taking the time to come in and talk with me. I believe I have all your numbers in the file in case I need to get in touch. I will let you know the outcome of my conversation with the DA."

Jill and Fred stood as the sergeant motioned toward the door.

Jill said as they were leaving, "Thank you for taking Fred seriously Sergeant. Let us know if you need anything."

With that they turned left as Sgt. MacDuff pushed the button to open the door to the lobby area.

Back in the car, Jill and Fred sat in silence for a few minutes.

Jill spoke first. "I wonder what extenuating circumstances there are that he can't tell us about. I also got the feeling he didn't not believe your story. When he started saying an ordinary case, I was afraid he was going to arrest you. But then he didn't. That strikes me as strange."

Fred said, "And that guy he mentioned, Ben something."

Jill corrected him, "His name was Brad Myers, or something like that. He said it so matter of fact and out of the blue I am not sure I heard it correctly. I agree that was a bit strange. This whole thing is so surreal."

Jill had a thought, "I wonder if this Brad guy is the same person the detective mentioned the night you went missing. If so, he may be important for some reason. The fact we said we did not know him wasn't really a surprise. Sergeant MacDuff moved right along as if it was just another insignificant detail. But I am not so sure. Especially if it is the same person. That would mean he has asked about him twice."

They sat there in silence for a few more minutes. Finally, Jill looked at Fred, took his hand, and said, "Let's pick up Kristine and go get dinner. Your choice!"

Fred turned the key and they headed toward home.

# CHAPTER THIRTY-EIGHT

Jill sent a text message to Kristine telling her they were on the way home and for her to be ready to join them for dinner. Two minutes later Kris responded.

"Kris wants to go to Jessie's. Okay with you?"

Fred thought for a minute. "Well, if anyone didn't know I am back, making an appearance at Jessie's will solve that."

This comment made Jill laugh out loud.

After picking up Kristine they headed to Jessie's for dinner. When they entered the restaurant Jean, the waitress, immediately recognized Fred and ran over and shouted, "Welcome back Mr. Bates!"

Fred said, "Thank you Jean. We would like to spend a quiet evening by ourselves. Anything available in a far corner?"

"Sure, there is a booth on the end. Will that work?"

Fred looked where Jean was pointing and said, "That will be fine."

"Great, follow me."

Following Jean, they made their way to the booth in the back of the restaurant and sat down. Fred and Jill sat facing the restaurant while Kristine sat opposite them. Fred looked around the restaurant and noticed a number of people stealing glances at him. When he met their eyes, they turned away embarrassed. Looks like he was correct about coming to Jessie's. The word of his return if not already known, would be soon.

When Jean came over to take their order, she looked at Fred and said, "Do you want the usual Mr. Bates?"

Fred looked at her then he looked at Jill then he looked at Kris and said, "No, I don't think I'll have the fish today. I'll just have a plain pasta dish. How about Rigatoni with meat sauce. And a couple meat balls."

After they ordered Kristine looked at Fred and said, "So where were you guys all day? You made me go to camp so we couldn't spend time together."

Jill said, "I had some errands to run and so did your dad. After that we had to go and talk to the detective. We texted you from the car when we were done. Besides, camp is important, and we are together now."

Once their orders arrived, they dug into their meals. Fred continue to glance around the restaurant. He noticed one particular woman that kept looking at him. He did not recognize her. He wondered why she kept looking at him. He whispered to Jill, "See that lady over there? She keeps glancing over at us. Do you recognize her?"

Jill looked at the woman without making it too obvious. She looked back at Fred and said, "Never seen that woman in my life."

A few minutes later, Fred noticed the same woman had gotten the waitress's attention and waved her over. He saw them talking in hushed tones all the while both taking furtive glances at Fred's table.

When they finish their meal, Jean came over to drop off their check and Fred said, "Who's that woman that kept asking questions? She appeared to be looking at me at the same time she was talking with you."

Jean said, "I don't know what her name is. She was asking me to tell her your name."

"Did you tell her my name?"

"No, I didn't. I told her that if she needed to know who you were, she needed to ask you. I don't think she liked that answer too much because she didn't give me much of a tip."

Fred smiled and said, "Thank you, I'll make up for the tip." He gave Jean cash to cover their food and a generous tip. "And we will see you the next time we come in." With that the Bates family got up and left the restaurant.

Once in the car Kristine said, "Dad, what was that all about?"

"I have no idea Kris. But I suspect there a lot of people that knew that I was gone, and are now curious as to what happened while I was gone. Now that I am back, they think maybe they'll get some answers."

"That wasn't much of an answer Dad. Something is going on that I don't understand. You and Mom are keeping things really hush-hush. People are gonna be asking me questions and I don't know how to answer them. That already started today at camp."

Fred and Jill exchanged glances. Jill said to Kris, "What did you say to the people at camp?"

Kris said, "I just told them Dad came home. I don't know any of the details, so I just told him he was too tired to talk much. So, I didn't lie."

Jill smiled. Kris really is a smart kid. She continued, "You did great. There are a lot of people that might not believe what your dad has experienced. There are still two people missing. The police are not sure if your dad had anything to do with their disappearances. Also, another person had gone missing earlier. People will want to know what's happening. Everyone that went missing was in the building where your dad works. So, that has people wondering. Can you understand?"

Fred started the car put it into gear but before he took off, he turned toward Kris and said, "Kris what happened to me, I'm not certain I even believe it. Certainly, I suspect it would be very difficult for you to believe. I know for a fact lots of other people will think that I'm crazy and therefore, they may want to see me locked away like I am some kind of lunatic."

Kris looked at her mother. "Do you believe him Mom? Do you know everything that happened?"

"Yes, honey I do believe him. Your dad has never lied to me. I have no reason to believe that he is lying to me now."

"Well then you guys need to tell me." Kris said almost like it was a demand.

Fred put the car back in park and turned off the motor. He and Jill both turned toward the backseat to face Kristine.

Fred said, "If we tell you anything more than we've already told you, you will have to promise not to repeat it. To anyone. Because they won't believe it, and we don't know how they're going to react. I am afraid that some people may look at you and think there's something wrong with you. And there is nothing wrong with you."

"What, were you with another woman or something? Why can't you tell me?"

"No Kris, it's nothing like that." said her mother. "I think we should go home and talk about it when we get there." Jill looked at Fred pleading for him to jump in.

He said, "Let's get out of here. I don't really want to talk about this in the car."

Jill mouthed "Thank you" toward Fred.

Fred started the motor again. He put the car in gear, pulled out of the parking lot, and drove home.

Kristine sat in the backseat arms folded across her chest, pouting the entire way home. When they pulled into the driveway of the townhouse, she got out of the car and bolted inside.

Jill looked at Fred and said, "What was that all about?"

"Well she is a preteen and you know how they are when they want something right now and they don't get it. They pout and run. Just like she did."

Jill took a deep sigh and said, "Yeah, I guess you're right. Do you think we should tell her the whole story?"

"I don't know. She is going to find out sooner or later. So, I think I would rather she hear it from me. That way she's going to hear my truth, the actual truth, and not someone else's exaggerated or made up version."

After another sigh Jill said, "I guess you're right. I'm just afraid that it sounds so fantastic. You hardly believe it. I believe it because you tell me that it's true. I don't know how she's going to react."

Fred and Jill got out of the car and headed into the house. Entering through the kitchen each one of them grabbed a drink and continued into the living room. When they got into the living room, they saw Kristine sitting in her favorite chair arms crossed. A determined pout still on her face.

Kristine said, "Well, are we going to talk about it?"

Jill said, "Yes, we are going to talk about it. But like your father said in the car, you cannot tell anyone. This is just inside the family. Even if someone brings up the topic to you, understand?"

Kristine looked at her mom and said, "I hear you. I don't understand why. But I will certainly keep it in the family."

Jill and Fred both sat down on the sofa facing Kris and put their drinks on the coffee table. Jill looked at Fred and said, "Do you want to do this, or do you want me to start?"

"I'll do it. That way I can fill in details when she has questions."

Now looking at Kris, Fred said, "What do you want to know?"

Kristine unfolded her arms and said, "Where were you? Why were you gone so long?"

Fred picked up his drink and took a big, long sip. He set the drink back down on the table and said, "Well, the day that I went missing I was off visiting a company that supplies engineering and software talent to our company. When I got back to our building, I got on the elevator. There was a group of guys on the elevator with me that work on the fifth and sixth floor. They pushed the five and six buttons. I pushed seven because I work on the seventh floor. As usual I was reading a book."

"They all got off on five. With my head down in the book, I didn't notice. The next time the door opened I just got off. It was six. The wrong floor. I looked up and noticed it wasn't the correct floor. I turned just as the doors were closing. Well, then the doors closed, and this is the part that people aren't going to believe. The hallway disappeared and I found myself standing in the middle of a meadow."

Kristine wide-eyed said, "What, you're no longer in the building? Where did it go?"

Fred said, "Well I don't know where. The strange part is I think the building is or was right where it is now. The problem isn't where, I think the problem is, when."

Now Kristine was really a bit flummoxed. "What do you mean? Are you telling me that you traveled in time in that elevator?"

Fred said, "That's the way it appears, and I'll tell you why I think that. Remember that monument down next to the waterfall?"

"Yes, I remember. We saw it the day we went walking next to the river. That was a few weeks before you went missing. In fact, it was the day that other guy went missing wasn't it?"

Fred smiled at Jill. He then said to Kris, "You have a good memory. Well, when I got off the elevator the river was nearby and the next day I went down and saw the river. Over the course of the time that I was gone I got to the spot where that marker is and it wasn't there, yet!"

The rest of the evening Fred and Jill and Kristine talked about the experiences Fred had while he was away, how the monument got made, and why and what the symbols on the monument mean.

When Fred was finally finished Kristine asked, "So, you really know what those symbols mean and how that monument got there because you were there?"

"Yes."

"And those other two people, Jason and Gail, right? They are still there, right?"

Fred took a deep breath and said, "Yes, they are still there, and I don't know what I'm going to do or can do about it."

Jill said, "So honey, now you know why we need to keep this a family secret because the story is very fantastic sounding and people just aren't going to believe it. We think the person that went missing before actually was at the same place as your dad."

Kristine said, "Well who is he?"

"We don't know. But it is getting late and you probably need to go to bed."

Fred said, "I agree with your mom. I'm getting tired. It is late we should all go to bed."

Kristine was not very happy the conversation was over. But she got up, gave her parents each a hug, and headed up to her bedroom.

When Kristine was in her room and the door was closed Jill asked Fred, "So, how do you think that went?"

"Well she's a really smart kid. I don't know what tomorrow's going to be like, but she seemed to handle it alright. I think she trusts us. And I think she knows that we're not going to tell her crazy stories just for the sake of telling crazy stories."

Jill nodded. She stood up, grabbed both of their empty drinks, and headed to the kitchen. Fred headed to their room and got ready for bed. A few minutes later Jill joined him.

Jill looked down at Fred who was sitting on the edge of the bed. "Hopefully, this will quiet down once the other two get back and we can move on."

Fred let out a sigh, "Man, I'm really tired. I don't know. Those few weeks away really took a lot out of me."

Jill said, "Yeah, it is noticeable. None of your clothes fit anymore!"

Fred looked up, "What?"

Jill just stood there next to him with a big grin on her face. "Well whatever you were doing there sure seems to agree with you. You have lost some weight. But not too much. Enough to make you look a little healthier than you were. Not that you were fat or anything."

"Thanks a lot. You mean you didn't like my masculine physique before?"

Jill looked down again and noticed he was also smiling and said, "We should go to sleep. We are both getting a little bit silly."

With that they both got into bed and wrapped up in each other's arms. Soon they were fast asleep.

Once again Fred was in the middle of the meadow hearing a bell. He saw an elevator door open. Now he was holding the door open yelling for Jason and Gail. But they were not coming. Where were they? He hoped they were not down at the river again. He started yelling, "Gail, Jason." Over and over and over again.

Everything went dark. The elevator disappeared and he was rocking back and forth like he was in an earthquake. Opening his eyes all he could see was dark. Then he heard Jill's voice. "Fred, Fred, wake up. You must be dreaming. Are you okay?"

Fred sat up. He felt his forehead and noticed that it was soaking wet, as was his pillow. "Yeah, I think I'm okay. What happened?"

"Well, you were shouting. It sounded like Jason and Gail over and over again like you were reliving something."

"I think I was wondering why they weren't coming when the elevator showed up. I hope these dreams don't happen often. I don't want to keep reliving that all the time."

Jill said, "Well if they do, you are going to have to go and see someone to talk about this. Otherwise, it may make you just as crazy as people will think you already are anyway.

Fred said, "Why do you think this happened to me?"

Jill gave him a hug and putting her pillow down in place of his nudged him to lie down. "I don't know. Let's go back to sleep."

"I don't know if I can. Or if I even want to!"

# CHAPTER THIRTY-NINE

Linda was in the lobby when Fred arrived to meet with Harry. She smiled and said "It is so very good to see you back Fred. Harry is on his way, feel free to go in and have a seat."

Fred went into Harry's office and sat on one of the chairs next to the desk. He had never really looked around the office before, so he got up to explore. The office was spacious while not being overly large. It had light blue walls. One wall was dominated by windows looking toward the front of the building. The desk was in front of the windows with Harry's chair next to the windows. He enjoyed the view but found it too distracting, so he now faces away from it. He can swivel his chair to look outside should he need a mental break, or to think.

Along one wall was a light brown leather sofa fronted by a glass topped coffee table. On the coffee table were some trade magazines and a large book of war planes. Two chairs were next to the desk. One of which he had been sitting upon. The chairs were made of maple and had been stained a color to match the sofa. They certainly were not what one considers as comfortable. Along the wall opposite the sofa was a credenza. The credenza was adorned with photographs of his wife, daughters, and grandchildren.

Fred seemed to notice for the first time the diplomas on the wall. Most of his previous conversations with the boss took place in his own office. There was also a frame hung on the wall with a signed picture of one of the local boys that had become a successful actor. He had been back home visiting family and was at the park walking their dog. Harry bumped into him in the park and had a photo taken. The actor told him to send it to him and he would sign it. Fred had never seen this before, or maybe just never noticed.

Harry interrupted Fred's exploration of the office. He asked Fred to sit down pointing to one of the maple chairs. Fred took this to be a bad sign.

Harry opened by saying "Fred, it has been weeks. No word, no call, no notice, no sign of you. Your wife didn't know where to find you. You wouldn't answer the phone and it went directly to voice mail."

Fred said "I know, I am very sorry. I can explain, but it sounds so fantastic I can't believe it and I was there."

Harry cut him off with a wave. "We can discuss that later. You have helped me build this company and I am grateful. As long as what happened will not bring dishonor to the firm we can move on. The last few weeks have demonstrated to me that you are a single point of failure. I need to fix that. We got along these past weeks burning up the backlog of courses you had scheduled. The backlog is nearly exhausted however, and you need to get back to work to get it back where it belongs."

"I also need you to take one of our other employees under your wing and teach them what you do, and how you do it. Your contacts, your processes, and how you manage to keep ahead of all the others in the same business. I am no longer comfortable with you having no backup."

Fred was a bit confused or maybe conflicted. He was happy he still had his job. He was not certain how he felt about training someone else to do that job.

Fred vaguely heard Harry saying "Fred … Fred are you okay?"

Fred snapped out of his thoughts and replied, "Yes, I don't know how to thank you."

At this Harry got up and walked around his desk. He placed one hand on Fred's shoulder and gave a gentile squeeze. He said, "Someday when you have had a bit more time to get it together, we will discuss the time you were away. Right now, I think it is more important for you to get back to work and resume something resembling your regular routine."

Harry continued. "I don't have a son of my own. I have two daughters." He pointed at the photographs on the credenza. "I have always thought of you as a member of the extended family. Go get reacquainted with your office. Don't worry about staying too long today. Be here bright and early Monday. We will talk again soon."

Fred stood up, mumbled a thank you, and walked trancelike to his office. It looked pretty much the way it had the day he disappeared. He closed the door, walked over to his chair, sat down, and put his head on the desk. He thought about his job and the strange conversation he just had with Harry. He thought about Jill and Kristine. His thoughts then turned to those he left behind. Gail and Jason. Where were they? When were they? Would they ever get back?

# CHAPTER FORTY

Fred's thoughts returned to his office. Looking around he noticed most everything was in its place. His credenza was open. This would be because the training materials were kept in there. Bob French had a key. Fred turned on his computer and monitors. He looked at the schedule for the day and noticed Bob was not teaching. He reached for the phone and gave Bob a call on the intercom.

The phone was answered after the first ring. "Hello, this is Bob."

"Bob, this is Fred."

"Fred! My God. Where have you been?"

"I will explain in due time. Do you have a minute?"

Fred heard some papers rustling. "Yeah, sure. Give me a couple minutes to finish something. I'll be right there."

Fred hung up the phone. While he waited, he studied what was left of the training schedule. The fog of being away was beginning to lift a little. Was it really going to be this easy to resume his life? That nightmare last night made him think otherwise.

Bob French appeared at the door. "What do you need boss. Boy, have I been ready to say that for a while. I didn't realize how much you do until I had to do some of it."

Fred looked up and gestured for Bob to take a seat. "I took a quick look at the schedule. We have a couple of corporate classes coming up. I won't be able to travel. Any chance you will be able to cover them?"

Bob studied Fred for a second. "I will check the calendar and get back to you. I think it will be okay. I don't have any family entanglements."

"Bob, there are some legal issues that are keeping from traveling just now. Since two other people have gone missing the police are keeping an eye on me."

"Really, what is going on? Are you in trouble?"

Fred paused before answering. "No, I don't think so. Jill and I met with the detective investigating my disappearance yesterday. He asked me to stay in town in case he had more questions. I have a couple things to do this morning, but I won't be here too long. I will be back full time on Monday."

Bob said, "Glad you are back. Anything else I can do?"

"No, how did the classes go this week?"

"We were, as you can see, only half full. Everything went great. I will catch up with you on Monday then."

Fred said, "Sounds like a plan. Have a great weekend."

Bob walked back to his office and Fred got up and closed his office door. He returned to his desk wondering what he should do now. The thought of the other guy popped into his head. Who was he and what is his story?

Fred went online to look up the news on the guy. He could not remember his name. He was not even sure if he ever knew it. Wait, the police sergeant asked if he knew some guy. Was it the same person? He typed "Missing Persons." He got tons of hits on missing people. Mostly children and teens. "Stupid, think before you type!" He scolded himself.

Next, he typed the address of the building, "1680 Hilltop Road." A number of articles popped up. Some of them were webpages for the companies in the building. Even the 13 webpage was on the list. As he scrolled down the list some older newspaper articles began to appear. Some were from when the building first opened. There were older lists of the tenants. He saw the listing for the sale of the building from the original owner. The list must be relevance ranked in some fashion since these articles all were mostly about the building. He remembered the search engines sorted the lists that way. What he was looking to find would be lower on the list because it was mostly about the person. What was his name?

Finally, he saw an article titled "Man Missing from Local Office Building." He clicked on the link. The article appeared in his browser window. It was from one of the local papers. There it was. His name. Brad Myerson. It listed the time and place he was last seen. He read Mr. Myerson's car was left in a visitor parking spot next to the building. Fred scrolled a little farther down the page. There he was. He looked quite different from when Fred had seen him in the parking lot. In the picture he had short hair. He was also clean shaven and a neat dresser! Fred did not recognize him as the same person.

Fred printed out a copy of the picture. He grabbed a pen and started to draw in a beard and extra unkempt hair. Soon the guy he saw in the parking lot that day began to emerge on the paper. He went back to the computer screen and hit the back button. He continued scrolling, looking for any news of his return. When he found a promising article, he clicked on the link to open it.

Brad's family did not believe him when he said he had gone somewhere in a time portal. They sued to have him committed to a hospital for the mentally ill. The family prevailed in the courts. Brad was sent to the State Center for Psychiatric Study.

Fred noted the name and returned to the search engine page. He entered State Center for Psychiatric Study on the search topic line and hit enter. A list of articles about the center and a link to a webpage appeared in the browser window. Fred selected the link to the center's webpage. The webpage contained many links. One was an overview of the facility. Another was contact information.

Fred selected the contact information first. He made note of the main phone number and the visiting hours. He went back to the main page and selected the center overview link. He read the overview. This page also included a bit more on visitation. While the visiting hours were listed on the contact information page, he read on this page, visitors were only allowed on Tuesday and Thursday. He thought it odd that would not have been included with the visiting hours.

# CHAPTER FORTY-ONE

With nothing much else to do, Fred decided to call and try to arrange a visit.

A pleasant voice answered the phone, "Center for Psychiatric Study. How may I help you?"

Fred answered, "I would like to visit one of your patients."

"Oh, we don't refer to them as patients. They are all residents of the center."

"Ah, very well. Then I would like to visit one of your residents."

The pleasant voice continued, "Let me pass you on to Mrs. Clark. She handles all our visitors. Allow me to transfer you." With that the line connected to some pleasant music. The volume was just right. Not too loud and no straining to hear it.

As the music played Fred waited to be connected to Mrs. Clark. He did not have to wait very long.

"Hello this is Helen Clark. I am told you would like to visit one of our residents. What is your name and who would you like to visit?" Helen Clark had been at the center for many years. She started out answering the phone like the woman with the pleasant voice currently at the switchboard. She worked her way up through various jobs. Now she was the primary interface between the center and the public. Even more so than most of the doctors. She was truly the residents' chief advocate, and in her mind protector.

Fred was about to experience Helen Clark just as everyone new to the center's residents does.

"My name is Fred Bates. I would like to visit Brad Myerson."

"Are you acquainted with Mr. Myerson?"

"No."

"Then why do you want to visit with him?"

"I am interested in hearing his story."

"Are you a reporter or someone wanting to write a book about him?"

"No, I work in the building mentioned in the articles about his disappearance and return. I actually saw him the day he returned. He was looking for his car. He was filthy and bearded and completely unkempt. He mumbled something to me, and I can't remember what he said. I would like to ask him what he remembers about our encounter, if anything."

Mrs. Clark continued, "Have you talked with his family?"

"No, do I need to?"

"Well, I would prefer it if you did, but it isn't mandatory. Please consider it. If you give me your contact information, I will pass it along to them. They may contact you. Then again, they may not."

Fred gave Mrs. Clark his contact information. He asked, "Are there particular times of the day best for a visit?"

"Mr. Myerson doesn't have fits or bad periods. In fact, he is quite the gentleman. If it wasn't for his insistence his story is true, he wouldn't even be here."

"When do you think I can visit?"

"Today is Friday. Unless I hear back from the family that they are against it, Tuesday lunch time would be the earliest."

Fred was checking his calendar for Tuesday. All was clear. "Okay then, unless I hear differently, I will see you on Tuesday. Is there anything he likes or needs? I can bring it with me."

There was a moment of silence while Mrs. Clark thought about Fred's question. She offered, "He isn't supposed to have soda pop, but I know he likes RC Cola. If you check out okay, I just might overlook it should you smuggle one in."

Fred noted RC Cola and replied, "Until Tuesday then." He then hung up the phone.

Fred straightened up the office and made a few calls to companies to let them know he was back on the job. After an hour, he decided that was enough for one day. He logged off his computer and turned off the monitors. He walked out of his office closing the door behind him. As he walked through the lobby he said to Linda, "Linda, thanks for everything. What you and everyone else did for Jill and Kris while I was away was much appreciated. I will be in Monday morning."

With a big smile Linda said, "Fred, we were happy to help. You have a wonderful wife and a beautiful daughter. You take care of yourself."

Fred smiled back and headed for the elevators.

# CHAPTER FORTY-TWO

Tuesday morning arrived. Fred was excited. He got up early and got dressed. He left the house earlier than normal. Jill asked why he was so rushed. He told her he had to pick up something on the way to work. Technically that was true. He needed to find a store selling RC Cola. Why then did he feel guilty about what he told Jill? Why didn't he want her to know where he was going today?

Fred had a hard time concentrating at work. His mind kept wandering to what he might discover during his talk with Brad Myerson. Would he be lucid, or would he rave like the lunatic his family believed him to be? Would he even agree to talk with Fred?

Harry poked his head into Fred's office. "Everything going okay? I noticed you were in a bit early."

Fred jumped a bit. "Sorry Harry I was pre-occupied and didn't hear you come in. Things are good. I do need to be out this afternoon. There are no issues upstairs. Everyone is situated. All of the classes for the week started yesterday without any problems."

"Well I guess we can do without you for an afternoon. Everything is running smooth now that you are back, and our backlog is growing again. Here, take your family out for a nice dinner on me." Harry handed Fred a gift card for Jill's favorite restaurant.

"Thanks Harry. You know there is no need for this."

"I do know that. Enjoy the dinner anyway!" With that Harry walked out before Fred could continue the objection.

Fred began to second guess his decision to visit Brad at the Center. Everything here was back to normal. Gail and Jason were still missing, but other than that all was good. The police appeared to be finished questioning him. Why is he still out and about and Brad is essentially locked up? Is it really only because Jill believes him and didn't press to have him sent to some institution?

He caught himself saying out loud the same thing he shouted in the woods, "I have the greatest woman in the world as my wife." The pangs of guilt returned. "Why didn't I tell Jill about Brad and my visit today? Is it really something needing secrecy?" He looked at his watch. He needed to leave soon.

# CHAPTER FORTY-THREE

Fred arrived at the Center for Psychiatric Study a few minutes early. He was not sure where to go or if he would have an in-person interview before meeting with Brad. He followed the signs for the main administration building.

The building looked like he imagined an Ivy League college building would look, grey brick with vines covering the lower half of one side. At one corner they snaked up nearly to the roof. White concrete stairs led up to the large double door entrance. Fred found an empty visitor parking space across from the steps. He was halfway across the driveway when he remembered the package he bought.

After retrieving the package, he climbed the twelve steps to the entrance. He pulled the door open and entered a spacious reception area. A large desk was immediately opposite of the door. The desk was a dark brown color and nearly obscured the young woman sitting in the leather chair on the other side. Fred walked up to the desk. The woman looked up from her computer monitor and asked, "May I help you?"

"Yes, my name is Fred Bates. I am here to visit one of your residents. His name is Brad Myerson."

She quickly looked at her monitor and typed a few keys. "Oh yes, I see you have a visitor appointment. Mrs. Clark would like a brief word with you before your visit. I will let her know you are here. You can wait over there if you like," she said pointing to a couple upholstered chairs to her right.

Fred noticed a name plate on the desk showing the woman's name to be Julie Cashman. "Thank you, Ms. Cashman."

"Oh, Julie will do here. We try not to be too formal. The residents are more comfortable that way. Mrs. Clark on the other hand, prefers the formality. I suspect you will understand once you meet her."

"Then, thank you, Julie. Thanks for the info." Fred gave her a wink and walked over to the chairs Julie suggested. They were brown leather – the same color as the chair Julie occupied. They looked to be more for relaxing than the desk chair. Fred selected the chair facing the entrance and Julie's desk, and sat down.

Fred looked around the reception area. All the furniture looked pretty much the same. It had a homey feel he suspected minimized the stress or apprehension some of the visitors may experience. He certainly felt at ease.

He had not finished looking around when Mrs. Clark appeared. She was an older woman with shoulder length hair beginning to thin. She was about 5 feet 6 inches tall with a slender build. She was wearing a light grey suit. When she approached Fred, her face broke into a wide smile. The smile was accented by a pair of large friendly blue eyes. She reached out with her right hand. "Mr. Bates?"

Fred stood and as he shook her hand said, "Yes, thank you again for allowing me to visit."

"Please, let's sit." She sat in the other chair. "We can talk here. We have a meeting room just down the hall for your visit."

Sitting back down Fred said, "I hope it isn't any extra trouble getting Mr. Myerson to the building?"

"No trouble at all. Mr. Myerson is not considered a threat to himself, or anyone else for that matter. I believe I mentioned that when we spoke on the phone."

She studied Fred for a long time before continuing. "The room we have for your visit is a room we had designed for visits like these. The residents allowed visitors are all familiarized with the room. We find it easier on them and the staff."

She went on, "What I would like to do for a few minutes before Mr. Myerson arrives, is learn a little more about you. I know you are not a reporter or an author. So, tell me about yourself. Where you work, your family, and interests. No need for too much detail but I like to know a little bit about our visitors."

Fred told her about 13 and his family. He also said he enjoys being outdoors with them like hiking. He talked for a few minutes and stopped when Mrs. Clark interrupted.

"Thank you, Mr. Bates, that will do just fine. I do have one more question. I took the liberty of Googling you and noticed you were reported missing some weeks ago. You also work in the very building Mr. Myerson says he was in when he went missing."

Fred interrupted, "I mentioned, when we talked earlier, I saw him the day he returned in the parking lot outside the building."

"Yes, I remember. You also said you were trying to remember what he said to you. My question is, is that the only reason you are here?" She was now looking at Fred like a parent that believes they have caught their child in a lie. She was waiting for him to come clean. Those blue eyes were no longer part of that smile, but part of a piercing gaze intended to intimidate Fred. It was working.

"What I told you on the phone is true. I do want to know what he said to me." Fred was a bit uncomfortable. He was not ready to discuss his ordeal with this stranger. "I know what it is like to be away from everything and everyone. I would like to hear how he coped with it then, and copes with it now. I am curious how he survived. I have had some training in survival, but I did not get the sense from what I read he did, before. I guess I just want to know how he got through it. I know it sounds strange, but I have this feeling in the pit of my stomach that I need to talk with him."

"No, that does not sound strange. You believe you have experienced something similar and therefore there is some type of a bond. You seem sincere in your desire to speak with Mr. Myerson. However, I am not completely comfortable with this. So, I am going to allow you to meet but I will monitor the discussion. You will have to sign a consent form. If I sense the topic is leaning toward your experience or if Mr. Myerson begins to get agitated, I will end the visit. Agreed?"

"Yes, no problem. Thank you."

Mrs. Clark looked at the bag next to Fred's chair. "What's in the bag?"

"Oh, you mentioned on the phone Mr. Myerson likes RC Cola. You know, not all stores carry this brand. I had to stop at a few. I got a six-pack. You can put five of them away for later if you like."

"Very thoughtful. I will do that. Mr. Myerson should be waiting for you by now." She rose and motioned for Fred to follow.

She reached for the bag and took one of the bottles. She handed that to Fred as they walked to the desk. She stopped at the desk and handed the bag to Julie. "Julie these are for Mr. Myerson. Please have them put in the fridge. Thank you."

She continued, "Do you have the form for us to sign?"

"Yes ma'am, it is right here."

"Mr. Bates, this form says we can record your discussions with Mr. Myerson and make a copy." She paused then added as she handed the form to Fred, "for legal reasons we have to keep a record."

Fred read the form. "Okay if I get a copy?"

"I don't know the answer to that question. I will find out. What format would you like should it be possible?"

"DVD or flash drive. It really doesn't matter. I can probably read any type of media you have available. I am assuming it will be a MP3 file."

"I don't know anything about that. Our admin takes care of those details. I will add one condition of my own, however. You must promise not to share this without Mr. Myerson's approval. It just may confirm his diagnosis to some people."

"That sounds reasonable." Fred said as he found the place on the form for his signature. Mrs. Clark signed the form as well.

The floor appeared to be empty except for the three of them. Mrs. Clark led Fred past two rooms finally stopping at the third. Standing just inside the door was a stern looking man in his late twenties. "That will be all John. I will let you know when we are finished."

The man nodded and without a word disappeared down the hall.

The room was large, and like the lobby, pleasantly decorated. Seascapes and country settings pictures were hung on the walls. Two large windows overlooked the well-manicured grounds of the center. Standing next to the windows was a slender man Fred recognized to be Brad Myerson. He had not gained all the weight back but looked just like his picture on the internet.

# CHAPTER FORTY-FOUR

Mrs. Clark spoke first. "Hello, Mr. Myerson. I am with the gentleman wishing to visit with you. His name is Fred Bates."

Brad turned to look toward the doorway. "Hello Mrs. Clark. Thank you for taking the time to bring him to me."

"It is no trouble at all. I am going to leave you two to your talk. As usual, I will be just up the hall in my office should you need anything." With that she walked out of the room closing the door.

"Hi, my name is Brad. All this Mr. Myerson stuff gets a bit old. Reminds me a bit like Cuckoo's Nest. Don't get me wrong, the people here are much nicer than Nurse Ratched on her best day. Please, let's sit. The view from this room is lovely." Brad pointed toward a pair of chairs near the windows.

Fred started for the chairs but stopped and said, "My name is Fred, Fred Bates. Mrs. Clark told me you like RC Cola. I got you some." He handed the bottle to Brad.

"You didn't have to do that. I would have still talked with you without the bribe." Brad walked over to a small refrigerator on the counter along one wall. He grabbed a plastic cup and filled it with ice cubes.

As he walked back to the chairs, he filled the cup with soda from the bottle. He swirled it a little to cool the soda. He winked at Fred, tipped the cup in his direction as if making a toast, and took a long pull from the cup. "Ah, that is something we don't get here. It isn't a beer, but it will do. Thanks!" He poured the rest of the soda into the cup and sat in one of the chairs. Fred sat in the other.

Brad looked at Fred closely. "You look familiar. Do we know each other from somewhere? I can't place you."

Fred replied, "I work at I3 on the 7th and 8th floors of 1680 Hilltop Road. I saw you the day you returned from your disappearance. You spoke to me in the parking lot as you were looking for your car, I think. The car had been towed well before you got back."

"I vaguely remember talking with someone. I was in and out of that building a lot, so I probably saw you from time to time. Mrs. Clark mentioned you wanted to talk about that day. Something about you not understanding what I said, or maybe you forgot. She wasn't sure."

"That is correct. I am curious what you said, and maybe also why you were saying it."

"Oh, yes. That may be the bigger question. Why. Do you know why I am here? I suspect you do but I need to ask."

"Yes, I know. Your family thinks you belong here because of the explanation you gave about your disappearance. About it being impossible, or something like that."

The door opened. Mrs. Clark poked her head in. "Everything okay Mr. Myerson?"

"Yes, Mrs. Clark. We are just getting started. Thanks for the soda. Please, call me Brad." Brad raised the cup to her.

"Alright, I am just up the hall." She closed the door.

Brad went on, "She does that sometimes just as a reminder she is listening. I don't really mind. She has heard it all anyway. As the visit coordinator she gets to sit in on some of the sessions with the doctors. With my permission of course. Heck it was all in the papers or court documents anyway, so what the hell."

Brad stopped to take another drink of the soda. When finished he continued, "Back to the topic of the day. What did I say to you in the parking lot? I must have looked like death warmed over."

"You were quite a mess. Hair was all ratty and your clothes all tattered. I told my wife you reminded me of Michael Palin at the beginning of the Monty Python TV show."

Brad gave out a laugh. "That is funny. I saw those shows on the internet. I guess I can see how you would have thought that. I had no comb or change of clothes."

Brad continued, "So, I think what I said was something like 'Sixth floor' and 'Use the stairs'. Does that sound about right?"

Fred said, "Close enough. You also mumbled something like 'Where is my car'. But like I said that was long gone."

"The car was taken to the police impound lot. My wife got it back about two weeks later. After they couldn't find anything in or on it to give them ideas to what happened. I do miss driving. It is a BMW convertible. Lots of fun on the back roads. What kind of car do you drive?"

"I drive a Ford Explorer. We have a lot of outdoor activities. My wife runs and I ride a bike a lot, so we need the extra cargo space. Do you ever get out for an hour or so to see the world or are you here full time?"

"We aren't supposed to talk about those things. So, to keep Mrs. Clark from popping in again, let's move on from that topic. Is that all you wanted to know?" Then after a short pause. "Wait, you also said you want to know why."

Brad looked at Fred for a minute and then said, "Are you really sure you want to know why? Because the answer is not at all simple, and you quite likely will agree with my family."

Fred returned the wait before speaking. He was worried how to continue without his disappearance getting included in the conversation. "I am curious what 'sixth floor' means and what does 'use the stairs' have to do with anything?"

Now Brad was wondering why Fred cared so much about his experiences. "Why do you want to know? It isn't like we are friends? You aren't a writer of any kind, so I see no reason why you should be here. Trust me, I don't mind the visit. I don't get many, and talking to someone that isn't a patient, oops, resident here is a real treat for me. But I do have to wonder a bit."

Fred thought about this. "Do you get to use the internet here?

"Not really. Most of the residents are better off not having access. So it doesn't look like I have special privileges, I don't have special privileges. Easier on the staff that way. Not much on the net I need while in here anyway. We do get to watch the news." He lowered his voice to a whisper and leaning over close to Fred said, "I think they edit the news to keep out items or stories that may upset some of the residents." He sat back in his chair.

Fred asked again, "Why the stairs? I assure you I am genuinely interested. I do not plan to write a book or an article or anything about your experience. I remembered we bumped into each other that day when I came across your story on the internet. I thought, 'why did he decide to talk to me? What did he mean by what he said?' He, being you. So, I decided to try and visit with you to find out."

Brad continued to study Fred, "How much time do you have? If I start, do you promise to hear me out?"

Fred said, "I have all afternoon. I promise I will listen and not dismiss anything you say. Okay if I ask questions along the way? Will Mrs. Clark let us talk as long as we want?"

Brad smiled, "We can have all afternoon. She leaves around 5 and I don't think she will allow you to be here if she isn't. And ask as many questions as you like. A conversation is better than a monologue."

Brad finished the soda. "Where to start."

# CHAPTER FORTY-FIVE

Brad started at the beginning. "That day I pulled into the parking lot and found one of the visitor spots open. Thinking it was my lucky day I parked there. They are usually taken when I get there. I think I was headed for the dentist on the eighth floor that day. They were one of my customers. You guys have classrooms up there or something don't you?"

"Yes, we do. I am in charge of the training center and all of the course material."

"Right, I got on the elevator?"

"Which one?" Fred asked a bit too quickly. He looked over at the door expecting it to open.

Puzzled, Brad said, "I think it was the far one on the left. It had all the padding covering the walls. I guess the owner prefers you use that one that one like a freight elevator. Anyway, after I got in three other guys got in. They were with the company on the fifth and sixth floors. I wasn't really paying attention."

"The elevator gave a little bump like they do sometimes. The three guys joked that it happened all the time. When we stopped at the fifth floor, two of the guys convinced the third to join them for a few minutes. So, he got off a floor early. The doors closed and soon they opened again. Without thinking I got off. I was the only one in the elevator and I guess I just assumed it was my floor. Well, it wasn't. It was the sixth floor not the eighth. The third guy had pressed the button for his floor. Then the doors closed."

"All of a sudden I was standing in the middle of a meadow!"

Fred said faking a bit of surprise, "A meadow?"

"Yes, a meadow. Remember, you promised."

"No, everything is okay. I wanted to make sure I heard you correctly. Is that why you said sixth floor?"

"Exactly, the sixth floor. And I said to use the stairs because the elevator is the key!"

"Wish I had realized that" escaped from Fred before he realized it. This was going to be hard. He suspected Mrs. Clark knew it would be hard.

"Sorry, what did you say?" Brad was looking at Fred suspiciously again.

Trying to change the subject, Fred asked, "You say the elevator was the key. What do you mean by that?"

Brad refocused on his story to the relief of Fred. "The elevator is what took me there. As you will see later it is also what brought me back!"

"Did you do anything special on the elevator to make it take you wherever you went?"

"Fred, I am not sure I follow your question. You want to know if I did something on purpose, to take me to a place where, as you will see, I barely survived and upon returning enabled my family to put me in this place. It is nice and all, but I would rather not be here. So, to answer your question, no, I don't think I did anything to make it happen."

Fred was a little embarrassed at how that question and answer turned out. "Sorry, when you put it that way it does sound like a pretty dumb question. I will try to think before I speak."

"Don't worry about it. One of my sisters actually asked the exact same question. My answer to her was a little less civil than the one just now. Now, where was I?" Realizing what he had just said made Brad laugh. "Boy, didn't that sound funny!"

"You just arrived at the meadow."

"Right, I couldn't believe it. I thought I was dreaming. I started yelling 'Wake Up', 'Wake Up', after a while of yelling and slapping my face. By the way, why do people do that? Do they really think if they are asleep, slapping their face in a dream will wake themselves? It hurts by the way."

"Anyway, after a while I looked around and I saw trees in the distance in every direction."

Fred interrupted, "Which way did you go?"

"What makes you think I went somewhere?" Brad had that suspicious look again.

"I don't know, staying out in the open in an unfamiliar place. Not sure I would do that I suspect. I would look for cover of some kind." Fred hoped, yet again, he had not summoned Mrs. Clark. Brad seemed to get over his suspicions.

"That makes sense. Have you ever had to do something like this? I mean be out in the elements and fend for yourself?"

Fred wondered if Brad was beginning to suspect something. He thought of the only thing he did when he was younger that came close to what Brad was asking. "Once when I was in scouts, our scout master had the idea we should all know something about living off the land, survival if you will. We spent months learning the skills. He even brought in some military folks to teach some of the lessons."

Fred continued, "After all the training was done, all of the scouts were asked if we wanted to have a survival camp out. Of course, we all said yes. All the older kids went, but some of the younger kids couldn't get the required permission from their parents."

Brad seemed satisfied with that answer and continued his story. "As it turns out, I did leave the meadow. I went straight toward the tree line I thought was closest. I guess it was a quarter or a half mile. I don't know anything about trees, but I thought there might be nuts or something in case I got hungry. Trees also provided some cover in case it rains. Well, I thought they did."

"Why do you say that?"

"It did rain the next day and I got soaked. When the leaves get wet, the water slides right off them. They only block so much."

"So then what did you do?"

"I built something like a lean-to. I think it is called a lean-to. Three sides and a roof."

"We would call that a lean-to. How did you know how to build one?"

"I didn't. I learned by trial and error. I think by the time I actually returned; the lean-to would hold up to all but the biggest storms. I sat through a couple doozies and the walls and roof held up."

"What did you use to make it?" Fred asked. Trying to keep Brad talking.

"I found some branches about 2 to 3 inches thick, about 7 or 8 feet long, and stuck them in the ground. I also found some underbrush I used as rope of a sort and tied full branches to cross branches to make walls and similarly across the top. I used a lot more on the top. After a few tries there were very few leaks."

"Did you take the bark off the support posts?"

"No why?"

"We were taught the wood will resist rotting longer with the bark removed."

"I didn't know that, and I was hoping to not be there that long. So, I had some shelter after a day or two. It got better and stronger as time went on as I learned more about what worked and what didn't."

Fred was beginning to get a little excited and impatient with the pace of the discussion. "Okay, you had shelter but what did you eat and what did you do for water?"

"Well, I guess that is the next topic. It turns out I was lucky to have picked this direction. When it got really quiet, I thought I heard water. About ten minutes into the forest was a river. The water tasted better than any I remember drinking. No chlorine, no pollutants. I had to go to the river whenever I was thirsty."

"There was nothing around you could use as a container for the water?"

"All of the logs around were quite rotten. I didn't dare use them. I had no tools. All I had was my cigarette lighter. Thank goodness for that or I would have had sushi every day." Brad laughed at his joke.

"Sushi? How did you go about catching the fish?"

"I learned very quickly fishing requires patience. At first, I was jumping and diving around after the fish I would see in the river. But as you can imagine they are better in the water than me. I sat on the bank and studied them.

Sometimes they just hovered in the sun and sometimes they didn't. I thought about all the movies I had seen, and the TV shows about people in Africa and the Amazon. It dawned on me they used spears."

"I went into the woods and looked for a sturdy stick. I picked one about an inch in diameter and about 9 feet long. I didn't have any tools so sharpening the spear proved to be problematic. For some reason popsicles came to mind. That morphed into just the sticks. We used to sharpen them into makeshift knives by scraping them on the sidewalk. I just went looking for a big rock. Soon I had a spear with a pointy end. It took some tries, but I got the hang of it and I had fish to eat."

Fred asked, "Weren't you afraid of starting a fire next to the shelter?"

"I didn't think about that. I built the fire next to the river. I feel sort of bad about just tossing the fish guts, heads, and bones back into the river. I tossed them downstream of where I fished and drank the water."

"That explains it." mumbled Fred.

"What?"

"I said that explains how you got food and water." Big sigh of relief. "Weren't you afraid of animals? Did you ever see signs of bear, deer, large cats, or anything else?"

"I did see some rabbits. I thought I heard a cat growl one night. That scared the crap out of me. The next morning, I made a few more spears. I kept a couple at the shelter and a couple next to the river. Fortunately, I never heard it again. Not much more to say. I never strayed from the path between the shelter and the river. Last thing I wanted was to run into that cat I heard."

"You never went up or down stream?"

"Only a little downstream when I was tossing the fish remains into the river. I guess I thought throwing them in the river would allow the fish to eat the leftovers.

Fred tried to move the story along. "What did you do when not at the river eating or drinking?"

"I needed to get back didn't I. I finally decided whatever mechanism dropped me there probably would come back. At least I hoped it would. So, I went back into the meadow to try and find where I started."

"I was lucky the grass in the meadow wasn't too high and the path I made was still visible. When I got back to the place I thought was it, I trampled the ground until the grass was almost dead. I wanted to be able to find it again."

Fred deadpanned, "You could have put a stick in the ground kind of like a flag."

"That would have been a good idea. I didn't think of it though. Anyway, I was able to find it even after a rainstorm. I would go back there every day."

Fred just smiled as that was exactly what he thought.

Brad said, "You are smiling about something."

"Well it obviously was the correct thing to do because you got back."

They both turned toward the door when Mrs. Clark appeared. "It is getting late gentlemen. You need to wrap things up. Another fifteen minutes, okay?"

Fred looked at his watch. It was nearly four in the afternoon. He looked at Brad.

Brad said back to Mrs. Clark, "Sure thing. We are nearly done anyway."

Mrs. Clark smiled and closed the door.

Brad returned to the story. "I sat there every day. It must have been at least 8 or 10 hours a day. Finally, I heard a bell. I looked up to see an elevator door. I never ran so fast in my life. I jumped in the elevator just as the doors started to close. It was empty. I pressed 1 as the door was closing. I caught a glimpse of the meadow just as it disappeared and the hallway on the sixth floor took its place just as the doors closed. It was more than surreal."

"I walked out of the building. My car was not in the space I left it. So, I wandered the lot looking for it. That must be when you saw me, and I spoke to you. The rest is a matter of record in the courts."

Fred was feeling mixed emotions. He was elated to know his hunch about Brad being the one to preceded him was true. He was anxious because Gail and Jason were still there. Were they still alive? The fact Brad figured out how to survive gave him some hope for Jason.

"Brad, thank you for meeting with me. I can't tell you how much this means to me."

"You are more than welcome Fred. Please come back again. I don't get many visitors. I really enjoyed our discussion. I almost feel like you believe me."

"I can honestly say, I believe every word. I hope someday you can get out of this place. I think we could be friends."

The door opened and the twenty something guy was back.

Brad said, "That's my ride. Thanks again for the visit."

"You are welcome. Brad, I really do believe you!"

Then the twenty something guy said, "Mr. Bates, Mrs. Clark would like to see you before you leave. Her office is across the hall."

Brad left with the twenty something guy. Fred watched as they walked to the end of the hall to the right. As they walked out the door, Fred saw a golf cart parked nearby. "I guess he really did mean his ride." After the door closed, Fred looked across the hall for Mrs. Clark's office.

# CHAPTER FORTY-SIX

The office was sparsely decorated with pictures, again similar to those in the visit room and the lobby. There did not appear to be any personal pictures or objects in the office. The furniture was like that in the lobby also. He knocked on the door frame since the door was open. Mrs. Clark looked up and waved him in.

"Let's sit over here." She said pointing to a large sofa along the wall.

Fred sat at one end. Mrs. Clark took the other. She started the conversation. "Thank you for keeping your promise. I am sure it was not easy for you. The little bit I listened to gave me the impression you were leading him sometimes."

"I am not sure leading is the way I would put it. I was just interested in how someone like Brad could survive that situation. I had a little training, and he had no clue. But he is a smart guy and he learned quickly using examples he had seen, and by studying his environment."

"You really believe him, don't you? Why?"

Fred couldn't keep it in any longer, the whole discussion with Brad made him want to burst. He just blurted it out. "Because I found his shelter. I made it bigger and stronger. His distances and descriptions were spot on. I explored more, but we sync'd up."

Mrs. Clark looked stunned. "You are saying the whole elevator thing happened to you?"

Just then a geeky looking guy came in and placed a small package on her desk. He turned and said as he left the office, "The DVD you requested. Two copies."

Fred waited until they were again alone. "Yes, it is true, I experienced the same thing. As did two others that are still there. I was asking if he did something special, so I could try to force the elevator to get them back. But he didn't know anything. I also do not believe he belongs here. Not my call, right?"

"Right." She stood and walked to her desk. She picked up the DVDs and looked at them.

"Here is the copy I promised you. I hope you keep your other promise. The one to not share this."

"Don't worry about that. I will not share it unless Brad gives his permission, and I do not intend to ask while he is here."

"Does your wife know your story?"

"Yes, so do the police."

"And she believes you?"

"She has no reason not to. I have never lied to her and she knows it."

Mrs. Clark walked to her door. Fred decided it was a signal time was up. He stood and followed her to the door. They walked in silence to the building exit. Fred noticed Julie's desk was empty.

Mrs. Clark opened the door. "I am intrigued. Would you come back and tell me your story?"

"Yes, but there will be conditions. It will have to wait until after the other two return. I also will not do it anywhere it can be recorded, and you will have to make the same promise as I to not publish." Fred said raising the DVD.

"That seems fair. I look forward to seeing you again."

"I will be back to see Brad sometime. Until then, thank you." Fred walked down the steps and climbed into his car. It took him a few minutes to focus on the car. He started the car, pulled out of the parking space, and headed home.

# CHAPTER FORTY-SEVEN

Still no sign of Jason or Gail. Fred was thinking about them as he walked into the lobby. He did not notice the "Out of Order" sign across the door to the first elevator on the right. He pressed the up button between the two on the left. He heard the bell ring and looked for the elevator doors to open. The door opposite the first elevator opened. He walked into the car and turned to press the button for the seventh floor. When the doors began to close, he looked up and saw the sign on the doors across the lobby.

Fred got to his office thinking about the out of service elevator. It was not the same one that had taken him on his journey. That elevator was in the opposite corner of the four. He sat at his desk and opened the file drawer. He looked for the folder. It was exactly where he expected it to be, between the one labelled "Breakfast Restaurants" and the one labelled "Career Planning." The label read "Building Information." He opened the folder and took out the sole sheet of paper. The top line on the paper read "Building Contact Information." Scrolling down the sheet he found the number for the building manager, Bill Kidd.

Bill answered the call after three rings. "Hello this is Bill how can I help you?" Bill's father was a huge fan of western lore and movies and thought it was cool to name his first-born son after one of the most misunderstood outlaws, William Bonney.

"Hi Bill, this is Fred Bates at 13. I noticed one of the elevators is marked out of service. What happened?"

"It is nothing to worry about. The elevator is getting its annual checkup. Each one will be serviced over the next month or so."

Fred answered back "But I don't see the technician."

"Oh, he won't be working on the first floor very often. He mostly works from one of the middle floors. Some of the time he will be on the roof, where the elevator shed is. He needs to have access to the top and underside of the car without having to move it. He has to disable the drive motors for safety reasons."

"The service man's name is Hyrum Zimmerman. He is an older gentleman. These elevators are old, and he is one of the last people, if not the last person, with the experience with this manufacturer and model. This elevator model has not been produced for over twenty years. The building owner is contemplating switching over to new elevators using newer technology. But that is expensive, and since these do still work, he is waiting."

Fred thanked Bill and rang off.

He carefully replaced the paper back into the folder and returned the folder to the correct place in the drawer. Before closing the drawer, he straightened the folders and made sure they were all evenly spaced.

He then got out of his chair and walked out of the office. He went straight to the elevators and pressed the down button. When the car arrived, he entered it, checked to see it was empty, and placed his hand across the safety bar on the door to keep it from closing. He made note of the manufacturer and model. He let go of the bar as he walked out of the car just as the warning buzzer was starting. As he returned to his office, he wondered why he had never noticed this information before, even after his journey!

Fred sat down and started to type on his keyboard. He typed "Elevator" in the search engine query box. The list returned had everything from elevator descriptions, history, and manufacturers.

Fred decided to start at the beginning. He read Archimedes built his first elevator in 235BC. That design was used in most elevators until the late 1800's. These elevators used ropes and pulleys to elevate or lower the car. Elevators were powered mostly by water, animals, or people, until electricity use became common. Werner von Siemens built the first electric powered elevator. Elisha Otis made many design refinements, including the special "breaks" that allow an elevator car to stop should the support cables or ropes break. One other important advance in technology was a method for opening and closing the doors safely. This was patented by J. W. Meeker.

Fred next looked at the technologies used in elevators. He read there are two primary types of technology. One technology, used in most buildings over six to eight floors, is traction elevators. These use cables or ropes with pulleys. There are different mechanisms for driving the wheels spooling or unspooling the cables or ropes. These elevators also use a counterweight to lessen the load of the driving mechanism. The most popular versions of these elevators have a machine room above the elevator shaft housing the motors and other machinery.

Growing in popularity is a version called the machine-room-less traction elevator. This version has the drive machinery over the top floor in the shaft. Building codes are slowly being adjusted to allow for this variant.

The second primary type of technology uses hydraulics. These elevators are limited to six to at most eight floors. They require a cylinder underneath the elevator. The cylinder moves by having a liquid (oil, water, or something else) forced into a chamber, thereby pushing the cylinder. With the elevator car atop the cylinder it is also forced upward. Removing some of the liquid allows the car to descend. The cylinder can either be one piece or can be of the telescoping variety. A hole is required under the building as deep as the cylinder is tall. Telescoping cylinders require a hole less deep. There are hydraulic elevators with the cylinders alongside the car instead of underneath. Hydraulic elevators are generally cheaper to install than traction elevators, but they are limited in the practical height achievable.

Fred saw a couple of interesting recent developments in elevators. One of the newer elevators, being used primarily in residencies, uses vacuum technology. These are essentially tubes using air pressure to move a cylindrical car up and down. The pictures in the article reminded Fred of the capsule used by banks at the auto tellers. You put the money and ID in and place it in the tube. It then gets sucked into the bank.

The last item Fred noticed was one from a German company stating they are working on an elevator that uses magnetic-levitation technology similar to the trains in Japan. This elevator will not be constrained to vertical motion. It will be able to go from side to side as well. Multiple cars will be able to utilize the same shafts or pathways at the same time, thereby reducing wait times. A prototype is under development. Fred thought about Willy Wonka and his "Wonkavator." Just push a button, and whoosh, off to that room you go.

Now with a rudimentary background in elevators, Fred typed the manufacturer name into the search engine. Everyone has heard of Otis, but he had never heard of The Sanderson Elevator Company. He had worked in this building for all this time, and the name on the elevators had never registered. His only excuse was he normally is reading something while going from his car to his desk. The search engine returned a list of sites answering his query. Again, Fred was amazed at what can be found on the internet.

Fred scrolled down the list of links until he found one he thought may be promising. The link sent him to a newspaper article that had been scanned. The article titled, "Sanderson Elevator Company Bought out of Bankruptcy" included a short history of the company.

> "The Sanderson Elevator Company of Cleveland, Ohio was purchased by the Midlands Technology Group. The purchase ended the fifty-six-year run of the recently troubled firm. The troubles began with the accident at the Glendale Insurance Company headquarters building in Dayton, Ohio. The accident occurred when one of the elevator cables failed. The car failed to stop and crashed in the basement. A young mother and her two-year-old daughter were both killed.

> "The subsequent investigation revealed the cause to be faulty installation of the elevator car braking system originally designed by Elisha Otis in the

1850's. The installation had used parts susceptible to wear outside of the safety specifications. Inspections of other facilities using the same elevator model uncovered the same parts being used on over 70% of the installations.

"The resulting wrongful death lawsuit and required repairs, caused irreparable damage to the company's cash flow resulting in the bankruptcy filing.

"Officials of The Midlands Technology Group have committed to maintaining the elevators installed across the country. They will, however, be recommending replacement with elevators from companies included in their conglomerate. They will retain the entire maintenance and repair staff. Sales and other employees will be retained where possible. There are no plans to retain the corporate management."

Fred skimmed through the article until he saw more of the history included near the end.

"Olaf Sanderson founded the company after recommendations of more efficient designs were rejected by his former employer. He moved to Cleveland from Sweden and formed The Sanderson Elevator Company. He was able to obtain a licensing agreement with his former employer to use their basic design, since they had little presence in America. He included his modifications to the drive mechanism improving the efficiency, thereby reducing the amount of electricity required for operation.

"The Sanderson Elevator Company successfully installed elevators across the United States. The majority were in the central section, from Pittsburg in the east, to Denver in the Midwest, and Houston in the southwest. Many of the installations were replaced over time as more modern elevators were developed."

Fred was interrupted when his phone rang. "Yes, this is Fred."

"Hello Fred. This is Linda. Harry asked me to call and see if you have time talk with him."

"Sure anytime."

"That's great. Should be no more than 30 minutes. He has a window starting in 15 minutes. Will that work for you?"

Fred iconified the browser windows and opened his calendar. He knew it would be open, but he wanted to make double sure. "That works fine for me Linda. I will pop in, in fifteen."

Fred could hear Linda typing through the phone receiver. "I will let Harry know. Bye now."

"Thanks Linda. Bye."

Fred wondered what that was all about. Normally when Harry wants to talk, he just walks over to Fred's office and sits down. Maybe since Fred had that session in Harry's office when he returned, it was now an acceptable place to meet. Is he getting paranoid? Now that he recommended Bob be his assistant, is he less valued by Harry?

Fred shook his head. He thought, "What am I thinking? I have built the backlog almost to the point it was before I went on my little journey. What possibly could Harry be upset about."

Fifteen minutes later he was knocking on Harry's door.

# CHAPTER FORTY-EIGHT

Harry looked up from his desk. "Ah Fred. Come on in." Harry stood and walked over to the sofa and motioned for Fred to have a seat. Harry closed the door then sat on the chair next to the sofa.

"Good morning Fred. There are a couple things I need to discuss with you."

Fred said, "Good morning Harry. What's up?"

"First, Bob French. You think he is a good person to backstop you? I really don't know him that well. You are the one that hired him."

Fred said, "When we talked about this I suggested, and you agreed, a companywide announcement of the position would be fair. This gave anyone in the company a chance to get the job. Four people in the company expressed interest in the position. One I dismissed out of hand since the employee was a recent hire and really didn't know enough about the company."

Fred continued, "The remaining three include one from the software development group, one from the business office, and Bob from the instructor staff. Each of the three satisfied some of the job requirements, and therefore would be able to contribute, at least partially. I think Bob is the better choice since he was already helping me, and he picked up the most while I was away. He and I get along quite well.

Harry said, "I see him around from time to time and at the company parties and such, but he spends most of his time in the classrooms. Tell me about him."

"Well, where to start. He is from Detroit. His parents came from Ethiopia. They are Christian and came to the US to get away from religious persecution. He went to school at Morgan State in Baltimore. He is married to a woman from his high school. I am not clear on the whole high school sweetheart thing, or if they got together later."

Harry interrupted, "How did you meet him? I don't remember you making any trips to Baltimore."

Fred said, "No, I didn't meet him in Baltimore. He had returned home to Detroit and was working for an insurance company in their IT department. The company is one of our clients. I was up there teaching a class. One of the senior managers of the IT department suggested I talk to him."

Surprised Harry asked, "Really, one of their people suggested he leave their company?"

"Yes, I think that alone speaks volumes. He told me Bob was wasted in their company. So, I met with him over lunch. I also had a follow up discussion over the phone after I got back. He started two months later. I must say, he is one of the best hires we have had since I have been here. He has a great work ethic and has a good understanding of the course materials. He has even made a few suggestions on how we can make some improvements."

"Really? Are they good suggestions?"

"Yes, I have implemented a few of them."

Harry thought for a minute. "Sounds like you have made an excellent choice. Do it."

Fred smiled, "Consider it done. Is that it?"

Harry looked at Fred. "No, there is another thing we need to discuss. We need to talk about your experience while you were away. I know I said we could do it on your schedule, but there have been a couple developments, so I need to talk about it now."

Fred looked a bit surprised by this. "Well, Linda said you only have thirty minutes. We have already used half of that. This is going to take a lot longer than fifteen minutes."

Harry got up and walked to his desk. Fred watched as he picked up the phone and dialed a number. "Linda, what is on my calendar for the next couple hours? That one can be moved to tomorrow. Yes, that one can be moved to next week. Gretta? That one is a bit harder. Please call her and explain I am with Fred and will get there as soon as we finish. Great. Thanks."

Harry hung up the phone and walked back to the chair. "We should have a couple hours and change, if needed."

Fred said, "You mentioned a couple developments. May I ask what has happened?"

Harry wriggled in the chair as if to get more comfortable. "I got a call from Sergeant MacDuff late yesterday. He wanted to make sure you were here working. I told him you have your old job back and were doing well. He didn't give me many details He did say the reason he was asking was because you are still a person of interest regarding the disappearances of two other people. He also said he has become aware someone has been making inquiries about you at the station."

"What sort of inquiries?" Fred asked.

"He wouldn't say. Has anyone contacted you about anything?"

Fred thought for a second. "You know, that is something that I have wondered about. Not one person from the news media has contacted me. I find that a bit strange. Now that you mention the detective has contacted you, it makes me wonder even more."

Harry said, "Okay, let's get to it."

Fred to a deep breath, "Okay, I want to say up front this all sounds very fantastic and unbelievable. Hell, I was there, and I have a hard time believing it."

"Language Fred!" Harry said with a wry smile.

"Sorry Harry. Do you remember the day we were on the elevator a couple months or so ago when the door opened on 6 and it sounded and smelled like it was raining?"

Harry thought for a moment. "Vaguely, why?"

"I will get there. I have to lay out a few background details that are important to the rest of what happened. Do you remember about the same time that another guy went missing? The cops were outside the building with yellow tape around his car in the visitor spaces."

"I do remember that. And after you went missing two other people went missing. The last place they were either seen or expected to be was this building. One, Gail Miller, was on her way to see me. Do you know anything about them?"

Fred continued, "The first guy that went missing, I saw him when he got back. He returned here. That is important. He looked quite ragged. His hair was a mess, and his clothes were all dirty and tattered like he had lived in them for a month."

Harry said, "He returned here? That doesn't make sense."

Fred said, "I hope when I am done it will make sense."

Harry apologized for interrupting, "Sorry Fred. I will try and keep the questions to a minimum so you can finish."

"Harry don't worry about the questions. I am more interested that you understand what happened, and if asking for clarification or additional information helps you understand, all the better. So, if I remember correctly, the day we smelled and heard the rain in the elevator was a few days after the first guy went missing."

Fred went on, "He went missing from the number four elevator. The reason I know this is because when I went missing, I was in the number four elevator. The car did that little bump between the second and third floors. It did that the day the first guy went missing. Anyway, I got off on the sixth floor by mistake. I was reading that darn book and didn't notice the other folks all got off on 5 like they do now and then. When I got off on six, by the time I noticed it was the wrong floor, the door was closing. When it closed completely, the hallway dissolved, and I was standing in the middle of a meadow."

"A what?" Harry asked.

"A meadow. I have to tell you I thought I was dreaming. I expected Jill to wake me up."

Harry asked again, "But a meadow. Like the one between here and the woods near the river."

Fred laughed a bit, "Sorry Harry, but yes a meadow exactly like the one between here and the river. In fact, I believe it is the exact same spot."

"How is that possible. The building is here."

Fred said, "This building was not always here."

"Hang on Fred. Are you telling me that ...?"

"Yes Harry. That is what I am telling you." For the next hour and a half Fred told Harry about his experience. Harry let Fred tell his story with little interruption. One such interruption was when Fred was talking about Jason's trip over the waterfall.

"That monument is about the three of you and his trip over the waterfall?"

"Yes, and I even know what the symbol means and why."

Harry again apologized, "Sorry Fred, go on."

Fred continued. He finished by telling Harry about the meeting he and Jill had with Sgt. MacDuff.

Harry said, "Well you were correct, it is quite hard to believe. I am not 100% convinced. I will have to think about that for a bit. And the detective has heard your story. I am surprised he didn't lock you up. I am glad he didn't by the way. What does Jill think?"

"Jill believes me. I have never lied to her. I see no reason to lie about this to her, or to you for that matter. You have been very good to me and my family. I know it sounds fantastic, but I am not the only one that says it happened. The guy that went missing earlier in the year. I have met with him. His story tracks exactly. I even asked him questions only someone that was there could answer."

"And?" was all Harry could say.

"He passed with flying colors. The only reason he is in the Center for Psychiatric Study is his family doesn't believe him and had him committed. I get the impression some of the staff members think he should be out, but it is not a decision for them to make."

"What about the other two? Any sign of them?" Harry asked.

"No. I am getting a bit worried. I did most of the gathering of the food and water. As for the shelter, it should be okay unless there are major hurricane force winds. The summer will be winding down soon, and I am worried about exposure. All they have to wear is what they had with them when they got on the elevator."

Harry looked at his watch. "Okay, I have to meet Gretta. Let me mull this over. For what it is worth I don't think you would lie to me on purpose. Do you mind if I discuss this with Gretta? She can keep a confidence so no worries about that."

"No problem. Let me know if either of you have any questions."

Harry stood up. "Alright, like I said I have to get going. Let's have lunch tomorrow. Ask Linda to make room if needed."

Fred got up. "I will do that on my way back to the office. Harry, thank you for not dismissing this out of hand. It means a lot to me that you are even considering the possibility this really happened. I have problems with believing it myself, and I was there. I will see you tomorrow."

Fred walked out of Harry's office. He wondered why the detective really called Harry. He also wondered who was making inquiries with the police. Why hadn't the newspaper reporters even called him? He was sitting at his desk before he realized he had not stopped by Linda's desk. He picked up the phone and called Linda.

# CHAPTER FORTY-NINE

"Fred what's wrong?" asked Jill. Fred was pacing around the house like a madman.

"A repairman is in the building for annual maintenance of the elevators."

"So, why does that have you so upset?"

"Jason and Gail have not gotten back yet! What if he screws up the elevator, and they end up stuck there forever?" Fred said this with a little more passion than Jill would have liked.

"Honey, come over here and sit with me." Jill sat down on the sofa and was gently tapping the cushion beside her. "Let's talk this through. How do you know he will fix it?"

"The last time he was here was about a year ago. No one ever went missing before then. Brad hadn't gone missing until after he finished. Now he is back and may undo what he did then. Did I say no one went missing before Brad?"

"Who is Brad again?"

"He is the guy I told you about a couple months before I went missing. I saw him in the parking lot. It was the day he returned. Remember? I think it is also the name Sergeant MacDuff mentioned the first time we met with him. He also mentioned that name to you when he met you the day I went missing."

"Oh yes, I remember now. I just forgot his name."

"I didn't know his name then. Anyway, his family had him committed to the State Center for Psychiatric Study. He has been a resident there since."

"Resident sounds voluntary." Jill pointed out.

"That is what they call patients there. I spoke with him just yesterday."

"What!" Jill exclaimed. "You didn't tell me about that!" Now it was Jill's turn to pace the floor. "Was he dangerous? A lot of those people in places like that are violent."

"They wouldn't have let me see him if he was violent. Besides, he is as sane as you and me."

"Then why is he still there?"

"Because he refuses to change his story. I know he is telling the truth. I know he was there." Fred was beginning to calm down. Jill sat back down.

"How do you know it was him? Maybe he made it all up and is really crazy."

"I tested him. I told him he talked to me in the parking lot the day he returned. He said 'Sixth Floor' over and over. He also said, 'use the stairs'. I asked him to tell me his story." Fred went on to recite Brad's story as best he could remember from his visit.

As Fred continued, he began to get more excited. "I quizzed him on little details, like how far the spot in the field was from the lean-to, and how far the river was. There were some other details also. He was spot on every answer."

"I believe you Fred. I just wish you would have mentioned it to me before. It isn't like you to keep things from me."

Fred remembered he was worried about Gail and Jason. "I don't know how to stop the guy from working on the elevators! I guess I could talk to the building manager. Of course, if I did, he would want to know why. I haven't told anyone outside of you two. Wait, Harry asked me to tell him the details earlier today. I need to find a way to stop the repairs."

Jill thought about this for a minute. "What if Brad figures it out and tells someone?"

"His family thinks he is beyond help. The staff at the center don't know what to make of him. He is normal in all respects except for his disappearance story. So, I guess they don't really think he is normal."

Fred thought a moment and then said, "I just remembered. Mrs. Clark at the Center knows!"

"How did she find out?"

"I kinda slipped up in my exit interview with her. She is the patient advocate. She meets with everyone that meets with one of the residents. I had to meet with her both before, and after my visit with Brad. You know, I think she believes him. All the visits are recorded. She gave me a copy."

"What do you mean, they recorded the visit?"

"The lawyers said they need to record all of the resident visits to protect the Center. The recordings are not released. I suspect if they were subpoenaed for them it would be different. I trust her."

"Okay, what if the repairman has already fixed it?" Jill knew the instant these words escaped from her lips it was a mistake.

Fred jumped up and exclaimed, "Oh my God! What if they never get back? They won't survive there very long."

Trying to undo the damage Jill said, "I am sure they will be able to get back. What elevator is he working on now?"

"Elevator one."

"And how long does he take with each one?"

"I think a week or two."

"Which one were you in when you went missing and returned? Was it the same one in both directions?"

"Number four, and yes it was the same one. But I don't know if he goes in numerical order, or how he does it. This is bad. Jason is not equipped to survive, and Gail is not much better. I did most of the work. I caught almost all the food. I did all the upkeep of the shelter. At least Gail took an interest in learning how I caught the fish. I am not sure if she remembers where all the animal snares are."

Noticing the time Jill said, "It is getting late. Let's sleep on it. You need your rest and I know I do. Come on." She gently took Fred by the hand and led him to their room. She climbed into bed next to him and snuggled close. Soon she was asleep.

Fred on the other hand took a long time to drift off to a fit filled sleep.

# CHAPTER FIFTY

The next morning Fred decided to ride his bike to work. He needed some time to think. The ride would also let him work off some of the nervous energy from the previous evening's discussion with Jill.

Fred packed his backpack with clothes for work, and a spare set of clothes for later. He slung the pack over his shoulders and wheeled his bike out to the sidewalk. He stepped on the left peddle with his foot, using his right foot, pushed off before lifting it over the seat to the other peddle.

As he rode his thoughts were racing from Jason and Gail, to Brad, to the elevator, to Jill and then back through the list again. What could he do about the elevator? How could he save Gail and Jason?

The ride to the office seemed to go faster, maybe because his mind was not on the ride at all. In fact, he didn't remember any details of the traffic, the roads, or stop signs along the route. It was as if he was on auto pilot or something.

When he rode into the parking lot of the building, he hopped of the bike, and walked it to the bike racks. He took his keys out of his shorts pocket and unlocked the cable he used to secure his bike to the rack. The bike secured, he headed to the office.

He pressed the up button for an elevator. The door opposite number 4 opened. He got in the elevator and pressed 7. During the ride up to seven, Fred realized he didn't know anything about this particular model of elevator. He knew about the manufacturer and the company that bought them out. He also knew about the maintenance arrangement providing Hyrum Zimmerman as the repairman. As he walked out of the elevator on 7, he decided he needed to learn more about this model just in case.

Linda noticed the backpack and his bicycle attire. "Good morning Fred. I see you rode to work today."

"It is a nice day and I thought, what the heck. Enjoy your day!"

Fred walked to his office and unlocked the door. He put his backpack on the table. He unzipped the bag and took out his work clothes. He headed to the restroom to get cleaned and dressed. He used the restroom on the eighth floor when he rode his bike to work.

Leaving the restroom with his cycling clothes in hand, Fred heard some strange noise coming from the elevator lobby. He walked to the elevators to see the door to car 1 open. Hyrum Zimmerman was standing on top of the car. Fred had no idea what he was doing. Fred walked over to the open door and looked into the shaft.

Fred said, "Good morning. I never saw the inside of an elevator shaft before. Aren't you scared?"

Hyrum looked at Fred. "Scared? Scared of what?"

"Falling I guess."

"This has no more chance of falling down the shaft than when you are riding from the first floor to this floor. If you would excuse me, I have work to do." Zimmerman turned away from Fred and got back to whatever he was doing.

# CHAPTER FIFTY-ONE

Fred stared at the repairman. Fred suspects he has been working on these elevators his whole life even though Fred only remembers seeing him in the building the last 6 months to a year. He has thinning light blond hair although it does not look like he is going bald. He stands about 5 feet 11 inches tall. Fred thinks he looks like a walking scarecrow. He reminds Fred of the character actor Mark Margolis.

Hyrum usually wears short sleeve button down shirts, grey work pants and low-cut work shoes. The shoes have steel toes and shanks to meet some OSHA requirement. They are black and look as if they are a little too big. That may be because of the steel toe and shank design.

Fred always gets a weird feeling when walking past the repairman. He always appears to look at the people in the building with a suspicious gaze. Almost like he has some secret, and he suspects everyone in the building is trying to find out what it is. When in fact, Fred does not think anyone really notices the repairman.

The type of elevator in the building is older. There are not many still operating that have not been replaced by a more modern elevator, so his workload has diminished over the last few years. He carries his tools in an old beat up tool bag. He has a tool belt he pulls out of the bag and puts on to do the work. The belt is quite worn and looks like it is in dire need of replacement. The tools for all the routine maintenance are held in his tool belt which his bulging with tools everywhere. The remaining tools in the bag are those he does not use very often.

Hyrum Zimmerman used to work for the Sanderson company, but now he works for another company that picked up repairs and maintenance for these elevators. Parts are hard to come by and building managers and owners are slowly replacing them as they breakdown. The owner of Fred's building has been contemplating that for some time.

One of the parts in particular is quite unique to this elevator. If it fails and cannot be repaired, the elevator will no longer work and has to be replaced. Hyrum is clever enough to fix the parts should they break. After they have been repaired three or four times, they become too unreliable to fix again.

# CHAPTER FIFTY-TWO

Fred shrugged his shoulders and walked to the stairs. Back in his office Fred put his clothes away. He sat at his desk and turned on his monitors. He logged on to his computer.

He brought up a browser window. "Where do I start?" Then he remembered the paper where he wrote the elevator information. He opened the file drawer and leafed through the folders. Finding the one he was looking for he pulled it out.

Fred opened a search window and typed the information in the query box. He looked through the list of hits from his search. He opened one. Not what he wanted. He opened another. Same. After opening 15 to 20 of the links he found a link with pages of diagrams. Once again, Fred marveled at the things one can find on the internet.

Fred paged through the diagrams. He saved the "PDF" files to his computer. He also printed a copy of the diagrams. When he was finished printing, he retrieved the copies from the big printer near the break room. Taking the printout to his office, he laid them out on the table. He was not sure what he was looking at. After a few minutes he gathered all the diagrams and put them in the folder. He put the folder back in the drawer. He would get back to them later in the day. Right now, he had work to do.

Fred met with his staff after the classes finished just after four in the afternoon. The meeting lasted for 15 minutes. Ten minutes later his staff had all left for home. Fred opened his backpack and took out the extra clothes he brought.

Fred closed his office door and locked it. He changed into the extra set of clothes. He called Jill on the phone and told her he would be at the office a little late. After hanging up, he opened the drawer and retrieved the folder with the elevator diagrams. Again, he laid them out on the table. He was not very good at reading diagrams. After several minutes he found a block highlighted. There was a caption in the highlighted section. The caption said, "Sanderson proprietary modifications included here."

Fred looked in the highlighted area but could not make any sense out of what he was seeing. He looked at the top of the page. The title of the diagram was "Electrical Drive Mechanism." Well that was a start.

Fred looked at his watch. It was now after five. Most of the offices and businesses would now be empty. Hyrum, the repairman, usually left the building around 3:30. He thought it would be safe. Walking back to his desk, he opened a different drawer and took out the flashlight he kept there. He picked up his phone and opened the door.

Fred peeked at the reception area and noticed Linda had left for the day. He walked through the reception office and walked to the elevator lobby. He pressed the down button. A minute later one of the elevators arrived.

Fred did not get on the elevator. Instead he rushed up to the eighth floor. He had watched Mr. Zimmerman open the outside doors on one of the elevators. He repeated the process on the doors to the elevator, now just one floor below. When the doors were open, he saw the top of the elevator just a foot or two below where he was standing.

Fred took out his phone and opened the camera app. He turned on the flashlight and pointed it at the top of the elevator car. He took pictures from as many angles as he was able from the doorway. He became frustrated at not being able to get pictures of the far side of the car.

Fred looked around. The dentist office was closed, and he was alone. He thought to himself, "Well, if Mr. Zimmerman can stand on top of these cars, I should be able to stand on them."

Fred put his phone and flashlight in his pants pockets. He grabbed hold of the door jam and sat down on the floor with his feet hanging down to the top of the elevator. He put his weight onto his feet and stood up all the while holding onto the door jam. He steadied himself and worked his way around to the opposite side. He retrieved the phone and flashlight from his pockets and repeated the process of taking pictures. Just as he was putting his phone away the outer doors closed.

Fred said, "What the hell? I didn't think they would be able to close."

Then it got worse. The elevator started moving. It was heading down. Fred nearly lost his balance. He grabbed for whatever he could to keep from falling. His hands found something hard and round. He was holding onto one of the elevator support cables.

The elevator continued to descend lower and lower. Fred looked up and saw the top of the shaft getting farther away. Just as suddenly as it started the elevator stopped. Fred once more had to fight to keep his balance.

The doors to the car opened and Fred heard two people enter. He could not understand what they were saying. One of them must have pushed a button for a floor because soon after the doors closed. The car was now going up.

Fred, still holding the cable, looked up to the top of the elevator shaft. He watched as the top got closer and closer. A thought came to him that he had no idea if there was room enough for him on top of the car if the two guys below him had pushed the button for the eighth floor.

The top of the shaft was getting close. Fred wondered who these guys were, and why were they coming into the building so late. The top of the shaft was creeping closer. Fred ducked down as far as he dared. The car stopped. The doors opened and the two guys got out. Fred heard their voices fade away as they walked through the elevator lobby one floor below. The elevator doors closed.

Fred waited for the elevator to move. It remained still. He waited a little longer, afraid to move in case the elevator moved. He remembered reading somewhere many buildings with multiple elevators have plans for efficient elevator movement. The cars have a sort of home floor. When they are not in use, they either stay where they are or return to their respective home floors. Studies had shown time and energy are saved using this method. Fred had no idea if that was in use in this building, and if it was, what floor this elevator should return to.

Fred waited for what he thought would be enough time to allow for those decisions to be made. He assumed the elevator was going to stay put unless someone pressed a button. He knew he needed to hurry. He made his way to the side of the car next to the doorway. He could not reach the switch that would let him open the outer doors. It was at the top of the doors and he was a couple feet lower.

Fred turned on the flashlight and looked around. How was he going to get out of here? He looked at the walls all around the shaft. Nothing there to climb on. He thought all those movies had it wrong. Next, he looked at the outer doors more closely. Maybe there was a duplicate switch closer to the bottom. The designers had to anticipate someone being stuck on top of the car, didn't they? He could not find anything to even try and use.

Fred pointed the flashlight at the top of the car. There was a lot of stuff on top. He noticed a square about 2 feet on each side. Could it be an escape hatch in the top of the car? Fred carefully made his way over to it. He found a small handle and turned it clockwise. After a quarter turn the handle would not go any farther. Fred lifted and the shaft was filled with light from inside the elevator car.

Fred placed his hands on either side of the opened hatch. He carefully lowered himself into the car. He had to drop the last two feet. Once in the car he looked up at the hatch. It was open and he could not reach it to close it. Now someone would know he or at least someone had been up there. How would he close it? He knew he must be tired because when it finally dawned on him, he thought the answer was far too obvious.

He pushed the button for seven. It was only one floor away. When the doors opened on seven, he looked around. Seeing no one. He ran to the stairs and up to the eighth floor. In the elevator lobby, he opened the outer doors. Just to his right was the open hatch. He sat down on the floor with his feet hanging over the side. He stepped down on the car and lowered the hatch. He turned the handle a quarter turn counterclockwise. He climbed out of the shaft and closed the outer doors.

After cleaning up in the restroom, Fred walked down the stairs and to his office. He put the flashlight back in the drawer. He took a cable out of the same drawer and plugged it into his phone. The other end he plugged into his computer. A few minutes later he had a folder on his computer full of the images he had taken on the top of the elevator car.

Fred printed all the pictures. After retrieving them, he put them into the folder with the diagrams. Looking at his watch he decided he needed to head home. He could look at the pictures another day.

He closed and locked the door and changed back into his cycling clothes from his morning ride. He packed his work clothes and the shirt and jeans he had worn in the elevator shaft. He logged out of his computer and closed his office.

He looked around the office and saw no one. He walked through reception and checked the other side. Harry was still in his office. He said, "Hi Harry just checking to make sure someone was here."

"Thanks Fred. Ride your bike today?"

"Yep. Heading out now. Have a good night."

"You the same. Say hello to Jill for me."

"Will do. Same for Gretta."

Fred turned and walked to the elevator lobby. He pressed the down button. The elevator he had just been photographing was still on seven. The doors opened. As he entered the car Fred noticed a layer of dust had settled on the floor to his right. There was a footprint he imagined matched the shoes he had been wearing. He brushed his foot against the dust, erasing the footprint.

# CHAPTER FIFTY-THREE

Fred's office phone rang. "Morning Linda."

"Fred, there is a Dr. Helen Clark on the phone. She says you know her. She was most insistent on talking with you."

Fred said, "Thank you, Linda. I will take it."

Fred switched to the incoming line. "Hello, this is Fred. Dr. Clark?"

"Yes, sorry we don't use my complete title at the center. Some of the residents might get confused thinking I am one of the medical staff."

"That is understandable. What do you need to talk about?"

Dr. Clark paused, "There has been a development with Mr. Myerson."

"Really? Is he okay?"

"He is fine, but he is troubled." Dr. Clark again paused. "I would prefer to have this conversation in person. Any chance you could come by tomorrow afternoon. I would like to explain the situation and Mr. Myerson would like a word as well."

This caught Fred a bit by surprise. "Brad wants to talk with me? What happened?"

"Yes, he does. I will provide all the details tomorrow should you visit. Will that be possible?"

Fred turned to his computer screen. "Let me check my schedule. I should be able to get there by 11:00. Can I bring anything?"

Dr. Clark smiled at this but said, "I can't ask you to do that. I will see you in the morning. Thank you."

"See you tomorrow then. Goodbye." Fred hung up the phone.

Fred sat back and wondered what that was all about. "Brad is troubled? What does that mean? How bad can it be if they are letting him meet with me? I guess I will find out tomorrow."

Fred picked up the phone and dialed Linda's extension. "Hi Linda. I need to leave before 9 in the morning. I am not sure what time I will get back."

"Does this have anything to do with the call from Dr. Clark? Is everything okay?"

"Not to worry. Everything is fine. She just wants to talk to me about someone we both know. Thanks for asking."

"Alright, I made a note about tomorrow. Enjoy the rest of your day." Linda hung up the phone.

The next morning at 11:00 Fred pulled into a visitor space across the drive from the building with the ivy growing up to the roof on one corner. He got out of his car and searched the windows to see if he could tell which two were in the visitor room. Unable to decide which were the two, he walked up the concrete steps to the large double door entrance.

He walked to the reception desk. "Hello Julie. I am here to see Dr. Clark."

"Oh, hi Mr. Bates. We don't use her academic title here. It may confuse the residents."

Fred said, "Ah, yes, I believe she did mention that to me yesterday on the phone."

Julie pointed at the lounge chairs to her right, "I will let her know you are here. Please have a seat."

Fred had barely sat down when Mrs. Clark appeared. "Mr. Bates let's talk in my office. Please." She gestured down the hall toward her office.

Mrs. Clark and Fred assumed the same seats as they had during the last meeting. The only difference this time was the door was closed. There were no changes to the décor. There were no personal objects anywhere to be seen. Fred wondered if this really was her office or just one that was used for meetings such as this.

She spoke first. "I suppose you are wondering why I asked you to stop by today."

"Yes, I am. I discussed it with my wife last night and neither of us could think of any reason. In fact, the most troubling aspect is the urgency of the visit. We both wondered why you insisted I come by today."

Fred continued, "Jill, my wife, was actually not in favor of this visit. She has serious reservations of me having a continuing dialog with Brad. Sorry, Mr. Myerson."

Mrs. Clark just smiled and said, "I don't think it is a problem if you refer to Mr. Myerson as Brad. The two of you seemed to get along quite well on your last visit. Your friendship may grow stronger today when you spend time together today."

This comment made Fred a little anxious and even more curious. "So, I take it from that comment you know why Brad wants to speak to me today."

Mr. Clark answered, "Yes, I do. He wants to speak with you because he has heard some of the details of your story."

"What, we had an agreement!" Fred blurted out.

"Mr. Bates, I can assure you I was not the source of those details."

"Then how? Who?"

Mrs. Clark continued, "I need you to calm down a bit before you meet with Mr. Myerson. I will explain the details as I know them. You have to promise to be calm because I do not want him to get unnecessarily excited."

Fred took a deep breath. "Alright, I am sorry if I seemed to overreact. The only people I told were my wife, the detective, my boss, my daughter, and you. I know Jill hasn't told anyone. My daughter is sworn to silence. I doubt very much she would say anything. I think my boss may have told his wife. She would not break that confidence."

Mrs. Clark interjected at this point, "You really told your daughter? That is amazing."

Fred said, "I would prefer she heard the truth from me. She is going to have to deal with it sooner or later. Besides, she deserves the truth. Seems like that was a good idea because now the story is leaking out. So, if you were not the source, that leaves the police."

Mrs. Clark said, "Unfortunately, that is where the information came from. It turns out one of Mr. Myerson's sisters knows someone in the Police Department and got some of the details. It turns out the same detective led his missing person case."

"I am going to have a few words with the detective about this."

"Sergeant MacDuff was not the source. You have to understand he is not the only person assigned to these cases. One of the others mentioned to Mr. Myerson's sister someone else had a similar story."

"The detective still needs to know someone is leaking information. What does she know?"

"Just your name, the fact you disappeared from the same building under similar circumstances, and that you believe you were transported to a different point in time to the same place."

Fred wondered if Brad's sister was the woman staring at him in Jessie's. "Well that is about all of the pertinent information. The rest is just filler. Damn. Sorry. My boss was reluctant to have me tell him what happened. I suspect he thought it was related to what happened to Brad and he didn't want to know the details. But, like I said, he does now."

Mrs. Clark said, "I discussed this with Mr. Myerson after his sister paid a visit. As a result, he wants to talk to you. I think he wants to compare his experience to yours. He also was a little angry you had that long conversation with him and didn't own up to being there. I explained to him you were under strict orders from me not to discuss anything related to your experience. I also explained that I knew none of these details before the two of you met. Had I known, there is a good chance I would have not allowed the visit."

"Why?"

"Well, if he found out you were claiming the same thing happened and were living at home and working, there was reason to believe he may react strongly."

"You mean violently."

"Not necessarily. In fact, I don't think it would have been violent. He does not strike me as someone to whom violence comes easily. I think it would have been more along the lines of making a fuss over being kept here. Depending on how that discussion transpired, it could have made it harder for him to be released in the long run. As I said, the last time you were here, his insistence the story is true is all that is keeping him here."

Fred sat for a moment. "So, now that his sister has heard someone else has a similar story, she might lobby on Brad's behalf to get him released."

Mrs. Clark gave a small shake of her head. "I don't think that is the direction this will take. If I had to guess, I would guess she would push hard to have you join him in here. She does not have any input into that decision, however. The only way she could do that is to have the police and the courts do it. The fact the other two people are still missing, and you have admitted to being with them, could become a problem for you if they remain missing. But that is way out of my lane."

Fred seemed stunned at this thought. "Do you really think she will push to have me detained in some fashion?"

"I can't say one way or the other. All I do know, is there is no movement from Mr. Myerson's family to have him released."

"So, what now?"

"Mr. Bates, Mr. Myerson would like to talk to you. If you still are willing, he is waiting in the meeting room across the hall."

Fred considered whether he should meet. "Will it be possible to have the meeting without it being recorded? I don't mind if you listen in like last time, but considering what you just told me, I would much prefer it not being recorded."

Mrs. Clark said, "I expected you might request this session not be recorded. I spoke with our legal department and they recommended it be recorded to maintain our protections, as I explained last time. Mr. Myerson's family has the right to know who he sees. If we do not have consistent recordings to match those visits, it will raise too many questions."

"Do they have the right to listen to the recordings?"

"They do not. They can sue to have them used in a commitment hearing. But, since Mr. Myerson is already here and they do not appear to have a desire to get him released, it would be extraordinary for that to be approved."

Fred now had to make a hard decision. He was concerned with his story being recorded. "Remember when we spoke last time, I said I didn't want this recorded. I really have a problem with this."

"You have no obligation to speak with Mr. Myerson. He will be quite disappointed, but I am sure he will understand."

Fred stood up and asked, "Would it be alright if I step outside and make a call? I will let you know when I finish."

Mrs. Clark looked at Fred with her piercing blue eyes and replied. "Sure, you can call from here and I can step out if you like."

"If it isn't a problem I would like to step outside and get some air while I talk."

Mrs. Clark stood and opened the door to the hallway. "I will walk you to the door. Just let Julie know when you are finished, and she will call me."

Once outside, Fred dialed Jill's office number. He had to wait a few minutes for her to finish with a patient. "Hello, Fred? Sorry I was finishing up with an Irish Setter. He is a beauty. What's up?"

"It turns out someone in the police department spilled the beans to one of Brad's sisters." He spent five minutes filling her in on all the details. "I asked them not to record my talk with Brad, but they are not willing to make an exception. I want to talk with him, but I really don't want it recorded."

Jill said, "I would certainly prefer that as well. But think of it this way. If the police are leaking the information in little pieces already, it won't be long before it comes out in detail. The Center can't release this per the agreement you signed. So, I say go for it. It is your decision though."

"Thanks, I always appreciate your opinion. I will be here a while. Love you!"

"Love you too!"

Fred hung up and headed back inside. Mrs. Clark appeared and walked Fred to the meeting room. She opened the door and dismissed the twenty something guy named John. "Mr. Myerson? Mr. Bates is here to talk with you. Let's try and keep this one a bit shorter than the last one. How about 2:00?"

Brad looked at Mrs. Clark and said, "2:00 sounds fine to me. How about you Fred? Is 2:00 enough time?"

Fred looked at Brad and then Mrs. Clark. "Whatever is allowed."

Mrs. Clark said, "Great, I will let you know about a quarter to 2:00, so you have time to wrap things. Enjoy your visit." With that, she left the room closing the door as she exited.

Brad studied Fred with a knowing smile. "So, let's sit down. Same as before. You were holding out on me!"

Fred said a bit sheepishly, "I was just following the guidance Mrs. Clark gave me. I was afraid she would end the discussion if I started talking about my experience."

"That's okay. She explained that to me. We are good."

Fred asked, "So, how much do you know?"

"All I know is, you were reported missing from the same building as me. You were gone around a month and two other people are still missing. You told the police you went back in time."

Fred nodded, "Yep that is the short version. The two people are named Gail and Jason. I am actually not allowed to leave the area because I am a person of interest in their disappearance. I admitted to seeing them after they went missing. By the way, I found your shelter and made some upgrades."

"Tell me everything you can in the time allowed."

Fred told Brad the highlights of his experience over the course of early afternoon.

When he finished, he looked at his watch. It was just after 1:30. "So, how did that match up?"

"You really fought a mountain lion? That's amazing. That monument at the waterfall. Is it still there?"

"Yes, if you ever get out of here you should go see it."

Fred thought about how to frame the next question. "You know they are recording this conversation and they recorded the last one."

Brad said, "Yes I know. No secrets in this room!"

"I asked for a copy of our last talk and it was given to me. I promised I would never let anyone listen to it without your permission. What I would like is permission to allow my daughter and boss to hear excerpts from our last visit."

"Do you really need to use our conversations? I am not sure. Let me think about that. I will let you know before you leave. Sound fair?"

"Yes, sounds fair. Do you have any other questions? I went through my experience pretty fast."

"No questions. I am amazed at what you accomplished. Making the tools and the buckets. I never could have done those things."

"Well, I had some training. What you accomplished was amazing. I was in awe of you when I left here last time. When I was younger, I had military experts teaching me how to survive. Granted it was only for a couple weekends. All you had was trial and error. It was remarkable."

Brad turned a bit red in the face at this last comment. "That was nice of you to say. Most of it seemed logical at the time."

Mrs. Clark opened the door to the meeting room. "Time to wrap things up gentlemen. I will be back in a few minutes."

Brad said, "Thank you we are nearly finished."

When Mrs. Clark was gone Fred said, "Brad, there is a problem."

"What's that? You look worried."

"The elevator repairman is doing the maintenance. I am worried the last time he did maintenance, he opened the portal causing all of us to be sent there, and you and me brought back. What if this time he "fixes" what he "broke" the last time? And, what if Gail and Jason don't get back before that happens?"

Brad said, "This is bad. Is there any way to delay?"

Fred went over to Brad and whispered in his ear, "We shouldn't talk about this we are being recorded!"

"Oh, you are right. Let's get back to the recording of our last discussion. Why do you think you need to use it?"

"Well our stories do sound a bit out there. Your family doesn't believe your story and I suspect they think I have copied your story."

"Your wife believes you. You told the police before you saw me. And, as far as I am concerned, you know way more details than we discussed in our first meeting."

"I wouldn't use the whole conversation. For one thing it is quite long. There are a few bits about the elevator, and the meadow and the return that I would focus on. Again, if you prefer, I won't use it at all."

"All of that is in the public record. My family makes me sound like I am crazy, so be careful how you present it. I guess I am saying that it's okay. Just use your best judgement on how much to share."

Fred said, "Brad, thank you. I will not use anything unless it collaborates my experience."

Brad got up out of the chair and said, "You are welcome. I hope we get to see each other sometime on the outside."

Fred also stood and shook Brad's hand. "I also look forward to that."

Brad walked to the door just as Mrs. Clark and John entered. "Mrs. Clark, thank you for letting Fred and me meet. I feel much better now. Fred, until next time, goodbye."

"Goodbye Brad."

Brad and John walked toward the end of the hall and walked out the door.

Mrs. Clark said to Fred, "Do you regret talking with Mr. Myerson today?"

"No. I am just concerned there is a recording of the meeting. No offence, but I wouldn't want to have that recording be instrumental in having me assigned to a facility such as this."

"No offence taken. The main reason I limited your time today, is that I have a meeting I must attend. Could you wait in the lobby for a few minutes? I have a little going away present for you. Do you mind waiting?"

Fred said, "I don't mind."

Mrs. Clark led Fred to the lobby. "I will leave you in Julie's capable hands. It was nice to see you again."

"Likewise. Thank you for the opportunity to talk with Brad again. Have a great afternoon."

As Mrs. Clark walked away Fred sat in the same chair he used earlier in the day and the first time he was here.

As Mrs. Clark promised, 5 minutes later, the IT guy Fred saw the last time he was here walked up to him and handed him a small envelope.

The IT guy said, "Mrs. Clark asked me to give this to you. I hope you have a good afternoon." He turned and returned from the direction he came.

Fred looked in the envelope and called after him to thank him, but he was already out of sight. Fred stood up and headed for the exit.

"Julie, he certainly is quick."

"Yes, he is. He pops up and before you know it, he has disappeared. Happens all the time."

Fred waved to Julie, "Have a great afternoon."

"You too."

Fred walked through the double door and crossed the road to his car. He opened the envelope and took out the flash drive. A note fell out of the envelope. He read the note.

> "Mr. Bates,
> Same rules apply as the last time. I hope your visit was fruitful.
> H. C."

Fred thought it was a little less formal than normal. He was not sure how he felt about that.

He put the note and the flash drive back in the envelope and tossed them on the passenger seat. He started the car and headed back toward the office.

# CHAPTER FIFTY-FOUR

When Fred arrived at the office, most everyone had already left. Traffic coming back from the Center was horrible and it took a lot longer than expected. Fred found a note taped to his office door. It was from Linda. He had gotten a phone call from Sgt. MacDuff.

"Gee, I wonder what he wants to talk about." Fred caught himself saying out loud with just a touch of sarcasm.

Fred unlocked his office door, grabbed the note, and walked to his desk.

Picking up the phone Fred dialed the number written on the note. Someone picked up before the first ring.

"Hello, this if Detective Sergeant MacDuff. How may I help you?"

"This is Fred Bates. I got a message you called."

"Yes. Mr. Bates. There have been some developments in your case. Any chance we could meet for a few minutes?"

"I guess. When would you like to meet?"

"There is a coffee shop about 5 minutes from your office on Center Street. Do you know it?"

"Yes, I know where it is."

Sgt. MacDuff said, "I can be there in ten minutes. I suggest you bring your wife with you if possible. She will want to understand this as well."

Fred a bit worried said, "I am not sure I can get her there in ten minutes. I will give her a call. I will be there for sure though."

"Great, see you in ten." Sgt. MacDuff hung up.

Fred sat there. He was just staring at the phone. He thought he knew what the detective wanted to discuss. Now he was not sure. The phone started making that busy signal sound when it has been off the hook too long. Hearing the busy signal made Fred hang up the phone. Using his cell instead, he called Jill.

Ten minutes on the dot, Sgt. MacDuff walked into the coffee shop. Fred was already sitting at a table in the back corner. The shop was mostly empty. Everyone else was sitting on the opposite side of the shop, so Fred and Sgt. MacDuff would have a little privacy.

The detective walked over to Fred. Fred stood and the two shook hands.

"Nice to see you again Mr. Bates."

"Sergeant MacDuff, you can call me Fred."

"Actually, since this is sort of an official visit I shouldn't. Did you order anything? I need a coffee."

"I got mine thanks." Fred said, pointing to his paper cup.

"Right, I will be back in a second."

Fred watched as Sgt. MacDuff walked to the counter and placed an order. After getting served, he walked back to the table with his own paper cup. He sat down across from Fred.

Fred said, "Jill is not sure she can make it. All depends on how long we are here. She will come over as soon as she can get away."

Sgt. MacDuff looked at his coffee and said, "Sorry for the short notice. There is some news. I thought it better if you hear it from me and not someone else. It is a little embarrassing actually."

"What do you mean embarrassing?"

Sgt. MacDuff said, "One of our officers that was assisting me with the missing person cases apparently mentioned some of the details of your case to a sister of Brad Myerson. Mr. Myerson is the person who went missing from your building a couple months ago. Maybe you will remember I mentioned his name during our interview."

"Is that it?"

"Yes why?"

"First, Jill and I could not remember the name of the person you mentioned during our meeting. So, I looked it up on the internet. I found out he is at the State Center for Psychiatric Study, a couple hours from here."

"Yes, I know that."

Fred continued. "If you remember I saw him the day he returned. He said something to me, and I couldn't quite remember what he said."

"Yes, I remember you telling me that. So, you put two and two together. Did you read about his story? It sounds a lot like your story, doesn't it?"

"Well, I did one better. I went to visit him."

"You what?" Sgt. MacDuff said this a lot louder than he should have. Everyone else in the shop turned and looked at him.

Fred said, "I went and saw him. I called the Center and a lovely woman named Mrs. Clark allowed me to spend an afternoon with him. I was not allowed to mention anything about my experience. I was only allowed to let Brad tell his story. He was quite willing to tell me. You know, it is quite remarkable that he survived. He had no training, and he did almost everything right. I was amazed. He is a very sharp guy."

Sgt. MacDuff now calmed down said, "So, you know everything. How his family got him put into that place. He shouldn't be there you know. That is off the record by the way."

"As far as I am concerned this entire conversation is off the record. I am sure we are meeting here in part because you are telling me things outside of official practices."

"You are pretty smart yourself. I don't know what is going on in that building of yours, but something weird is going on. The fact you and Mr. Myerson have such a similar tale intrigues me."

Fred said a bit surprised, "So you believe me? I mean us?"

Sgt. MacDuff shifted a bit uncomfortably in his chair. "I am not sure what happened. I do know something did and neither one of you guys strike me as someone that would just up and leave for three or four weeks without telling anyone. Especially you. I can't imagine you leaving your family like that. I can read people. That is how I got this far in the police department. You and your family have something special. No way you would just up and leave without them knowing it."

Fred said, "Thank you detective. You can't imagine how much that one statement means to me. By the way, there is more."

"What do you mean?"

"I got a call yesterday from Mrs. Clark. Did you know she has a PhD? It isn't a medical degree, so she doesn't use it at the Center. Anyway, she told me she needed to see me right away. In addition, Mr. Myerson was asking to see me again. I found this strange, because I didn't think they allowed residents to ask for specific visitors. Well maybe family, but I am not family."

"Did you go and see them?"

"Jill and I talked it over and decided I should at least find out why Mrs. Clark wanted to see me."

All Sgt. MacDuff could say was, "And?"

"Mrs. Clark told me one of Brad's sisters had visited him. His sister told Brad she found out about me and some details of my story. Mrs. Clark wanted me to know. Brad wanted me to tell him what happened to me. We talked for a couple hours. I was there when you called. I saw a note you called when I got back to the office and returned the call straight away. Now, we are here."

Sgt. MacDuff sat back in his chair and took along sip of his coffee. "I guess I didn't need to tell you after all."

Fred took a sip of his drink and said, "I am glad you did. I have to say, I was really pissed off when Mrs. Clark told me. I did calm down. She wouldn't have let me talk with Brad if I didn't. I thought the details of investigations are supposed to stay private."

"Well that is the embarrassing part. They are. The officer in question has been reprimanded. I had a very long talk with him. I made him understand how a leak like this could jeopardize an investigation. A judge and the DA would certainly have something to say if a mistrial or acquittal resulted. That would not be an issue in this case."

Fred was a little concerned. "Do you think he will take this out on me and my family?"

"I don't know why he would. You had nothing to do with it. I found out because Mrs. Clark also phoned me. She was quite upset. This type of thing could have a huge impact on Mr. Myerson and his situation."

Fred nodded, "Yes, Mrs. Clark and I talked about that. So, where do we go from here?"

Sgt. MacDuff said, "Well you are still officially a person of interest in the disappearance of Gail Miller and Jason Lake. I still need you to stay in the area. I did talk with your boss. Seems you have picked up right where you left off at work. That will help."

Fred looked at the front door to the shop. "Here comes Jill."

Both men stood as Jill approached the table. Fred said, "Can I get you anything?"

Jill shook her head. "No, I don't want anything. What's up."

Sgt. MacDuff looked at his watch and said, "Mr. Bates and I are about finished. I need to be across town soon, so I will leave Mr. Bates to fill you in on the details. Nice to see you again."

The detective turned and walked to the door. He tossed his now empty coffee cup into the trash can just outside the door. Fred and Jill saw him get into his unmarked car and head down Center Street.

"Fred, what the heck was that all about?"

Fred spent the next thirty minutes telling Jill about his talk with Sgt. MacDuff and his visit to the Center.

# CHAPTER FIFTY-FIVE

Fred was becoming concerned with how many people were aware of his experience. He wondered what people must think now that two people had similar stories. He wondered what they would think when Gail and Jason return and add their experiences to his and Brad's.

These thoughts were occupying his mind as he was walking into the building. He did not notice he was following Hyrum Zimmerman until he was almost to the front door. Seeing the repairman, Fred's thoughts returned to doing everything he could to make sure Gail and Jason would be able to get back. He watched the repairman head toward the stairwell at the back of the building as he waited for an elevator. Fred wondered how the repairs were progressing on the elevator. He wondered how much time he had to figure out what to do before it was elevator number four's turn.

Fred found himself unable to concentrate on his work. Finally, he pushed away his computer keyboard. He stood up and paced around his office. He soon tired of walking around his office and walked out to the cubicle area where his team sat when not teaching a class. He walked through the area as if checking to make sure everyone was working.

Fred did not notice anyone. Some looked up to see him, but he just walked to the next desk and then the next. When he reached the back of the building, Fred opened the stairwell door and walked up to the eighth floor. He walked to the elevator lobby to see if Mr. Zimmerman was there. He was not. Fred retraced his steps to the stairwell. He walked down to the sixth floor. As he walked down the steps, he wondered why Mr. Zimmerman did not ride the elevators. Could it be Mr. Zimmerman knew something? This thought began to take root in Fred's mind.

When he stopped to open the door from the stairwell, he realized he had walked past the sixth floor, and the fifth floor, and the fourth floor. He was on the third floor. Fred decided since he was on three, he would look at the elevator lobby. No one was there. Shaking his head, he pressed the up button.

Back in his office, he wondered how Mr. Zimmerman tested the elevators. He had to ride them sometime. Why did he, of all people, use the stairs.

Fred stood up and began walking around his office again. He looked at his watch. Not even lunch time. There was a knock on the door. Fred turned his attention to the doorway. Linda was standing at the door.

She said, "Everything okay?"

"Yes why?"

"No reason." She turned and walked toward the lobby.

Fred wondered what that was all about. He shook his head as if to clear his thoughts. He went back to his desk. He pulled his keyboard closer and put is fingers to the keys.

Nothing. He could not think of anything to type. Maybe he shook his head too hard and really cleared all the thoughts out. No, he was thinking about the elevator, Gail, Jason, and why Mr. Zimmerman took the stairs. Where was he?

Fred decided to get an early lunch. He got up and walked to the stairway instead of the elevator. He walked down to six. He did not miss the door this time. He checked the lobby. No repairman. He repeated this all the way to the first floor. He had to be somewhere. Fred did follow him into the building. Fred bought lunch and took the elevator back to seven.

Fred took his lunch to his office. He sat back with his sandwich and the bottle of tea on his desk. He turned around and headed back to the stairs. He walked up to eight again. He walked by each of the classrooms and peeked in each. After he walked by the last one, he headed to the stairs. Instead of heading back down to seven he went up.

Fred paused at the door to the roof. He had never been up there before. He was not sure if it was alarmed or not. But if the repairman was out there, the alarm would be turned off. Wouldn't it? He thought for what seemed to be an eternity. His heart was racing. He did not expect that to happen. Finally, he decided to go for it. He turned the knob on the door.

He pushed the door slowly. The door was barely open a foot when he saw Mr. Zimmerman. Mr. Zimmerman saw the door begin to open.

Fred heard him say, "Who is there? Get away from here! I am busy. Shoo!"

Fred closed the door. He hoped the repairman had not seen him. He ran down the stairs as fast as he dared. When he reached the bottom, he glanced back up the stairs. The door was still closed. He exited on eight just to get out of the stairwell.

His timing was not completely perfect. He came out of the stairwell just as one of the classes was taking a break. The area between the classrooms and the stairwell was full of students going to and from the restrooms and the break area.

Bob noticed Fred at the stairway door. "Everything okay Fred?"

"Yes, why does everyone keep asking me that today?"

Fred turned back to the stairway and hurried back down to the seventh floor. He grabbed his lunch from his office and headed to the elevators.

As he passed Linda, he lifted the bag and bottle so she could see it. He said, "Linda I am going to sit outside for a bit."

"Enjoy your lunch."

Linda watched him leave. After he entered the elevator, she picked up her phone.

# CHAPTER FIFTY-SIX

The next day, Fred got to work early. Just before 11, he decided to take his mind off work and those he left behind for a few minutes and headed down to Clara's. He noticed Linda was not at her desk as he walked through reception. Taking the elevator down to the first floor he headed into the shoppette.

Lara saw him come in and waved. "Hey Fred. How are you doing?"

"Oh, as well as can be expected. Trying to get back into the swing of things at the office and at home."

Lara finished ringing up one of the guys from the insurance company. Fred was left as the only customer. "So, what are you having today?"

"Just the usual. I will grab a soda from the fridge as well."

Fred almost always ordered the same thing. It was a ham and swiss on rye bread with lettuce and spicy brown mustard. While Lara was making the sandwich, Fred wandered over to the refrigerator with the glass door and took out a soda.

After he paid for the sandwich and drink, he was about to leave when Lara said, "Fred, are you okay? You seem so distracted the last few days. I know you have experienced something but there is something else weighing on you. I can see it and some of the other folks have mentioned it. Take care of yourself okay!"

Fred didn't know what to say except, "Thanks Lara. I will be okay. I appreciate your concern. Catch you tomorrow." He headed out of the shoppette in time to see Linda struggling with a couple boxes at the front door.

He walked over to the door and walked out to give Linda a hand. "Need a hand? If you carry this, I will carry that." Fred said as he held his sandwich and drink in front of him.

Linda said with a big smile, "That would be wonderful. They aren't that heavy just awkward."

The two of them switched loads and headed into the lobby. As they approached the elevators, they saw Bill Kidd and the elevator repairman putting a sign in front of elevator number four.

Fred hurried over to find out what was going on. "Bill, what is happening?"

"Hyrum here has to shut down one of the elevators because he needs a part for the one he is working on. It will take him awhile to find a replacement or if he can't find a replacement to fabricate one. So, we thought number four was the logical one to close since that is the one next on his list."

Fred said a lot louder than he should have, "NO you can't do that!"

Bill and Linda were shocked at his outburst. Hyrum the repairman seemed to not even notice.

Bill said, "Gee Mr. Bates, I am not sure I expected that reaction from you. I assure you it will be okay."

Fred gathered himself. He had to think quickly. If they turned off number four Jason and Gail would not be able to get back. Looking at Linda and then the packages he was carrying for her an idea came to him.

"Bill, number four is the one the owner has designated as a sort of freight elevator, right? Seems to me if you turn that one off you will have to designate a different one for that purpose. That one would then be exposed to all the hand trucks the delivery folks use. The potential to scrape up a second elevator car seems a bit unnecessary. Sorry if I reacted a little strongly. It was just a bit of a surprise."

Bill thought about this. After a few moments he began to nod his head in agreement. He looked at the repairman and said. "Well Mr. Zimmerman can you use the part from one of the other elevators? Mr. Bates has a good point. I don't think the owner would want to risk getting another car scratched up."

Hyrum Zimmerman looked at Bill and then Fred, then scratching his cheek said to Bill in a scratchy voice, "I don't really care which one we shut down. You tell me which one, and I will do it."

Bill looked at the cars across the lobby and pointed at the one closest to the rear of the building. "Use that one."

Hyrum said, "Okay." He picked up the sign and walked across the lobby and placed it in front of the selected elevator.

Fred said to him, "How long will you be away?"

Hyrum still scratching his cheek said, "Oh, I don't know. A month or so. These elevators are old. Parts are hard to find." With that he headed for the stairs. Still not riding the elevators he serviced.

Fred pressed the up button and soon the door to elevator 4 opened. Since he was with Linda, and he had just made a fuss over using it for deliveries, Fred had to go in. Linda followed. She pressed the button for seven.

After the doors closed, she looked at Fred and said, "Fred, what was that all about. I don't think you really care that much about the appearance of these elevators. Does this have something to do with your disappearance?"

Before Fred could answer a look of knowing crossed Linda's face. "Oh, my. Everyone that went missing went missing from this building. Do you think this elevator had some role in that somehow?"

"Linda, I really don't want to go into details, but as far as I know everyone that went missing including me was last seen in this elevator car."

Linda started looking around the car suspiciously. The car stopped and the doors opened. Fred looked at the lights at the top. Number 7 was lit. Floor seven in both normal lettering and Braille was visible in the hallway.

Fred said, "I think this is our floor."

Linda slowly got out of the car followed by Fred. Just to the right was the door to the I3 reception. Linda let out a deep breath.

Fred said, "Where do you want these?"

Linda took a second to compose herself. "Just set them next to my desk. I will take care of them later."

Fred did as she asked. Linda handed him his ham and swiss sandwich and soda. She sat heavily in her desk chair. Fred looked at her. She was shaken.

"Linda, are you okay?"

"I don't know what to make of what you just told me. I guess I knew you all went missing from the building, but I didn't know anything about the elevator."

"Well not to add to your consternation but I will never use number four again if I can help it. If you were to ask me for my opinion, I would tell you not to either. If you do, make sure you get off on seven. Oh, Linda, please don't worry about it. I can see you are upset, and I feel bad I am the cause of it."

Linda sat watching Fred. Fred was deciding if he should stay with her or head to his office to have his sandwich.

Finally, Linda said, "Fred, I have no idea what happened to you. I know you are struggling a bit. I can see you pacing from time to time. You never used to do that. There is something on your mind and I suspect it is because two other people are missing. Piecing together everything you said to me the last five minutes I think you think that elevator is important for their return. That must be why you reacted the way you did."

Now it was Fred's turn to be stunned. "My goodness Linda you are one smart lady. Please do me a big favor and keep this to yourself. The only one here I have told anything to is Harry. I am sure he told everything to Gretta and I trust both of them with my life. The first person to go missing is now in the State Center for Psychiatric Study. I really don't want to join him."

Linda, now composed, reached out and patted Fred's arm. "Don't worry Fred. I can't blab what I don't know. And besides, there are certain things and people I would never talk about. You and your lovely family are on that list. I understand very well why Harry and Gretta picked you and Jill to be part of the 13 family. Go have your lunch."

Linda smiled her big smile. As he turned toward the door to go to his office, he marveled at her. Harry was lucky to have her. So was he!

While he ate his sandwich, he realized he had prevented a disaster. However, should Gail and Jason return soon, the elevator would still be able to take someone else away. He had to figure out a way to disable the elevator in the event the two of them got back. He needed to do it in such a way that even Hyrum Zimmerman could not fix it.

# CHAPTER FIFTY-SEVEN

Fred was lost in thought when he heard someone knocking at his office door. Looking up he saw Bob French standing in the doorway. "Fred, are you okay? I knocked three or four times."

"Sorry Bob. What's up?"

"I took care of checking all the classrooms. They are ready for tomorrow. I am heading out unless you need anything else from me."

Fred looked at his watch. He did not realize it was so late. "No, I can't think of anything. Have a great evening. See you tomorrow. I will be right behind you."

Bob said, "Thanks. You too!"

Fred watched as Bob headed toward the lobby. The afternoon had gone by quickly. He had no idea how long he had been distracted by his thoughts. Linda noticed he is having some problems. Lara has noticed. Now Bob probably knows something is going on. Bob is a smart guy. That is why Fred had the company hire him.

Fred's thoughts returned to Gail and Jason. He truly hoped they would return soon. He had to come up with something. Even if he did, what could he possibly do with Mr. Zimmerman here. These elevators are quite old. That old repairman must be some sort of an elevator genius to have kept them running so long. What could Fred possibly do that old man could not fix, probably in his sleep!

Fred turned off his computer and closed his office. He made his way through the now empty lobby and pressed the down button. He rode an elevator to the first floor and walked to his car. All he could think about was Gail, Jason, and elevator number four.

The next thing Fred new, he was parked in the driveway next to the townhouse. He realized he was shaking. He turned off the car and sat there. Shaking.

A few minutes later Jill came out. She looked at Fred through the windshield of the car. Sensing something was amiss she walked around to the passenger side of the car and opened the door.

"Fred, are you alright?"

Fred just sat there, shaking.

Jill got in the car and closed the door. "Fred, you are scaring me. What's wrong?"

Jill touched Fred's right arm. This seemed to snap him out of some sort of a trance. He looked at Jill. "Look at me. I am shaking like a leaf in a strong breeze."

Jill said, "What happened?"

Fred took a deep breath. "It has been strange day."

Fred told Jill all about the plan to shut down the elevator and how he reacted to the news. He also recounted his conversations with Linda, Lara, and then Bob.

Fred then said, "All I could think about this afternoon was what if I can't stall the repairman long enough and Gail and Jason don't get back. I am not sure how that will affect me. I am already a mess."

Jill said, "I am sure they will get back. Mr. Myerson got back. You got back."

"I know, but I can't stop thinking about them. I don't even remember the drive home. It was almost like I was on auto pilot or something. I must have gone through a stop sign. The one near Miranda and West. I vaguely remember hearing someone yell, "Nice stop asshole." Good thing there were no other cars or people crossing. Who knows what would have happened otherwise."

Jill thought for a minute. "Fred, I know you are worried about those other people. But you have other people you need to worry about. One of them is at the table in the house waiting for us to come in so she can have dinner. I have a strange feeling those two are going to be back soon. Once that happens everything will be better, and we can get back to normal."

Fred took Jill's hand and squeezed. "I never regret the day we bumped heads. Thanks. I needed that. I love you more than anything."

Jill leaned over and gave Fred a kiss on the cheek. "Let's go inside."

Fred grabbed the keys from the ignition. "I will follow you in a second."

Jill opened the door and got out. "Okay but don't take too long. Dinner is getting cold."

Fred watched Jill walk into the house. He thought it strange he was watching people walk away from him. First Bob and now Jill. Did that mean anything? His thoughts are so muddled he was not sure of much of anything. He still could not get those thoughts out of his head.

What if Jill is right and Gail and Jason do get back. How could things be normal when that damned elevator was still working? Nothing would ever be normal until no one else would be able to disappear from 1680 Hilltop Road.

Fred got out of the car and headed into the house.

# CHAPTER FIFTY-EIGHT

The next morning Fred was running a few minutes late. He called Linda at the office.

"Hello, 13, this is Linda may I help you?"

"Yes Linda, this is Fred. I am running a couple minutes late. Would you let Bob know? I don't have any classes today."

"I will tell Bob. Fred, there was a gentleman here this morning from downstairs. He left your briefcase. He said you left it behind. Do you know what he is talking about?"

Fred nearly dropped his phone. "Jason was there?"

"Yes, that was his name. Jason Lake. Do you know him?" Then it dawned on Linda, "Oh my, he was the guy from downstairs that went missing. Of course you know him! Fred? Are you still there?"

But Fred was not there. He was running out of the house. He got into his car and headed toward Jason. When did Jason get back? Is Gail back? "I don't even know her phone number." A million things were all fighting for time in his thoughts.

Fred pulled into the parking lot. He had no idea how he got there. He parked in his normal parking spot. He got out of his car and practically ran into the building. He pressed the up button and rushed into the first arriving elevator. It was not until he was on the way up to his office that he noticed the walls were covered with tan padding. He was in car number 4. Realizing where he was caused him to take a breath and slow his mind down.

When the elevator stopped, the door opened, he checked which number was illuminated at the top. It said seven. He then checked the door frame. He saw the number seven, as well as the Braille representation. He was taking no chances. Satisfied he was on seven, he walked into the hallway. He turned right and opened the door leading to the 13 reception office. Linda was nowhere in sight, neither was his briefcase.

Fred walked around Linda's desk and headed toward his office. Just as he was passing through the door from reception, he saw Linda come through the opposite door to the executive suite.

Linda saw Fred, "Fred I dropped your case in your office. I hope you don't mind. Mr. Lake also left a note. I put that on your desk."

"Thank you, Linda. No problem. I may be out for a bit this morning."

Linda smiled, "I suspected as much."

Fred walked to his office. Linda had locked the door. He reached in his pocket for his keys which he promptly dropped on the floor. After retrieving them, he opened his office door. Once in his office, he closed the door. There, on his table, was his briefcase. He walked over to the table and sat on the chair. When he picked up the case, he felt a little bump come from inside. When he opened the case the source of the bump was revealed to be his cell phone.

Fred removed all the contents of the case. There was the cell phone, a couple CDs of the course slides, and the remaining pieces of paper from the hard copies. Most of the pages had been used to help start the fires.

The book was there. He had forgotten about the book. He already went to the library and told them he lost the book. He offered to buy them a new copy. They told him they had plenty of copies and were actually taking a few of them off the shelves so no harm done.

Lastly, there was the box of matches. Fred let out a small laugh as he opened the box to find two matches left. Once Jason arrived with a cigarette lighter there was no need for the matches.

Fred put the box of matches back in the case. He put the CDs and course materials into the company proprietary trash can. He plugged the cell phone into the charger. He no longer needed a phone because he had gotten a new one. However, he wanted to make sure he knew what was on the phone before throwing it away.

Finally, remembering Linda mentioned a note, he went to his desk. Sitting down, he found an I3 envelope with his name written in Linda's perfect hand propped up against his computer monitors. Taking out the note, the first thing he noticed was it was not written in Linda's perfect writing.

The note said Jason and Gail were back and for Fred to call Jason. Jason's number was at the bottom of the note. Fred felt a bit uneasy after reading the note. He stared at the paper for a long time. Finally, he decided to call Jason. After all, the note said for him to call but he had a strange feeling about it.

Fred picked up the phone and dialed the number written on the paper. The phone rang once, twice, three times, finally after what seemed like for ever there was a voice after the fourth ring.

"Hello, this is Jason."

Fred's heart was pounding. He had to repeat the first couple of words. No words would come out of his mouth even though his lips were moving. Finally, "Jason, this is Fred."

"Ah, Fred. How are you?"

"I am glad to hear your voice. How are you?"

There was a short silence on the other end. Finally, Jason said, "I am as good as can be expected. I would like to see you."

Fred said, "Are you in the building?"

"Yes, I am in my old office. There is a chance I may get my old job back."

"Great, let's meet at the picnic tables." Fred did not want to meet in his office or Jason's office. He thought the picnic tables were neutral enough. He still had a weird feeling he did not understand.

Jason thought for a minute and finally agreed. "Alright. I will meet you there in five minutes." Jason hung up before Fred had finished saying goodbye.

Fred dialed Jill's cell. After three rings it went to voice mail. "Jill, this is Fred. Jason and Gail are back. I am heading to see Jason now. Call me when you get a few minutes."

Fred hung up the phone and headed down to the picnic tables. Again, he was lost in his thoughts and did not hear Linda as he passed through 13 reception. He did not notice which elevator he was on as he rode down to the first floor. He walked out to the picnic tables and sat down. Jason was not there. Had it been five minutes yet? Was Jason late or was he early? Why was his heart beating so fast again? Why was he having trouble catching his breath?

Then Jason was walking out of the building. He looked just like he did the day he fell over Gail except he was a little bit thinner. Fred did not think he looked very happy.

Fred stood and walked toward Jason with his hand outstretched. Jason ignored his hand and walked past him to the tables and sat down. Fred turned and followed sitting down opposite Jason.

Jason spoke first. "I gotta tell you, we were pissed you left without us. Gail is still so mad she doesn't want to see you or even talk to you."

Fred finally able to breath said, "I called for you until the door forced itself closed. I was pushing as hard as I could, but the door was stronger than me. Where were you guys?"

"We were down at the river. Why should that matter. You should have stayed."

Fred looked at Jason, "Let me ask you. If you were in my place would you have stayed?"

Jason said, "Damn right I would have stayed?"

"Stayed for me or for Gail?"

Jason was not at all happy with that question. "What do you mean?"

"If Gail was not there and it was just you and me, would you have stayed?"

Jason was not expecting this and had no answer.

Fred reacting to the silence said, "I thought as much. Listen, in hindsight we all should have been in the meadow together. I thought it would be boring for everyone to always be there. I guess the shelter and therefore the river were just too far away. It looks like everything turned out okay anyway."

Jason his voice now back said, "Everything turned out okay? Really? You left us alone. You were the survival expert and you left us alone!"

"Wait a minute, Gail was already very good at catching the fish. There wasn't much left that needed to be done. The shelter was pretty solid, there were plenty of water buckets. You had your lighter should the fire go out."

Jason stood up and walked around the table. "Who had the only blade out of the three of us? Huh! Sure, Gail could catch the fish, but you had the knife to clean them. Did you leave that behind with us? Huh! No, you had it with you. I took your briefcase to your office. The knife wasn't in it was it?"

Fred dropped his head, "No, I had the knife in my pocket where it always is. Sorry, it never crossed my mind until you mentioned it just now."

Jason was now letting his anger get the best of him. "Oh, you never mentioned to me anything about the large cat you tangled with before Gail and I got there."

"So, the topic never came up. I did mention it to Gail though."

"Exactly, no thought of mentioning it to me. Just maybe it would be a good thing for me to know about. I guess that never crossed your mind either."

"Well, I never saw or heard it again after the encounter, so you are right it never crossed my mind."

Jason got real close to Fred and said, "Do you remember what the cat sounds like?"

"Yes. I don't ever want to hear it again."

"Well, a couple days after you left us behind, both Gail and I heard it. She has not been the same since. She was petrified. She told me about the scar on your back and about your fight with the cat. She never went anywhere alone. I even had to go with her if she needed to relieve herself. She squatted over the ground with a spear in one hand. Not only was she scared, she was embarrassed I had to be with her. She needed you to be there!"

Fred was stunned to hear Jason say this this, "Wait a minute. You two were, are, a thing. She didn't need me. She has you."

332

"Come on Fred we both know she relied on you for all the survival stuff. Sure, we have an intimate relationship but that is much different. You spent a lot of time together before I arrived. She thinks of you as a brother, more than a brother. Then you left."

Fred said, "Where is she now? Is she okay?"

"She is at her place. She needs the familiar surroundings. I tried to get her to stay at my place but she can't. She is a mess."

"We should go and see her."

Jason looked at Fred, "Fred, she doesn't want to see you. I am not sure she will ever want to see you again. She feels absolutely betrayed. You left her."

"Does my family get any consideration? I do have a wife and daughter. I had been away for quite a while with no word." Now Fred was getting upset.

Jason said a bit a defensively, "At least you have a family. All Gail and I have is each other."

Fred sighed, "Well at least we are all safe. And yes, we all have issues to deal with as a result of our experience. By the way have you notified the police of your return?"

"The police? Why?"

"There were missing person reports filed for each one of us. I met with the investigating detective the day after I returned. You both need to talk to them so they can close out their investigations."

Jason thought about what Fred had said. "I am not sure I want to do that. I don't know what to tell them."

"Tell them the truth."

Jason exclaimed, "What and have them think I am crazy. Who would believe what happened? They will put me in an institution somewhere. What did you tell them?"

Fred looked at his hands for a minute before answering. "After my wife and I discussed it I told the detective everything."

Fred was expecting a reaction from Jason, but he was not expecting the right cross that broke his nose.

"Jason, what the hell!" was all he could get out. He backed away a couple steps. His nose was beginning to ooze blood. He pinched the nostrils together to try and stem the flow.

Jason said, "I can't believe you told the police what happened and where we were. What were you thinking? What does that make me and Gail look like?"

Fred said, now in a strange voice, "It makes you look like you had a life changing experience. You have returned from it and can move on. I actually think the detective believed me. But, I need you guys to talk with them. Since I told them I had been with you after your disappearance I am a person of interest. I have been asked not to leave town."

Jason sat heavily on the picnic table bench. "Why on earth would anyone, especially a police detective, believe what happened to us?"

"Well I think it was because he heard the same story from the guy who originally built the shelter we used. He asked my wife and I if we knew this guy. We couldn't remember his name after we left so I Googled missing persons and found him."

"So, where is this guy? What is his name?"

Fred said, "Now that is where it gets a little complicated. His name is Brad Myerson. The problem is he told his story to his family and his sisters had him committed to a facility."

"That is just great. I told you. They are going to put me away, I know it."

"I don't think they will. They didn't force me into one."

Jason asked, "And why do you think that is?"

Fred said, "I think it is because of two things. First, Jill believes me and said so to the detective. Second, the detective knows something odd is happening in this building and as farfetched as the explanation is, he is open to it. Now with the two of you saying the same thing he will have to believe it."

"I don't know Fred. I am not sure I can tell that to anyone let alone the police. Hell, I am not sure I believe it."

Fred finished wiping the blood from his nose on his shirt, stood up, and took it off. He turned his back on Jason and said, "See that scar? That cat cut me. I smacked it across the head with a club and it ran away. You heard it. Gail heard it. Are you telling me we dreamt all this? All three of us with the same dream? No, Jason, it was real. It was strange, but, it was real."

Fred put his shirt back on. He continued. "I talked with Brad. Twice. The people where he is, told me in confidence they don't believe he belongs there. He is not a danger to anyone. The only reason he is still there is his family. I don't think we need to worry about that. What we need to worry about is that elevator."

Jason said, "What do you mean?"

Fred smiled, "The problems began after the repairman was here to fix the elevator. It was six months to a year ago, I guess. Elevator number four had issues. Brad went missing a after the repairman was here. The problem is all four elevators are due for their overhaul. The repairman showed up just after I got back."

Jason said, "So that is good. Maybe he will fix it so no one else will go missing."

Fred said, "That is a good assumption except up until yesterday you were not back. I couldn't let him fix it before you returned."

"Oh yeah, didn't think of that. What happened?"

"Well we got lucky there. One of the elevators on the opposite side of the lobby broke down. I researched the manufacturer and model. It turns out these are very old and out of production. There is one particular part that can't be swapped with anything. If it fails, the elevator will not work. The repairman is very good at fixing these parts, but he can only do it so many times."

Jason said, "And the elevators in there are wearing out?"

Fred said, "Exactly. He had to stop working on the elevators. He is trying to find another part somewhere. Now that you are back, we have a separate problem."

"What's that?"

"Elevator number four is still working. We have to do something about that before someone else goes missing."

Jason said, "How do you propose to do that? You aren't seriously proposing to break the elevator. Are you?"

Fred started walking toward the building. "I need to do something about this mess you made of my face and change my shirt. As for the elevator, I don't know. I do know we can't let anyone else disappear. Call the cops! Stay in touch."

Fred walked through the door and to the elevators. He pressed the button and the one working elevator on the side opposite number four opened. He got in and rode to his floor.

When walking through reception Linda looked up and gasped, "Fred what happened?"

Fred laughed, "Ah yes, Jason and I disagreed on a point or two during our discussion. I think we got passed it. I am going to get cleaned up and change my shirt. Is Harry in?"

Linda said, "Yes, Harry is in. He won't be very busy today. Do you want to schedule something?"

"Yes, I will call him when I finish. I want to see if he can have lunch."

# CHAPTER FIFTY-NINE

When Jason returned to Gail's house that evening, she was waiting for him at the door. "So, how did your discussion go with Fred? Why did he leave us there?"

Jason said, "He said he called for us until the doors were closing. He couldn't hold them open anymore. You know when that alarm goes off and they start to close."

"Why didn't he stay with us?"

"He said he had to think of his family and that we had each other."

"Yeah, but he was the one with all the skills. We could have died."

Jason put his arm around Gail. "He said you were good at everything we needed to survive."

"Well, I still think he abandoned us. What else did he say?"

"He said we should talk to the police. There are missing person investigations open on both of us."

Gail said, "Seriously? Talk to the police? What would happen to us if we tell them what happened? No way."

"That is what I told Fred. But he said he told them everything. And he is still working and is out and about. He is a person of interest in both our cases because he mentioned he was with us."

"He told the police we were with him? Why would he do that?"

"He said he thought the truth would be best. His wife agreed."

Gail thought for a few minutes. "Well, if we have to talk with the police, we will not be telling them we went back in time. I am not interested in people thinking I am crazy when I had no control over the situation."

"What do you mean? We are going to make up a story? What about what Fred has already told them?"

"It will be two against one won't it. They won't believe Fred."

"He said he thinks the detective believes him."

Gail said, "How can anyone believe that story? I was there and I don't believe it."

Gail and Jason spent the remainder of the evening coming up with a story and doing a little research. The next morning, Jason called the police station to tell them he had returned. A little later Gail did the same. They did not want the police to know they were together.

Gail was the first to hear back from the detective. She scheduled a meeting with him later that afternoon. A soon as she hung up from the call, Jason's phone rang. He scheduled his appointment with the detective one hour later.

Jason dropped Gail at the front door of the police station and drove away. She walked into the lobby. The desk sergeant on duty was the officer Jill and Fred met on their visit. Gail was led into the same conference room as well. She was looking at the same picture of the waterfall when Sgt. MacDuff entered the room.

He said, "Hello I am Detective MacDuff. I have been leading the investigation into your disappearance. I see you are looking at the picture of the waterfall in the park. Have you seen it before?"

"No, I haven't. I am Gail Miller. We spoke on the phone earlier today."

Sgt. MacDuff took out his notepad and began writing. Then he pointed at the table and chairs. "Sorry, please let's sit down. Hopefully this won't take too long."

They sat on opposite sides of the table. Gail asked, "What do you want to know?"

"My first question is where have you been? Follow that up with who were you with and were you there voluntarily?"

Gail answered in order, "I was at the North Pines Park about three hours north west of here. I was with Fred Bates and Jason Lake. Yes, I was there voluntarily."

"How did you know these two gentlemen and for how long?"

"We all met at the building where Fred and Jason work. I guess we knew each other for about six months."

"Why did you leave your cars at the building and leave on different dates?"

"Well, Fred mentioned some guy went missing from the building. If we left our cars there, people may think our disappearances were related to whatever happened to that guy. He also thought he should go first to get the site at the park ready for the rest of us."

Sgt. MacDuff was writing furiously in his notebook. When he was caught up, he looked at Gail. "Why did Mr. Bates go without his family?"

Gail was not ready for this question. Taking a little longer than she would have liked she said, "He said they didn't want to go. The trip was going to be a long one and his wife didn't want to be away that long."

Sgt. MacDuff found this response a bit curious. He made some notes in his book. "I see. I guess I wouldn't want to be away that long either. Were there any incidents? Did anyone get hurt?"

"Yes, Fred fell down the ravine and a tree branch cut his back. Also, Jason fell as well and bruised his left leg. Other than that, I can't think of anything."

The conversation went on until only five minutes was left of the hour. Sgt. MacDuff said, "I only have one more question. Why did Mr. Bates leave so much earlier than the two of you? Afterall, you staggered leaving, but you and Jason returned together."

"Jason and I formed a closer relationship while we were there. I guess Fred was a little uncomfortable around us. It also made him miss his family, so he went back. Jason and I were enjoying each other so we stayed a bit longer."

Sgt. MacDuff made a couple final notes in his book and stood. "I want to thank you for coming down today. I am glad you have returned safe and sound. Do you have any questions for me?"

Gail stood. She was anxious to leave. "No, I don't have any questions."

Sgt MacDuff took a card out of his coat pocket and handed it to Gail. "Please give me a call if you remember anything you think may be important. I will show to the lobby."

He led Gail out of the conference room and turned left to walk the short hallway to the lobby door. Once in the lobby he shook her hand and said goodbye. He noticed a man in a suit in one of the chairs. The man and Gail exchanged glances as she walked out of the building.

Sgt. MacDuff turned to the man and said, "Are you Mr. Lake?"

Jason stood and said, "Yes I am. Jason Lake."

"I am Detective MacDuff. Please, follow me."

Sgt. MacDuff looked at the desk sergeant with a nod. The desk sergeant pressed the button for the door. The was a click and Sgt. MacDuff opened the door and led Jason to the conference room. "We will be in here for our discussion. I need to get something from my desk I will be back in a minute."

While the detective was away Jason walked around the small room looking at the pictures on the wall. As if it was destiny, Jason was looking at the picture of the waterfall when Sgt. MacDuff returned. The detective smiled imperceptibly. "I see you are looking at the waterfall. It is at the park near the building where you work. Have you ever seen it? I hear it is quite lovely."

Jason turned to the sound of the detective's voice. He was unconsciously massaging his left leg. "Ah, no, I don't recall ever going to the park. When I get off work, I am not interested in hanging around the office."

"I certainly understand that. Please, let's sit down. I hope you don't mind if I take notes. I am a detective after all" The detective took out his notebook and sat down. Jason followed on the opposite side of the table.

Sgt. MacDuff skimmed a couple of the pages from the interview with Gail. He did this for two reasons. First, he wanted to make sure he asked the same questions in the same order. Second, he noticed Jason was uncomfortable and wanted to increase his anxiety a little. He noticed Jason reaching for his leg at the mention of the waterfall. He had reread his notes from Fred's visit to prepare for these two interviews and was reminded Fred had mentioned Jason fell over the falls. Gail also mentioned Jason fell but dismissed it as no big deal and gave no details.

Sgt. MacDuff finally started the questions. "My first question is where have you been?"

"I was at the North Pines Park. It is north west of here."

After making a note Sgt. MacDuff looked at Jason. "Who were you with and were you there voluntarily?"

Jason answered out of order, "I was there voluntarily with Gail Miller and Fred Bates."

"How do you know these two people and for how long?"

"We all met at the building where Fred and I work. I guess we knew each other for about six months."

Sgt. MacDuff wrote some notes and then turned back to the notes from the interview with Gail. He made a mental note and flipped forward to where he made his last note.

"Why did you leave your cars at the building and leave on different dates?"

"Well, Fred mentioned somebody went missing from the building. So, we left our cars there, maybe people would think our disappearances were related to whatever happened to that guy. Fred wanted to go first to get the site at the park ready for the rest of us."

Sgt. MacDuff was writing furiously in his notebook. "Why did Mr. Bates go without his family?"

Jason paused a beat. He and Gail did not talk about this. What if his answer did not match her answer? Finally, he said, "I am not sure. I don't think they wanted to go."

Sgt. MacDuff smiled a smile that was imperceptible to anyone that did not know him. The officers watching the video feed noticed. He made a few notations in his book. He continued. "Did anyone get hurt?"

"Yes, Fred fell down the ravine and got cut. That happened before I got there. I also fell and bruised my left leg. Just a Charlie horse. I was fine an hour or so later."

Like the conversation with Gail, Sgt. MacDuff kept asking questions until the time allotted for the interview was nearly spent. He said, "I only have one more question. Why did Mr. Bates leave so much earlier than the two of you? Afterall you left on different days, but you and Gail returned together."

"Gail and I got into a romantic relationship. I think that made Fred miss his family. Gail and I decided to stay."

Sgt. MacDuff made a few final notes, closed his notebook, and stood. "I have no more questions. Do you have any questions for me?"

Jason asked, "Does this mean the investigation to my disappearance is closed?"

"Well, I have to do a little background checking and I need to compare your answers to what Mr. Bates and Ms. Miller told me, but I think it can be wrapped up pretty soon. Here is my card. Call me if you think of anything else that you may remember."

Jason stood and took the card. The detective led him out of the room and back to the lobby. After shaking hands and bidding Jason goodbye Sgt. MacDuff went straight to his office and picked up the phone.

He heard three rings at the other end of the line and then a women's voice.

"I3, this is Linda, how may I help you?"

"This is Police Detective MacDuff. I would like to speak with Fred Bates."

# CHAPTER SIXTY

The phone in Fred's office rang. "Hi Linda, what's up?"

"Fred, Detective MacDuff is on the phone."

"I will get it, thank you."

"Is everything okay?"

"I don't know. I guess I will find out when I talk with him. Thanks again."

Fred pressed the outside line on the phone. "Hello Sergeant."

Sgt. MacDuff said, "Mr. Bates. I have interviewed both Gail Miller and Jason Lake. I am glad to see they have both returned safe."

Fred said, "I saw Jason yesterday and told him to get in touch with you. I am glad to hear they have talked with you. That should clear up the missing person cases."

Sgt. MacDuff paused, "Well, it may not turn out to be that simple."

"Oh, how so?"

"I met with each of them separately this afternoon. In fact, Mr. Lake just left."

"They didn't meet with you together? I am surprised. They do everything together. In fact, I think Jason is staying at her place."

Sgt. MacDuff said, "I would not have met with them together. I always need to hear from everyone separately. That way I have everyone tell me what happened in their own words. You said they are staying together? That is interesting."

"Why?"

"I can't go into this over the phone. Any chance you can come down to the station for a few minutes. I can fill you in on what I can here."

"I guess. There isn't anything pressing here. I can be there in fifteen minutes or so."

"Sounds good. I will see you in a few minutes." Sgt. MacDuff hung up.

Once more Fred wondered why the detective wanted to talk to him. Was it related to the interviews with Gail and Jason? What did they say? Why was MacDuff interested in their staying together? He closed his office and headed out.

Linda seemed to be worried about him leaving shortly after getting a call from the police. She asked, "Is this related to you and the other people that went missing?"

Fred said, "I am not sure. The detective didn't want to talk over the phone. I don't know how long I will be gone. I guess assume I will be out the rest of the day. Bob can take care of anything that pops up."

"Okay Fred, take care."

Fred walked to the elevators and pressed the down button. Funny, he never thought about if people disappeared on the way down. Everyone he knew about, disappeared on the way up. He left the building and headed for the police station.

When he arrived, he was directed to the same conference room by Sgt. Bland. Sgt. MacDuff was a minute behind him.

"Hello Mr. Bates. Thank you for coming straight away."

Both men sat down in the same chairs they used before.

Fred said, "What has happened?"

"Like I mentioned on the phone I talked with Ms. Miller and Mr. Lake this afternoon. Unfortunately, their version of what happened is quite different from your version. Have you ever been to a park called North Pines Park?"

"Sorry? North Pines Park? What does that have to do with me?"

"Have you ever been there?"

"I have never heard of it. Why?"

Sgt. MacDuff was making notes. "Both Ms. Miller and Mr. Lake say that is where they have been since they went missing. I looked it up. It is about three hours north and west of here."

"You mean they said I went to a park three hours from here and never told my wife and daughter. You know they are lying."

"Well their story does not involve time travel as your story does. That in itself gives it more of a sense of believability than your version. They said it was your idea. They also said your wife and daughter opted not to go because of how long you planned to be gone."

Fred was getting a little annoyed. Jason had hinted he would not tell the truth. "Well, if you talk to Jill and Kristine, they will tell you I never asked them to go on an outing to … what was the name of the park again?"

"North Pines Park."

"How did they explain my car being at the office? Why did we all leave on separate days. How did we get there if our cars were left behind? I don't get it?"

"They had explanations for all of that. I am afraid it will be your word against theirs."

Fred snapped, "This is bullshit. They are making up this crap so they won't sound crazy. I never knew either of them except to see them in the building to say hello. I didn't even know their names until they showed up in the meadow."

"Mr. Bates, I need you to calm down. I know this is unsettling. Conflicting versions of events just need to be investigated. I am sure eventually, the truth will come out."

"Right, but now you and your officers have even more doubts about what I told you. That would mean I lied to you which I think is a crime. I didn't lie to you by the way. I get whisked off to some other place I didn't want to go, for a hell of a lot longer than I would want to be away, and there is now a real possibility I will go to jail? I am not happy."

"Mr. Bates, I can see you are not happy. Unfortunately, what I am about to request will make you even less happy."

"What do you mean?"

"Remember when you and your wife came by the day after you returned, and you agreed to a psychiatric evaluation? Well that is now being requested. I am afraid you will have to be evaluated. Since you have volunteered, you can select the facility as long as the cost is within the limits set by the city."

Fred was now really worried he was going to end up in a place like Brad. "I really need to do this? There are no other options?"

"I guess I could arrest you for lying to an ongoing investigation. I don't think that would be a good use of resources or anyone's time. You would also have that on record and we at the department think this evaluation is a better way to proceed at this time. The DA agrees."

Fred just sat in his chair. He did not know what to think. Finally, he said, "When would this have to happen? Now? Today?"

"No, you will need to select a facility and then we need to get it scheduled. Do you have any ideas about where you prefer to have this done?"

"The only place I know anything about is the Center where Mr. Myerson is. I do trust those people. Is that a possibility?"

Sgt. MacDuff said, "I will check to see if they have the proper evaluation protocols. I suspect it will take a day or two. I am done here. Do you have any questions?"

"No, I am not sure what to ask. I need to talk with Jill."

Sgt. MacDuff said as he stood, "That is a great idea. Go home and talk with your wife. I will walk you out."

Fred stood up. At first, he didn't notice Sgt. MacDuff leading him out of the station. They were on the sidewalk outside of the station when he realized the detective was still beside him.

Sgt. MacDuff said, "Where is your car?"

"Around the corner."

"Are you okay to drive? I can have an officer drive you home if you prefer."

"No, I will be okay."

Before he knew it, they were next to his car. Sgt. MacDuff leaned against the car essentially blocking Fred from getting in. "I have something to say I did not want to be on the recording in the interview room. I don't for one minute believe Ms. Miller and Mr. Lakes version of events. Their answers to my questions were too perfect. The reasons they gave for doing things didn't make any rational sense to me. I will do whatever I can to keep you from being locked up or put in a facility."

"Thank you."

Sgt. MacDuff moved away from the car to let Fred open the door. Fred got in and rolled down the window. "I will call you tomorrow morning will that be okay?"

Sgt. MacDuff moved closer to the car window and looked in all directions as if to make sure no one was listening. "That will be fine. I am heartened you are going to do this evaluation. I pretty much know what will come of it already. And Fred, take care of yourself and your family."

Fred was surprised the detective used his first name. He started to say something, but the detective was already headed back to the station. Fred turned on the car and headed home. Along the way he wondered why he was in this position. All he wanted to do was have a happy life with Jill and Kristine. All he was getting was grief because of that damn elevator.

Fred pulled into his driveway to find Jill's car already there. He looked at his watch to find it was nearly 7. He had not called. She must be worried.

He walked into the house through the kitchen door. He found both Jill and Kris at the table. He said, "Sorry I did not know the time. I know I should have called. I have been talking with Detective MacDuff."

Jill said, "Don't worry about it. You must have done something right because that detective is looking out for you. He called me as soon as you left the station. He thought you were a bit out of sorts. What happened?"

"Gail and Jason were interviewed today. Their versions of what happened are different. They made up a story that is pure crap. But it is their word against mine. Well, for the most part. Sergeant MacDuff told me in confidence he doesn't believe them. But, he and the DA have requested I get a psychiatric evaluation."

Kristine said, "What? They think you are crazy? That is just stupid."

Jill tried but could not stifle a laugh. "Kris, I have to agree with you, it is stupid. Are you going to do it?"

"I really don't think I have a choice. I volunteered the last time we met them. The detective and the DA both want it. Since it is considered voluntary, I get to choose the facility. I think I would like to go to the Center. I like the people there and I think we can trust them. And the city is going to pay."

Jill thought for a moment. "I guess if you are comfortable. I know there are horror stories of what goes on in places like that."

"Well the Center has a good reputation. I read all about it when I was researching Brad. Brad seems to think the place is okay. I also think Mrs. Clark likes me. That may also be a good thing. She is the patient advocate.

"Okay, when will this all happen?"

"Sergeant MacDuff said it would take a couple days to get everything arranged."

Jill said, "Okay, are we all agreed?"

Fred nodded. Both he and Jill looked at Kristine. She said, "What, do I get a vote?"

Fred smiled, "Absolutely. You are a member of the family. We want to know your opinion."

Kristine said, "I think it is stupid. You are not crazy. Why do you have to do it?"

"The police and the District Attorney are requesting it. I believe if I refuse, they may press charges for lying to a police investigation."

Kristine protested, "But you didn't lie. You told them the truth. The other two people are lying."

Jill said, "Kris, calm down. Your dad needs to do this to prove he is not crazy. Then hopefully we can put this spring and summer behind us."

Finally, Kristine said, "Okay, but I will miss you."

# CHAPTER SIXTY-ONE

The next morning Fred arrived at the office early. Linda was at her reception desk when he arrived. She looked up as he entered the lobby. "Good morning Fred. How did everything go yesterday?"

Fred being a little distracted said, "Sorry, not sure what you mean."

"You know, with the detective. Sorry if I am being too nosey."

"Oh that. I don't mind. Just keep this to yourself. I have to get a psychiatric evaluation."

"Good lord. Why?"

"It turns out the other two people made up a story about our little adventure that is totally different from what happened. Now, the police don't know what to believe. I volunteered to be evaluated the first time I met with the detective. Now the DA and the police want me to do it."

"They made up a story. Do the police believe it?"

"Well, it doesn't involve the elevator at all. I can see where some of it seems logical, but I think it is full of holes and I think the detective doesn't believe it."

Linda smiled and said, "I think you will do fine. Just stay calm and tell the truth."

Fred said, "Thank you Linda. Oh, by the way I will need to tell Harry. Would you find a few minutes on his calendar this morning?"

"Absolutely. And our conversation didn't happen." She winked at Fred.

Fred headed for the door toward his office. Linda remembered something. "Oh, Fred. I meant to tell you. I was talking with Bill Kidd this morning. He told me the repairman; I think his name is Zimmerman."

"Yes, Hyrum Zimmerman."

"Right, that is what Bill said. Anyway, apparently, Mr. Zimmerman has had a serious accident. He fell and is in the hospital. Bill said the company Mr. Zimmerman works for says he may not be able to return to work. Bill is all worried because the elevators may not be repairable without him. At least he finished the first elevator. Now only the one he borrowed a part from is not working. According to Bill he was going to start on that one next."

A look of panic crossed Fred face. He was not sure if Linda noticed or not. He turned away from her quickly. He said as he was walking through the door, "Thanks Linda."

Fred fumbled with his keys as he tried to unlock his office. His hands were shaking. Finally, he got the door opened. He went into the office and closed the door. He put the keys on the table and started pacing around the room.

Fred was thinking as he was pacing. The more he thought the faster he walked. What will happen if the repairman never comes back? How long will it take to replace the elevators with more modern versions? Would the owner even do that? Three are still operating, would he just let them run until they failed and then replace them? One at a time?

What if someone goes missing and then the elevator stops working? Or, is turned off and gets replaced before they can return?

Fred said aloud. "I have to do something. But what?"

Fred was pacing around his office trying to come up with an idea. He thought he heard something familiar. Suddenly he realized the sound he was hearing was his office phone ringing. He walked to his desk and picked up the receiver.

"This is Fred."

"Fred, this is Linda. Are you okay? The phone rang about 8 times. You always pick it up on the first or second ring."

"Sorry Linda, I was thinking about something and didn't notice the phone. What's up?"

"Harry can meet with you now if you have time."

"That sounds fine. I will head over to his office. Thanks."

"No problem."

Fred put the receiver back in the cradle and grabbed his keys from the table. He walked through the reception area on his way to Harry's office. Linda examined him as he entered. She said, "Don't worry he has no idea why you want to talk. I didn't tell him anything."

"Thanks again, you're a great friend!"

This made Linda turn a little red. Now it was her turn to look away in hopes Fred would not see her face.

She need not have bothered because Fred's thoughts were elsewhere. He was trying to figure out just how to break this news to Harry.

Fred arrived at Harry's door. It was open. Fred knocked on the door jam.

Harry looked up from his desk. "Fred! Come on in and have a seat."

Fred walked in and sat in one of the chairs.

Harry said, "Linda said you want to talk about something. She didn't say what it was, but that it is important."

Fred said with a bit of a smile, "Leave it to Linda to say a lot without saying anything."

Harry laughed. "Yes, she is particularly good at that. What do we need to talk about?"

Fred looked at his hands. He noticed he was wringing them. He suddenly stopped and looked at Harry. "I met with the detective again yesterday afternoon. As you probably know, the other two people have returned."

Harry said, "Really, I did not know that. When did they get back?"

"They both returned a couple days ago. I met with one of them, Jason, the day before yesterday. I told him, he and Gail, the other one of the two, needed to go to the police because they had been reported missing."

Harry said, "And, I assume your meeting with the police came after their meeting with the police."

"Yes. The detective met with each of them separately. He called me right after he finished talking with them and asked if I could meet him. I headed to the station and we talked."

"The discussion was about what the other two told him, correct?"

"Yes, again. The problem is, Jason and Gail, made up a huge lie instead of telling the truth. So now the police have to decide if they are telling the truth or if I am telling the truth. I think the detective believes their story is bullshit."

"Language Fred!"

"Sorry Harry. You have to admit, and so do I, that the truth sounds too fantastic to really be the truth."

"I agree what you told me is difficult to believe. But, I talked it over with Gretta. We have decided just because we don't understand how it could be possible, doesn't mean it didn't happen."

"Thank you, Harry. I can't tell you how much it means to me, and Jill, that you believe me. Tell Gretta thank you as well."

Harry continued, "You think the detective is more inclined to believe you. Interesting. So, what happens now?"

"Well, the police and the DA want me to have a psychiatric evaluation."

"Really?"

"Yes, I guess they want to know if I am totally off my rocker. The evaluation will take a few days and I have to report to the State Center for Psychiatric Study in a couple days. I will probably be out the office for at least two."

"I am not worried about you being out of the office. You have built up an amazing back log of classes since you have returned from your 'adventure', I think you call it."

Fred added, "And Bob French is fitting into his new role wonderfully. I have full confidence in him."

"That makes me feel even that much better. Is there anything I can do for you?"

"No, you, as always have done a lot already. Your understanding and support…" Fred couldn't finish.

Harry got up and walked over to Fred. He helped Fred out of the chair and gave him a big hug. "Fred, you go do whatever it takes to clear your name. Your I3 family will be here to help however we can."

Harry led Fred out of his office and watched as Fred headed back through the door to reception.

Fred walked back to his office thankful, he decided work for Harry. Once back in his office, his thoughts returned to the problem of the elevator. What was he to do?

He opened his file drawer and pulled out the internet printouts he made from the diagrams of the elevator. He laid them out across his desk. He was not sure what he was looking to find but hoped he would know when he did. It was like when he was looking for things in the woods. He always seemed to find what he needed, even if he did not know what to look for.

He looked over the diagrams of the car and the car control panels. He did not see anything there he thought would be useful. What was it that made these elevators unique? He thought about that for a few minutes. Fred took the pages for the cars and the control panels and put them back in the drawer. He seemed to remember the change Mr. Sanderson made was in the controller for the lifting mechanism, the drive motors, or something like that.

Fred found those diagrams and put the rest back in the drawer with the car and car control panel diagrams.

Once he found those diagrams, he studied them for close to an hour without finding what he was looking for. He looked at the clock. It was late morning. He had not even logged on to his workstation yet. Since he was not making any headway with the diagrams, he decided maybe a few minutes away would help him get a fresh start a little later.

He logged on and looked at his calendar. His calendar was clear for most of the day. He did see a meeting with Bob French the day after tomorrow. He would need to move that meeting up since he would be away. He brought up Bob's calendar and re-scheduled the meeting. He needed to let Bob know he would be out for a few days.

The classes for the rest of this week and for next week were all arranged and staffed. No additional materials needed to be printed or obtained. He and Bob had a good rhythm in place and all those details were well in hand. He was glad Harry had asked him to bring someone else into the management team. Bob was, as he mentioned to Harry, working out wonderfully. Just as Fred knew he would.

When he finally finished going over the calendars, Fred decided to get an early lunch. He headed down to Clara's. There he ordered his usual and headed back to his office thinking lunch may give him a new outlook on with the diagrams.

He opened the wrapper around his sandwich and opened the bottle of iced tea. He took a bite of the sandwich. He took the diagrams of the top of the car back out of the folder. He stared at them while he ate. Then he saw it. Just like in the woods.

He saw a transformer. There must be a part needing a lower voltage. Could this actually be the part of the elevator Mr. Zimmerman was able to rebuild? It is in one the sections on the diagrams labelled as changes made by Mr. Sanderson all those years ago.

Fred had found the unique part. How could he disable it so it could not be repaired? Could the transformer be a clue? While he finished his lunch, he thought about what he knew about electronics, which was not very much. He was a software guy.

Then it came to him. He remembered when he was a kid, he had a portable CD player. One day, he ran out of batteries. He searched the house for two batteries but could not find any. While rummaging around, he found a lamp his mom was going to throw away. He remembered thinking, why not try it? He took the lamp apart and unscrewed the power cord. He went back to his room and took the battery cover off the CD player. He attached one of the lamp wires to the positive lead and the other to the negative. He plugged the lamp cord into the wall socket.

As soon as the plug was in the socket Fred had learned an important lesson. The CD player started smoking. He quickly unplugged it, but it was too late. His bedroom now smelled like an electrical fire because he just fried his CD player.

Fred's thoughts returned to the elevator. Could it be that simple? He opened the drawer again and took out the pictures he took of the top of the elevator car. "Where is that guy?"

Fred was looking for the part on the photograph corresponding to the part on the diagram. Finally, he said, "There you are."

Fred began making a list. He had some shopping to do.

# CHAPTER SIXTY-TWO

The next morning, Fred packed his backpack with everything on his shopping list. After saying goodbye to Jill, he drove to the office. He parked in his normal spot. He took the elevator to the eighth floor. He did not want to explain to Linda why he had a backpack but was not dressed in his usual bicycle clothes.

Arriving at the eighth floor, Fred walked to the back of the building and headed down the stairs. Few of his team were in and those that were paid little or no attention to him as he walked to his office.

Once inside his office, Fred placed the backpack on the floor behind his desk. He was glad to get it off his back. The contents were bulky, and the weight distribution was uneven. His left shoulder was sore after bearing most of the load.

Later in the morning, Fred met with Bob French to let him know he would be away for a few days. Bob suggested they have an impromptu team lunch in one of the classrooms not being used this week. Fred agreed. They had not had a team lunch since Fred returned and it was clearly overdue.

"Don't you worry about a thing I will take care of the details. You have a lot on your mind, especially today. See you in a bit." Bob said over his shoulder as he left Fred's office.

Fred sat at his desk and thought about the suddenness of the team lunch suggestion. He wondered if Linda or Harry may have had something to do with it.

Fred's suspicions were confirmed when both Linda and Harry popped into the classroom about 30 minutes after everyone else. Neither made any mention of Fred's impending evaluation. Fred appreciated that. He was not sure just how many people he wanted to know about the next few days. He was realistic, however. This type of thing would not stay quiet for long. Office gossip always seems to find out this type of news quickly, and it does not take long before everyone knows everything.

After Harry and Linda left the party, Fred called for everyone to be quiet. "I have a few things to say. First, I want to thank everyone. You have done fantastic work the last couple of months. Especially while I was away. I will talk about that with you sometime after I return. I will be away for a few days. I have met with Bob and I don't think there will be any issues. I will tell you the few days I will be away is related to the investigation of my disappearance as well as the two people that disappeared while I was gone and have since returned. Because of the investigation I am limited to what I can say and to whom."

As the party wound down, every member of Fred's team professed their support to him and said they would do whatever was needed in his absence. Fred already knew that was the case, but he was happy to hear it. By the time Bob said the same, Fred was nearly in tears. He excused himself and headed back downstairs to his office.

Fred needed to collect himself. He needed a clear head this evening. He thought to himself as he sat at his desk, "I have a great job with wonderful people working for me and around me. I have the best woman in the world as a wife and our daughter is all I could have asked for. Why in hell has all this shit happened to me? Am I being punished for having a great life?"

Fred's thoughts were interrupted by the phone ringing. "Hello this is Fred."

"Fred this is Linda. You have a call from Dr. Clark. I wasn't sure if you were in your office or still upstairs with your folks."

"Thanks Linda, I left them to finish without me. I will take the call."

There was a faint click on the phone and then Fred heard Dr. Clark's voice. "Mr. Bates? This is Helen Clark."

"Hello, how are you today?"

"I am fine, thank you. I am just calling to confirm your arrival tomorrow."

"Yes, I am still planning to be there tomorrow. I have a few things to finish up here today before I can leave."

"That sounds good. I look forward to seeing you tomorrow. Goodbye." Dr. Clark hung up before Fred finished his goodbye.

Fred placed the handset in its cradle and sat heavily in his chair. He heard himself say out loud, "That was a very strange phone call."

What did Dr. Clark mean when she said, "I look forward to seeing you tomorrow."? Was that a common thing to say to someone about to visit the Center for a psychiatric evaluation? Was he making too much out of it? Then again, did she personally call everyone in his situation to confirm the visit? He began to wonder about this visit. He had a weird feeling about it. He just could not put his finger on it.

While he was thinking, he noticed he was opening his backpack. Focusing more on his backpack than the visit to the Center, Fred examined the items. Not being able to really see them with the backpack on the floor Fred got up and made sure his door was closed and locked. He emptied the contents carefully on his desk.

When his backpack was empty, he took a mental inventory. He had a headlamp, two extension cords, a one to three receptacle attachment, a small fan, a $CO_2$ fire extinguisher, a multimeter, and a small toolkit.

One of the extension cords was 100 feet long and with three prongs. The one to three receptacle attachment was plugged into the end. If all went as planned, he would only use two of the three. The other was a short two wire cord. Fred had cut the end with the receptacles off. The exposed wires had the insulation stripped back. Fred had soldered alligator type clips on them.

Just in case something went wrong, Fred bought a $CO_2$ fire extinguisher. He bought the smallest one he could find. It was a five-pound model with a red exterior. There was a tag wired near the handle indicating this particular unit had been tested and was approved for use on electrical fires in this state. Class C was written in big letters on the side. There was a small horn shaped nozzle where the $CO_2$ would come out should he need to use it. He was glad to have learned the CO2 (Carbon dioxide) would not leave any residue should he need to use it. He read somewhere,

> Carbon Dioxide Fire Extinguishers meet many hospital medical equipment requirements. CO2 Extinguishers are also used for mechanics and factories as they leave no residue.

Fred was not sure he would need the tools in the kit, but again better to have them. He also was not sure the multimeter would be needed but same there. The last item, now on the desk, was a fan. Remembering his experience with the CD player, he wanted to make sure any smoke generated was quickly dispersed. He was not sure there were smoke detectors in the elevator shafts. The fan had a blade diameter of eight inches. Fred thought this would be big enough. Besides, anything bigger would not fit in his backpack.

Looking at the pile of stuff on his desk, Fred wondered if he had forgotten anything. He started putting everything back into the backpack. Too late now if he did forget something. He unlocked his door and opened it. Most of his team were back at their desks working.

By five in the afternoon, everyone had left for the day. Most of them said a quick goodbye to Fred as they left. Seems like word was beginning to circulate around the office already.

Fred opened his file drawer and took out the folder with the diagrams and pictures of the elevator. He took out the pictures he had taken. He found the one with what he thought was the transformer. He studied the picture. He needed to find where he thought the best place to clip on the wires.

Fred did not want to be on top of the elevator car any longer than necessary. It would take a couple minutes just to get everything out and positioned. He was hoping the elevator mechanism would act like his CD player. Meaning it would only take a fraction of a second for the damage to be inflicted. He could then turn on the fan and blow the smoke away. If there was any. He thought, "there has to be some."

Fred got up and walked to the eighth floor. He checked all the classrooms. They were all empty. He checked the dentist office. It was closed. He paced off the distance from the nearest electrical outlet to the number four elevator door. He had plenty of extension cord.

He walked back down the stairs and went to his office through the I3 lobby. He was checking to make sure Linda had left for the day. He was glad to see her desk was locked up and she appeared to be gone. He walked back to his desk and grabbed his backpack.

He went back upstairs and put his backpack in the classroom closest to the elevator lobby. He then went back down to the seventh floor. Fred thought to himself he was getting a workout going up and down the stairs. He went to the elevators and pressed the down button. The wrong elevator arrived. He went into the car and pressed all the buttons. He then left the car.

He waited until the doors closed and he could hear the elevator descending. He then pressed the down button again. This time elevator four arrived. Fred hoped it would stay put. He waited for the doors to close. After a few more seconds he did not hear it start to move so he headed back to the eighth floor.

He went to the classroom and retrieved his backpack. He unzipped it on the way to the elevators. He took out the long extension cord and walked around the corner and plugged it into the receptacle. He played out the cord behind him as he walked back to the elevators. Just as he thought, he had plenty left over. He unwound the end with some extra and placed the remaining cord coiled next to the number four door.

Fred tried to open the door. It would not open. He placed his ear up against the door and listened. It sounded like it was moving. What luck. Someone was using the elevator. Fred thought it was late enough so there would not be much traffic. He picked up his backpack and returned it to the classroom. He left the extension cord. It would save some time when he came back.

Down on the seventh floor he recalled elevator number four. Again, he had to wait for the second elevator. This time he ran up the stairs to the eighth floor. He went straight to the elevator door and opened it. This time the elevator was where it was supposed to be. Now the doors were opened, Fred retrieved his backpack from the classroom. He took out the headlamp, the fire extinguisher, the fan, the other extension cord, the multimeter and the tool kit. He put the multimeter and toolkit next to the door. He put the headlamp on his head and turned it on.

He picked up the fire extinguisher and stepped down to the top of the elevator car. Fred looked around for the transformer. Locating it he placed the fire extinguisher on a flat spot nearby. He reached up and took the fan and the extension cords. The fan he placed where it would blow air away from the transformer. He plugged the fan into one of the receptacles at the end of the long cord.

Fred looked at the transformer. It looked a lot newer than the rest of the machinery on top of the elevator car. He wondered if this was part of how Mr. Zimmerman had been able to keep the elevators running. There was one wire, or cord, coming out of the transformer. There was a barrel connector at the end of it. Fred did not think barrel connectors would have been around when this elevator was built. But he really did not know, after all, he was a software guy.

Connected to this wire was something that looked a bit out of place. It was another wire coming out of the barrel connector. This one spilt into two wires. Each of these was connected to two other wires with wire nuts. They looked a bit too clean to be standard issue from the days the elevator was built. The two wires ran to two screws on the outside of what looked to be some type of motor housing. Not being mechanical at all, Fred was not at all sure.

Fred picked up the small cord and tried to fasten the two alligator clips to the screws on the outside of the housing. They kept falling off. He decided to clip them on the other end of the wires. He carefully, one at a time, unscrewed the wire nuts. He placed the clips on the end of the wires leading toward the housing.

Fred turned the fan on low and felt the slight breeze now coming from the fan. He picked up the fire extinguisher and pulled the safety pin out of the handle. He unhooked the horn shaped nozzle and laid it close to the motor housing. He picked up the ends of the two extension cords and stared at them for a long few seconds. He took a deep breath and said, "Well, no time like the present."

He plugged the small cord into the long cord.

There was a bright flash and a large puff of smoke. Fred saw a small yellow flame in the motor housing. He unplugged the cord and grabbed the fire extinguisher. He squeezed the handle and blew $CO_2$ all over the motor housing and transformer. The flame was out in an instant. Fred could smell the familiar scent of burning electronics.

After putting the fire extinguisher down, he turned the fan on high to blow the smoke better. Satisfied the smoke was dissipating, he took the alligator clips off the ends of the wire. Now finished with that cord, he tossed it up to the floor next to his backpack.

Fred then reattached the wires with the wire nuts. He picked up the fire extinguisher and set it on the floor. He let the fan run for a couple minutes. When he thought it had been enough time to clear the smoke, he unplugged the fan and put it and the cord on the floor. He looked around the top of the elevator car to make sure he had not left anything behind. Seeing nothing, he climbed out to the floor.

He quickly put everything into his backpack. He closed the elevator door and then walked down to his office.

He set the backpack down and then walked to the elevator lobby. He pressed the down button. A moment later an elevator appeared. He went in and pressed all the buttons. He repeated the operation with the next car that came by. Now with what he hoped were the two remaining working elevators stopping at every floor, he pushed the down button again. He waited. Finally, an elevator appeared. It was the same as the first one. Fred thought this meant number four was out of commission. Had number four been working it should have opened immediately. Fingers crossed; mission accomplished.

Fred went to his office and grabbed his backpack. He locked up his office and headed home. When he walked into the house Jill looked up from the table.

Jill said, "Well, success?"

"I think so. I dropped the one extension cord into a trash can near the convenience store on the way home. I am not sure what to do with the fire extinguisher."

"We should have one. Why don't we just put it under the sink?"

Fred nodded and put the fire extinguisher under the sink.

# CHAPTER SIXTY-THREE

The next morning, Fred and Jill rose early. Kristine soon followed. They ate a leisurely breakfast without much talk. Afterwards, Fred went to the bedroom to put a travel bag together. He was allowed to bring a change of clothing and pajamas. He packed his toothbrush and toothpaste. He also packed his electric razor. He was not allowed to bring a blade razor. He also packed a comb and shampoo. He grabbed the book he was reading and tossed it in the bag as well. He could not think of anything else.

When he was finished packing, he took the bag to the kitchen and set it on the table. Kristine and Jill were just finishing the breakfast dishes.

Jill looked up from the sink and said, "What time do you need to be there?"

"They are expecting us at 1. It is a couple hours away. We should leave a little before 11 just to have some buffer in case there is traffic.

Kristine put her towel on the handle of the oven, using it like a makeshift towel rack. She went to Fred and gave him a big hug. "I don't want you to go away again Dad."

"Don't worry. It is only for a few days. I will be back early next week."

"Why do you have to go?"

Fred sat down and had Kristine sit in one of the other kitchen chairs. "We talked about this. The police have requested this evaluation. Your mom and I think we should do it for a couple reasons. First there is nothing to hide. Second to get the doctors opinions."

Kristine was not giving up so easily. "But you told them the truth, right?"

"Of course I did."

"Then why did those other two people say you lied to the police?"

Fred smiled at Kristine, "Well, you have to admit my version of events sounds a lot more unbelievable."

"But that doesn't mean it is a lie."

"No, it doesn't. I think everything will work out in the end. Don't worry about it."

Fred stood up and walked over to Jill. Whispering in her ear he said, "Sorry about this. Please take care of our little girl while I am gone."

Jill smiled and nodded. Looking at the clock she said, "It is nearly 10. We all need to get cleaned up and dressed."

Kristine got out of her chair and went to her room. Fred and Jill went to their room.

The two of them showered and dressed. When they came out of their room, they found Kristine dressed and ready to go.

Picking up his bag, Fred headed toward the kitchen door. Jill grabbed her keys from the counter. Kristine was already a step behind her dad. Jill, last out the door, locked it and pressed the unlock button on her car remote. Kristine got in the backseat. Fred put his bag on the back seat opposite Kristine. He got in the passenger seat. Jill was driving. She started the car and they started the two-hour drive to the Center.

Arriving at the Center, Fred got out the instructions for where to go to be admitted. He would not be going to the administration building where he met with Brad. The building was easy to find. Jill parked next to the door to the admissions office. The three of them got out of the car and walked into the building.

The room looked like a small version of an emergency room lobby. There were a few chairs in a waiting area. At the side of the room opposite the door there was a desk. Behind the desk was a gentleman in his thirties.

As Fred, Jill and Kristine entered the room, the gentlemen looked up. He said, "Are you Mr. Bates?"

Fred said, "Yes, I am."

"Great. We are expecting you. Please have a seat." He pointed to the chairs near the windows.

Fred, Jill, and Kristine sat in the chairs opposite the desk. The gentleman behind the desk picked up his phone. He talked with someone on the phone for a minute.

As he hung up the phone the gentleman stood, picked up a clipboard, and walked over to the chairs. "Mr. Bates, there are a couple forms you need to sign. I also have one for Mrs. Bates."

Fred and Jill took the forms and read through them. They were the standard forms required for a short-term volunteer admission. When they finished reading them, they signed in the space provided. Fred stood up and walked the forms over to the desk.

The gentleman looked them over and said, "Someone is on the way to take you to your room. You should say goodbye to your family. They will not be allowed to join you."

"Thank you." Fred turned and walked back to the chairs.

Jill stood and said, "Do we have to leave?"

"Yes, you can't come with me."

Kristine stood and jumped into Fred's arms. Now crying she said, "Dad, I don't want you to go."

"It will be okay. I already told you I will only be here a couple days. We are just checking a box, remember?"

Jill joined them making it a family hug. She broke from the hug and taking Kristine by the hand, said goodbye. She then led Kristine out the door. Fred watched them through the window as they walked to Jill's car. This time, Kristine got into the front passenger seat. Fred watched as Jill backed out of the parking space and drove away.

A few minutes later, the door behind the desk opened and in walked the twenty something guy named John. "Hello Mr. Bates. Please follow me."

Fred picked up his bag and followed the twenty something guy through the door. They walked down a hallway and out through another door. Parked next to the door was a golf cart. They got into the cart and headed toward the building where Fred would be during his stay.

John stopped outside the building and led Fred inside. They took an elevator to the second floor. Exiting the elevator, John turned right. They passed a few rooms with the doors closed. Stopping at the fourth door on the right, John opened the door and motioned for Fred to enter.

John said, "Mr. Bates please feel free to put your change of clothes in the chest of drawers and your toiletries on the counter in the bathroom. We ask you stay in your room this afternoon unless asked to leave. This afternoon, you will be left alone to get acclimated to the room. You may have an examination before dinner. You will have a meeting with one or two doctors sometime after dinner. I am not sure if that will happen during my shift. If not, someone else will take you to the interview room. I am not sure, but someone may stop by to provide more details. Do you have any questions?"

Fred replied, "I guess, I got here after lunch. We didn't stop on the way. Is there any way I can get a bite before dinner?"

John said, "I will see what I can do. It won't be much."

"Anything would be appreciated. And thank you."

John smiled and left closing the door.

Fred looked around the room. There was a bed, a small chest of drawers, a lounge chair, and a night table. There was a ceiling light and a lamp on the nightstand. There was a window next to the lounge chair. The window had a nice view of the grounds. A door next to the chest of drawers led to the bathroom. The bathroom had a sink, a toilet, and a shower. Nothing fancy, all functional. Same for the rest of the room. Painted a pleasant light gray. There were a couple paintings of local landmarks on the walls.

Fred unpacked his bag putting the clothes in a drawer and the rest on the bathroom counter. The unpacking finished, he put his bag in the corner and sat down in the chair and stared out the window. He wondered if he was doing the right thing.

# CHAPTER SIXTY-FOUR

Fred was reading the book he brought with him when there was a knock at the door.

"Yes?"

The door opened revealing Mrs. Clark. She said, "May I come in?"

"Sure."

Mrs. Clark came into the room with a manilla folder in her hand.

Fred put the book down on the nightstand and stood up. "Would you like to sit down? There is only one chair. I can sit on the edge of the bed."

Mrs. Clark walked over to the chair and sat down. Fred sat on the bed.

Mrs. Clark spoke first. "I want to go over the evaluation process we use here at the center. Since you are here voluntarily the process is a little less structured. Make no mistake we will do a thorough evaluation."

Fred said, "I have no doubt about that. That is one of the two main reasons I selected the Center. You have a wonderful reputation."

Mrs. Clark said, "Well that is very good of you to say. What is the other reason?"

"Both times I have been here I have been treated with respect. I have seen how you treat your residents. I feel comfortable here."

"That is also good to hear. Your being comfortable will help with getting an accurate evaluation. Shall we begin?"

"That is why I am here."

Mrs. Clark opened the folder. "Part of the evaluation is a series of family history questions. We could ask them during the face-to-face with the doctors, but we find it saves time to have them review it before you meet with them. That way they can concentrate any follow-on questions on any of your answers they think need clarification or more discussion."

Fred said, "Are those the questions in the folder?"

"Yes, there is also a smaller subset we would like your wife to fill out. Her name is Jill correct?"

Fred said, "Yes her name is Jill. How will you get them to her? She went back home as soon as she dropped me here earlier this afternoon."

"I already contacted Jill this afternoon. I emailed the questions to her. She will overnight them to us. We need to start with a physical examination. I have scheduled that for 4:00 this afternoon. We prefer not doing that after a meal. The first meeting with a doctor will be this evening. It is scheduled for 7. That should give you plenty of time to finish dinner."

Fred said, "Okay, is that all?"

Mrs. Clark said, "No, there are a couple rules I need to confirm you understand. First, since you are only here for a short time and to lesson any impact to our residents you will not be engaging with the general resident population. You will be given options for your meals and they will be brought to you here."

"I understand. That was in the forms I had to sign when I arrived."

"Yes, I am glad you remember. There will be another meeting with at least one doctor tomorrow morning at 10. Depending on how the physical and two meetings go there may or may not be more."

"Does Brad, I mean Mr. Myerson, know I am here?"

"No, there is no reason for him to know. He is not in this building so there is little chance you will accidentally bump into each other. In fact, I need to make a note." She took out her phone and typed a memo to herself.

Mrs. Clark stood up and headed for the door. Fred stood as well. She said, "That is all for now. I hope your stay with us is a pleasant one given the circumstances."

Fred said, "Thank you for everything."

"You are welcome." Mrs. Clark walked out of the room and closed the door.

There was a knock on the door at precisely 3:55. "Mr. Bates? This is John. I am here to take you for your physical. Please bring all of the papers Mrs. Clark left for you."

Fred picked up the questionnaires and walked to the door and opened it. Sure enough, John, the twenty something guy, was waiting just outside. Fred fell in behind John closing the door behind him. There was no golf cart ride. John led Fred to the elevators. He pressed "B". The elevator descended slowly to the building basement. When the doors opened Fred saw what looked to be a small doctors' office. There were examination rooms and various medical machines on rolling carts.

John led him to one of the examination rooms. "There is a gown on the table. Please get undressed and put on the gown. When you are finished please open the door. I will be back when they are finished."

Fred said, "Thank you John."

Fred undressed and put on the gown and then opened the door as John told him. A few minutes later a nurse came in.

"Hello Mr. Bates. My name is Debbi. I will be taking your vitals and getting an EKG. The physician will be in after I finish. If all goes well, you should be out of here in less than an hour." Debbi Wilson was a few inches shorter than Fred. She was dressed in green scrubs. She was older than Fred and had a touch of grey in her brown hair.

Debbi went about collecting Fred's vital signs. She then had him lay on the table and attached all the EKG wires to his arms, legs, and chest. It took her more time to attach the wires than it took to run the test.

Debbi started pushing the cart out of the room, "The doctor will be with you shortly. I will come back when he is finished. I may have to draw blood and I know they will want a urine sample."

Fred watched her leave and wondered why they would want blood and a urine sample.

Debbi spoke true. The doctor entered the room a few minutes after she departed. He held out his hand to Fred.

"Good afternoon Mr. Bates. I am Dr. Dewey." Dr. Clifford Dewey appeared to be in his mid to late forties. He was nearly six feet tall and had jet black hair cut short. He also had dark eyes. He was wearing black slacks and a white shirt with a blue tie. He was wearing a white waist length lab coat as well.

Taking the doctors hand Fred said, "Good afternoon."

Dr. Dewey said, "May I have the paperwork you filled out?"

Fred handed him the papers. The doctor selected a few of the pages and read through Fred's responses.

Dr. Dewey said, "I see nothing out of the ordinary except the one for recent injury. You say you were attacked by a mountain lion and received a wound on your back."

"That is correct."

"Let's have a look. Please turn around."

Fred turned around so his back was facing the doctor. The doctor opened the gown and examined the scar from the cat claws.

"Well, I am not an expert on wounds of this nature, but it looks to be about a month or so old. It is healing nicely. You say it was a mountain lion?"

"I think so. It was light brown, almost tan, and about the size of a female German Shephard. And yes, it was just over a month ago."

"Do you mind if I take a picture of this and send it to a colleague that has done some work with wild animal attacks?"

"No, I don't mind."

"Wonderful." Dr. Dewey said. He took out his phone and typed in something.

"While I wait for Debbi to come in with the hi-rez camera let's get on with the rest of the exam."

When nurse Debbi arrived with the camera, Dr. Dewey was nearly finished. He took the camera and snapped a couple pictures.

"Debbi, please download these to Mr. Bates folder. I would like to have them ready to send when I am finished."

Debbi took the camera and walked out of the room.

When the exam was finished Dr. Dewey said, "That is all for me. I will have Debbi come in and get a urine sample. I was informed blood work would not be required today. There is a chance it may be necessary later. I will see you again before you leave. Good afternoon."

Fred said, "Good afternoon Dr. Dewey, and thank you."

A few minutes later Debbi arrived with a plastic cup. After he provided the sample, John magically appeared to return him to his room. When he arrived, his dinner was waiting.

There was a knock at Fred's door at 6:55. Fred answered the door. A young man in his twenties was just outside in the hallway. He said, "Mr. Bates? I am Lawrence. I am to take you to see Dr. Straub. Follow me."

Fred fell in behind Lawrence. They went to the elevators but this time they went up two floors. When the elevator doors opened Lawrence turned left and started down the hallway. The hallway looked much like the administration building hallway. Lawrence led Fred to the last door on the left. Lawrence knocked on the door.

"Come in."

Lawrence opened the door and motioned for Fred to enter. Lawrence said, "Dr. Straub, this is Mr. Bates. Please let me know when you are finished."

Lawrence turned around, closed the door, and walked away.

Dr. Straub was sitting behind a desk next to the windows. He was wearing a three-piece blue suit with a striped tie. His hair was light brown, almost blond. He had blue eyes and looked to be nearly six feet tall. His height was confirmed when he stood to welcome Fred. He said, "Good evening Mr. Bates. Please have a seat."

Dr. Straub was pointing to one of the two chairs opposite the desk. Fred sat in the one on the left, Dr. Straub the one on the right. Fred noticed the office was decorated much the same as the visitor room. Pictures on the wall were seascapes. There were no personal items in the office. Fred wondered if this was really Dr. Straub's office or just a meeting room.

Dr. Staub spoke first. "My name is Dr. Straub. I am the senior Psychologist here at the Center. Are you being treated alright Mr. Bates?"

"Yes. Everyone has been quite nice. Thank you."

Dr. Straub continued. "What do you think the reason is for you being here?"

Fred said, "To find out if I am telling the truth because what happened to me sounds unbelievable."

"Ah, I can see why you would think that. You are not here to find out the truth. You are here to be evaluated from a mental health point of view. Put another way, my colleagues and I will need to make a recommendation to the authorities. That recommendation will be either a belief you are a danger to yourself or others and therefore should be remanded to a facility such as ours until such time as that is no longer the case, or the belief you are not a threat to yourself or others. In the latter case our recommendation would be for you to not be remanded to a facility such as ours. Do you understand our task?"

Fred thought about the question. "So, I understand your task, as you put it. I was hoping to be able to convince you all that I am not lying as some people have intimated."

"Well, Mr. Bates while I said our main task doesn't specifically mean we will accept your truthfulness, it doesn't necessarily mean we won't believe you either."

Fred said, "Thank you. That is good to hear."

Dr. Straub opened a notebook and set it in his lap. "Let me describe how this session is going to work. I will start by asking you a series of questions. Some of the questions may be familiar as they were on the questionnaire you filled out when you arrived. Some clarification or discussion will help my understanding of your response. We will end with a discussion of your time away. Since we are doing this as part of a legal process, I have listened to both recordings that were made on your visits to Mr. Myerson."

Fred was surprised by this admission. "Really, I didn't think those recordings would be heard by anyone unless you were being sued or something like that."

"You are quite right. This is one of the cases that falls into what you called "something like that." Let's wait to talk about that until a bit later. Alright?"

"Sure. I am here to answer whatever questions you have. I hope I didn't give you the impression otherwise."

"Not at all. Let us begin. Are you comfortable?"

Fred adjusted his position in the chair. "Yes, you have the best chairs here."

"Thank you. We find the results of our examinations are better when the subject is comfortable. First question, are you having any issues with doing the standard daily activities like showering, brushing your teeth, getting dressed, driving, etc.?"

"No everything is fine. I did run a stop sign the other day. My mind was on something and I blew right through it.

Fortunately, no other cars or people were at that intersection."

Dr. Straub jotted down something in the notebook. "What were you thinking about?"

"As you know from listening to what happened, I returned before the other two people. I was thinking about them. Would they get back and were they okay. Things like that."

Dr. Straub made more notes. "Did those thoughts go away or are you still dealing with them?"

"They are gone. The other two people are back."

"I see." He made more notes.

Dr. Straub continued, "I see you are married. Children?"

"Yes, my wife and I have a daughter."

"How would describe your relationship with your wife and daughter?"

"My wife and I are soul mates. We tell each other everything. As for my daughter, other than my wife she is the most important person in my life."

Dr. Straub asked, "Do you have any problems maintaining relationships with other people? For example, do you have any friends you have kept in touch with for a long period of time?"

"I think I get along with people well. I have known my boss for over 14 years. Jill and I have been friends with Harry and his wife Gretta ever since we met them."

Dr. Staub was making more notes. "Since you mentioned your boss, what kind of work do you do?"

"I am the lead of our software and training departments. I oversee the maintenance of our software products. If I have time I may even help with the changes. I also manage the team responsible for training our customers how to use our software products. Another of my responsibilities is to sell our training."

"How do you think your boss would rate your contributions?"

"I actually know how he feels. We had a long discussion after I returned from my adventure. He likes what I do but is concerned I am, or was, a single point of failure."

"What do you mean was?"

"Harry asked me to hire an assistant and train him, or her, on what I do. I selected someone from my team."

The next hour Dr. Staub continued to ask Fred questions from his list. The doctor finished with this question, "I read in your answers your father died when you were sixteen. How did you cope with his death and did you get any counseling?"

Fred said, "Yes I was sixteen. My mom was a bit old fashioned I guess because going to a therapist was out of the question. But I don't think it would have mattered that much anyway. My two brothers, my mother, and I were and still are quite close. I got a job at a hardware store to help pay for college. That paired with school and scouts kept me busy. Did I miss my dad? Sure. I still do."

Dr. Straub said, "Now, I would like to hear your version of what happened while you were away. I think you called it your adventure. Would you spend, oh, fifteen minutes going over the highlights?"

"Sure."

The highlights took twenty minutes. Dr. Straub only interrupted Fred a couple times.

Dr. Straub said, "Thank you for that summary. That is all I need for now. After you meet with Dr. Murakami in the morning we will decide if another session is warranted."

As if on cue there was a knock at the door. Lawrence came in.

Lawrence said, "Mr. Bates, if you will follow me, I will return you to your room."

Fred stood up to leave.

Dr. Straub said, "Good night Mr. Bates."

Fred said, "Good night." He followed Lawrence back to his room.

Just before 10 the next morning there was a knock at Fred's door. John, the twenty something guy was outside. Fred followed John as they went up the elevator two floors, turned left, and walked toward the far end of the hallway. John knocked on the door opposite the room Fred had met with Dr. Straub the night before.

A soft "come in" came from the other side of the door. John opened the door and they went in. A small dark-haired woman in her early fifties said, "Thank you John. I will let you know when we are finished."

John turned and closed the door as he left.

The small woman said, "Good morning Mr. Bates. I am Dr. Akiko Murakami. I am the senior Psychiatrist here at the Center. I am also the senior mental health professional. All major decisions related to our residents are cleared by me. Please have a seat." She pointed to the chair on the left.

As he was taking his seat Fred looked around the room. It was identical to the room from the previous evening apart from the pictures on the wall. This room has landscapes instead of seascapes.

Dr. Murakami sat in the other chair. She was wearing a suit with grey slacks, a grey jacket, and a white button-down blouse buttoned to her neckline. Her dark hair was pulled back into a ponytail. She was no more than 5 feet tall and could not weigh more than 100 pounds.

Dr. Murakami also placed a notebook in her lap. She opened the notebook and looked at Fred. "Mr. Bates, you are here voluntarily. What do you want as an outcome of your time at the Center?"

Fred was expecting the same opening question from the previous session with Dr. Straub and was caught a little off-guard. "Um, I was hoping to convince everyone I am telling the truth. But last night Dr. Straub told me I am being evaluated to see if I should be admitted to a place like this. So, I guess what I want has changed a little. While I would still like to be believed, I would really prefer to not be admitted."

Dr. Murakami said, "Yes, you stated our purpose quite succinctly. I do appreciate your desire to be believed."

THE LIFT

She continued, "Like Dr. Straub last night, I have a series of questions. While there will be some overlap, my questions for the most part will have a different focus. I have listened to your sessions with Mr. Myerson."

Fred interrupted, "Dr. Straub said the same thing last night. Do you really think that was necessary?"

Dr. Murakami wrote in her notebook. When she was done, she said, "I believe for us to perform a credible evaluation, we need to have at our disposal any information that may be relevant to your situation. Those two recordings, in my view, are central to your situation. Having listened to them will also save some time. You will not have to recount your story in such detail during these sessions. They were heard by only four people Mrs. Clark, Dr. Straub, Dr. Dewey, and of course me."

Dr. Murakami looked at her notes. "Unless you have any questions we should get started."

Fred said, "No questions. I am ready."

Dr. Murakami began, "Is there a history of psychiatric hospitalization in your family?"

"No."

"Do you know about any suicide attempts in your family history?"

"No."

Dr. Murakami asked, "Have you ever had any symptoms related to the present situation?"

Fred thought for a moment. "I am not quite sure what you are asking. I was a bit anxious for a couple weeks just after I returned."

Mr. Murakami said, "How do you mean anxious? How did it manifest itself?"

"I was worried about the other two people. They had not returned. I had a few nightmares. I was, at times, distracted at work. I paced around the office. The lady at our reception desk noticed it and said something to me. I had not realized I was doing it. I also ran a stop sign once because I was distracted."

"Is this anxiety still present? Are you experiencing any of the symptoms you described?"

"No, the two other people have returned safe."

"Other than the nightmares you mentioned, are you having any difficulty sleeping, have there been changes to your appetite, or has anything else changed from what were your normal day to day activities?"

"The only thing I can think of is I won't be eating fish for a while."

"Why is that?"

Fred smiled, "While I was away my diet was almost 100% fish."

Dr. Murakami was writing in her notebook. "Are you on any medication or under any medical treatments at this time?"

"No."

She continued writing in her notebook. When she finished she looked at Fred. "Do you have a history of alcohol and other substance use?"

Fred said, "My family didn't drink. So, I never really started. The people I hung with in college weren't what I would call drinkers either. Then I met Jill and rest is history."

"What do you mean by the rest is history?"

"Oh, sorry. After Jill and I got together my life was consumed by school and her. Sure, I did some other things, but I had no desire to go out to bars or go to big parties. Come to think of it I really didn't do that before I met Jill. Being with her, then and now, is all I really want to do."

Dr. Murakami said, "Let's move on. Do you know of any history of serious illness in your family?"

"The only serious illness I know about is the one that took my father. As far as I know he was the only one in his family that died young."

Dr. Murakami and Fred spent another hour talking. She asked questions and Fred provided answers. Dr. Murakami looked at the clock and said, "I only have a couple more questions. Do you engage in any high-risk behaviors?"

"What do you mean by that?"

Dr. Murakami said, "There are many types of behaviors that can be considered high risk. I am most interested in those that may have consequences to your health and the stability of your family. Here are some examples: unprotected sex outside of your present relationship, taking illegal drugs, reckless driving, and any other activities for which you are not properly trained. Think thrill seeking activities."

"None of those things. I guess I lead a pretty boring life."

Dr. Murakami made some more notes in her book. "Mr. Bates, I don't think there is anything boring about working at a job you obviously like and raising a family with a partner you call your soul mate. Sounds pretty idyllic to me. I did not mean to infer anything by my question."

Fred thought about this for a minute. Did Dr. Murakami really just say that? That did not sound anything like a comment he expected to hear in this setting.

Dr. Murakami must have sensed his confusion about her last response. She quickly said, "One last question. Other than your current situation, have you ever had any significant dealings with the courts or police?"

"No, I have never even gotten so much as a parking ticket."

Dr. Murakami wrote something in her notebook and then closed it and set it on the desk. "Before we finish would you describe to me in your own words what happened when you were missing?"

"But you heard it all on the recordings."

"I know, it is a fascinating tale and there are a few details I would like to explore."

When they were finished discussing his disappearance, just as the evening prior, there was a knock at the door.

Dr. Murakami said, "Come in John."

The twenty something guy named John opened the door and said, "Mr. Bates I will take you back to your room."

Fred and Dr. Murakami stood. Dr. Murakami said, "Mr. Bates thank you. I will see you again soon."

Fred fell in behind John and returned to his room.

# CHAPTER SIXTY-FIVE

The next morning Mrs. Clark knocked on Fred's door.

"Come in."

She said, "Good morning Mr. Bates. How are you today?"

"I am fine. How did I do?

"That is why I am here. At 11 this morning we will be having a review of your case. This is a very unusual case and the process we are using is a little out of the ordinary. The staff here has been in contact with the DA's office and the Police Department. All have agreed to the process we have followed up to this point and to the decision to be made at the review later this morning."

Fred thought about this for a minute. "I thought I am here voluntarily. Do I get a say?"

"Your input will certainly be considered. I must caution you, however. The city has paid for this evaluation and therefore they have a considerable interest in the outcome. Do you have clean clothes to wear this morning?"

"Yes, one of your staff came by yesterday afternoon and collected all of my clothes. They were brought back to me just a short time ago, clean and folded."

"Wonderful, John will come by just before 11 to collect you. We will be meeting in the visitor room today. We have configured it a bit differently than your previous times here. I will be attending the review so I will see you at 11.

Mrs. Clark left the room and closed the door. Fred looked at the time. It was 8:30. He had two and a half hours to wonder how the meeting, Mrs. Clark said review, would turn out. Did this mean there is a chance he will not be going home? He promised Kristine he would only be gone a few days.

Fred showered and got dressed. He spent the rest of the time waiting for John staring out the window or pacing back and forth. He had not done that since before he found out Gail and Jason had finally returned.

As promised, there was a knock on the door at precisely 10:55. The twenty-something guy named John was at the door. Once again Fred fell in behind John. This time they walked outside of the building and rode the golf cart to the administration building.

Mrs. Clark was waiting at the door when they reached the administration building. "I will take him from here John. I will call when we are finished. Thank you."

Mrs. Clark opened the door and motioned for Fred to enter. As they walked to the visitor room she said, "I have a little more information on what you can expect this morning. Each of the doctors you have seen since arriving will be in the room. I will also be there. There will be someone representing the DA's office and Police Department. I believe you know Detective MacDuff. There is one other person we have invited to attend."

They had reached the door to the visitor room when Fred noticed Mrs. Clark motioning for someone in the lobby to be brought to the room. Julie walked over to the chairs. To Fred's surprise, the person Julie was now walking beside toward him and Mrs. Clark was Jill. Fred looked at Mrs. Clark. She smiled and nodded. Fred walked to Jill and gave her a huge hug.

He said, "What are you doing here?"

Before she could answer Mrs. Clark said, "Thank you Julie." Then to Fred, "I called her yesterday and suggested she should attend the meeting today at 11. The rest of the people attending have been meeting since 9 this morning. We should go in and get started."

The three of them entered the room to find four people already sitting at a conference table. It was a standard looking table with three seats on either side and room for one on each end. Only one end had a chair. Mrs. Clark led Fred and Jill to two empty seats on one side of the table. She took the seat at the end of the table.

Mrs. Clark spoke first. "I would like to start off stating the purpose of this review. The purpose of the review is to state for the record the results of the psychiatric evaluation of Mr. Fred Bates. Mr. Bates is in attendance. Because all parties in the review are not known to all other parties, I will make introductions. Going around the room clockwise we have Dr. Dewey our physician, Dr. Straub one of our Psychologists, Dr. Murakami one of our Psychiatrists, myself, Mrs. Clark, our Patient Advocate, Detective

MacDuff of the Police Department, Mrs. Jill Bates, wife of Mr. Bates, and Mr. Fred Bates, as I mentioned the person of interest for this review. I believe Detective MacDuff has something he would like to say before we start. Detective?"

Sgt. MacDuff stood. "Thank you, Mrs. Clark. I have been duly authorized by both the Office of the District Attorney and the Chief of the Police Department to act on their collective behaves in this matter. If anyone has objections to my participation, please say so now."

The last sentence he said looking directly at Fred. He then sat back in the chair next to Jill.

Picking up on this and looking at Jill, Fred said, "I, no we, have absolutely no problems with Sergeant MacDuff in the role he mentioned."

Mrs. Clark said, "Very good. We will now go to the examining Doctors for a summary of their findings. We will start with Dr. Dewey for his summary of the physical examination."

Dr. Dewey rose from his chair. "We had Mr. Bates fill out an extensive health history form upon his arrival. Part of that was a family history. We also provided a shorter version to Mrs. Bates which she promptly completed and returned. There were only two items of concern in either the forms or the actual physical examination performed two days ago. One issue was provided in the family history. That was the untimely death of Mr. Bates' father. I believe Mr. Bates was 16 at the time. I saw nothing in my examination raising concerns to his physical wellbeing as a result of his father's death. I will leave the mental questions to my two colleagues."

Dr. Dewey continued. "The only thing I found interesting in the physical examination may actually have a bearing on the outcome of this review. I will leave the interpretation again up to my colleagues.

The interesting find was a wound on Mr. Bates' back. He told me it happened a month or so ago. Looking at how it is healing I concur with the approximate time frame. With Mr. Bates permission, I photographed the wound and sent copies of the photographs to a colleague of mine with substantial experience with wild animal wounds. Mr. Bates stated he received the wound when he was attacked by a mountain lion. My colleague has stated the wound in the photos I sent to him are as close to a 100% match to what he would expect a month-old mountain lion wound to look like. So, it is my opinion the likelihood Mr. Bates is telling the truth in this matter is extremely high. Everything else is documented in the formal documentation provided."

With that Dr. Dewey returned to his seat.

Sgt. MacDuff said, "Dr. Dewey do you have a copy of the photographs available? I would like to see one."

"Yes, of course. They are included in the formal documentation I mentioned, but I do have copies for you to look at." Dr. Dewey passed three photographs to Dr. Straub who in turn passed them around the table.

After taking a quick look at the pictures Mrs. Clark spoke again. "Thank you, Dr. Dewey. Next, we will hear from Dr. Murakami. She will summarize the findings of both her and Dr. Straub's examinations. Dr. Murakami?"

Dr. Murakami stood and walked to the end of the table opposite Mrs. Clark. "Thank you, Mrs. Clark. First, I want to thank everyone in the room for cooperating in these examinations. The reason for the examination is quite fantastic and I applaud the professionalism with which everyone has endeavored to maintain. I also want to thank Mr. and Mrs. Bates for their prompt responses to our requests even if they may have at the time seemed more invasive than necessary. Their candor is a necessary component to a successful outcome."

"There is one additional question I need to ask. We all agreed to wait until this session to ask the question. This way we will all hear it at the same time. Mr. Bates, your list of events is almost the same as what Mr. Myerson has provided. I, we, find that a bit coincidental. Can you explain that to us?"

Fred was expecting this question. He expected to be asked during the one-on-one sessions though. He took a deep breath and started. "Yes, it does track quite closely with Brad's, sorry, Mr. Myerson's experience. There is a reason for that. I ended up at the same place just a little after he had returned."

Dr. Murakami interrupted, "Yes, we understand that from what you said. But how do we know you did not fabricate this whole story after you and Mr. Myerson met?"

Fred was not sure if he was now in a confrontational setting. "I did not meet Mr. Myerson until I had been back from my experience for around a week. During that week, I had told my wife what happened. I also told a shortened version to my daughter. The day after I returned, my wife and I met with Sergeant MacDuff. I told him everything I have told you. So, you can see at least three people knew some or all of the details before I met with Mr. Myerson. I know most, if not all, of you have listened to the recordings of my meetings with Mr. Myerson. You will note the questions I was asking him during the first meeting were very pointed."

Dr. Murakami said, "Pointed? How so?"

"Well, I was there. I suspected he had also been there. I was asking questions to verify it was him. By the way, I was amazed at how he adapted. He did almost everything the way I was taught when I was younger, and he never had any training."

Dr. Murakami looked at Dr. Straub, Dr. Dewey, and Sgt. MacDuff. All three nodded almost imperceptively. She then said to Fred. "Thank you, Mr. Bates. I think your description of the timeline of events answered any lingering questions."

She went on, "Dr. Straub and I took separate routes in our evaluations. There was obviously some overlap, but we have our areas of expertise. Also, we relied heavily on the General Medical History from Dr. Dewey's examination. Dr. Straub concentrated on what we call a Functional Assessment; a Developmental, Psychosocial, and Sociocultural History; and Mr. Bates' Occupational History. I, on the other hand, concentrated on his Sensorium and Level of Cognitive Function; Childhood Development Issues; Mental Issues Surrounding the Current Situation; Past Mental Health and/or Substance Abuse Problems; and lastly, a Review of Systems. We both documented Mr. Bates behavior during the interview process. As for that aspect of our examinations, we both agree Mr. Bates was a perfect gentleman. He answered all of our questions with what we both believe to be a high level of candor."

Dr. Murakami continued. "Mr. and Mrs. Bates, I will not go through all of the results of the examinations in this review, as the rest of us in the room have spent all morning reviewing our examinations and the conclusions to the same. All the input and conclusions are included in the formal documentation Dr. Dewey has already mentioned. What I will do instead is give the two of you our conclusion and the high-level basis for that conclusion. Should you have questions when I have finished, we have plenty of time for those to be addressed to your satisfaction."

Dr. Murakami spent the next ten minutes providing an overview of both her examination and Dr. Straub's examination. "In conclusion we both agree there is no reason for Mr. Bates to be held in a facility such as ours. He does not pose a danger to himself or others. We would like to keep him here for the duration of the time recommended. I believe that is for him to be released first thing the day after tomorrow. We were not present during his self-described adventure. It seems fantastic if it really happened as he described it. As you know, there is one other person with a similar story. We will be reviewing his case sometime soon. But we cannot go into any of those details here. Suffice it to say, we believe Mr. Bates belief in his version of what happened to be currently of little or no consequence to his ability to function in society."

Dr. Murakami walked back to her seat and sat down.

Fred looked across the table at the three doctors. They all were smiling.

Mrs. Clark said, "Thank you Dr. Murakami. As you know, this psychiatric evaluation was requested by the Office of the District Attorney and the Police Department. Detective MacDuff, would you like to say anything to the group now Mr. and Mrs. Bates have heard from the doctors?"

Sgt. MacDuff said, "Outside of this set of examinations I have contacted Fred's employer, Harry Esposito. Mr. Esposito had nothing but good things to say about Mr. Bates. He has no plans to terminate Mr. Bates' employment.

In fact, Mr. Bates is an integral part of the company. I believe he is a part owner as well. Based on my investigations of the disappearances of Mr. Bates, Ms. Miller, Mr. Lake, and Mr. Myerson, I have no objections to the findings of the panel of doctors assembled here today. I, speaking for the City Police Department and the Office of the District Attorney, accept these findings and will abide by your stated recommendation."

Mrs. Clark stood, "Thank you, Detective MacDuff. Dr. Dewey, Dr. Straub, and Dr. Murakami thank you. I believe we are finished here."

The three doctors left the room. As they left, they shook hands with both Fred and Jill and wished them luck in the future.

Sgt. MacDuff stood. He said to Fred, "Fred, please give me a call when you get home. There are a few things we need to clean up before we can officially close your case."

Fred said, "Sure thing. Thank you."

The detective smiled as Mrs. Clark led him toward the door. She said, "Mr. Bates, I will take the detective to the door and let John know we are finished. I will leave you and Mrs. Bates to have a few minutes together."

After the door closed Jill said, "Did that really just happen? Seemed a bit odd it went so fast and so well."

Fred laughed a bit, "I certainly hope they have been recording everything in here today. I would love to have a copy of this one."

Jill and Fred sat in their chairs quietly holding hands until John appeared at the door.

Fred said, "Love you, see you in a couple days."

# CHAPTER SIXTY-SIX

The next morning at precisely nine o'clock the phone in Fred's room rang. Fred was still in his pajamas, sitting in the chair next to the window, admiring the landscaping. He stood up and walked around the bed and sat down. He answered on the third ring.

"Hello, this is Fred."

"Mr. Bates, this is Mrs. Clark. I am sorry to call so early but you have a visitor request. Since you won't be here on a normal visiting day, I am wondering if you want me to make an exception. The gentleman seemed quite anxious to talk with you."

"Who is it?"

"His name is Jason Lake."

"Really?" Fred said with a touch of sarcasm and surprise.

"Yes, he was most insistent. Would you mind meeting with him?"

Fred did not answer right away.

As Fred was taking too long to answer, Mrs. Clark asked, "Mr. Bates? Are you still there?"

"Sorry, yes I am still here. I will meet with him. Would it be alright if you and I meet in your office for a few minutes before I meet with him?"

Now it was Mrs. Clark's turn to think for a moment. She wondered why Fred would want to meet with her. She decided it could not hurt. "I think that can be arranged. It is just after 9. Mr. Lake said he could be here by noon if you agreed to the meeting. Shall we say 11:30 in my office?"

Fred said, "11:30 sounds fine with me."

"Very good. I will have John pick you up just before 11:30."

Fred got up from the bed and headed for the bathroom to shower and get dressed. While he was talking to Mrs. Clark, an idea started to form in his head, leading to his request to meet with her first.

While in the shower, he thought about what he wanted to accomplish at the meeting with Jason. Would Mrs. Clark agree to help him? He truly believes she likes him and believes what both he and Brad have recounted of their respective adventures.

He knew Gail and Jason had lied to the police. That is why he is here at the Center. Yes, he was going to be leaving in a couple days, but everyone now is not sure if he was telling the truth or lying. Now he has a chance to set the record straight.

Would Mrs. Clark help? He thought so. If not, he would not be worse off than he already was.

Five minutes before 11:30, the twenty-something guy named John knocked on his door. "Mr. Bates, are you ready?"

"Yes John. On the way."

Fred walked beside John down the hallway toward the side entrance. They walked through the door and got on the waiting golf cart. John drove to the administration building and parked at the back door. They both got out of the cart and headed up the short stairway to the door.

Mrs. Clark was in her office when John knocked. "Yes?"

"Mrs. Clark, I have Mr. Bates with me as you requested."

"Thank you, John. I will take him to the meeting room when we have finished. I will give you a call when it is time for Mr. Bates to return to his room."

John, now dismissed, turned and retraced his steps to the back door.

Mrs. Clark motioned for Fred to come into her office. She then pointed to a chair next to the sofa as she said, "Mr. Bates. Come in. Please sit down."

Fred did as she asked and sat down in the chair. Mrs. Clark sat behind her desk. She smiled and her blue eyes had the friendly look about them he had seen when he first met her.

"So, Mr. Bates. You asked to meet with me. What is on your mind?"

"Mrs. Clark, I know you have heard my complete story. Not necessarily the way we had discussed the first time I was here. Since you have heard the story you must know who Jason Lake is."

"Yes, I know he is one of the two people you said were left behind when you returned. I also know their story does not line up with your story leading to you being here today."

"Precisely." Fred said.

Mrs. Clark asked again. "What is on your mind?"

Fred thought for a second and decided to just go for it. "Will you be recording our conversation?"

"Of course. I told you at our first meeting the reasons why. I have to record the meeting."

Fred, sensing she was thinking he did not want it recorded said, "I don't mind. In fact, I really want this one recorded."

Mrs. Clark said, "Mr. Bates, if you want it recorded and if we are planning to record it what is the problem?"

"There is no problem. I would like to ask you a favor."

Intrigued Mrs. Clark said, "Go on."

"I plan to find out why he is here. Then I want to lead him to contradict his version of the story they told the police."

"Why does that matter? You are going home soon."

Fred said, "I want to get him on record in the lie. I want Jill, Kristine, Harry, and everyone else to know I am telling the truth. That matters to me. I also want Sgt. MacDuff to know the truth. That should not only matter to me, but to him."

Mrs. Clark smiled. "I see. I think the truth is very important."

"It is not just me. I am also thinking of Brad. Mr. Myerson. He doesn't belong here either."

"I agree with that, he is not a danger to anyone. Is there anything I can do other than what I normally do anyway?"

"I know you listen in from time to time. When you hear Jason contradict his story, if you could stop in to check on us. You know, like you always do. When you do come in, shoot me some signal you heard him. It would set my mind at ease and I would know I could stop pressing him."

Mrs. Clark thought about that. "Well, I will have to play that by ear, so to speak. I am not sure I should take sides in your disagreement."

Mrs. Clark looked at her watch. "It is almost noon. You should be in the visitor's room. I don't want Mr. Lake to see you coming out of my office. I don't normally meet with residents here."

She got out of her chair and walked around the desk toward the door. Fred stood and followed. She led him across the hall to the same room where he met Brad both times they talked. The room was returned to the visitor configuration.

She said, "I will be back with Mr. Lake as soon as he signs the release for the meeting to be recorded. If he is on time, it should only be about five minutes."

Mrs. Clark walked out of the room closing the door behind her.

Fred walked over to the window looking out on the Center grounds. He could see the parking space where he had parked both times he was here to meet with Brad. There was a car in one of the spaces. The car was empty. Fred turned away from the window and saw the same two chairs arranged facing both the window and each other.

Six minutes later there was a knock at the door. The door opened. Mrs. Clark came in followed by Jason. "Mr. Bates, your visitor, Mr. Lake, is here."

Fred walked to the door to meet them. Jason entered the room looking more at his shoes than at Fred. They shook hands.

Mrs. Clark said, "Well, since you two already know each other, I will leave you to your discussion."

Fred thought he detected a sly wink as she left the room. He dismissed it as being a bit out of character, and therefore he must have imagined it. He turned to Jason and said, "Hello Jason. Please have a seat."

Fred walked toward the chairs and took the one on the left. Jason sat in the chair on the right. Fred turned a little crooked in the chair, so he was looking directly at Jason.

Jason, looking at the floor, spoke first. "I know you must be angry at me because you ended up here and I am on the outside."

"Jason, I am not angry. Not really. I just wish you would have told the police what happened."

Jason looked up at Fred, "I did not come here to talk to you about that."

"Gee, Jason, I am not sure there is much else for you and me to talk about. We don't work together. We have never socialized. The only time we have been together is during our, shall I say, adventure together. Oh, sorry, then there was the day after you returned when you punched me in the nose."

Jason looked back down at the floor. "Yeah, sorry about that. Like I said, Gail and I were pretty upset."

Fred said, "So, if you don't want to talk about our little journey together, why are you here."

"I want to talk about the elevator."

"What about it?"

"Has the repairman fixed it yet?"

Fred stopped him, "Wait a minute. What has the elevator got to do with anything. According to what Sgt. MacDuff said about your story, I had arranged with both of you to meet someplace and I decided to leave a couple weeks before you. So again, what does the elevator have to do with any of that?"

"I just want to know if it has been fixed."

"I don't think the repairman has been back. Why don't you tell me what you told the police? I am not sure I heard the whole story."

Jason looked surprised. "You really want me to tell you that story?"

"Yes, I do."

"Okay, but there really isn't much to tell." Jason spend twenty minutes telling Fred everything he and Gail had told the police.

Fred did mislead Jason a bit. He had heard the whole story. Sgt. MacDuff did not really believe them. There were some inconsistencies. Their answers to the same questions were too close to being the same almost like they were rehearsed. That sent up some flags.

When Jason was done, Fred said, "That all sounds wonderful Jason. But why would I have arranged to meet you and Gail a week apart from each other? Why wouldn't we all just go at the same time?"

"Ah, that was Gail's idea. She said if we all went at different times people would not think we were all together. It would make it harder for someone to find us."

"But having to explain all of the cars being found at the building. More deception to throw of their tracks?"

"Exactly."

"I still don't know why you just didn't tell the truth. Both Brad and I did that."

This caught Jason off guard, and it made him a little angry. "I told you when we met before that was a non-starter. You and Brad are now here. I told you I did not want to be here."

"So, you and Gail made up the other story just to keep you both out of a place like this." Fred said as a statement not a question.

"Yes."

"But now everyone thinks I am crazy and lied to the police. So, not only am I in here, if I ever get out I am facing a charge for lying to the police. My boss isn't sure whether to believe me or to believe that bullshit story you two told."

Jason had indeed forgotten he was being recorded. "Do you really think I was going to tell anyone I went back in time? In an elevator? No way am I telling anyone. I will be sticking to the story Gail and I came up with. That is what is on record with the police."

Fred has a huge smile on his face. "Really. The two of you are resigned to telling that story. Nothing I can do to convince you otherwise?"

"Nothing."

There was a knock at the door. Mrs. Clark opened the door and poked her head in. "Everything okay you two?"

Fred looked around at the door. Jason just hung his head. "Everything is okay Mrs. Clark. I suspect we will be finished in a few minutes. You can let John know he can start back over."

Much to Fred's surprise, Mrs. Clark entered into the room and walked over to him. She bent over and whispered in his left ear, "We got it."

Fred looked at her. This time there was no mistake at the wink. He smiled.

Mrs. Clark turned and headed toward the door. She said, "I will have John here in 5 minutes."

After she left Fred turned to Jason. "So, one last time. Why did you come by today?"

Now Jason looked petrified. "Gail went to meet with your boss the day before you came here. She never got there. Gail is missing!